Blood
Possession

by Tessa Dawn

A Blood Curse Novel
Book Three
In the Blood Curse Series

Published by Ghost Pines Publishing, LLC
http://www.ghostpinespublishing.com

Volume III of the Blood Curse Series by Tessa Dawn
First Edition Trade Paperback Published April 15, 2012
10 9 8 7 6 5 4 3 2 1

ISBN-13: 978-1-937223-03-8
Printed in the United States of America

Author may be contacted at: http://www.tessadawn.com

This is a work of fiction. All characters and events portrayed in this
novel are either fictitious or are used fictitiously. Any resemblance to
actual persons, living or dead, business establishments, events, or
locales is entirely coincidental.

Ghost Pines Publishing, LLC

Acknowledgments

"Mersi."

Lidia Bircea ~ Romanian Translations

Reba Hilbert ~ Editing

Miriam Grunhaus ~ Cover Art

Also, to my lifelong friend and cousin Carla, thanks for coming to my rescue; what a way to spend our birthdays!

The Blood Curse

In 800 BC, Prince Jadon and Prince Jaegar Demir were banished from their Romanian homeland after being cursed by a ghostly apparition: *the reincarnated Blood of their numerous female victims*. The princes belonged to an ancient society that had sacrificed its females to the point of extinction, and the punishment was severe.

They were forced to roam the earth in darkness as creatures of the night. They were condemned to feed on the blood of the innocent and stripped of their ability to produce female offspring. They were damned to father twin sons by human hosts who would die wretchedly upon giving birth; and the firstborn of the first set would forever be required as a sacrifice of atonement for the sins of their forefathers.

Staggered by the enormity of *The Curse*, Prince Jadon, whose own hands had never shed blood, begged his accuser for leniency and received *four small mercies*—four exceptions to the curse that would apply to his house and his descendants, alone.

Ψ Though still creatures of the night, they would be allowed to walk in the sun.

Ψ Though still required to live on blood, they would not be forced to take the lives of the innocent.

Ψ While still incapable of producing female offspring, they would be given *one opportunity and thirty days* to obtain a mate—a human female chosen by the gods—following a sign that appeared in the heavens.

Ψ While they were still required to sacrifice a firstborn son, their twins would be born as one child of darkness and one child of light, allowing them to sacrifice the former while keeping the latter to carry on their race.

And so…forever banished from their homeland in the Transylvanian mountains of Eastern Europe, the descendants of

BLOOD POSSESSION

Jaegar and the descendants of Jadon became the Vampyr of legend: roaming the earth, ruling the elements, living on the blood of others...forever bound by an ancient curse. They were brothers of the same species, separated only by degrees of light and shadow.

Prologue

800 BC

"Napolean, run!"

The ten-year-old child stumbled backward, his eyes wide with fright. His father's commanding voice shook him to his core.

"Run, son, go quickly!"

"No, Father. I don't want to leave you! Father, please—"

"Go now!" Sebastian Mondragon clutched his stomach and fell to the ground. His hands and fingers curled into two twisted balls, and his body contorted in an agonizing spasm. The transformation had begun. Writhing in pain, the once fearless warrior panted the warning a third time. "Napolean...son...please, run! Hide!"

Napolean heard his father's words as if from a distance. He wanted to flee, but he was frozen in place. Mesmerized by the horror that surrounded him, he swallowed hard and simply watched as the thick, inky fog swirled around his father's writhing body. Long, skeletal fingers with hooked claws and knobby knuckles clutched at his father's throat, raked deep gashes along his chest, and dug mercilessly toward his innards. Blood seeped from Sebastian's mouth as, inexplicably, his canine teeth began to grow, assuming the shape of—

Fangs.

But it was his father's unrelenting cries of agony that finally forced Napolean's retreat.

Napolean ran like he had never run before, his little heart beating furiously in his chest, the need for air burning his lungs. He weaved through the morbid courtyard, dodging fallen bodies and clasping his hands to his ears to block out the endless wails. All around him, males fell to the ground, cursed, and moaned. Some died immediately from the shock...or pain. Others drew their swords from their scabbards and took their own lives. Still others succumbed to the brutal torture, helpless as the darkness embodied them.

BLOOD POSSESSION

They were being punished.

Changed.

Transformed into an aberration of nature by the ghostly spirits of their victims.

The Blood Curse was upon them.

Napolean focused his eyes straight ahead, never losing sight of his destination: the imperial castle, a would-be fortress. He and his friends had hidden there so many times in the past, playing hide-and-seek, avoiding angry parents, hoping to catch a glimpse of a member of the royal family. Napolean knew the grounds like the back of his hands, and so he pressed on, desperate yet determined to get there, resigned to hide as his father had bid him.

At last, he arrived at the familiar gray castle gate.

He scurried into a small hole beneath the fortified wall and drew himself into a tight little ball. He tried to become invisible. Although he could no longer see the carnage in the village, the haunting cries continued to batter his ears like thunder against a stormy sky.

Napolean shook, remembering the moment Prince Jadon had emerged from the castle, his dark onyx eyes glazed with fear. He had gathered his loyalists to his side to explain the pronouncement—their punishment—what was soon to become a new way of life.

With so little time to prepare his men, Jadon had tried the best he could. Napolean had understood none of it, save one thing: The followers of Jadon needed to pledge their loyalty to the twin monarch as quickly as possible, before the transformation began, or they would meet a much worse fate.

Though Napolean's father had served for years in the royal one's secret guard, fighting to defeat the ever growing armies of Prince Jaegar, Napolean had been too young to join. Consequently, it had been imperative that he formally align himself with the right twin—for those who followed Jaegar were to receive no mercy.

And so, like all of the others, Napolean had knelt to kiss Prince Jadon's ring—recited the sacred pledge of loyalty before it was too late—and braced himself against what was to come...

Napolean shivered, bringing his attention back to the present moment.

He wanted to be brave, but fearful tears stung his eyes.

Then all at once, he heard cruel, disembodied laughter, the sound coming closer and closer, assaulting his ears.

"No. No. No," he whimpered, drawing further into the hollow cavity for protection, quivering so hard his bones rattled in his skin.

The fog swirled into a miniature cyclone, rose up from the ground, and dipped low as if it had eyes that could see...

Him.

Hiding.

"You think to escape, child?" the ghostly aberration hissed, laughter ricocheting through the small cavity. Flames exploded from the center of the darkness. "Die, little one! And be reborn the monster that you are!"

Napolean screamed so loud the sound became a cosmic explosion in his ears, yet the fog kept coming. It wrapped itself around his meager body, entered his mouth, and descended into his chest.

And then the pain began.

The excruciating, unrelenting, unbearable pain.

Acid flowed freely through his veins. Fire consumed his internal organs. Bones reshaped. Cells exploded. His entire composition changed, transformed...died.

He heard his own shouting as if it belonged to someone else, someone wretched and pitiable. He clawed at his skin, hoping to tear it from his body. He bit through his hand and pounded the ground. He writhed, thrashed, and tried to crawl away, but nothing stopped the assault.

Dear Celestial Gods!

He prayed for death, but it wouldn't come.

How much time had passed before the agony subsided, he had no idea. Had it been minutes? Hours? Perhaps days? It could have been a lifetime for all he'd endured before it had ceased...and the craving had begun.

A gnawing, all-consuming, primal thirst.

For blood.

It was the craving that had brought him out of the hole, crawling along the ground like an animal, stumbling through the darkness, searching for his father.

Now, as bitter tears stung his eyes, he absently wiped them away, only to find smears of blood on his hand.

Great goddess Andromeda, what had he become?

BLOOD POSSESSION

Finally reaching the village square, he staggered to a halt beside an aged stone well. As his vision adjusted to the darkness, he caught a shadow out of the corner of his eye: No, it couldn't be.

Please gods, no!

The grisly scene unfolded in slow motion as Jaegar Demir, the evil prince, hunkered over his father's body. The prince's eyes were wild with insanity as he bent to Sebastian's throat, tore into the flesh—as if it were mere parchment—and drank his fill of...blood. Napolean could neither move nor turn away as the macabre scene unfolded before him. As the evil prince drained his father's already gored and tattered body of life.

And then...

Horrified, trembling, and defeated, Napolean watched like a coward as Prince Jaegar withdrew his sword and took his father's head.

When at last the terror released him, he fisted his hands and howled at the heavens.

"Noooooooo!"

He shouted until his throat bled: "Father! Father! Father! Father..."

Buzzzzzz.

Napolean Mondragon hit the button on the alarm clock hard. He sat up and wiped the sweat from his brow. *Great gods, not again.* He swung his feet over the edge of the large canopy bed and rested his elbows on his knees, his face in his hands.

This was the third time this week he'd had the nightmare.

As the sovereign lord of the house of Jadon, the only remaining male living from the time of the Blood Curse, the memories occasionally plagued his sleep, but never this often. *Hades*, the nightmares must have been provoked by the sight of the male he had seen in the shadows just a few weeks back: the one who, impossibly, looked just like his murdered father.

The father who had been dead for twenty-eight hundred years.

Napolean rubbed his eyes and wrinkled his brow. *Gods*, he

could use the sweet affection of the princess right now—the touch of her gentle hand, the gaze of her compassionate eyes, the warmth of her soft lips against his.

"Ah hell, Napolean. Why torture yourself?" He wrung his hands together and shook his head. Vanya Demir had been a bright light in an otherwise dark, unending life. Her presence in the mansion had brought song and laughter and joy to a heart that had known nothing but duty and solitude for twenty-eight hundred years. The attraction between them had been magnetic, undeniable. She had become the best reason he'd had for rising in the morning in centuries.

And that was part of why she had left.

That, and the invitation she had received to go live with Marquis, her sister, and their newborn baby. Family was everything to Vanya, and she was not about to pass up the chance to help raise her nephew...or to be with her sister. In addition, Napolean had begun to mean far too much to the female, and she had been afraid that she might fall in love with a male she couldn't have—a male who was destined to only one woman in an eternal lifetime.

A woman who wasn't her.

Vanya was not Napolean's true *destiny*, and she had lost too much in her life already to risk losing once again.

Napolean shrugged, forcing his thoughts elsewhere. What difference did it make why Vanya had left?

She was gone.

She wasn't coming back.

And that was that.

Rising from the bed, he headed toward the shower and turned on the water. No, he would not obsess over the princess again. He had far too many pressing concerns with the recent discovery of the Dark Ones' colony. With the recent string of dead—no, *murdered and drained*—human bodies showing up all over the place in Dark Moon Vale.

And hell and brimstone, if that damnable nightmare was not beginning to unnerve him. Why now, after all these years, would his memories come back to haunt him so? Would he never be free of the guilt? Would he always feel ashamed of the day his father died?

And just who was that male he had seen in the shadows?

one

Brooke Adams smoothed her pencil skirt, flipped a wayward lock of ebony hair out of her eyes, and turned back to her PowerPoint presentation. It was Friday morning, the last day of the weeklong sales conference, and this was her moment to shine.

Her eyes scanned the audience.

Good. Tom Halloway seemed visibly impressed, and he was the one she needed: the CEO of PRIMAR, *Professional Image & Marketing, International.* Jim Davis, on the other hand, was noticeably confused, but what was new? He was in way over his head in the department anyhow, and there was no way to explain such a complex—and if she dare say so herself, *brilliant*—marketing strategy to the likes of *Jimbo*, a name he had chosen for himself. And Lewis, well, Lewis was…distracted. His beady eyes bounced back and forth between the large, drop-down screen and Brooke's breasts like an out-of-control yoyo—up, down, drool; down, up, drool; drool, stare, drool…

Annoyed the heck out of her, really. But the presentation was far too important to interrupt now. She had put too much time and energy into this moment. She didn't dare break her rhythm to chastise Lewis-hit-on-everything-with-legs-Martin. Not today. Unless, of course, he raised his hand.

Which he just did.

Seriously?

Raised his hand?

What was this, kindergarten?

"Yes, Lewis?" She put on her best professional smile.

His beady eyes narrowed, and he licked his lips. Probably had some drool to catch. "Could you unbutton your blouse?"

Brooke gasped. "Excuse me?" Her eyes darted around the room, waiting, as she fully expected one of her male colleagues

1

to come to her rescue, snatch Lewis up by the collar, and escort him out of the meeting—that's if Halloway didn't fire him right on the spot first.

No one moved.

In fact, no one seemed even the least bit offended by Lewis's request. *What in the world?* She swallowed a lump in her throat. Apparently, it was up to her. Squaring her chin, she gave Lewis her best I'm-gonna-mop-the-floor-with-you sneer and nearly snarled. "I beg your pardon, you little jackass, imbecile, son-of-a—"

And that's when her alarm had gone off, mercifully ending the nightmare.

For the love of Pete, this presentation was going to be the death of her.

Brooke wrapped the soft, Egyptian-cotton towel around her head and swallowed an aspirin: Such strange dreams always gave her headaches. Or maybe it was just the anticipation of the actual presentation. She glanced at the bright blue numbers on the digital clock. In less than one hour, she would be standing in that hotel conference room, all eyes focused on her, as the annual event came to a close, pitching the largest marketing proposal she had ever dared to envision to the entire PR department, head honchos included. And Tom Halloway, the company's CEO, would be sitting right there in the front row.

Good Lord, what if Lewis really did ask her to unbutton her blouse? How would she handle such an unexpected hiccup?

Yeah, right. Get it together, Brooke.

She reached for her cell phone and punched in the number of the most reasonable person she knew, her favorite coworker and trusted confidante—who also happened to be her best friend for the last ten years—Tiffany Matthews.

Tiffany picked up on the second ring. "Hey. What's up, Brooke."

"I think I'm completely losing it, Tiff. I had a dream that I was in the middle of the presentation when Lewis asked me to unbutton my blouse."

Tessa Dawn

Tiffany's laughter echoed through the phone. "Sounds about like Lewis."

Brooke frowned and peeked out the hotel curtains to check the weather: cool but clear. A perfect day for her presentation. "Tiff, it's not funny. I swear, I think I'm caving under the pressure."

"You're not caving, Brooke. And you're not going to cave." She sounded amused.

Brooke bit her lower lip, a nervous habit that just reinforced her point. "How do you know?"

Tiffany sighed. "Because you're the best presenter we have, and other than some insane, repressed paranoia you tend to harbor, you never bomb on anything. *Miss perfect?* Are you kidding? Halloway is gonna love your idea, and hey—if for some reason, he doesn't, your dream already told you what to do."

"Huh?" she asked, confused.

"Unbutton your blouse!"

Brooke couldn't help but laugh. "Yeah, that would be great. Halloway could fire me, and then he could ask me out on a date."

Tiffany snickered. "True. True. Maybe not the best idea." She paused then. "Brooke?"

"What?"

Tiffany's voice was all at once serious. "Girl, tell me you are dressed and out of bed...please."

Brooke rubbed the towel over her thick, shoulder-length hair to speed up the drying process and stared at the ruffled hotel sheets beneath her.

"Brooke?"

"What?"

"Brooke!"

"I'm out of bed."

"Oh hell, Brooke; you aren't, are you?"

Brooke sighed. "Okay, okay, so maybe I climbed back in bed, but I've already showered and washed my hair...and I'm getting back up...right now."

3

BLOOD POSSESSION

"Brooke! I swear—"

"I'm up! *I'm up!*"

"I'm coming over," Tiffany said.

"No, you're not." This time Brooke spoke with authority.

"What's the room number again?" Tiffany asked, her voice heavy with insistence.

"Tiff, don't. I'm twenty-nine years old! I think I can dress myself by now."

"*Room number?*" Tiffany's tone brooked no argument.

Brooke absently glanced at the plastic key-card on her nightstand: *Dark Moon Lodge, room 425.* She rolled her eyes. "How many times have you been to my hotel room, Tiff?"

"Don't get smart with me, Missy," Tiffany warned.

"Fine," Brook said. "Four—two—five."

"Be there in ten."

Brooke laughed. "Make it fifteen and bring me a doughnut? I need some sugar." She put an extra ounce of pleading in her voice.

Tiffany huffed her annoyance. "Now just where am I supposed to find a doughnut shop in Dark Moon Vale? Have you actually seen one since we've been here?"

"No," Brook admitted, feeling the promise of a nice, sugary-sweet pastry rapidly slipping away. "But I'm sure they have a bakery somewhere. If not, maybe try a local coffee shop or the grocery store. *Please?*"

"Oh, good grief," Tiffany grumbled. "The conference starts in forty-five minutes, you're not even dressed, and your top priority is finding a doughnut!"

Brooke stifled a laugh. "Think of it this way," she said, ignoring the anxiety-producing reference to time, "maybe you'll get lucky and there'll be a specialty souvenir-slash-pastry shop right next to the lodge, fully staffed with big, handsome mountain men." She groaned. "Big, *naked* mountain men with huge…axes."

Tiffany sniggered. "Yeah, that's going to happen." She sighed, ruefully. "With my luck, it'll be fully staffed with

4

toothless, mutated psychopaths, all recently transplanted from *The Hills Have Eyes.*"

Brooke couldn't really argue: Tiffany's luck with men was just that bad. "Just get me a fresh chocolate éclair if you find one, 'kay? Pretty please with a cherry on top?"

"Maybe," Tiffany teased, trying to sound maternal. "In the meantime, you just get dressed and concentrate on your presentation. Think about what you're going to do with all that bonus money when Halloway falls in love with your proposal and offers you the director of marketing position."

Brooke smiled. Now *that* would be the perfect outcome. Not that the idea of hot, naked mountain men serving pastries—with big axes—didn't also rank pretty high on the list. "Oh, and Tiff?"

"Yeah?"

"Bring your black stilettos in case my navy pumps don't work with my skirt."

Tiffany giggled on the other end.

"What?" Brooke asked, failing to get what was so funny.

"You have an IQ over 140, yet you still rely on sexy legs to give yourself an edge."

"Hey, Mama didn't raise any fools, right?" The moment the words left Brooke's tongue, she regretted speaking them. Not only were they untrue—Mama hadn't cared enough to raise anyone—but her *mother* was a subject better left alone. And thoughts of the heartless woman were not about to steal her joy—or her confidence—this time. Not today. She deliberately made her voice cheery. "Every possible advantage, right?"

Tiffany cleared her throat. "I'm telling you, Brooke, you're not gonna need it. Anyhow, hop to it; I'll be there in a few."

"Okay," Brooke replied, "see ya soon." She hung up the phone smiling and took a deep, cleansing breath. She might not have much in the way of family—and boy, was that the understatement of the century; outside of her precious grandma Lanie, there was virtually no one related by blood who cared for her—but she had struck gold when it came to finding a best friend.

And, who knows, maybe Tiffany was right: Her presentation was going to be a knock-out. Halloway was going to fall in love with her ideas, every bit as much as her sexy shoes. And the conference in Dark Moon Vale was going to go off without a hitch.

Brooke rubbed the towel energetically through her still damp hair, tousling the thick, heavy strands as she grinned. If all went well, in less than ten hours, she would be headed home to San Francisco with a tentative contract in her hand and an even brighter future on the horizon.

Tiffany was absolutely right.

What could possibly go wrong?

two

Salvatore Nistor raised his arms languidly above his head, crossed his feet at the ankles, and sank deep into the comfortable mattress in his underground lair as he replayed the events of the previous night in his head. He could still see the female he had used...and exterminated...so vividly in his mind. He could still taste her fear, and the thought hardened his groin even now.

She had been standing beside her car in a grocery store parking lot, fumbling with her keys, so tempting and unaware. Her ample chest had risen and fallen with each shallow breath, such a willing victim just crying out, *Take me! Choose me!*

And Salvatore had been quick to oblige her.

In one lightning quick move, he had snatched the human by her arm, sent her groceries scattering to the ground in random piles of rubbish, and flown the two of them behind the building to a nice secluded area.

"Please," she had whispered in a terrified voice as desperate tears had rolled down her cheeks.

Salvatore licked his lips as he remembered how he had snarled back at her, "Please what!" The female had been as beautiful as she was...stupid. But that was to be expected, as all humans were pathetically inferior to vampires. Salvatore had pressed his finger to her lips and made a shushing sound, glaring at her with eyes he had known were gleaming red. "Quiet. Not a word," he had commanded. "Do not move, and do not speak a word."

He had allowed his fangs to elongate then—slowly, for effect—before lifting her trembling wrist to his mouth and dragging the sharp points of his canines lengthwise across her vein. A small line of crimson had trickled along the creamy white skin of her forearm, and he had quickly lapped it up with his

7

tongue, groaning at the exquisite taste of freshly drawn blood.

Mmm, he moaned even now, growing restless on the bed.

He let out a deep breath, remembering how he had invaded her mind, forcing his way into her memories in order to retrieve her name.

Jane.

Ah, yes, his delectable prize had been named Jane.

He could have sworn Jane's knees had literally buckled as she had swayed before him then, nauseous from the sight of her own blood, nearly passing out from fright.

But she hadn't passed out.

She had stood perfectly motionless. Deathly quiet. *Like an obedient female should.*

"Good girl," he had murmured, impressed.

He had scanned her fine features next—her soft lips and pale blue eyes, the high inset of her cheekbones, which gave her a model's appearance—and then he had frowned, thinking it a pity that he would have to kill her before he could thoroughly enjoy her—say, for at least a week or more—if he could avoid getting her pregnant that long.

He sighed, releasing the pang of regret; after all, duty was duty, and time had been of the essence: Oskar's orders were to kill, not capture.

In fact, Oskar Vadovsky, the Dark Ones' new chief of council, had made all of his instructions explicitly clear: "Drop enough bodies in the streets of Dark Moon Vale to terrify the local humans; create enough pandemonium in the towns to rile up the hidden vampire-hunting societies; and let the humans come after their foolish enemies—the sons of Jadon, who live on the surface—while we, the sons of Jaegar, remain safely hidden beneath the earth." In other words: *Exact revenge on Napolean Mondragon for the damage he inflicted on the colony.*

Salvatore snarled, remembering the wretched king of the house of Jadon and all he had wrought upon the house of Jaegar—the *utterly humiliating* ass-kicking he had given all of them the day he and a handful of his warriors had come to rescue

Tessa Dawn

Princess Ciopori from Salvatore's lair. The day Marquis Silivasi and his crew had slaughtered *fifty* of the Dark Ones' children, even as the young ones had slept in their cribs.

A deep growl reverberated in his throat, his desire for revenge rising like bile.

As if the murder of their children had not been enough, Napolean Mondragon had single-handedly slain *eighty-seven* of their soldiers as the males had chased him through the tunnels on his way out of the colony. The haughty king had harnessed the power of the sun—*underground, of all things*—in order to incinerate his pursuers deep in the heart of their own home—where they should have been safe from burning!

Salvatore ran his tongue over his canines and tried to force the memory from his mind...back to more pleasant recollections.

Back to the night before...

Back to Jane and the way he had snarled at her like a feral animal when she had tried to back away, whimpering at the pain in her wrist.

"You think to escape me, female?" he had thundered.

She had not been such a good girl after all.

"I'm sorry," she had whined like a baby, clearly not understanding what *quiet* meant.

Salvatore had cuffed her then, and the impact of his blow had sent spittle mixed with blood spewing from her mouth. "Not a word!" he had repeated, searing her with a harsh glare.

Horrified, she had covered her mouth with both hands, struggling to stifle a scream, and then her legs had given way and she had fallen to her knees, shuddering like an idiot. For a moment, Salvatore had simply watched her—kneeling in the dirt, squirming like a worm—but his patience had not lasted. Jane had moved when he had told her to be still. She had spoken when he had warned her not to make a sound. And she had more or less worn on his last nerve...just because she had. He had been determined to punish her for her insolence.

He laughed now, thinking about it.

9

BLOOD POSSESSION

They had been such minor infractions, really.

But it simply didn't matter.

Defiance was defiance, and his enemies never went unpunished.

His lips twitched, and he sat up on the bed, contemplating the importance of that truth: Napolean Mondragon would not go unpunished either. *He could not go unpunished.* The Dark Ones would have their revenge, and Salvatore would benefit, politically, in the process. He would pay Marquis Silivasi back for taking Ciopori from his lair. He would appease Oskar Vadovsky by demonstrating his superior knowledge of Dark Magick. And he would regain the respect of the remaining council members— the two who had witnessed his own unspeakable *degradation*—by doing what had never been done before: He would kill Napolean Mondragon, the ancient, heretofore invincible leader of the house of Jadon.

His plan couldn't fail.

It was too well constructed.

Salvatore had paid too much homage to the Dark Lords of the underworld for their favor in the matter—their assistance in his wicked scheme—and the demon lords would help him. So far, they were delivering handsomely.

Salvatore exhaled.

He stretched his arms and rolled his shoulders, allowing the tension to ease. All in good time. It would all happen in good time.

Once again, he returned his attention to the night before, conjuring the image of a delectable silhouette: the body of the squirming woman still kneeling beneath him, trying desperately to crawl away.

The game had become fun then.

Salvatore had waved his hand, turned on his heels, and started to walk away—pretending as if he were finished with the night's festivities: He had intentionally given Jane a small measure of hope, a slight window of time in which she almost believed she might escape.

Tessa Dawn

"*Ha!*"

He laughed aloud, recalling the scene in exquisite detail, the way that Jane had played along so beautifully. She had leapt to her feet—quite adeptly, actually—and taken off running with a strength of purpose that was…well, shocking. And kudos to her for trying. She had even let out an ear-piercing scream, a cry for help so desperate it might have possibly reached the heavens.

But her god hadn't come to rescue her, and neither had anyone else.

Salvatore lifted the tip of his finger, extended a jagged talon to his mouth, nicked his bottom lip, and tasted the blood, sighing.

The memory was positively erotic.

The female had taken five solid steps—five enormously wide strides—before Salvatore had caught her. He had grasped a handful of her fine, strawberry blond hair in his fist and yanked her back against him. And then he had spun her around by the shoulders, clutched her by the neck, and forced her to face him. "Look at me!"

It had been an imperious command, possibly a little overdramatic.

Of course, he had also scanned the area around them for the presence of others—not that he had been worried about humans; he could always erase their memories if he had to—but he had to be wary of the sons of Jadon, the *privileged* vampires. If one of them had heard her scream, Salvatore would have been forced to fight. And she was hardly worth it.

Confident that her cries had gone unheard, he had tightened his grasp on her throat, hauled her solidly beneath him, and bent to drink from her neck.

She had truly become hysterical then, beating her hands against his chest and twisting her torso back and forth in a frantic attempt to break free; and all the while, her heart had pounded like a bass drum, threatening to explode in her chest as her tears had fallen like raindrops.

She had begged for mercy, her entire being consumed with

terror.

And then instantly, albeit noiselessly, a puddle of pale liquid had pooled on the ground beneath her. Annoyed—actually, *disgusted*—Salvatore had withdrawn his fangs and quickly shuffled out of the way. He had been wearing a brand-new pair of Testoni Norvegese shoes—not to mention a six-hundred-dollar pair of black linen pants—and the last thing he needed was some human urinating on his crisp, expensive outfit.

He had to admit, the female's inability to control her bodily functions had really been a buzz-kill; she had almost completely squelched his desire to play.

Almost.

He sighed, musing. If only he could terrorize Napolean Mondragon the same way. Imagine, forcing the arrogant king to wet himself and beg for his life...before killing him: Now that would be worth all the spells in the Blood Canon!

Salvatore's hands slowly curled into fists at the mere mention of the ancient book of Black Magic. He had possessed the Blood Canon for nearly eight hundred years, and the dark treasure had been his greatest acquisition. His most prized possession. He ground his teeth together. Nachari Silivasi had stolen the book the same day Napolean had killed eighty-seven of the house of Jaegar's warriors.

In fact, Nachari Silivasi, along with that headstrong tyrant Marquis, had murdered Salvatore's beloved little brother Valentine even before then—

Stop! Salvatore told himself.

Do not go there!

Not now.

He was surprised by his pathetic lack of discipline. He was getting far too worked up when he needed to stay focused on the here and now. The others would pay.

They would all pay.

One at a time.

Starting with their insufferable king.

Oh, to hell with it, Salvatore growled. He would not restrain his fury! He would not control his thoughts! He would ruminate on his hatred. Feed his sweltering thirst for revenge until it grew into a living, breathing entity with a life of its own.

He would continue to delve into the heart of Black Magick, to beseech the assistance of the dark lords to mess with Napolean's head—sending him nightmare after garish nightmare, day after endless day—conjuring ever more vivid images of the ghostly apparition Napolean believed to be his father until the worthless king's mind was so twisted with guilt and confusion that he didn't know which way was up, what was real and what was illusion.

Napolean Mondragon would ultimately bend to the will of Salvatore Rafael Nistor just as the useless human female had bent to his will last night!

His chest heaved with the raw power of his conviction, and he salivated over his final tryst with Jane, turning each delectable detail over in his mind, savoring the memory of every precious moment one last time. He had punished her for wetting her pants by slowly carving a macabre outline into the delicate flesh of her throat…watching…anticipating…while blood streamed down her neck, across her shoulder, and along the swell of her right breast. Oh, how he had relished the taste—sucking the tender flesh of her nipples as they had slowly marinated in her blood.

The female had opened her mouth to cry out in anguish, but no sound had come out. Salvatore had stolen her voice, and *damnit, if her silent pleas hadn't turned him on.*

He had thrown her down to the ground then—careful to avoid the noxious puddle she had made in her moment of weakness—as he tore off her soiled clothes. Gazing down into her pale blue eyes, he had brought his lips to hers and kissed her harshly—a small token of mercy as women liked that kind of thing—and then he had pierced her bottom lip with his fangs so he could drink from her mouth as he took her.

The union had been perfect.

Shocking, painful, uninhibited.

BLOOD POSSESSION

She had begged him to kill her—and he had almost shed a tear.

"Soon, my lover. *Very soon*," he had whispered in her ear.

Salvatore wiped the sweat from his brow. The memory had inflamed him almost as much as the real thing, and now that his state of arousal was too great to deny, he would require a physical release. He wondered if one of his fellow Dark Ones had a female captive close by, but then he realized that his need went beyond what a woman could provide.

Salvatore craved extreme adrenaline, violence, and pain—the erotic strikes of venomous snakes, the awareness of the serpents' lethal poison being attacked by his own, and the sweet sensation of nimble scales slithering over his warm flesh, bringing him to satisfaction again…and again. He rose from the bed and headed for the colony's Chamber of Cobras.

As he glided through the underground halls, his thoughts returned to Napolean one last time. Indeed, the wretched king would die this time, too. With the help of the dark lord, Ademordna, Salvatore Nistor would accomplish what no other Dark One had been able to do in twenty-eight hundred years: He would end Napolean Mondragon's life. He had finally found a way to make it happen. As he entered the final hall that would lead him to his erotic fantasy, Salvatore picked up his pace and laughed at the brilliance of his plan…

Napolean Mondragon would continue to be haunted by endless nightmares.

Confusion, guilt, and *insanity* would torment him relentlessly…until it finally wore him down. Salvatore would never let up until he broke him. Until at last, the ancient one could bear his existence no longer. And then—when Napolean was agonizingly desperate, confused, and completely vulnerable—the ghost of Napolean's father would offer him a way out of the madness…an opportunity to atone for the one great sin of his past. The one thing he had never shared with his people.

The shameful secret the dark lords of the underworld had

revealed to Salvatore, alone.

In exchange for freeing the ghost's eternally tormented soul, Napolean's father would order Napolean to take his own life. And at last, no one would need to defeat the unconquerable Napolean—because the all-powerful king would be the instrument of his own demise.

Napolean Mondragon would kill himself.

At his father's command.

three

Brooke took a large gulp of her coffee and slammed her mug down on the short, round table in the corner coffee shop. "Well, so much for a bright, promising future."

Tiffany smiled sheepishly. "Now, Brooke. It wasn't *that* bad. In fact, I think it was one of the best presentations I've ever seen." She added a second package of cream to her own vanilla latte.

Brooke glared at her friend, resenting her pitiful stab at compassion. "Yeah, I'd say so: Brooke Adams, up and rising star of PRIMAR—dressed to the nines in a sleek, smoky gray suit, mind you—walks confidently to the front of the room, gathers the hushed anticipation of all eyes, clears her throat, turns toward the presentation screen, and breaks a four-inch stiletto heel, falling promptly on her ass in front of everyone!" She gestured wildly with her hands. "But does she simply catch her balance and readjust? Nooo, of course not. That would be too easy. She has to put on a complete jackass clinic: flailing her arms like some kind of spaz while grasping wildly at the whiteboard, only to take it down with her—*on top of her*, mind you—before hitting the ground, spread-eagle, with her skirt jacked up to her waist as she shares her...*assets*...with the whole room." She dropped her head in her hands. "Yeah, I would say it was quite the *presentation*."

Tiffany sighed, trying hard not to laugh. Again. "Aw, Brooke. It really wasn't...I mean...I don't think anyone thought—"

"Thought what?" Brooke whimpered, her bottom lip jutting out in a pout. "That I was a complete idiot? Or that I'd make a great stripper if things ever went south as PRIMAR?"

"Now, Brooke."

"Hey, red g-string, black stilettos, bared ass to a room full of

17

men—if it walks like a duck…"

Tiffany frowned, her eyes soft with compassion. "Brooke, it was an accident. No one thought less of you. In fact, everyone was really concerned for your safety."

Brooke glared at her friend—a real threat emerging in her expression this time. "*Stop*. Just stop. You know as well as I do that the men got a cheap thrill, and the women—well, they probably loved witnessing my downfall. No pun intended." She shook her head slowly back and forth. "Oh God, just kill me now."

"Brooke—"

"Did you see Halloway's face!" she exclaimed, her voice rising in proportion to her anxiety. "His eyes were wide as saucers! Like a five-year-old kid at a carnival. And his mouth? It was literally hanging open! I don't think he knew whether to laugh, help me up, or—or stuff a dollar bill in my waistband." She banged her head softly against the tabletop three times. "How many people actually got up and left the room just to keep from laughing?" She moaned.

Tiffany shook her head, feigning ignorance. "I really didn't notice anyone leaving the…"

Her voice trailed off before she could complete the…lie.

Taking a deep breath, Brooke sat back in her high-backed, wooden chair and brushed a sprinkling of sugar crumbs from the table, her eyes averted downward. She rubbed her temples then, wishing she could transport herself to another universe. "No one made eye contact with me the entire presentation, Tiff. I was so mortified! Oh my God, why did I have to wear a g-string today? I mean, really? What are the odds of something like this happening? *Ever?*"

Tiffany gently grasped Brooke's forearm. Her sea-green eyes were muted with kindness. "Oh, sweetie…okay, so it was an…unfortunate moment. A *very* unfortunate moment. But honestly? The presentation was really, *really* good—once you got back on your feet." She bit her lip to keep from laughing.

"Don't you mean, once I got back on my *bare* feet?" She

18

brushed Tiffany's arm away and took another slow sip of her coffee. "Oh hell, I think I took the entire women's movement back a century today." Despite her gallant attempts at humor, her eyes welled up with tears. "I have never been so humiliated in all my life. That presentation meant so much to me!" Her shoulders sagged and she curled into herself, dropping her head down on her arms.

Tiffany stood up then. She hurried to the other side of the table, sat down next to her friend, and brushed a wayward lock of brunette hair away from her face. "Listen to me, Brooke…"

Brooke frowned.

"I mean it. *Listen!*"

"What?"

"Are you listening?"

"*Yesss—what?*"

"You know as well as I do that what made the presentation important was not the delivery but the information. You showed Halloway a solid way to make a boatload of money, and you backed it up with concrete facts and figures. You introduced an entirely new way of thinking about things that the top brass never even considered, and *that*, more than anything, got their attention." She sat back and crossed her arms. "So you had an unfortunate moment—so what? Money talks, Brooke, and that presentation spoke loud and clear. As far as I'm concerned, you took a ground-breaking idea, sold it in a half an hour, and wrapped it all up in a gorgeous silk bow—namely, *a really great ass!*" She smiled broadly. "Add a little *damsel-in-distress* theme to the mix, and frankly, there wasn't a man in the room that wasn't sold. And the women? Well, luckily for you, Halloway has the final say. You mark my words: This whole incident is going to end up working in your favor."

Brooke peeked at her friend from beneath her hands. "You have the strangest way of looking at things, Tiff. Do you really think I still have a prayer?"

"Yes," Tiffany answered emphatically. "Are you kidding me?"

BLOOD POSSESSION

Brooke sat up a little straighter. "Man, I really hope so." She offered a halfhearted smile. "At the least, I hope Halloway doesn't hold it against me."

Tiffany laughed then, her kind eyes brightening with a twinkle. "You know, for such a smart woman, you can really be dense sometimes."

Brooke frowned.

"What is Halloway?" Tiffany asked.

Brooke wrinkled up her forehead. "The boss?"

"*What is Halloway?*"

"The CEO—"

"No! Before that. *After that.* What is Halloway?"

Brooke shook her head.

"He's a *man*, Brooke."

Brooke rolled her eyes. "Maybe, but a very discerning, professional man—who I doubt makes decisions based on some primal, male instinct."

"Agreed," Tiffany stated. "And if your ideas and your presentation sucked, then I don't think standing in front of the room buck-naked would've helped you. But that's not the case. And all things considered, you really do have a great ass."

Brooke laughed then. She couldn't help it. Leave it to Tiffany to find the silver lining in every cloud. "I kind of do, don't I?" At least she hadn't flashed anything she had to be ashamed of.

Tiffany smiled. "See, there you go!"

Brooke sighed, feeling a little better. *A little.* "I guess we'll just have to wait and see."

"Trust me, darling," Tiffany assured her. "You won't be waiting long."

Brooke shrugged then. She crumpled up her napkin and tossed it in a large gray wastebasket just behind their table. "I think I've had enough caffeine for a while." She stood up, walked to the bin, and dumped her coffee, careful to brush an errant crumb of coffee cake off her skirt before turning back to face her friend. "You ready to get out of here?"

Following suit, Tiffany cleared her place and dumped her trash. "Yep. Two more sessions this afternoon, then we're home free."

Brooke cringed, not wanting to think about facing her coworkers so soon. "Can we take a little break before we go back to the conference?"

Tiffany smiled. "Sure. Maybe we can do a little sightseeing before we turn in the local rental car...get back to the lodge. It gets dark fairly early around here, so let's try and visit some of the historical sites while there's still some daylight."

Brooke nodded. She retrieved her itinerary from her purse and gave it a cursory glance. "I have Time Management from noon to two and three, short breakout sessions between three and five. What about you?"

Tiffany shrugged and held the door open for her friend. "I think I'm in the noon session with you, and afterward, I have to do some teaching—the PRIMAR branding concept, integrating the new software system, that kind of thing. Either way, we should be packed, in the cab, and on our way to the airport no later than six."

Brooke stepped into the brisk mountain air and took a deep breath. "I hope no one mentions the...incident again," she said.

"They won't," Tiffany replied, almost convincingly. She reached for her keys to the rental car. "You just hold your head up and expect good things to happen. Trust me on this one, Brooke."

Brooke nodded and tried to look on the bright side. They only had seven more hours to go. She could do this. She had certainly dealt with far worse things in life. And what was a little embarrassment among professionals, anyway? She winced. *Yeah, whatever. It sucked.* But she would get through it. Besides, once she allowed herself to look past the humiliation, she knew Tiffany was right: The presentation itself had been stellar. Unless Halloway was a truly shallow individual, he had to see the brilliance of her strategy.

Forcing herself to project confidence, Brooke deliberately

raised her chin, drew back her shoulders, and climbed into the passenger seat of Tiffany's rental.

A few more hours in Dark Moon Vale.

Then back to San Francisco.

Napolean glanced up at the high, pearl-white ceilings in the dimly lit meeting room of the ancient Hall of Justice. Lantern light was still used to illuminate the circular space, and the muted glow cast ghostly shadows against the surrounding stone walls as the males gathered to discuss the business of their enemies.

Napolean drew in a deep breath and counted backward from ten to one as he felt the life-affirming energy fill his lungs. He regarded Marquis Silivasi with a stern look and slowly exhaled. "The boy is simply too young to attend the warrior's meeting, Marquis," he repeated for the third time.

"Nonsense," Marquis grumbled, shifting the smiling infant on his lap and repositioning the slobber-covered rattle in his hand.

"He's four weeks old," Napolean reiterated.

Marquis smiled then, the grin of a proud father, and it was a welcome sight to Napolean's eyes, a rare expression of unqualified joy on the face of a male who had lived a very difficult life…until recently. Marquis had met his *destiny* just over one month ago, and she was a beautiful and strong mate, not to mention one of the original females of their celestial race. Perhaps this was why Napolean had let the discussion go on this long: The male was a valued Ancient Master Warrior, the closest thing Napolean had to an equal in the house of Jadon, and the mate of an original princess: Vanya's sister.

"He's sitting up by himself," Marquis explained, gesturing toward the boy's straight—well, semi-straight—back. "And he has the grip of a gladiator."

As if arguing for his own right to stay, the child looked up at his Sovereign and cooed.

Napolean sighed. Indeed, little Nikolai Silivasi was strong and alert—clearly bright, and unnaturally handsome, even for a vampire—as Marquis was quick to remind anyone who would listen. But the truth remained—he was not the only baby ever born to the descendants of Jadon, he was clearly far more interested in cutting his teeth on his rattle than strategizing on how to organize teams of executioners to hunt Dark Ones, and Marquis would have to come back to earth soon or they would all lose their sanity.

"Do not worry. You're perfectly sane!" Marquis argued, inadvertently reading Napolean's thoughts.

Napolean growled a subtle warning—purposeful or not, the mind of another vampire was sacred ground, not to be tampered with—to which Marquis simply waved a dismissive hand. Napolean stepped back, more than a little surprised by the casual license his subject was taking with him: Had the entire world gone mad?

"Marquis! You will do well to remember your place, warrior; and you *will* take your son home to—"

"*Milord...*" A soft voice interrupted the exchange before it could become heated, not that Marquis—or any other male in Dark Moon Vale for that matter—would dare to openly defy the ancient ruler.

Napolean looked up just in time to see Ciopori Demir-Silivasi saunter into the chamber and make her way down the narrow, center aisle toward her mate, a look of solemn purpose and apology on her face. "Greetings," she sighed as she stopped before the two of them. "How it pleases me to see you this night, my king." She kissed Napolean softly on the cheek.

In front of his men.
In front of Marquis.

Marquis's eyes flashed red, and Napolean groaned inwardly. True, it was an instinctive male reaction that Marquis—or any other male vampire, for that matter—could hardly be expected to restrain. They were territorial creatures to put it mildly;

nonetheless, the room full of warriors perked up, watching with apt fascination and more than a little amusement as Napolean hissed beneath his breath, warning Marquis to control himself.

Truly, the world was out of alignment.

"Please forgive me," Ciopori continued, seemingly unconcerned by the not-so-subtle displays of dominance and aggression. "I asked Marquis to keep Nikolai for the afternoon while I went out to do some shopping. I'm afraid I lost track of the time—"

"And refused to answer your cell phone!" Marquis snapped, feigning irritation.

"Now, Marquis," Ciopori said in a sweet, cajoling voice.

"Don't Marquis me!" he replied. "You also failed to answer my telepathic calls, woman. This is not acceptable."

Ciopori laughed, a carefree, lyrical sound, and smiled. "Oh, stop your grumbling, warrior. You seem none the worse for the experience. Besides, sometimes a woman needs a moment to herself." With that, she reached down and scooped up the baby, who immediately began to wriggle his arms and legs in excited anticipation of his mother's embrace.

Napolean felt the energy around them stir and knew that the two of them were finishing their conversation telepathically. He had no intention of interfering—Ciopori was perhaps the only individual in the valley who was a true match for Marquis Silivasi and his...*socially challenged*...personality. She could give as good as she got.

Once the energy settled down, Napolean nodded at Ciopori, conveying his understanding. After twenty-eight hundred years, he was not a male of infinite patience—and the order he kept in the house of Jadon was not a small matter—however, he had a hopeless soft spot for the surviving female children of King Sakarias, and there was no point in pretending he did not. Truly, after so many years of believing all females of their race to be extinct, all the males in the house of Jadon treated the princesses with infinite respect and awe. It was still hard to believe the two females had survived that terrible time.

Napolean blinked, bringing his thoughts back to the present. "I understand, of course, Princess. Thank you for coming for Nikolai."

"Of course." Ciopori reached out and gently touched Napolean's arm, and a collective hush settled through the room.

Few beings touched Napolean so casually.

Few of his subjects took such informal liberties with the most ancient and feared of their kind, and it was still a bit unsettling for the males to witness such a simple—yet powerful—connection with their leader. Indeed, the princess rarely shied away from him.

Marquis stirred in reaction.

A low, almost inaudible growl resounded in Marquis's chest, and Napolean instinctively displayed a lightning-quick flash of deadly fangs. It was a clear, unambiguous threat...a prominent, unequivocal show of dominance. Normally, Napolean found humor—if not delight—in the possessive ministrations of his males, but he would not be challenged, warned, or corrected in front of an assembly of his warriors, not even by Marquis.

Not even if the male couldn't help it.

"Blessed Andromeda," Ciopori sighed, rolling her eyes. "Vanya and I must get working on an anti-testosterone spell immediately. There must be some magic-spell in the coffers somewhere..." Her voice trailed off.

Napolean smiled.

Marquis growled. "Go home, woman. We have important things to discuss here."

At that, Ciopori punched him in the arm, and to her credit, she didn't draw back her fist to rub bruised knuckles. "Do not push your luck, warrior," she chastised softly, still smiling. Then, she swung around, bent down, and planted a sound kiss on Marquis's lips before sauntering out with Nikolai in her arms.

Marquis's face remained hard, but Napolean could have sworn he saw the corner of his mouth turn up in a smile. This was good—very good. All was well with the Silivasi family for the first time in years.

BLOOD POSSESSION

Returning his attention to the room, Napolean crossed his arms and regarded the warriors as a whole. The males quickly stood at attention. "If there are no more interruptions," Napolean said, "then I would like to get on with the meeting. Ramsey, do you have the report I requested?"

Ramsey Olaru pushed off a large column he was leaning against and slowly removed a thin reed of grass from between his teeth. As he made his way to the front of the room, he rolled his head from side to side, popping his neck to release tension, his cold, calculating eyes staring straight ahead.

The six-foot-five sentinel was a stormy combination of tightly wound energy and barely leashed aggression in his most relaxed state of mind, a countenance at complete odds with his looks: While, for all intents and purposes, one could argue that something had gone terribly wrong in Ramsey's childhood—perhaps he had taken a dark turn during his studies at the University—he had the face of a GQ model. A very large, dangerous, somewhat unstable GQ model. His massive shoulders were contrasted by a fall of chin-length, dark blond hair that he kept flawlessly tapered to frame his face; and his solid frame of titanium muscle was encased in baby-smooth skin that remained perpetually tan, though he made no effort to keep it that way. And while women might faint at the sight of his rather…sensual…mouth, every warrior in Dark Moon Vale knew the guy would just as soon rip your head off with his bare teeth than look at you. There was nothing mellow or soft—or GQ—about Ramsey Olaru.

"Evening, milord," Ramsey drawled, turning to face the other warriors.

Napolean nodded and stepped to the side, careful to keep Ramsey in his sights. Not that any of the valley's three sentinels were anything but loyal to the death, but it simply went against instinct to turn one's back on a wild tiger.

Ramsey placed one foot on the seat of the nearest chair, rested an elbow on his knee, and glanced at the notes he held in his hand. "Got a few stats," he said, and then his eyebrows creased and his face went deathly serious. "As best we can project, based on the schematics Marquis, Santos, and Nathaniel drew up, we believe there are at least fifteen hundred of our Dark Brothers living beneath the Valley."

Someone whistled low beneath their breath, and a few of the warriors shifted in their seats. Resulting from the abduction of Princess Ciopori by Salvatore Nistor, the discovery of the Dark Ones' underground colony had been a shock to everyone. For centuries the sons of Jadon had believed their Dark Brothers to be scattered, nomadic, and living out of caves, yet nothing could have been further from the truth. And now that they had been discovered, the Dark Ones were wreaking havoc in the local towns and villages.

"There have been at least seven murders that we know of since we rescued the princess—and that's just within the last thirty days."

Marquis Silivasi clenched and released his fists, and Napolean gave him a reassuring nod. *You will have your revenge, warrior.* The king spoke on a private bandwidth. *We all will.* He held Marquis's stare for a moment before turning back to regard Ramsey. "And you believe the purpose of these murders is to stir up fear among the humans, to place suspicion on those of us who live on the surface, who walk in the sun?"

"We do." Ramsey nodded.

"Or just for the hell of it," Nathaniel Silivasi added from the back of the room.

Napolean made a tent with his hands and pressed his fingers to his lips. "And how well is this being contained?"

Saxson Olaru, Ramsey's fraternal twin and another one of the three sentinels, stood up and bowed his head in deference.

"Speak freely," Napolean urged.

One by one, Saxson made eye contact with the other males. "The new crews are working pretty well." He gestured toward a tall male with a dark, military buzz cut sitting next to Kagen Silivasi. "Our teams of trackers and medics are getting to the murder scenes and analyzing the evidence—time of death, type of injuries, etc.—fairly quickly, usually before the humans find the bodies. But in those rare cases where we don't get there first, our cleanup crews are containing the scenes, erasing the memories of the local authorities, and taking control over the situation in less than twelve hours…max. Once we have the bodies incinerated and the DNA cleaned up, our wizards go in to deal with the families and friends—they create new scenarios to explain the deaths, add memories of funerals…relevant histories…whatever is necessary so we don't end up with a missing persons epidemic on our hands. But I have to say, this is the really difficult and time-consuming part: The tendrils of a life are like the branches of a tree, touching dozens of others, sharing an intricate system of roots. It takes a lot of time and energy to flush out all the central relationships of one human being: best friends, family, lovers, teachers…those who are going to care enough to make some waves." Saxson glanced at Nachari Silivasi, who was sitting next to his brother Nathaniel, listening with rapt attention. "Right now, it's a full-time job for the wizards, and that can't be sustained."

Napolean followed Saxson's gaze. "Nachari?"

The youngest Silivasi brother and the only Master Wizard present at the meeting stood up.

"Do you have anything to add?" Napolean asked.

Nachari lowered his head in a slight decline, a gesture of acknowledgment and deference to the king, and then he let out a deep breath. "Saxson is right, but it's more than just a bit exhausting—I don't think any of the practitioners of Magick would complain about that piece of it. The real problem is the risk being taken by our community as a whole…the resulting vulnerability."

Napolean knew exactly what Nachari was referring to. The energetic cost of supplanting human memories was higher than that of simply erasing them. Such a feat required the vampire to take blood from each person whose memories he or she wanted to manipulate, and the more blood a *wizard* took, the more random energy that wizard absorbed from the host. A Master

Wizard needed to keep his vibration in perfect alignment with the universe at all times in order to perform Magick at will. Should the Master's energy be too…compromised…at any given time, he might not be able to perform a much more important duty when called upon. In other words, Magick required alignment; alignment required pure Celestial energy; and pure Celestial energy required a balanced Wizard. Consuming the blood of dozens of scared, confused, and potentially grieving humans altered that balance. And *that* altered the Wizard.

Napolean began to pace back and forth in front of the room as he considered the dilemma. "Nachari, explain what happens to the other warriors."

Nachari nodded. As was so characteristic of all the Silivasi brothers, his thick, dark hair fell forward as he began to speak. "As you wish, milord." He turned to face the other males. "Whenever a wizard attempts to alter complex memories…"

As the bright young wizard continued to speak, his words and image began to fade out.

It was as if the room had become a scene in a 3-D movie, and the director had suddenly retracted the lens and zoomed out of the picture…

And then a much narrower image began to come into focus, a strange, unsettling frame containing the shadowed figure of a man, an ancient being who had died over twenty-eight hundred years ago: Napolean's father, Sebastian Mondragon.

Napolean swallowed a gasp, hoping to conceal his alarm at the sudden, unexplained appearance of the apparition in the room. Similar manifestations had been occurring far too often recently, and he was beginning to wonder if he wasn't suffering from some sort of exhaustion…or paranoia…if his years on earth were not beginning to warp his mind.

He could still see Nachari speaking out of the corner of his eye, and all the males seemed to be focused on the young vampire, carefully weighing his words. No one seemed to notice the dark, imposing man at the back of the room

Father? Napolean tried speaking to the male using telepathy.

BLOOD POSSESSION

The shadow turned his head quickly in an angry, undulating motion, his eyes locking indelibly with his son's. *Yes,* he answered.

Napolean took a step back.

Son... The being spoke again.

Napolean blinked rapidly, trying to erase the image from his vision, but the man still stood there...looking young and alive...much like he had the last time Napolean had seen him. Right before he had been beheaded.

Napolean swallowed a lump in his throat. *Is it really you?*

The being laughed. *Why did you let the Dark Prince murder me, Napolean? Was I not a good father to you? Could you not have attempted to save me?*

Napolean was utterly stunned by the words, and it took him a moment to reply. *I...I was only ten years old, Father.*

You were a Mondragon, son! The future leader of our people! There was so much I still needed to teach you—so much life left to be lived—yet you stood there like a frightened child...and watched as I died!

Napolean was flabbergasted. *I didn't watch. I didn't...know. I didn't understand.*

The tall male slowly shook his head and gazed down toward the ground, his face revealing such grave disappointment.

Napolean swallowed hard, and his heart sank into a hollow place in his chest. He had to make his father understand. He had to convince him. *I couldn't have saved you, Father. I was too far away. It happened so fast—*

Sebastian raised his hand to halt Napolean's speech. *Do you think you were the only one who felt fear in that moment? The only one who suffered on that fateful day?*

Napolean felt the breath leave his chest. *No—of course not.* "No!" He didn't realize he had spoken aloud.

Sebastian looked up and smiled, and then his expression dimmed. *Oh son, how I have regretted your weakness in that fateful moment, mourned for the courage you did not possess. Wondered how I failed you.*

Napolean staggered back.

"Milord." Someone spoke his title.

Did I not teach you the ways of our people—the ways of a warrior? his father continued. *After so many years—preparing at my side for combat on the battlefields—even at ten years old, your first instinct should have been to confront the enemy.*

"No!" Napolean argued. "You...you wanted me to run...when it all began...you told me—"

Oh, Napolean... The image of his father wavered, flashing in and out. *I wanted to live, son!* And then, he simply faded out of view, his voice—and disappointment—echoing through the hall like a ghost's lament.

"*Milord.*" The voice seemed to belong to Marquis Silivasi, but Napolean could not divorce himself from the confrontation with his father long enough to tune it in.

"Wait!" Napolean shouted. He stepped forward. "*Father?*"

"Milord!" This time, Marquis Silivasi reached out and grabbed Napolean by the arm; then he just as quickly let go.

Startled, Napolean turned to face Marquis: The warrior's face was ashen and his brow was deeply furrowed. He blinked rapidly, staring at the ancient warrior.

"Napolean?"

Ramsey stepped to Marquis's side and reached out a steadying hand. He placed it on Napolean's shoulder.

Napolean stepped back. "Do not!" He waved them both away. "I'm fine," he muttered, working quickly to regain his composure. "I'm fine." His eyes swept across the room. The hall had become deathly silent, and the realization of what he had just done—speaking aloud to the ghost of his father—was almost as distressing as the look of alarm on the faces of his warriors.

All eyes were transfixed upon him.

Except for one vampire's...

Nachari Silivasi stared pointedly toward the back of the room, measuring the empty space where the apparition of Napolean's father had just stood, a subtle look of wariness in his eyes.

31

BLOOD POSSESSION

The wizard had seen something, too.

Just what, Napolean was almost afraid to ask.

Almost.

Gods, he hoped Nachari had not heard his father's words, but he had to know: There was no point in avoiding the possibility. *Did you hear something, Nachari?* He spoke on a private, telepathic bandwidth, his psychic voice both stern and unyielding—an unspoken command to reply with the truth, no matter what it might be.

No. Nachari was quick to reply—almost too quick. And although he appeared to answer honestly, there was a slight hesitation in his voice, and his deep, forest-green eyes darkened with intensity.

Napolean sighed. He might as well face the subject head-on. "Do you wish to say something, Nachari?" He spoke loud enough for all the males to hear. If something was going to surface, it might as well come out here and now. He would rather go on the offensive than wait around to hear whether or not the youngest Silivasi had witnessed *any form* of his shame.

Nachari paused for what seemed an eternity, and then he slowly shook his head. "No, milord." But there was an odd curiosity in the wizard's eyes: a deeper wisdom emerging.

A question not yet answered.

Nachari might not have seen Sebastian, but he had sensed *something.*

"What's going on, milord?" Ramsey asked, his voice heavy with concern.

Napolean shook his head and held up his hand. "It is finished," he said, and that was that. *No one* would question him further.

Ramsey and Marquis exchanged curious glances, but neither spoke a word.

"Now then," Napolean said, clearing his throat in an abrupt change of subject. "I would like five teams of warriors to go out into the local towns tonight in hunting parties. If the Dark Ones are bent on their murdering rampage, we will be there to meet them." He turned to regard Kagen. "Master Healer, there is word that another human was found, the body of a woman, raped, murdered, and drained behind the corner grocery in Silverton Park. The remains were taken to the basement of the lodge for analysis and incineration. I would like to meet you there tonight—I want to see what was done for myself."

Kagen nodded.

Napolean turned to Nachari then. "Master Wizard, you will personally attend to the family of this victim. Until we have a better option, supplanting memories is still necessary. I have shared our predicament with the high council in Romania, the fellowship of wizards, and they share your concerns. If we cannot find an adequate solution to the problem of energy imbalance, they can at least send us more Master Wizards to help until the crisis is over."

Nachari nodded and took his seat. "As you wish."

"Very well," Napolean continued, eyeing the other males in the room, "if it is possible to capture a Dark One alive, then do so. However, it is our goal from this day forward to see to their ultimate extermination. If we cannot destroy the colony beneath us without significant risk to the earth or its human inhabitants, our way of life, we can at least exterminate our enemy one by one." He turned to face Marquis, who was still standing in front of him. "Marquis, you and Ramsey see to the ongoing training of the hunting teams. You will share command of the tactical units and adjust strategy as necessary."

Marquis nodded and turned to Ramsey. "Can you remain for a while after the meeting? I would like to go over some unfinished details."

Ramsey agreed and reluctantly went back to his seat, his cold, calculating eyes taking full measure of Napolean one last time with a note of apprehension before he turned away.

Napolean straightened his shoulders and raised his chin. "If that is all, this meeting is adjourned."

As if perfectly choreographed, each warrior stepped back on his left foot with military precision and placed his right hand over his heart. All eyes remained respectfully averted while Napolean left the room.

Relieved to be out of the stifling hall and done with the meeting, Napolean immediately headed for the door that led back to his manse.

What in the hell had just happened?

As he reached for the ornate iron handle, he slowly exhaled, remembering the look in Nachari Silivasi's eyes: The male had answered him honestly, and he had shown the proper respect, but he knew how the wizard's analytical mind worked. Nachari may not have seen or heard Sebastian clearly, but he had picked up on the errant energy, and he wouldn't stop turning it over in his mind until he put two and two together.

Celestial gods, this could only mean one thing, Napolean thought.

The image he had seen was real.

As impossible as it seemed, somehow, the father he had failed to save on that wretched day when the sons of Jadon and Jaegar had been cursed was back.

And he was deeply ashamed of Napolean's cowardice.

Napolean hung his head in disgrace. *Dear gods*, was he really responsible for his beloved father's death?

four

Brooke tossed her luggage in the back of the cab and joined Tiffany in the backseat, ready to head to the airport. The day had gone better than expected, and for all intents and purposes, the annual conference had been a hit.

She settled into the stiff vinyl seat and tried to get comfortable for the long ride to DIA. Their plane didn't leave until 11:00 the next morning, so they would have to spend one more night in a hotel by the airport. But she didn't mind so much. The view was spectacular this time of year, so many auburn, rust, and yellow leaves dotting the landscape as groves of aspen and evergreen trees lined the narrow mountain roads on the way down from the pass. The ride would be a gift of sorts, a gentle reminder of the power...and unabashed beauty...of nature, of her humble place in the whole scheme of things.

Brooke liked being reminded of the big picture.

It was easier to reconcile her past—and all the pain she had had to find a way to live with—when she chose to rise above the fray, so to speak, when she reminded herself that there was a wonder and a design to this life, a purpose that reached beyond one's circumstance of birth.

As she looked out the cab window at the towering mountains around her, she marveled at the magnificent peaks dotted with snow and their expansive bases thick with pine. There was simply no way to doubt the power of the universe around her. She could feel it as much as see it, and the knowledge—the possibility—of such greatness gave her hope for her own life.

Sighing, she patted Tiffany on the thigh and gave her best friend a reassuring smile. "Good week in the end, huh?"

Tiffany patted her back, a gesture of camaraderie. "I think

so." And then she turned to look out her own window.

Knowing each other as long as they had, Brooke knew that Tiffany had learned to flow with her quiet, contemplative moods, to simply understand her sudden bouts of silence or introspection, and to share the space without the need to fill it with noise. All qualities Brooke appreciated immensely.

As the cab slowly made its way along the extended, curved driveway, Brooke sighed with contentment.

Napolean stood at the edge of the Dark Moon Lodge loop, waiting for several rental cars and a slow yellow cab to pass. The crystal lake shimmered in the moonlight behind him as he thought about the body of the human female he was about to view…and all that it meant for his kind: the ongoing scourge of their Dark Brothers. He was so lost in thought that he barely noticed the sky blackening above him, until the moon visibly dipped in the sky.

Instinctively, he looked up.

Indeed, the moon was dancing as it were…changing…from a brilliant halo of white to the softest dusty rose. His stomach did a strange flip, and his pulse increased as the unconscious awareness registered in his body before his mind.

The dusty rose was deepening now.

It was growing darker. *Much darker.* Into a deep, burgundy red.

Was this simply an astrological event, or was he actually viewing the start of a Blood Moon, the ancient Omen that signaled to his people—the males in the house of Jadon—the arrival of their *destinies*…the one human woman in a lifetime chosen by the gods to be a vampire's mate?

Napolean shut out the world around him. He closed his eyes and sent all of his senses seeking outward, heightened and alert. He was the sovereign lord over the house of Jadon, the only remaining male from the time of the original Blood Curse. And as the king, he knew the lives...the very heartbeats...of every male under his command. He had taken the blood of every Fledgling, Master, Warrior, Healer, Justice, and Wizard in Dark Moon Vale, and he knew each one intimately as a result: He could feel their very DNA.

Napolean felt for the identity of the male. He tried to read the energetic imprint of the moon, yet nothing clear came to him. *Odd*, he thought, opening his eyes. He looked toward the sky. If it was indeed the Omen, then the stars would soon reveal the chosen one in the formation of a distinct constellation.

He watched in anticipation as the dark canvas began to take shape, and one by one, the brilliant stars began to weave an intricate pattern in response to the beckoning of the Celestial Gods. Twenty-eight hundred years, and the phenomenon never ceased to amaze him. Enthrall him.

And then all at once, he drew in a harsh breath, unbelieving. The hair on the back of his neck stood up, and his heart began to pound in his chest, even as his mouth went dry. It couldn't be.

It simply couldn't be!

It had never happened before, and as far as he was concerned, it was never going to happen. Napolean was an...exception to the Blood Curse, at least he had come to believe he was. After so many years of wishing, waiting, hoping—after having found the princess Vanya and knowing he could never act on his deep feelings for the original Celestial female—Napolean had convinced himself that he was meant to be one thing—and one thing only—the leader of the house of Jadon.

He was meant to be alone.

Forever.

His blood heated as the stars nestled into their final resting place and the inevitability of what he was seeing settled upon him, although it still did not quite register: Andromeda.

Napolean Mondragon's own birth constellation was shining

as bright as the noonday sun in a clear sky, illuminated by the most beautiful shade of red he had ever seen. It was his own Blood Moon that appeared in the sky above him.

His head turned instinctively to the left and then the right. His vision became even more acute as he scanned the nearby environment. Who was she? Had they met before?

Where was she?

And then, like a gleaming spotlight piercing a dark stage, the moonlight filtered into a narrow cone and shone down on the backseat of the yellow cab slowly inching its way along the Dark Moon Lodge driveway. *Slowly taking her away from Dark Moon Vale.*

Time stood still.

Napolean had to act quickly, but there were people around. His hand went reflexively to his mouth in an effort to cover—to restrain—his elongating fangs: the primal instinct that was quickly rising within him. His inner voice screamed, *Claim her, take her, stop her!*

Now.

He shifted his weight to the balls of his feet, prepared to move in an instant, even as he sent an imperious telepathic command to his sentinels, Ramsey and Santos Olaru. *Warriors, you are to come to the lodge courtyard at once. I need your assistance with the humans.* Not only would he require their help in keeping order—considering what had to be done—but he would need them to erase the memories of everyone present, to take control of the scene.

After all, he had only one objective, one dire edict, to claim his mate and get her to safety as quickly as possible. His very life depended upon it, as did the welfare of the house of Jadon. This was not like any other Blood Moon. There was no room for error, no time for niceties. He was the king of the Vampyr, and his queen would be the most coveted prize his enemy had ever sought.

We see the sky, milord. Ramsey's deep, raspy voice penetrated Napolean's thoughts. *It is true then—your destiny has finally come.*

38

Tessa Dawn

Do as you must; we will contain the area.

Even before the warrior finished speaking, Ramsey materialized in the courtyard, tall, strong, and proud. His brother Santos appeared quickly behind him. The warriors gave Napolean a silent nod, and he responded in kind.

Taking a deep breath, he leapt the distance between himself and the cab, perching perilously in front of it just as it began to accelerate out of the drive. The driver hit the brakes, causing them to squeal as he wrenched the wheel to the side, trying to avoid striking the man who had just appeared in front of him. Napolean placed his hand on the hood of the vehicle, bringing it to an instant halt and, unfortunately, leaving a palm-size dent in the metal.

It mattered not at all.

His eyes focused like laser beams on the backseat of the cab, where he observed two women: a skinny, well-dressed blonde, and a tall brunette with haunting blue eyes. His gaze dropped to their left arms, furiously scanning their wrists…

And there it was.

Andromeda.

Holy Celestial Beings, this just couldn't be!

Every intricate line of the ancient constellation was etched indelibly into the brunette's wrist, and she was holding it up, staring at it with a look of wonder—as well as terror—in her eyes.

Great gods, was this really happening?

The brunette looked up then, and her eyes met Napolean's through the front windshield—even as her mind began to process what had just happened to the cab. Reflexively, she reached over and locked the door, barking a harsh command to the other woman to do the same. As Napolean rounded the cab, her mouth fell open and she scooted away from the window toward her friend.

Gods, this is awful, he thought. What a way to meet one's destiny.

Humans were beginning to gather around now, gawking at

the scene, pointing and whispering at the dent in the cab. A tall man with broad shoulders started to walk briskly toward the chaos, shouting a command at Napolean to leave the women alone, but he was quickly intercepted by Santos, who sent him in the other direction with nothing more than a tap on the shoulder and a mental suggestion. Napolean shook his head to clear his mind. The people around him were not his concern right now. This woman was. And based upon the look of sheer terror on her face, she wasn't about to answer a polite knock on the door.

Napolean took a deep breath, glided to the side of the cab where the woman sat, reached for the handle, and wrenched the door open, trying mightily not to rip it from its hinges.

He failed.

And the woman gasped in fright.

And then she flailed wildly, trying to back-pedal away from him as if she were running on an invisible treadmill. He could hear her heart pounding in her chest, and it sounded like a bass drum thrumming in a five-hundred-watt subwoofer.

"Come to me," he beckoned, reaching out his hand.

He wasn't sure if her response constituted a shriek, a yell, or a growl—but he pretty much got the gist: *No!*

"Please," she whispered, her magnificent blue eyes glazing over with the onset of panicked tears, "take our money. We don't want any trouble. Just take whatever you want and go. Leave us alone."

Napolean's upper lip twitched, no doubt revealing a hint of fangs, and he felt the heat in his eyes—knowing they were glowing red. He could hardly speak. "Come, or I'll take you." His voice was pitched low in an imperious command, removing any ability she had to refuse. He was an Ancient—his power unmatched among all the Vampyr—and knowing this, he tried to soften what he did.

She was trembling uncontrollably now as she began to scoot toward the door, her body betraying her will.

"Brooke! What are you doing? Get away from the door!" The blond woman grabbed her friend by the arm and tugged her back, pulling her into the center of the cab. "Go away!" she yelled at Napolean, her sea-green eyes ablaze with defiance. "Leave us alone!"

The door to the other side of the cab opened, and Santos reached in and placed his hand on the blond woman's shoulder. Her head lolled to the side, her eyes fell shut, and he laid her back gently against the seat. She was fast asleep.

The brunette screamed a god-awful cry as her friend fell silent. Leaning back, she kicked at Napolean, screaming for help all the while.

Damnit. This was simply too public of a scene. "Shhh," he whispered. "I am not going to hurt you. Come now." He ushered her forward again, and like a programmed robot, she got out of the cab, her eyes wide as saucers as she lost her ability to resist his voice.

Napolean froze then, his eyes taking her in.

She was lovely.

Positively stunning.

Her hair was ebony silk, the length of her shoulders. It was impossibly thick and straight as an arrow, expertly cut in a soft, modern sweep so that the pieces in front were angled slightly longer than the back, accentuating her stunning features. And her eyes—they were so outrageously blue—as brilliant as sapphires with such incredible depths. This woman was neither simple nor shallow. She had lived through much in her lifetime, and there was a stark wisdom and keen intelligence in her gaze, despite her fear.

Napolean reached out to touch her.

He couldn't help himself.

"I am Napolean," he said, his fingers gliding through the wisps of her hair. "What is your name, milady?"

Brooke swallowed hard and blinked, as if coming out of a trance.

When she refused to answer, Napolean gave her a gentle thrust with his mind.

"Brooke," she whispered.

BLOOD POSSESSION

Napolean closed his eyes and repeated her name like a prayer: "Brooke."

Brooke.

Napolean opened his eyes again just as Ramsey pulled up behind them in Napolean's black Toyota Land Cruiser. He pitched his voice low and made his tone as soothing as he could. "Brooke, you will come with me now, and all will be explained to you soon." He bent to her ear to speak a gentle but powerful compulsion. "Please know that I will not hurt you."

The stunning woman—*Brooke*—swayed. Her face grew ashen and pale, and Napolean had to steady her before they could begin walking. "Be at ease, milady," he purred, taking a firm grasp of her arm.

And then he quickly led her to his truck.

five

As the Land Cruiser made its way along increasingly narrow, steep dirt roads, Brooke scooted as far back into the beige seats as she could, and molded her body against the cold, unyielding leather. The night had grown intensely dark and ominous, and the looming mountain peaks, with their endless trails and hidden chasms, seemed to be closing in around her. Her eyes darted around the inside of the cabin like a frightened deer's, taking in her surroundings and studying her abductors: The driver was an imposing-looking blond with chin-length hair that fell in paradoxical soft waves around the frame of his face. He had the body and intensity of a pit bull and the stalwart will of a Rottweiler. She wanted nothing to do with him.

Sitting next to him in the passenger seat was another male with an unusual mixture of black-and-blond hair beneath a soft widow's peak. Several of the blond tendrils gleamed snow-white, and his eyes were a sharp, crystal blue, harboring a deep chasm of intensity in their depths.

Swallowing hard, she brought her attention to the backseat and the giant of a male who sat as silently as an owl beside her. Like a wizened bird of prey, he glanced at her often—staring straight through her eyes to the seat of her soul with his penetrating gaze—and it was as if she knew on some fundamental, cellular level: *These men were not human.*

She blinked rapidly and struggled to dismiss the thought.

No.

Do not go there.

Her sanity would not survive *going there.*

So what if the one the driver had called *milord*—he had called himself Napolean—had strange, vivid eyes that alternated between a deep, galaxy black—with odd silver speckles in the centers—and an otherworldly...*red?* That didn't mean he wasn't

43

human. Of course he was human! What else could he be?

And so what if Napolean's harshly beautiful face, with all of its sculpted planes and smooth angles, was accentuated by a strong, purposeful mouth that sometimes revealed a hint of...fangs.

Fangs!

Oh, hell...

What were these men?

Brooke shut her eyes and forced her attention on her breathing.

In and out.

Deep breath in.

Slow breath out.

Do. Not. Hyperventilate.

As long as there was life, there was hope, and she wasn't dead yet. She had to keep her wits about her. Any chance of survival depended upon it.

Slowly, and with deliberate intent, she opened her eyes and forced herself to hold the Great One's gaze. *Great One?* Where in the world had that come from? Her eyes swept down from his magnificent face to his long, flowing hair—impossibly beautiful, straight hair—that fell all the way to his waist yet appeared in no way feminine. The very strands seemed to sway in silent motion, imbued with kinetic energy, flowing gracefully as if entwined with a gentle, unseen wind.

As if they were a living part of the nature of wind, itself.

Brooke cleared her throat and looked away.

Okay, she really was losing it.

Elemental creatures with inhuman beauty...eyes that sometimes glowed...and fangs?

He reached out his hand to touch her, and she almost flew backward through the window, banging her head sharply against the glass. "Ouch!" she cried, stretching her neck to avoid his touch. "Don't touch me!"

He leaned toward her then, and his eyes captured hers in a chillingly hypnotic gaze. His powerful hand swept the length of her jaw, traced the curve of her mouth, and gently tipped her chin to maintain their eye contact. And then he focused on her like a snake-charmer, mesmerizing with his stare: "Look at me, Brooke." His voice was beautiful, powerful, so deep and alluring...

So very, *very* dangerous.

She squeezed her eyes shut, resisting the inherent potency of it with all of her will. *No. Don't do it, Brooke. Do not look at him.*

He pitched his voice an octave lower and repeated the words: "*Look at me.*"

Though her every instinct protested, she opened her eyes and looked at him.

And then, he threaded his fingers through her hair, and heaven help her but she could have sworn a current of electricity shot through his fingers, and she wanted to crawl into his lap and immerse herself in the peace he was offering. He began to rub soft, gentle circles along the base of her scalp, directly over the area she had thumped against the door, and the pain subsided instantly—as if it had never been. What was this power he had? This inhuman ability to soothe, heal, and coerce? It had to be bad. Some sort of voodoo or sorcery.

"Don't," she whispered again, the sound drifting softly from her lips. "Let go of me." Even as she spoke the words, her head lolled back against his hand, betraying the fact that she wanted more of his touch.

And then a deep wave of serenity flooded her entire body.

It swept down from the top of her head, spread out through her neck and shoulders, and traveled along the length of her torso, grounding at her feet. If she hadn't known better, she would have sworn someone had just pumped an IV full of Stadol into her veins—and he had done it with only his touch. No one should have that much power. No man. No animal. No earthly being should possess that much control. And she knew, instinctively, that he did.

Oh, did he ever—

Far beyond what she was seeing now.

BLOOD POSSESSION

It was painfully evident in his countenance—in his eyes and his mannerisms—that the man possessed some sort of raw, uninhibited power. He wore it like some men wore clothes...in the proud way he held up his head, in the hard, absolute set of his jaw, in the strength and regal stature of his shoulders, and in the infinite wisdom reflected in his eyes.

Who was he?

What was he!

Brooke shifted her weight and gently shoved at his arm to break their contact, hoping she would not provoke his wrath. Dear God in heaven, what would anger look like in a man like this? "Please, don't touch me," she said, wishing there had been more authority in her own voice.

"If that is truly your wish." He drew back his arm, sat back in his seat, and turned to look out the window, seemingly unaffected.

Brooke doubted there was much that could affect this man, if anything.

If that is truly your wish?

Had he actually complied that easily?

Was he really that agreeable?

She bit her bottom lip and almost dared to hope. "Could you take me back to the hotel, please? Napolean?" She spoke respectfully, using his name for effect—somehow understanding that he was accustomed to being addressed with great deference.

"I'm sorry, I cannot." His eyes were kind but stern, his resolve unwavering.

Brooke frowned, and then she shook her head, trying to throw off the mesmerizing cadence of his voice. "Um, why not?"

He smiled then, and it was as if the full glory of the moon had taken residence in the car. "Because you are my *destiny*, and there is much we must learn about each other in a very short amount of time."

Brooke jolted. "Excuse me?" Before he could answer, she started to protest. "Um, I can pretty much guarantee you that

46

whatever this destiny thing is, I'm definitely not that person. I mean, no offense; you seem like a really…interesting guy and all, but"—*stop it, Brooke*—"truly, I just want to go home." Her eyes started to fill with tears. *Damnit*, she did not want to cry. She did not want to appear as afraid as she was. Brooke knew better than to give a predator an invitation to pounce—not even one who projected utter nobility and self-control.

She shivered as she lost the battle with her emotions, and the wet evidence of her fear began to roll down her cheeks. "Please…" Her voice trembled. "*Please*…I just want to go home now."

The phrase, once spoken, had a transformative effect, jolting her from the present, catapulting her into a distant, painful past…

I just want to go home now.

These were no longer the words of a twenty-nine-year-old woman—the request of a confident, accomplished professional—but the pitiful plea of a six-year-old child who had spent seven days in a small, secluded cabin by a lake…with a predatory stepfather.

These were the words of a smart, resourceful kid who had flattered, cajoled, and pleaded her case—for six long, excruciating nights—in a desperate attempt to outlast, outwit, and outmaneuver a sick, twisted grown-up into taking her back home to her mother…in a life-and-death battle to survive.

And these were also the words of an eight-year-old girl who, two years later, had sat on a hard, wooden bench in a cold courthouse in order to testify against that same evil man—to tell the world what had happened in that cabin and how she had survived—in order to insure that the monster was locked away in a dungeon for a very long time. She had repeated the entire grueling ordeal only to watch her own mother turn away from her in disgust, never to speak to her again…as if somehow, she had been to blame. If it hadn't been for her late grandma Lanie, who took her in and raised her as her own, Brooke would have had nowhere to go.

BLOOD POSSESSION

Her tears fell like raindrops now, and she looked away, once again feeling very much like that frightened, abandoned little girl.

"Brooke."

She heard her name as if from a great distance, but she was too far away to respond.

"Where are you, Brooke?" The man's voice was soothing yet commanding at the same time.

Brooke blinked, then wiped her nose, staring blankly at the man in front of her. "Huh?"

She felt a sudden push...an invasion...like her mind being filled with stiff cotton, and then just as abruptly, the sensation disappeared, and the man's expression hardened, his features a mixture of anger and resolve.

"Please," she whispered, despising herself for her weakness. "Please let me go. I just—"

He touched his forefinger to her lips and slowly shook his head. "Shh."

Somehow, his touch brought her back from the past. Supplanted the girl with the woman. Replaced yesterday with today. And as her bearings came back, her temper flared.

She would rather be dead than grovel!

She would rather risk her abductor's rage than ever...*ever*...beg another man for her well-being again.

Brooke squared her chin and forced her tears to stop falling. Staring Napolean straight in the eyes, she gritted her teeth and spat her words. "If you think you're going to hurt me, you will have to kill me first. So maybe you had better find a different plaything—*destiny*—because I'd rather be dead than a victim, and I will fight you to my last breath."

The man's expression was unreadable. He regarded her thoughtfully, and then his lips drew back and his canine teeth began to lengthen.

Brooke shrieked in surprise. She tried to hurdle the seat into the rear of the truck, but he caught her with one hand and easily placed her back beside him. As she sat there stunned, panting, and wishing like hell that she had a gun, he placed his hand over

48

his mouth, closed his eyes, and then slowly lowered it back down in order to speak.

The sharp, ivory fangs were gone.

"I have no doubt that this is true, my angel, but you must trust me when I tell you—you are not a plaything. And this is not a game. I have no intention of harming you."

Brooke opened her mouth to speak, then closed it. *Sometimes silence was golden.*

"Rest now," he whispered in a rich, singsong voice. "There is so much I need to explain to you, and I will. I promise. But you are in no state of mind to receive it just yet. Sleep, and be at ease."

Brooke felt her eyelids grow heavy, and she yawned unwittingly. "But...I don't..." Her words drifted off as exhaustion overwhelmed her. She thought she saw the man reach out for her; and then all at once, she felt a tender tug, and her head fell back against a strong, well-defined arm. As her consciousness faded, she became vaguely aware of his commanding presence, the power of his touch; and she could have sworn she heard his voice drifting all around her, floating as if inside her, asking her strange questions about her stepfather—his name, his occupation, his birthday...

Why his birthday, she wondered.

The strange question faded away as she gently nestled into his beckoning warmth and drifted off to sleep.

Brooke's stepfather was named Angus Monahan.

Adams must have been Brooke's mother's maiden name.

And his date of birth was October 13, 1956.

Napolean let the information settle into his consciousness, seep into his pores...knowing he possessed the power to do what no other vampire could do—kill a human being from a distance. He sat back in his seat and pondered: What was he to

BLOOD POSSESSION

do with Angus...

As the sovereign leader of the house of Jadon, and an Ancient Master Justice, his primary obligation was to maintain harmony between the Vampyr and their human counterparts, see to a just balance among the earth's inhabitants. Like all vampires, he was a predator who had to feed to survive, but he rarely killed—even when it was warranted. Should there be an enemy that needed to be destroyed, he called upon his Master Warriors to see to the task; and up until recently, he had even kept conflicts with the Dark Ones to a minimum in order to avoid creating a ripple effect of natural disasters: The earth's response to a vampire's emotion was simply too volatile, and Napolean was simply too powerful.

But this was an entirely different matter. This was his *destiny*. *His woman*.

As her chosen mate, Napolean was honor-bound to protect her. As a member of the house of Jadon, a male who understood and upheld the laws, the right of Blood Vengeance was his. He could always attend to the matter later, but truth be told, seeing through Brooke's mind that the despicable man was still alive really ticked him off.

A low, feral growl rose from Napolean's throat, and Ramsey peered through the rearview mirror to glance at both of them, no doubt sensing Napolean's predatory energy. To his credit, the male held his tongue.

Napolean closed his eyes and gave full vent to his psychic power—an unparalleled command of the laws of nature that few, even among his own kind, could even comprehend. He was quantum energy in motion, ruler of the force which created worlds. As his heart rate slowed and his breathing grew deeper, he began to explore the precise date of Angus Monahan's birth: the distinct cosmic imprint of the stars and the particular alignment of the planets associated with the day he was born.

Although few humans understood the depth of their connection to the world around them, as a descendant of Celestial Beings, Napolean knew that energy amassed in a very

50

specific way whenever a soul entered a physical body—that the unique configuration of variables existing on that date, in that predetermined moment, was neither random nor unrelated.

It was a direct reflection of the soul, itself.

A psychic fingerprint, as traceable as it was recognizable.

Napolean sighed and entered an even deeper state of awareness. Thoughts were also powerful markers. Their individual vibrations created eternal imprints as every thought ever projected existed forever, vibrating in the nonphysical realm, either active or inactive. Taken as a whole, a being's name, their nature, thoughts, and actions left as clear of a stamp on the cosmos as their individual fingerprint on a piece of paper.

All Napolean had to do was search the universe. Align the energetic fingerprint that was Angus Monahan with the universal database in which the disgusting man had projected his thought, intention, and action.

Napolean sent his spirit seeking.

He scanned the planet at enormous speed, dividing the vast expanse into quadrants so he could search one at a time. He had taken all the information he needed from Brooke's memories—analyzing each vibration of fear, helplessness, and disgust from the week she had spent in terror with her stepfather—and reactivated the imprints using his own strong, otherworldly focus. Now, he was searching for the other participant.

A high-pitched humming began to ring in his ears as the vibration increased. He threw back his head and sent the full power of his nonphysical senses in the direction of the vibration until he was almost in perfect alignment with the darkness he had tapped into. His stomach roiled as his body fought to reject the intense hatred and confusion that personified the being that was Angus Monahan. And then just like that, a full connection was made.

Napolean locked onto Monahan's energy and followed it like a bloodhound, onward...forward...as if he were entering a dark tunnel and spinning at an enormous rate of speed. As his ethereal form emerged from the tunnel, he quickly took inventory of his surroundings in an effort to reorient himself in time and space: Invisible, he had emerged in a small, dingy, one-room apartment on the east side of Detroit, and the place stank like body odor and rotten garbage. Somewhere in the kitchen, there was old meat or produce that had gone bad. Napolean scowled with disgust. And then he saw him. The male who had terrorized the woman he had waited centuries to love.

Angus Monahan was short but burly, the result of being born with a very large frame. It was obvious that he had become lazy over the years, and his once robust appearance was now portly and slack. He sat on an old, grungy couch with his bare feet up on a torn ottoman. He held a beer in his left hand and a remote control in his right. Snorting to drag some phlegm from his lungs, he spat into a nearby trash can and flipped the channel from professional wrestling to hard-core porn. He sank deeper into the tattered cushions and smiled.

For the first time, Napolean noticed that the top of the man's jeans were unbuttoned, and although he was now staring at naked women, his thoughts were of naked girls. Rage swirled through Napolean's head like particles in a dust cloud. Still invisible, he sent a thin bolt of electricity from the tip of his fingers into the television set, instantly shorting it out...

And then he waited.

Angus sat up on the edge of the couch and cursed, his layered belly protruding far below his dirty T-shirt. He glared at the TV screen and slammed the remote on the rickety wooden coffee table. "Damnit," he spat. "I paid good money for that damn box—it better not be broken!"

Although Napolean had no intentions of drawing the scene out, he wanted Angus to know what fear felt like...before he left the earth. Drawing on his primal, animal nature, he released a low growl from the bottom of his throat and followed it with a slow, drawn-out hiss like that of a snake...but far more haunting.

Angus spun around. "Who's there?" He turned rapidly in every direction, his wide eyes searching the corners of the room anxiously. "What the hell?" He got up and headed toward the kitchen, where he peeked around the corner and glanced low, beneath the table and chairs. When he still saw nothing, he checked behind the soiled garbage can, opened several cabinets, and then headed for the bathroom. Before returning to the living room, he flipped the dead bolt on the front door and latched the chain lock, peeking through the eye hole for good measure. His heart was still beating rapidly when he returned to the television and slowly ran his finger over the burnt power cord. "How the hell…" He grimaced and gave it a hard tug, quickly yanking it out of the wall.

He cocked his head to the side like a confused canine as he measured the broken glass along the front of the screen and sniffed at the remaining wisps of smoke. "Shit, I need another drink."

Low, taunting laughter echoed through the room.

It crept up the walls, swirled along the ceiling, and dropped down again to envelop the man where he stood. Angus jumped back and threw up his fists. "What the hell kind of game is this? Who's there! Show yourself, you asshole." He hurried back to the kitchen, threw open a cabinet door, and retrieved what appeared to be an old Smith & Wesson revolver, and then quickly returned to the living room, waving it in front of him. "I've got a gun, you prick. Still want to play with me?"

Still invisible, Napolean silently approached the filthy man and then abruptly slapped him across the face with an open hand. Angus's nose shattered like a walnut beneath a nutcracker, and several teeth shot out of his mouth as his feet rose up from the carpet and he flew backward into the wall. The revolver flew out of his hand as he hit with a thud, and something in his hip snapped, crackled, and popped.

He screamed in pain. "What are you? Where are you? I don't believe in ghosts!" The words came out gurgled as he choked on his own blood and struggled for air.

Napolean chuckled, although the lethal sound was devoid of humor. Having divided his life-force into two separate spaces, he now projected his image into the ethereal energy that stood in Monahan's apartment. "I'm right here," he whispered, coming into full view with deadly fangs, protruding claws, and glowing eyes.

"Holy shit!" Angus's eyes shot open and he scrambled about the floor, favoring his broken hip, searching the room for his weapon.

Napolean took one step forward and stomped the revolver with his foot, reducing it to smithereens as if it were nothing more than a puny insect.

"You're not real," Angus panted. He rubbed his eyes and then patted the center of his face where his nose used to be. He stared at the empty beer bottles on the floor by the couch. "I've had too much to drink."

Napolean closed the distance between them in three stealthy strides and towered over the human with fury in his eyes. "Oh, I'm very real," he taunted. He snatched him by the neckline of his shirt and yanked him onto his feet. "Stand up!"

Urine trickled down Angus's leg, and tears poured out of his eyes, making it next to impossible for the man to breathe. "Please, please, man...I mean, what the—"

"Shut. Up." Napolean pressed the heel of his hand to Angus's windpipe, and the man's remaining teeth literally chattered.

"Please..." He wept like a baby.

Napolean scowled. "Is that how Brooke cried? Did she say *please*?"

Angus's eyes narrowed and his brow creased as he appeared to search for meaning in the words. "What? Who? Brooke?" He shook his head furiously. "No...no...no, man; you've got the wrong guy!"

Napolean froze then. He closed his eyes and held his breath, taking most of the air out of the room with him. The bastard didn't even remember. "You don't know the name of your stepdaughter?" He lowered his head until his fangs brushed against Angus's throat, and then he growled against his skin.

"You don't remember what you did...*to Brooke*...at the cabin...by the lake?" He met Angus's blank stare and then forced his way into the human's mind like a surgeon, rousing the memory with such precision and strength that it must have felt like a scalpel slicing into his brain.

Angus clasped his head on both sides and cried out. When his eyes met Napolean's, they were so laced with dread—and understanding—that the pupils had dilated. "How do you know Brooke?" he whispered, shaking.

Napolean considered the question for the briefest of moments, wanting to couch the answer in terms the man would understand. "She is my wife."

Angus slumped against the wall. "Oh, hell...shit...look...I'm sorry. I never meant...I just..." His eyes bounced around the room haphazardly, unable to meet Napolean's scrutinizing gaze. "Look, man, I'm sick. Really, I didn't...I never meant to hurt her. I mean, it's just...honestly, I'm glad Brookie finally found someone...nice...like you. She was always such a good girl." He nodded furiously, clearly so frantic to talk his way out of the situation that he would say just about anything—however absurd. "What...what's your name? I mean, I'd really like to be friends...you and me. It's probably best for Brooke...so I can make amends...with you...you know, together—"

"Shh." Napolean placed his finger over Angus's mouth. "I'm afraid I have very little time for new friends these days." He ran his tongue over his fangs and smiled.

Angus whimpered like a wounded animal—the pitiful sound growing increasingly high-pitched and desperate—as Napolean bent ever so slowly to his neck to enact his final wrath. In one feline motion, Napolean ripped out the human's larynx with his teeth and spit the hunk of flesh on the ground. "I have been called many things over the years; however, *nice* is not one of them."

Stunned, Angus grasped at his throat. He opened his mouth to scream, but all that came out was a gurgle as he choked.

Napolean did not prolong the end.

BLOOD POSSESSION

He drove his fist through Angus's chest, extracted the still-beating heart, and held it up before him. "My name is Napolean." He tossed the offensive organ aside and watched as Angus's life slipped away. "But my enemies call me *justice*."

As the heartless body toppled to the floor—a worthless heap of blood and flesh—Napolean withdrew his spirit from the room. He entered the same swirling vortex he had followed to get there and swiftly traveled back...

Back to his body.

Back to the SUV.

Back to the avenged *destiny* that awaited him.

six

Brooke held the steaming cup of tea in her hands and tried to control her trembling. The last thing she needed was to scald herself with a hot brew of chamomile, mint, and jasmine tea. She risked a glance at the imposing figure sitting across from her in a huge, dark blue chair—the size of a love seat—and quickly looked away.

He was just too intimidating. The entire situation was just too horrifying. Here she was, in the heart of the Dark Moon Forest, sitting in the living room of a fierce stranger's mansion, afraid to speak...afraid to remain silent. She decided to distract herself by studying the details of the room...

The ceiling was an intricate dome of moldings, textures, and coffers, framing a hand-painted mural of Zeus and Apollo seamlessly crafted onto the grayish-blue canvas. The furniture was exquisite, plush, and clearly custom-made, no doubt costing more than her entire house, and there were tastefully placed art nooks as far as the eye could see, each one boasting a softly lit treasure from an evident time gone by, many of the possessions undoubtedly priceless artifacts.

The windows were made of frosted glass, also adorned with scenes from battlements and pictures of what appeared to be Greek or Roman gods, each depiction etched beautifully into the glass.

For a psychopathic lunatic—who thought he was a vampire—the man had incredible taste. And obviously, a shitload of money. Brooke cleared her throat and gathered her courage. "So..." The word came out hoarse, so she cleared her throat, steadied her hands, and tried again. "*So.*"

Her kidnapper, who called himself Napolean Mondragon, leaned forward in his chair, his every movement graceful and smooth like that of a predatory animal. "So?" he repeated.

BLOOD POSSESSION

Brooke forced a smile. So far, he hadn't killed her, molested her...*or tried to bite her neck*. Rather, he had offered her a blanket, kindled a fire in the enormous hearth, and brought her a steamy cup of chamomile tea. Better to try and worm her way out of her predicament with words and niceties than confrontation and struggle. The mere thought of a physical altercation made her wince: The man was a Viking. Never mind his solid, six-foot-four frame, made of all hard muscle and impassive girth, his face—*his eyes*—said more than his body ever could...

Napolean Mondragon looked as if he could drop someone right where they stood with no more than the blink of an eye.

Like he could kill with his intention alone.

His features were wickedly handsome, and his smile was subtle and kind...but just beneath the surface—and not so deep that one would have to go very far to find it—there was something else, something absolute and harsh, something unforgiving and implacable. He was very much like the god he had painted on his ceiling, and Brooke half expected to see a bolt of lightning shoot out of his hand any moment now.

No, discretion was definitely the better part of valor now. She didn't stand a chance in a physical struggle with this man.

"So?" Napolean repeated. His voice was infinitely gentle, like a soul who had practiced patience in a dozen lifetimes until he had mastered it as a mind-body-spirit art form, and he purred his words when he spoke in that characteristic deep, husky drawl.

Brooke swallowed hard and set her mug down on the coffee table. Then she quickly snatched it back up, replaced it on a coaster, and grimaced. "Sorry."

Napolean smiled a devastating grin. He gestured toward the teacup and chuckled. "You need not worry about the furniture—or anything else around here, Brooke. Make yourself at home."

Brooke blinked rapidly.

Okaaay.

She nodded. "Thanks...I think."

He sat back, shifting in that sultry, animalistic way again.

"You're welcome."

She cleared her throat...again. "So, let me get this straight: You think you come from an ancient race of people—celestial *gods*, is it? And humans who sacrificed all of their women—and I really don't even want to know how—to the point of extinction, and then they were cursed?"

"Correct," he said in a clear, matter-of-fact tone.

She laughed then, a humorless sound. What episode of *The Twilight Zone* had she landed in? "So, you don't have anything to...clarify...about the ancient race of celestial people thing?"

He shook his head and held her gaze.

It was too unsettling. She had to fight the urge to get up and run. "Or the fact that your race was then punished and turned into...vampires?"

He sat quietly, impossibly still, just waiting—watching.

Brooke shifted uncomfortably on the sofa. They weren't getting anywhere. "And now each of you has a *destiny*—a woman the *gods* have chosen for you, and over the last twenty-eight hundred years you have been waiting for...me?"

Napolean nodded and sat forward again, his eyes darkening with intensity, his forehead creased with seriousness. "Brooke..." He practically purred her name, and she had to catch herself from being swept up by the hypnotic cadence of his words. "You are unbelievably intelligent and have memorized all that I have told you impressively, but I think we are at an impasse..." He held out his hands, palms facing up, as if offering her...what? "Until you can merge your ability to memorize the information I give you with an even faint belief in its authenticity, we aren't going to get anywhere."

Brooke swallowed her fear.

Get anywhere?

That was just the point: She was not his long-awaited bride, and—*God help her, please*—he was not going to *get* anywhere with her.

Despite a valiant attempt to remain emotionless, her eyes began to fill with tears...again. If he was going to kill her, she almost wished he would just get it over with and end her suffering, because the not knowing, the anticipation, this whole insane hospitality routine was unbearable. God, where was Tiffany? Where were the police?

How was she ever going to get out of this?

Her eyes swept deftly around the room, measuring the windows, making note of the locks—judging the distance between Napolean and the front door. If she could just get to that door. If she could just scream loud enough. But then, where in the forest were they? Was there anyone close enough to hear?

Napolean stood up abruptly, and she almost jumped out of her skin. "Stop!" she cried, instinctively holding out her hand. "Sit back down. Let's talk. Really—we should talk some more."

Napolean ran his hands through his long hair and shook his head in what appeared to be frustration. He did not sit back down but very slowly, carefully, backed away from the sofa, leaving an even greater distance between the two of them in what appeared to be an effort to reassure her.

Brooke watched his every movement like a hawk. "Please, can you just...call me a cab...*please*."

He sighed. "Brooke, look at the fireplace."

She blinked. "What?"

"Look at the fireplace."

Brooke slowly turned her head to the giant hearth situated on the other side of the living room; a roaring fire blazed in a large pit beneath a hefty marble mantel. Above the mantel was an ancient bronze statuette of a horse and rider, and it appeared to be watching over them.

Napolean waved his hand, and the dancing flames became shards of ice, cracking into a hundred little pieces before crumbling to the fire-pit floor.

Brooke inhaled sharply and gawked at him. She looked back at the hearth—where the fire had just been—then back once more to Napolean. "What...what is this?...some kind of magic trick?"

He waved his hand again, and blue streams of fire shot forth from his fingers. The blaze roared back to life.

Brooke gasped and jumped back on the couch. "How did you do that?"

"Your teacup," he said.

Despite her fear and revulsion, she quickly glanced downward, her eyes riveted on the simple clay mug, and she jolted when it began to rise from the coffee table and slowly move across the room, floating effortlessly into Napolean's hands.

"Forgive me," he said next, "but you must understand that my words are true." She heard a sharp crack, like the sound of wood splintering, and a brilliant pair of enormous wings sprang forth from the center of his upper back and spread out behind him. When he turned to look at her, his eyes were glowing red once again—just as she remembered from the hotel parking lot—and his canine teeth began to grow.

Two sharp ivory fangs extended from his mouth, and he turned his head to soften the visage. And then he simply vanished out of thin air, only to reappear once again across the room, looking like an ordinary, handsome man in a pair of blue jeans and a black silk shirt.

Brooke had seen more than enough.

She leaped up from the couch and bashed her shin against the coffee table in a desperate attempt to hurdle it on her way to the front door. *To hell with this!* Her lungs burned from the sudden exertion even as her heart pounded in her chest.

Then just like that—he was there. Standing in front of her. Blocking the door.

Holy shit, she hadn't even seen him move.

A shriek of unbridled terror escaped her throat, and she back-pedaled as fast as she could, heading for the other side of the room. She stopped abruptly. He was there, too. Once again, standing in front of her, blocking her path.

"Nooo!" She screamed like a madwoman, striking out wildly with a fist that landed somewhere between his chest and his right bicep.

BLOOD POSSESSION

A window. She had to get to a window.

Snatching an ornate glass vase from an art niche on her way to the window, she tossed the heavy object as hard as she could against the glass and ducked as it exploded outward, shards shooting in every direction. A sharp piece of glass embedded in her thigh, but she was too frantic to feel the pain. Yanking desperately on her jacket, she wriggled out of it, wrapped it around her fist, and began to punch out the remaining shards of glass.

Napolean was there in an instant. He grasped her by the shoulders and pulled her away from the window. "Brooke, don't. You'll cut yourself."

Panic overwhelmed her. "Let go of me!" She spun around swinging violently, her eyes wide with fright. She reached for a jagged shard of glass and thrust it at him, lunging with all of her might. The sharp tip caught the inside of his forearm and instantly drew blood.

Now was her chance.

She kicked at his groin, and he instinctively *flew* backward...avoiding her foot and releasing her. To hell with the glass. It was now or never.

She climbed into the small window pane, praying she was small enough to wriggle through it, and started to shimmy out the hole, wincing in pain as the sharp, pointed edges sliced at her body, and then—as if a pair of invisible hands had grasped her—she was forcefully pulled out of the window...only Napolean stood several feet away.

Dear God, was he doing it with his mind?

Moving her with only a thought!

She didn't stand a chance against this...*thing*.

Rage consumed her. She reached for a nearby brass candlestick and hurtled it at his head. Then she followed it with a set of stone coasters, tossing them one by one, screaming her defiance as they flew.

"You can't just take a person!"

Crash!

"You can't just have me because you want me!"

Boom!

"Do you hear me?"

Thud.

One at a time, Napolean blocked each object in midair, side-stepping as they crashed to the floor. He took a step toward Brooke, and this time, he didn't just look like a fierce, dangerous predator. She knew, unequivocally, that he was one.

"No!" she shrieked, shuffling backward and tripping over a pile of glass. He caught her before she hit the hardwood floor, and she beat at his chest. "Let me go!"

He restrained her arms effortlessly. "Brooke, stop! You're hurt."

"*No!*" She struggled valiantly, twisting this way and that—kicking, turning, dropping to the floor—and trying desperately to crawl away.

"You're bleeding," he whispered. He pitched his voice in a soft, sultry lilt that clouded her head. "Please, stop."

"No," she whimpered as he knelt down on the floor beside her and reached for her hands. "*No.*" Tears ran down her face in rivers, and her shoulders shook from the weight of her frustration—the overwhelming helplessness she felt. "I can't do this. I can't do this…again."

He turned her hands over and studied all of her wounds. As she shook from the pain, frustration, and exhaustion, he began to pull thin shards of glass from her palms, her arms, and her legs…removing each one with exquisite gentleness and care.

She blinked up at him, confused by the compassion in his eyes, but desperate to make him understand. "Don't you get it? I can't fight you. I can't! I can't struggle to keep you away…and lose. I can't be a victim again—only to have to tell the whole world what happened someday in a courtroom. I'd rather die." She sobbed. "I *can't* do this."

Napolean reached out and cupped her face in his hands. "Brooke, look at me."

She shook her head and tried to pull away.

BLOOD POSSESSION

He tightened his grip and tilted her head upward. "*Look at me.*"

Her eyes met his, and she shuddered. "Please—"

"I am not your stepfather."

She grew pale. "What?" Her voice was a mere whisper, sounding foreign even to her own ears.

"I am not your stepfather. And I am not going to harm you. Ever."

How in heaven's name did he know about her stepfather? She had never said anything. Well, she had *thought* about it in the truck, but—

Did this creature read minds?

Could he possibly hear her thoughts?

"Yes…and yes," he whispered.

"How? How is that even possible?" she asked, dumbfounded.

"Shh." He caressed the side of her cheek with his thumb. "Be at ease."

Before she could panic anew, his incisors elongated in his mouth; he lifted her hands and dripped a clear fluid into her palms. It was then that she realized the mind-reading was not going to be a problem—she would die of a heart attack before she had time to process that latest bit of information. The man had just dripped…saliva…on her hands. On purpose!

She watched in rapt fascination, and more than a little terror, as his fangs receded and he began to rub the saliva—no, venom—into her wounds.

The cuts healed as she watched.

She sniffled and sat extraordinarily still as he repeated the process, healing one wound at a time…easily. Effortlessly. And then all at once, it occurred to her: *Napolean was a vampire.* And she was a human being—who was clearly bleeding in front of him.

Why wasn't he biting her?

"I've already told you. Because I *will not* hurt you."

Brooke looked up at him then—really stared—assessed the

sincerity in his eyes. They were soft with compassion, heavy with concern. *Genuine.* "I don't understand," she whispered.

He smiled then, faintly. "I know you don't, but you will…in time."

She shook her head absently. "But I want to go home."

Napolean grasped her hand in his, raised it slowly, and held it to his cheek. "This is your home now, Brooke. I am sorry this is so hard on you. It is what the gods have chosen—for both of us."

She sighed in exasperation. "Well, why can't you—why can't *we*—just choose something else? I mean, you could let me go. I won't tell anyone."

Napolean shook his head. "You don't understand. I cannot. To do such a thing would cost me my life, and it would cost you yours as well."

"Mine?" She drew back like he had burned her. "How would your letting me go endanger *my* life?"

Napolean seemed to weigh his words carefully. "I have powerful enemies, Brooke. Now that I have claimed you, you must remain under my protection."

Brooke's head was spinning. Claimed her? What did he mean by claimed her? And what kind of enemies could this…vampire…possibly have? What in God's name could be a threat to *him*? She reached up and grasped her head with her hands as if she could simply will the thoughts—the reality of the situation—out of her mind. "No." She shuddered. "No, no, no…" She shut her eyes and began to rock slowly back and forth, displaying the soothing behavior of a child. She was beyond all adult reasoning—this just wasn't real. *It couldn't be real.*

Vampires didn't exist.

Napolean didn't exist.

None of this was real.

Finally, after what seemed an eternity—Brooke rocking back and forth while Napolean lightly caressed her shoulders, her arms, her cheeks—she finally opened her eyes and spoke timidly: "And what if I would rather die than be your…hostage? Will you

BLOOD POSSESSION

deny me that choice, too?"

Napolean did not dismiss her words, nor did he frown at them or try to argue with her reasoning. He actually considered her feelings. "I have many warriors in my care, and all are strong, valiant males who would die for their families, for the house of Jadon...for me. And it is a nobility I respect infinitely, but I do not live for myself alone. My death would have enormous consequences—just as your life does now. So no, I could not allow such a thing."

Brooke shook her head. "I still don't understand."

"I am not just a vampire, Brooke."

She shook her head, confused. *Just* a vampire?

"I am the only remaining male from the time of the original curse. I am the appointed leader of the house of Jadon; I am their king."

Brooke sagged against the wall, and then she began to laugh rather riotously. After a time, she quieted down and simply sat with the information. When Napolean stood and extended his hand, she took it and allowed him to help her up. He immediately stepped back, placing ample space between them, but if he was hoping to appear nonthreatening, it wasn't working.

"Would you like to shower and change? Perhaps you are not up to eating quite yet, but I could make you another cup of tea."

Brooke looked down at her bloody, disheveled clothes, and considered how badly she needed to be alone for a minute. "I don't have any clothes."

"Ramsey brought your luggage," Napolean offered.

Brooke sighed and forced herself to remain in the moment. To stay calm. "You will let me go...shower...alone? Because there's no way—"

"Of course," he assured her. "I will be close by, but your privacy will be respected."

Brooke swallowed a lump in her throat and slowly nodded her head.

Napolean raised his eyebrows. "Yes, then?"

Brooke ran her hands up and down her arms as if warming her body from a sudden chill. "Yes."

Napolean gestured toward the hall. "Come then: Let us go get your bags."

Brooke gathered her courage and forced her feet to move, intentionally placing one in front of the other, concentrating on the rote placement of each step in a straight line.

Just walk, Brooke.

One foot in front of the other…just walk.

She sent up a silent prayer to God: *Please let me be doing the right thing. Please don't let this vampire hurt me.* She hesitated briefly before heading toward the hall, careful to keep a moderate distance between the two of them. As they rounded the corner, she glanced over her shoulder once more to look at him: He was watching her carefully, like an owl or a hawk, a bird of prey with wise eyes…always surveying…

What?

His carrion?

"Napolean," she said, her voice barely a whisper.

He waited.

"What are you going to do with me?" There was no hiding her trepidation. She had to know.

The vampire closed his eyes and pointed toward a black and burgundy suitcase sitting in the hall just outside of a bedroom. "Should the gods allow it—and should you give me even the slightest opportunity—I hope to spend every ounce of my considerable power making you happy."

She bit her lower lip and drew in a sharp breath before completely turning around to stare at him in wonder. When after several seconds, he neither spoke nor turned away—just held her gaze with a steadfast promise in his eyes—she slowly exhaled and reached for her bags.

BLOOD POSSESSION

Napolean rested against the bathroom door, his head falling back against the sturdy wood.

Brooke.

Brooke Adams, according to the name affixed to her luggage.

His *destiny*...at last.

Despite the impossibility of the situation, a tentative smile curved along the corners of his mouth. How had this happened? When had this happened? When had the gods finally decided to bless him?

He let out a slow, deep breath—one he had been holding metaphorically for centuries—and briefly shut his eyes: *Gods, he had been so alone for so long.*

He ran his hands through his long hair and shook his head, trying to clear the cobwebs. In all his long centuries, he had shared his bed less than two dozen times with a human woman, and then, only when the loneliness—the existence of a life without any physical contact—had become unbearable. The relationships had all been short-lived, ending with his guilt and the woman's memory erased for both of their protection. And the sex? Well, it had been hollow at best, a physical release, an emotional larceny. He had always had to use such enormous restraint, such incredible concentration, to avoid hurting the human; and the care that had to be taken to avoid an accidental pregnancy was beyond daunting. Such an error with any woman who was not a male vampire's true destiny was an unspeakable tragedy, ending in her ultimate death.

The idea of it had been one of the reasons he had finally let go of Vanya—let go of the idea that they might have a future. He had lived so long, had seen so many blood moons, he had known from the beginning—deep in his soul—that she was not his true *destiny*. But their attraction had been so magnetic. So powerful. So intense. They had shared a yearning based on a common history, an understanding of loyalty and duty, a longing to stand in greatness with another being. And of course, a physical hunger to touch the core of what each one of them was in another: original beings begotten of the celestial gods and

68

their human mates.

But to chance hurting Vanya?

It had been just too much to risk.

Injuring her body—or breaking her heart—would have been unfathomable.

Unforgiveable.

Napolean tuned into his senses and let the sound of running water—of Brooke merely breathing—fill his soul and touch the emptiness.

She was real, and she was here.

Gods forgive him, because in that moment he wanted nothing more than to open that door, make a beeline to the shower, and take her from the spray to his bed. To make love to a woman he could not hurt. To feel complete abandon. To satisfy her fully…again and again. His groin hardened and he shifted his weight, trying to find a more comfortable stance.

Blessed gods, it would be so easy to take her…to have her.

With his considerable powers, it would require nothing more than his desire—a single word from his lips—to place her in a trance. With one suggestion—and perhaps a well-placed touch of his hand—she would be longing for their union…on fire for him.

He cursed beneath his breath and shook his head.

No.

Absolutely not.

That wasn't what he wanted.

If nothing else, Vanya had shown him that much…

Napolean wanted a woman who came to him of her own accord. An equal. He wanted a mate that he could rule with, someone who would truly understand him…and stand at his side. And he wanted to give her the same.

He heard Brooke turn off the spray in the shower, and he stepped away from the door. She would be out again soon, and they had a very long way to go. Bowing his head, he closed his eyes and raised his hands in supplication: a Vampyr king beseeching a celestial queen: "Goddess Andromeda, help me

BLOOD POSSESSION

touch her heart. Show me how to reach her."

He knew Brooke Adams would continue to resist him…try to escape if she could. The beautiful human would protest and struggle, but, ultimately, to no avail: Napolean Mondragon had never been defeated in his long life. And in this, he knew he would remain implacable, no matter what occurred. His will had been like iron for twenty-eight hundred years, and in this matter it was absolute—

Napolean would die before he would ever let Brooke Adams go.

seven

Tiffany Matthews sat up abruptly, grasped the messy covers at her waist, and anxiously scanned the dark corners of her bedroom. She was trying desperately to reorient herself in time and space. As her eyes shot wildly from the left to the right, scanning for only god-knows-what, her mind finally began to separate the elements of her dream from her reality.

Tiffany was what her grandmother had called a *Dream Weaver*: someone who walked through dreams in a purposeful manner. Someone who could dream the future, sort out the past, and uncover endless secrets through the process of dreaming.

It really wasn't as cryptic as it sounded.

She simply had a gift for *knowing*. And that knowing came through information she received in her dreams—a universal language of symbols—the unconscious mind delving into the collective universe and making sense out of it in a night-time, moving picture.

She drew in several deep breaths and listened to her heart pounding in her chest.

Vampires.

Existed.

And they had the ability to erase memories…implant new ones…control the minds of humans.

Brooke had been taken by one of them the last night of their convention, stolen away from the cab like nothing more than a door prize waiting to be claimed. And the one who had taken her was dangerous—formidable—someone with more power than Tiffany's human mind could possibly comprehend. He had been beautiful, fierce, and absolutely determined.

The thought made her stomach churn in fearful waves of dread. She ran a dainty hand through her short, harshly layered hair and shook her head as if clearing out the lethargy. She had seen it all in her dream. Her Dream Weaver had illuminated it all so vividly. But her mind was still having a very hard time grasping what it had seen...

When Tiffany had returned from the Dark Moon Vale convention, it had been with a fuzzy recall of the last day's events, the belief that Brooke had decided to stay on for a couple of weeks to simply unwind, enjoy the scenery, and figure out what her next professional move was going to be with regard to PRIMAR and where she wanted to take her career. It had seemed odd at the time. More than that, really. It had been out of character for her best friend, but Tiffany had accepted it without question, almost as if her mind had been programmed to accept it.

And it had.

She shivered at the knowledge. At the memory of dark, feral eyes boring into hers, telling her what to think and what to remember, commanding her to go home...without Brooke.

"Oh God," she whispered, feeling lost and overwhelmed. What was she going to do? That man...that vampire...had ripped the door right off the cab. He had wanted Brooke, but why? Where had he taken her? What had he done to her?

Every movie she had ever watched—*Dracula, Nosferatu, The Lost Boys*—played through her mind at record speed, almost propelling her into a full-fledged panic. She reached for the bottled water beside the bed on the nightstand and took a sip, desperate to regulate her breathing.

Think, Tiffany. Think!

If vampires were real—and she had been dreaming too long to doubt the accuracy of the information that came to her through her subconscious, especially when it was played out so vividly—then others had to know about their existence. Somewhere, somehow, someone knew about these mythical beings and could help her.

She swallowed a large gulp of water and steadied her resolve. Brooke was like family—the sister she had never had. She couldn't simply leave her to the whims of some undead monster.

She hugged her knees to her chest and shook, but she resolved not to let fear stop her. Brooke would never leave her to such a fate. Never.

She had to be careful who she approached, who—if anyone—she told. Not only was her story unlikely to be believed, but she could hardly back it up with, "But I saw it all so clearly in my dream." If her Nana was still alive, she would believe her; she would know what to do. Or would she?

Tiffany bowed her head and said a silent prayer, and then she did something she rarely chose to do out of respect for her gift: She decided to consult her dreams intentionally—to seek the information she needed. Opening the top drawer of her nightstand, she withdrew a small writing tablet and a pencil, and she wrote down a question: *Is there anyone else who knows that vampires exist? And if so, who are they and where are they? How do I find Brooke?*

She underlined each word slowly, meditating on each question one at a time before stuffing the tablet underneath her pillow—a reminder to her subconscious mind that the questions were there. Then she reclined on the bed, pulled the covers tight, all the way to her neck, and tried her best to get comfortable. One way or another, she had to fall back asleep. She had to dream. The answers she needed were somewhere in the universe, floating freely out there in the collective unconscious.

She had to reenter the Dream Weave.

Nachari Silivasi stood on the porch of an old pastoral duplex in Silverton Park and double-checked the address: 219 Horsetail Lane, #A. Yep, he had the right address; although, since when was "A" considered a number? He kicked the dirt off his heavy boots and drew in a deep breath. He hated this part of his duty, having to deal with the family members of those the Dark Ones killed so randomly...so needlessly. He had already taken care of the woman's parents—Jane Anderson's mother and father—replacing their memories of a living daughter with the memories of a child who had died several months back in a skiing accident, implanting recollections of a wake and a funeral, knowing that the grief would be a source of great confusion to them, despite his expert magic: The memories would be months old, but the grief would be fresh and unbearable.

And now, here he was, ready to do it again. Ready to erase the memory of an innocent human and replace it with something false. Only this time, he would do it to Jane's sister.

Nachari swore beneath his breath. He knew all too well how precious one's memories were, especially of a sibling. He couldn't imagine losing one single moment of his twin's life, let alone someone changing any of the events surrounding Shelby's death, however horrible it had been. Knowledge was power, after all, and it was the knowledge of Valentine's wicked scheme to take Shelby's *destiny*, Dahlia—to impregnate and kill her—that had allowed Nachari and his eldest brother Marquis to ultimately seek vengeance...to finally put an end to the evil one's life. Nachari shook his head, causing his heavy raven hair to sway. He clutched the amulet around his neck—the one Shelby had crossed over from the Spirit World to give him—and took courage. Then he knocked three times on the door, three steady, long drums echoing in the otherwise quiet night.

The girl who answered was thin and slight. She had medium-length auburn hair, cut in a side bob, and large brown eyes that were red and puffy from crying.

"Jolie?" Nachari asked, pitching his voice in a deep, hypnotic cadence. "Jolie Anderson?"

She stared at him as if she were transfixed. Her mouth opened to speak, but no words came out. Her eyes swept over his face, memorizing his features—each one in turn—then down to his toes and back up to his intimidating shoulders. Her lips quivered in surprise.

Nachari waited.

It wasn't as if he hadn't witnessed the reaction of human

females to his presence a thousand times before. His mother—
may she rest in peace—had called it *arresting*: "*Nachari, you must be
careful not to abuse your power where women are concerned. You are my son,
which makes me a little less than objective, but trust me when I tell you,
your beauty is arresting. It is as shocking as it is surreal, and it will give you
undue influence over the fairer sex. Do not misuse such a gift.*" Nachari
had laughed at his mom and responded to his brothers with
mock arrogance when they had called him *pretty boy*, always
teasing. But over the centuries, his mother's words had come to
be as wise as the woman who spoke them. With practiced ease,
he averted his eyes, breaking the hypnotic stupor he had over the
human female; then he gently sent a short wave of energy into
her heart region, a lightning-quick zap of electricity that shocked
her Anahata—her heart chakra—back into the present, jolting
her out of her fog.

"Um...y...y...yes," she murmured. "You're...Jolie. I mean,
I'm Anderson. *Jolie.*"

Nachari nodded and smiled. "Do you have a sister named
Jane?"

All at once, Jolie's eyes became dark with trepidation, and
her brow creased with concern. "Yes," she whispered, visibly
holding her breath. "Do you know something about Janie?" Her
already red eyes glazed over with the onset of fresh tears.

She knew.

Somehow, deep in their souls, on a level known only to their
unconscious minds, humans always knew.

"Can I come in?" Nachari asked.

Jolie looked uncertain. She worried her lower lip with her
teeth, and her eyes darted around the porch as she considered
his question.

You desire to let me in, Nachari suggested, pressing a light
nudge against her mind. There was no need to go too deep...yet.

Jolie blinked three times. "Uh, yeah...sure." She took a step
back from the door, clearing the threshold for his entry.

Nachari smiled a wickedly tantalizing grin. The next entreaty
would have to be hers alone, free of compulsion: "I would feel

better if you invited me in." A vampire could not enter the threshold of a human's home without an invitation, at least not the first time.

Jolie paused but only for a millisecond. "Of course, please— *come in.*"

Nachari stepped past the entryway into the small living area, where he quickly surveyed the contents of the room. It was sparingly but tastefully decorated, mostly in creams and beiges, and the inexpensive furniture revealed the fact that the apartment was occupied by two young roommates starting out on their own for the first time. How did he know there were only two people living there? Because everything was purchased in doubles: two armchairs beside two matching end tables by the sofa, two bar stools just outside of the kitchen, two eating chairs tucked under a small dining room table, and two doorways facing outward toward the hallway, with one bathroom clearly at the end.

Nachari noticed several photos on the end tables and an ornately framed eight-by-ten photo of Jolie with her arm around another girl—the same height with blond hair—on the wall: It was Jane, her sister, and obviously, her roommate. By the look of their smiles, their body language, and the laughter they shared in the photographs, the two were very close. Nachari swallowed his bitterness. There was an address book next to a cell phone on the coffee table and a small pad of paper with names written in neat penmanship—and then crossed out—in a series of rows: Jolie had obviously been making calls—probably to everyone they knew—searching for Jane.

"You know something, don't you?" Jolie's faint, uncertain voice interrupted his thoughts. "About Janie?"

Nachari took a deep breath, focused, and stepped into his duty. "Yes."

"That's why you're here?"

He nodded. "Yes."

She shook her head as if to dismiss his answer—as if she could dismiss the reality and stop the train wreck about to happen. "No," she muttered, and the tears began to fall. She cleared her throat, raised her chin, and clearly summoned all of the courage she had. "Are you a police officer?"

"Something like that," Nachari answered, hating that he had to lie. He knew that the human was too distraught to question him...to check his background. Besides, his position was irrelevant. What mattered was his information.

He extended his arm, holding out an open, beckoning palm. "Come to me, Jolie." The words were a magnetic compulsion laced with compassion, his voice as deep as the ocean, as compelling as the night sky.

She swallowed hard, some primal part of her beginning to recognize that she was in the presence of a dangerous being—a predator—but his coercion was undeniable: an effortless feat for a five-hundred-year-old vampire and Master Wizard. She moved toward him, her eyes open wide and transfixed on his. Cautiously, she took his hand. "Where is Janie?" she whispered through trembling lips. "What's happened to her?"

Nachari gave her hand a gentle tug, pulling her slightly off balance. As she fell into his enormous frame, he gently spun her about so that her back fell against his broad chest, and his heavy, muscular arm encircled her from behind, holding her tight to his body. She fit inside of his large frame like she had been molded to him. Her heart raced, and her legs quivered.

"Shhh," Nachari soothed, his lips just above her right ear. He tightened his grip with his right arm while stroking her hairline with his left hand, all the while soothing her with his rhythmic voice. He hated this coercion, this ruse, knowing that in the breadth of one moment—the blink of an eye—Jolie Anderson's world would change irreversibly. She would go from cautious hope—a life filled with her cherished sibling's love and friendship—to deep, unrelenting grief. She would go from *together* to *alone*. From sharing a life to remembering one, lost. Her world would be forever, tragically changed.

Nachari's amulet began to glow softly at his chest, and he felt a flood of reassurance envelop him. His own sibling. His own twin. Reaching out from the Valley of Spirit and Light to remind him that death was not a permanent separation but an entry into another realm. To assure him that the love between souls lived on.

Nachari inhaled Jolie's scent, just above her jugular, and then he carefully coaxed her head to the side: Erasing a human's memories was so easy, too easy; it required nothing more than a strong mind probe, psychic invasion. But to replace memories in a matter this complex—to create what was never there to begin with, rewrite the neuropathways—required a deeper connection, one that could only be forged through the exchange of blood and venom: her life force into him, his life force into her. The first would be painless and simple—feeding was an art form to a full-grown vampire—it could be accomplished in seconds, if desired, the prey never realizing what had occurred. But an inoculation of venom was always painful. Luckily, she would only require a few drops.

"Relax," he whispered into her ear. "Lay your head against my shoulder, Jolie...and relax."

Her head lolled back, and her eyes fluttered closed, even as her body grew limp against him. It was no effort, whatsoever, to hold her up with one arm; she couldn't have weighed more than a hundred and twenty pounds.

Nachari tuned into the alluring sound of her pulse, a slow, steady thrumming in her neck. He parted his lips and let his canines lengthen into two sharp points. Jolie shuddered—as if she sensed his intention, but a soft nuzzle to her neck brought her quickly back to submission. Nachari struck with aged precision, sinking both fangs deep into her jugular in one smooth, flawless motion, his mind circumventing her fear—and her pain—before it could register through the complex somatosensory cortex of her brain.

She twitched violently and her body began to convulse, but that was a normal reaction, one that would subside in as little as thirty seconds.

Nachari drew several deep, heady gulps of the warm, rich

substance from her vein and analyzed it as it slid down his throat: her character, her needs, her hopes, and her fears, the current DNA—as well as the timeless genetic memories—that made Jolie Anderson the distinctly unique person that she was.

And ultimately, what it would take to implant memories that would be real to her senses—to her distinctive way of being and knowing—that would stick. When he had taken enough, he gently retracted his fangs, allowing his incisors to lengthen in their place. The two drops of venom that leaked out sealed the puncture wounds, but there was no way to inject a larger dose that would be equally gentle or painless. Knowing that her suffering would cease the moment he erased the memory, Nachari chose to just do it—get it over with quickly.

He clamped both arms around her waist and held her tightly like a vise, seizing her vocal cords so she couldn't cry out as he struck swiftly above her collarbone at the base of her throat. He pumped the venom out quickly—there was no point in prolonging it—and she began to struggle in earnest. Her eyes betrayed her panic, and her arms flailed, betraying her pain.

"No...stop..." She groaned the words, a stark look of desperation etched into her features.

Nachari closed his eyes and focused.

Just a little more...

He felt for the threshold—that magical place of bonding where his essence was intertwined deeply enough with hers to begin creating in her reality. Not only were human beings endowed with freewill by their creator, but their physical laws enabled them to create with their minds...with their thoughts and their words. Though they rarely knew they were doing it, they literally thought and spoke things into being over great periods of time; however, the ability to do so was limited to one's own circumstances: Since a human could not create in any reality other than their own, a merging of essence—of souls as it were—was necessary to create in Jolie's mind.

As the pain became unbearable and her resistance severe, Nachari felt a sudden surge of energy: the imprint of the soul that was Jolie flowing freely through his own DNA. He swiftly retracted his fangs, wiped the pain from her memory, and clutched her mind—her full consciousness—in his psychic grip. Like the Master he was, he began to weave new branches along old dendrites, imparting vivid memories of an accident, a horrible loss, a funeral, and a new life constructed without her beloved sister. He made it real, impressing each memory upon all five senses, weaving the essence of it into her soul.

Jane Anderson's remains would be buried in the local cemetery, and when her family went to visit, they would remember several such trips that didn't truly exist. Fortunately, the final resting place and the connection would be real from this moment on. Nachari appeased his conscience by reminding himself that the Dark Ones had taken Jane's life—not him or his brothers—that she could not be brought back to life, and it was necessary for the safety and anonymity of his kind to continue cleaning up the Dark Ones' messes...at least until they could be hunted to smaller numbers.

When he was done replacing Jolie's memories, he erased any knowledge of his visit and actions, gave her a soft command to sleep, and carried her to her sofa, where he covered her with a nearby throw blanket. Tucking her in, he mouthed the words *I'm sorry* against her temple and slowly backed away.

It took less than five minutes to make the necessary changes in the apartment—to make it appear as if Jane had not lived there for months.

Ramsey, he reported telepathically to the sentinel in charge of the house of Jadon's clean-up teams, *I am done with Jane's family.*

Good, Ramsey replied. *I'm afraid we have found two more bodies. Your work this night is not yet done, wizard.*

Nachari sighed and rubbed his eyes. He was tired of all the death and grief; it still hit too close to home. His mind flashed back to the earlier warrior's meeting with Napolean—and the king's bizarre behavior. There had been something unseen—unspoken—in that room, a subtle taint of black magic...of evil. Whoever the practitioner was, they had tried to cover up their murky fingerprints, so to speak, but Nachari had felt…something…so amiss. And whatever this thing was, it was after their Sovereign. It was being used against Napolean.

And it was working.

Nachari had more questions than answers, certainly not enough information to go to his brothers with…just yet, but of one thing he was certain: If he continued to dilute his own blood and energy with the blood of so many humans—so many sad, grieving, and confused humans—his power would be diminished at the very time it was needed most.

Ramsey, he said, his voice thick with resolve. *It has become too much for me to handle the difficult cases on my own. I cannot explain right now, but energetically, there is a growing danger to the house of Jadon with each human I bite. Let Napolean know that I wish to make an appeal to the Council of Wizards at the Romanian University. I wish to request the presence of two more Masters—my classmates Niko Durciak and Jankiel Luzanski—to assist me in serving until this crisis is over.*

Damn. Ramsey's tone reflected the gravity of the situation. *Are you sure?* The sentinel had to know Nachari would not request assistance unless it was absolutely necessary.

Yes…I'm positive.

Very well then, Ramsey said. *I will advise our Lord of your decision. Can you take care of the other families tonight? Until your colleagues get here?*

Nachari glanced over his shoulder at the sleeping female on the couch. He clenched his eyes shut, stroked his amulet, and then slowly headed out the door, shutting it quietly behind him. *Of course; I will do whatever is required of me.*

Raising his eyes upward to the beautiful night sky, he added a prayer to his divine guardian, Perseus: *Grant me wisdom, Lord, to understand what is going on with Napolean. And until then, please—bring my fellow wizards soon!*

eight

It was early Sunday evening, two days after Napolean had taken Brooke from outside the Dark Moon Lodge—two days since she had discovered her fate as the predestined mate to an ancient vampire king. Napolean rotated Brooke by the waist until her shoulders faced squarely east, and then he took a quick step back, wanting to give her ample room to breathe.

He had been doing just that ever since she had relaxed enough to take a shower at the manse: allowing her space to maneuver and silence to think. Beyond that, he had also given her full access to the annals of his people, the complete records in the Hall of Justice, recognizing that she was analytical by nature: Brooke Adams would do better reading the history of the house of Jadon than sitting through a detailed lecture. She would make more sense of the Blood Curse by sifting through the vital statistics records of marriages and births—of *destinies* and sacrifices—than listening to Napolean try to explain a strange and ancient people. It was a lot to take in all at once, and Napolean had gambled on the belief that Brooke would understand the story of Prince Jadon and Prince Jaegar best by reading a full account herself.

And being left alone to do so.

She had needed to process such a vast quantity of information, and Napolean had given her the peace, quiet, and space to do just that.

It seemed to have helped.

Brooke had digested, or at least consumed, more literature than Napolean had ever seen any human read in the space of two days. Donning an endearing pair of designer, black-rimmed glasses, she had nestled into his study beside a quiet fire and devoured every piece of literature he had brought her. It was almost as if reading the truth had kept her at arm's length from

83

having to face it. As long as she held it in a book, it might remain fiction.

But it wasn't fiction.

And the beautiful human's sporadic tears, occasional gut-wrenching pleas to be released...allowed to go home...to call her best friend Tiffany had tugged at Napolean's heart-strings. A few pieces of furniture had been dented and a few priceless artifacts destroyed when the overwhelming urge to flee had struck her on two separate occasions, causing her to struggle valiantly for her freedom; but all and all, Brooke had handled the distressing situation with as much grace and civility as Napolean could have asked for.

"Are you ready?" he asked, gently removing her hands from her eyes, still surprised she had allowed him to lead her into the canyon without her sight.

"As ready as I'm going to be." She blinked several times, slowly raising her head, and then she drew in a crisp breath of air and her mouth fell open.

Napolean smiled, pleased at her reaction. "It's beautiful, no?"

Brooke spared him a glance over her shoulder and then turned back to gaze at the magnificent two-hundred-foot waterfall cascading out of a deep crevice of a red cliff. The water fell in rushing waves, each spray surging harmoniously, one after the other, in a hypnotic rhythm as it splashed brilliantly into a deep pond at the base of the cliff. "It's...amazing," she answered, absently taking a step forward as if drawn by the enthralling sound.

Napolean kept his distance. "This canyon"—he gestured toward the jutting rocks all around them—"is my own private sanctuary of sorts." He leaned back against a large, smooth stone and crossed his arms in front of his chest. "There's a ward around it—"

"A ward?" Brooke asked, staring up at the looming mountaintops, completely unaware that she was beginning to freely ask him questions.

Tessa Dawn

"Yes," Napolean answered. "A protective spell—a very subtle but powerful boundary that warns others away."

Brooke turned toward him then, her deep sapphire eyes cloudy with consternation. "Do you mean the...*Dark Ones?*"

Napolean shrugged. "Well, yes, but not just them. I mean the house of Jadon as well. The ward keeps all explorers away. Until now, no one has seen this particular ravine but me. It's my private stronghold."

Brooke swallowed hard, and Napolean could hear her throat work alongside the steady pulse beating at her neck. He steadied his breathing. "I wanted you to see a...softer...side of my world."

Brooke frowned. "Softer? Sacrifices ... Dark Ones ... curses ... hmm." She turned around and took several steps toward the waterfall, planting both hands inside her blue-jean pockets. Her soft, silky hair sashayed as she moved, swaying high above the graceful arc of her back. She was truly beautiful, and Napolean watched her with growing appreciation. Staring out at the water, she cleared her throat. "So, it's okay then...now that we're here...for me to ask you some questions?"

Napolean didn't move.

Not one muscle.

He was too afraid of frightening her...or dissuading her. He had told her he was taking her someplace peaceful so they could talk—someplace where she could ask all the questions she wanted—and it appeared as if the setting was encouraging just that. Between the roar of the waterfall, the ample distance between them, which allowed her to keep her back protectively turned to him, and the innate serenity of a warm autumn evening in one of the Rocky Mountain's most beautiful valleys, there was nothing imposing about the environment: In fact, it offered both power and peace to the observer.

If Brooke was willing to take advantage of the moment—whether because she felt less trapped and was running out of time, or perhaps because she knew this was as good as it was going to get—Napolean would eagerly welcome their first, truly open conversation. "Yes." The word was but a whisper.

"Okay," she responded, removing her hands from her jeans and tightly folding her arms against her waist. "What I—I don't really understand…" Her words trailed off, and she shivered as if her courage was already waning.

"You don't understand what, Brooke?" His voice was gentle yet encouraging.

"I don't understand *how*…how did you manage it? I mean, my coworkers? Tiffany? Aren't they going to miss me? Come looking for me?" There was a note of hope in her voice, and although Napolean regretted her loss, he knew it wasn't going to happen. No one would come to her rescue. Besides, he couldn't bear to lose her now.

He kicked a small pine cone that lay at his feet and rested further against the rock, surveying the uneven rows of evergreens and quaking aspens that littered the ravine, the wild rye grass growing around the circular pond. "Ramsey implanted memories in Tiffany's head so that she would alert your colleagues at PRIMAR." He made the explanation short and sweet. "As far as they are concerned, you stayed an extra few weeks at the lodge to…*de-stress*…enjoy the spa, take in some horseback riding, perhaps recharge your batteries before returning to the day-to-day grind."

Brooke ran her hands up and down her arms as if it were cold, though it was blissfully warm. "Tiffany knows me better than that. She knows I wouldn't stay here by myself…not that long…there was too much going on at work. She'll wonder, and she'll come looking. I know she—"

"Brooke…" Napolean had no intentions of playing games with this woman or misleading her. Her fate was with him, and he would never release her. He would not encourage her to maintain false hope. "Tiffany will believe whatever Ramsey suggested because that is the power we possess as Vampyr. I'm…sorry. She will not search for you—neither will anyone from work." He sighed because the truth was not what she obviously wanted to hear, and he so desperately wanted to win her affection. "And you must know by now, there is not a human alive who could successfully take you from me."

Brooke spun around then, her stunning eyes flashing with anger. "And you would take that from me, Napolean? My best friend? My job? *My career.* All that has been my life up until this moment?"

Napolean advanced forward, and Brooke took a startled step back, her eyes darting back and forth across the ravine as if searching for an escape route—a place to run.

"Do not," Napolean instructed, holding out his hand. "I am not going to hurt you."

Brooke held her thumbs up to the corners of her eyes in an effort to block her tears. "Damn you, I don't want to cry anymore."

"Then don't," he implored, stopping several feet in front of her so she would quit backing up. "It is my hope that you will keep your dearest friendships, especially Tiffany. I have seen your memories: I know what she means to you. Once you have stopped searching for a way out, accepted your fate—*our* fate— we will welcome her into our lives."

Brooke laughed then, an insincere sound. "Oh yeah, I can really see that working. Hey Tiff, meet my new boyfriend...the vampire king. Wanna hang out on Friday? Maybe we could go to a blood-bank or something." The moment the words left her mouth, her countenance changed. She grew tentative and afraid—like someone who had inadvertently opened the doors to a cage containing a dangerous tiger.

Napolean frowned and waited for her to see that he wasn't a rabid animal...or even an unstable vampire. In her presence, he was just a helpless male, unable to make her understand how much he could give...if she would only let him. He felt his frown deepen along the corners of his mouth. "Boyfriend?" he scoffed. There was a hint of irritation in his voice.

"It was just a word," she explained, sounding frustrated. She started to roll her eyes and gasped when he suddenly appeared at her side—facing her and close enough that their arms were touching. "What are you doing?"

He leaned in and lifted her chin. "Look at me, Brooke."

She tried to meet his gaze, but she couldn't hold it for more than a second. "What?"

"I am many things," he murmured, "but I am not a boy."

She shook her head as if to dismiss his words...her casual use of *that* word.

His hand tightened, though not enough to cause her pain. "I am centuries old. I have seen things you cannot conceive of and survived things you will never encounter. I carry a weight beyond your imagination, the lives of hundreds of men—families—in my care; their duties, fears, hopes...souls. I protect the humans of this valley from a power that could annihilate them at the mere whim of my warriors, and I seek a balance for this earth—for your kind—so that the extinction of your species does not become inevitable as a result of my own." He brushed his hand softly along her cheek. "I have not yet earned your respect...or your love...but I am not a boy, nor is any of this a game."

To his great surprise, she squared her shoulders and raised her chin, and then she stared him straight in the eyes and began to speak in her own, no-nonsense tone. "All right then, *milord*. Isn't that what you're called?"

Napolean winced, but he didn't answer. *Gods, the woman was tough.*

"Then let's be completely honest with each other. If you are all these things..." She paused. "*Since* you are all these things, then what do you want with *me*? If I cannot imagine or fathom...or understand your world, then how can I fit into it?"

Napolean shook his head and briefly shut his eyes; when he opened them, he knew they were beginning to glow—though not with anger—with power. "The gods are never wrong; you fit me, Brooke. Of this fact, I have no doubt."

"No!" She waved a desperate hand. "I don't!" Her hands rested on her hips. "You lead warriors every day. I...I create marketing   campaigns   to   sell...soap...and underwear…and…pizza! Hell, paper products sometimes! I know nothing about leadership and honor and fighting darkness."

Napolean whistled low and smooth.

"What is that for?" she asked defiantly.

He measured his words carefully. "Do you think, by now, that I have not glimpsed your memories? Asked my men to provide me with information about your background and your life?"

Her eyes grew wide, and she looked offended.

He shook his head. "*Brooke*, you must come to understand— I am not just any male, and you are not just any female. The things we do must always be in the best interest of many. I am not afforded the time another warrior might be afforded to court you, to learn all about you. There is too much at stake with our…mating. Too much low-hanging fruit for my enemies. I will always protect you, and I always will protect the house of Jadon—at the expense of etiquette."

Brooke stiffened and took another step back, her foot resting in a patch of soggy grass at the edge of the pond, only inches away from the swirling water. "I—"

"You are twenty-nine years old. You have been with your company for less than two years, yet you are the senior most account rep in PRIMAR. Over fifty percent of the company's revenue within the past year has been earned on your accounts, *your* original ideas, and *your* innovative campaigns—for which the company has registered patents. You've carried your department and fostered the relationships that have kept PRIMAR's clients satisfied—and still doing business with the company, I might add. You came to this conference already outperforming all of your competition in order to present a new, revolutionary concept in marketing—a simple but brilliant approach that would triple the corporation's bottom line in less than five years." He stepped back and tried to keep his voice even. "And all of this, you have done under the constant strain of sexual harassment and the ignorant—inexcusable—dismissal of your brilliance simply because you are female." He growled low in his throat then, trying to contain his disgust. "Yet you stuck with it out of sheer determination, knowing that it would one day pay off." His eyes drifted to her full bottom lip, the curious look of surprise on her face. "You know a great deal about leadership, Brooke."

He turned away then, hoping to hide his anger from her view. "And you know a great deal about honor and fighting darkness."

Brooke swallowed a lump in her throat, and he could sense a rise in her anxiety, as if she knew exactly where he was going next.

"How old were you, Brooke?" he asked her directly. The subject was too important to treat with any less significance. "When you fought that monster?"

"What monster?"

"You know what monster."

She paled. "Don't, Napolean."

"Your stepfather. How old were you?"

Brooke shook her head. She started to step back, but there was nowhere to go. Stuck, she looked up at him and, for the first time, appeared helpless. "Please...don't."

"Don't what?" he whispered, his voice as solemn as the subject demanded. "Don't remind you that you were a six-year-old girl"—he gritted his teeth, grinded his molars—"locked in a cabin with a forty-two-year-old man, a monster as dark as the night and far more evil?" She tried to turn away, but he reached out and held her gaze with his hand resting beneath her chin. "You fought like a warrior, Brooke, and you outsmarted him; you outlasted him. You walked away *alive*."

Tears began to stream down her face, and her narrow shoulders trembled.

"And honor?" he continued. "You knew your mother was not as strong as you. You knew she could not face the truth your testimony would expose in that courtroom, a mirror which would reflect her own weakness for all the world to see, yet you knew it was right. And you did it anyway. You sacrificed the security of family and the hope of reconciliation to do what was honorable, and you sat in a room full of leering adults and showed enormous courage through a six-day trial." He stopped and sighed. "You were beyond brave, Brooke. You were *heroic*."

Brooke could clearly take no more. Desperate to get away, she forgot her perch and stepped backward, falling off balance into the pool. Before a shriek could leave her throat, Napolean had her in his arms, the two of them floating just above the water, drifting ever so slowly back toward solid ground.

Involuntarily, Brooke grasped for his shoulders, and then let out a series of plaintive sobs. "How could you know that?" She averted her eyes and shook her head. "You invaded my most intimate memories?"

"No," Napolean insisted. "The night we met in the cab...your fear...you were broadcasting your past, Brooke. You are my *destiny*. How could I not hear such anguish?"

Her chest shook beneath the weight of the recollection. Desperate, she wiped her eyes with the back of her hand and continued to cling to his shoulders, though they were now standing on solid ground.

"Courage and leadership," Napolean said, "they are not about brute strength—or even being a superior species. They are about standing when everyone else is sitting. Facing adversity when others would choose to run away. Charging confidently into battle so those who come behind you believe victory is possible."

Her tears rolled silently down her cheeks, her head rested on his shoulder, and she leaned against him, whimpering softly, as if seeking his comfort.

"How long did he spend in prison, Brooke?" Napolean asked. He had not retrieved that memory, not wanting to take more than she had broadcast, but the knowledge of what she had been through cut him like a knife. "How long?"

She shook her head, rubbing her nose against his arm. "Let's just say, it wasn't worth it—the trial. There was no justice."

"How long?"

She looked up then and met his eyes. "Two and a half years."

Napolean stood deathly still, allowing her words to sink in before drawing her tightly against him and holding her in a firm, unyielding embrace. And then he whispered in her ear, low and lethal, "I am justice, Brooke. For you, there will always be justice."

She froze against him. "What did you say?"

He shook his head. "Nothing. It doesn't matter."

She let out a deep sigh. "Yes, it does. What did that mean?" The words were mumbled into his chest. "What are you saying, Napolean?"

"I am saying that the one who harmed you no longer walks among the living."

She gasped but didn't speak, and he knew that she was finally listening…

"Hear me, Brooke," he purred, his voice a sultry promise of his commitment to their union. "You must understand who— and what—you are destined to mate. I am the sovereign king of an ancient race, begotten of gods and man. *I—am—justice.*"

Brooke Adams felt the reverberation of Napolean's words deep in her soul, and the power of his revelation somehow awakened another memory.

A vision?

A dream?

A make-believe childhood friend conjured up by a little girl in a time of desperation.

"Oh my God!" Brooke suddenly gasped, pushing back against Napolean's chest so she could look at him.

"What?" Napolean asked, sounding all at once concerned. "What is it?"

She shook her head in disbelief. "You. It was you!" She looked up into his eyes and stared at him, really stared at him, as if for the first time, wanting—no needing—to take in every microscopic detail of his handsome face. Unwittingly, she reached up and touched his hair. She rubbed it lightly between her thumb and forefinger to test the texture, and then she gently let it go. "Were you there with me?"

Napolean shook his head. "I'm sorry…I honestly don't know what you're referring to."

Brooke looked off into the distance, yet she remained oblivious to the scenery before her: What she saw was not in the canyon but somewhere much, much farther away—a memory from the past.

"When I was a child"—she swallowed hard—"in the cabin with my stepfather, I imagined so many things…whatever I had to in order to get through it. Survive."

Napolean reached for her hand and held it firmly in his own, and for the first time, his touch didn't startle her.

She didn't pull away.

She heard a hollow sound as if from a distance, a miserable croon like the murmur of a child, and realized that it had come from her own throat. She steadied herself, needing to get through this. "Sometimes, late at night, he would corner me. You know, want to touch me…" She struggled to maintain her focus, and his eyes dimmed as if he were struggling, too— desperate to contain some deeply primal emotion.

"And?" He spoke through gritted teeth.

She swallowed. "And I would imagine that I was someone else—someone really strong that he could never hurt. A boy. No, that's not true. A man." She looked down at the ground, feeling that familiar ache of shame. "I was less vulnerable that way…at least in my mind."

Napolean nodded. "Of course." The kindness in his eyes was unfathomable.

She whispered then, knowing it was the only way to get out what she needed to tell him: "My name was…*Napoleon*." Her eyes filled with tears, but her voice became stronger. "Like the two-time emperor of France—you know, the military commander. We had just learned about him in my first-grade social studies class, and in my imagination, he was this formidable personality." She blinked rapidly, sending several wayward drops down her cheeks. "I can't believe I forgot...all these years. It was such a big part of how I made it through."

For the first time since she had met him, the king of the vampire appeared speechless. In fact, he stood as still as a statue, his eyes boring into hers as if he were viewing her very soul, and in that frozen moment, he appeared every bit a Greek god, the full embodiment of power and strength—of absolute, unequivocal dignity—as if he were a figure in a museum preserved from antiquity. And his magnificence was alarming.

Brooke glanced at the strong hand gripping her own with such compassion and intensity and felt suddenly self-conscious, like she couldn't bear his touch. She gently tugged against him, forcing him to let go. "In my head"—she tapped her forefinger against her temple—"I carried this mighty sword—the Sword of Andromeda—and I would imagine myself stabbing my stepfather through the heart over and over, cutting off his hands, and—"

"What did you say?" Napolean's voice was barely audible, and his eyes were practically burning with intensity, the center of his pupils reflecting a deep, crimson red, that she was oddly drawn to despite their feral appearance. "Your *make-believe* sword—what did you call it?" he repeated.

She cleared her throat, trying to concentrate. "Andromeda."

His eyes were positively luminescent now; and if she hadn't known better, she would have sworn that the temperature around them rose a couple degrees, as if the universe had turned on an invisible heater. The leaves in the trees began to slowly rustle around them, and nearby birds left their perches in swaying branches. Not knowing if this was good or bad, she softened her voice. "Maybe I should stop—"

"No," he argued, "please...tell me." His voice played like a lyrical instrument over her ears. "You called your sword *Andromeda*..." His tone urged her to continue.

She nodded. "Yes...Andromeda...and you know what was the craziest thing?"

He shook his head. "No, what?"

She started to answer but suddenly lost her train of thought. For some inexplicable reason, she just couldn't stop staring at those eyes.

"What was the craziest thing?"

God, he truly was magnificent.

"Brooke?"

Her heart raced in her chest as she continued to stare at Napolean. This man—no, this *vampire*—had kidnapped her, thrown her into a world so frightening and bizarre that her mind still failed to grasp the breadth of it, and refused to let her go. Every survival instinct she had insisted that she resist him—implored her to somehow, someway, escape him, and she was biding her time until she could do just that—but right here and now, in this pregnant moment, he was the strongest and the most beautiful thing she had ever seen. It was as if he had unwittingly cast a spell over her.

"Brooke!"

His dark, haunting eyes were like two piercing lasers—adorned with thick, dark lashes, softly rounded in the subtle shape of almonds. Why hadn't she noticed this before?

"*Draga mea*, can you hear me?"

His perfect, angular jaw was harsh with iron determination yet softened by an unnaturally smooth complexion. Heaven help her, he was...*breathtaking.*

"Where did you go?"

His wizened brow was faintly creased, yet the lines only enhanced an already strikingly handsome face. Like catching an unexpected vision of the sun setting over the horizon in a purple sky, her eyes simply could not turn away.

"*Brooke...*"

She heard her name as if from a great distance and forced

herself back into the moment. The conversation? What had she been saying? *Oh yeah…the crazy thing was…* "The crazy thing was, he would stop."

Napolean blinked, and his dark brows rose in a subtle question. "Your stepfather?"

She clenched her eyes shut and nodded. "Yes. I would imagine swinging that powerful sword over and over in my mind until it felt like there was a blaze of fire around us, and he would slowly back away—almost like he was afraid—until he was no longer…touching me."

Napolean swallowed hard, and his jaw unclenched. "Then he never actually—"

"No." She shook her head adamantly. "But it wasn't for a lack of trying."

He reached out ever so tenderly and cupped her face in his hands. All at once, it felt as if the same warm breeze wafted over her, and her skin, beneath the pads of his fingers, tingled with electric energy. He smiled at her, and the adoration—the conviction—in those hypnotic eyes was unmistakable: In his mind, he believed she was already his. He pulled his hands away from her face, leaving her feeling momentarily bereft, and then he took her forearm in his left hand and quietly traced the lines etched into her wrist with his right forefinger. "Do you see these markings?" he asked.

She looked at the odd *tattoo*, for lack of a better word, the strange configuration of lines and patterns that had appeared on her wrist the night Napolean had taken her…the night the moon had turned the color of blood. It was a distinct engraving of a woman facing head down at an angle with her left arm outstretched and her right arm bent about ninety degrees. She appeared to be floating in the sky.

Brooke nodded. "Yes, I see them." Then she remembered what Napolean had told her: It was a sign from the gods—the same image that had appeared in the stars when he had found her. "It represents a vampire's…ruling constellation," she murmured, remembering the numerous histories she had read in his library.

He smiled then. "Yes, Brooke. Your grasp of so much information—so quickly—is amazing. But this"—he pointed at the unique image stamped in her arm—"is so much more."

She shook her head, not understanding.

Napolean rubbed his thumb reverently over the outline of the woman. "This is the goddess *Andromeda*. She is *my* reigning constellation, and it is under her protection and her Blood Moon that our souls have been brought together. She is the one who chose you…for me."

Brooke tilted her head slightly to the side, her mind working hard to process what Napolean was saying.

"And the Sword of Andromeda is not an imaginary thing," he continued. "It is the only family heirloom I possess that was handed down from one generation to the next, taken by me after the death of my father. Do you understand what I am saying, Brooke?"

Brooke stared at him intently, measuring every subtle line in his face, following every nuanced fluctuation in his voice. She did not fully understand…yet, but she wanted to. "Help me to understand," she whispered.

His smile was positively radiant. "It was not a coincidence that your stepfather yielded to your imaginary sword's power—to Andromeda's power. The goddess was with you, Brooke. All those years ago. Protecting you for me. You and I were destined, even before your birth."

Now *she* was speechless.

His radiant smile softened into a warm glow of pure, unconditional affection. "Will you not even entertain the possibility that this"—he held out his arms, gesturing to encompass himself and all that was around them—"is not only real…*but right?*"

Her breath escaped on a sigh.

Napolean.

His name was a whisper in her mind.

A biological imperative in her cellular memory.

BLOOD POSSESSION

Napolean Mondragon: keeper of the Sword of Andromeda.

She blinked up at him, and her heart filled with wonder. This couldn't be real. He couldn't be real. How could an entire world exist outside of her knowledge—an entire species separate from the human race—prospering outside of the knowledge of most of the world's population? She looked once again at her wrist...

It seemed very real.

And that fateful night—the night of the Blood Moon—it had been real, too.

So had the stars in the sky...Andromeda.

Her imaginary sword.

She slowly shook her head as the full realization sank in: God knew, her week in that cabin with her stepfather had been real...and all of the years she had lived alone without a family since.

She felt Napolean's scrutinizing gaze and met it head-on, trying to discern the truth from his eyes. "I don't know what to believe," she whispered truthfully. "It all seems so impossible." Her eyes watered, and she started to shiver. "I'm so...afraid." There. She had said it out loud. "Of you," she continued, gathering her courage. "Of the world you come from—of all of this." Her breath came in short gasps. "I feel like I've been capitulated back in time—like I'm at the lake again—locked in a cabin against my will, and I—I..." She choked on a sob. "I promised myself that I would never be in that situation again. I don't know what to do."

Napolean released a slow, steady breath and held out his hand. "*Ingerul meu*—my angel—come to me. Brooke...listen to your heart...and let me take this fear from you, forever." He opened both arms and held her gaze. "Just one step forward."

Brooke looked at the enormous male standing before her with his arms stretched wide. He was an ancient predator, more powerful than anything she had ever encountered and twice as deadly, yet he looked so...gentle...vulnerable...welcoming.

But she knew better.

He had *fangs*.

He had…intentions.

"You're going to bite me at some point," she murmured, surprised that she had let the words slip.

Napolean didn't flinch, nor did he deny it. "Just one step, *Draga mea*."

"You're going to hurt me."

He shook his head. "Life has been…unkind…to you, but your refuge is right here. Come to me, Brooke."

"You're going to ask me to face things…do things…horrible, scary things that I'm not ready or able to do."

"Tomorrow will take care of itself. You cannot make sense of everything in this one moment, and I'm not asking you to. But you can relinquish your fears. I can take that from you…if you'll let me."

"That's mind control," she protested.

"Compassion," he argued.

She sighed. "*You're a vampire.*"

"And you are my *destiny*, chosen of the gods. We have no say over our fate, Brooke: only over whether we fight it or embrace it."

"I'm scared," she repeated in a whisper, restating her original—and most compelling—argument.

"Just one step," he replied, restating his.

Brooke closed her eyes. What would it be like to let go of her fears…if only for a moment? To trust someone other than herself? She looked up at him, and there was a deep longing in his eyes: the look of someone who knew exactly what it was like to walk through the world as an island unto yourself: always strong, always in control, always making the hard decisions based on an indomitable determination—not just to survive but to triumph in the end.

Always—and ultimately—alone.

She didn't understand what was happening—why the earth had suddenly shifted on its axis and thrown her off course in opposition to the very gravity she depended upon to live—but she did believe, deep down in her soul where all truth lived, that some sort of simplicity...if not a preordained *destiny*...stood only inches away from her now.

That she was being given a rare and indescribable opportunity...

And she no longer had to bear her fear...alone.

Summoning every ounce of courage she possessed, Brooke Adams took a single step forward—into the indomitable strength of Napolean Mondragon's waiting arms.

nine

Tiffany Matthews ran her hands through her short blond hair, smoothing the sleek, stylish tresses back into place, and pulled her beige cashmere sweater down over her hip-hugging jeans, then stared at the heavy metal door in front of her.

It was hard to believe she was standing at the back of a filthy warehouse, about to meet with some covert member of a vampire-hunting militia, but...such was her reality. She swallowed her fear, squared her shoulders, gathered every ounce of chutzpah she could muster, and knocked on the door. *Ouch,* that hurt her knuckles.

The door opened slowly on a creak and a grind, and a tall, fairly thin man with short, dark brown hair stood in the shadow of the doorway. He was dressed from head to toe in dark camouflage military fatigues, which somehow looked starkly out of place on him. "Matthews?" he grunted.

Tiffany had a sudden urge to bolt and run, but she held her ground...even extended her hand. "Yes, sir. I'm Tiffany Matthews."

He stuck his head out the door and quickly looked both ways before drawing back. "David Reed," he said, giving her a thorough once-over from head to toe. He smiled appreciatively. "Come in."

Tiffany glanced over her shoulder in a reflexive action: What was he checking for? Other humans...or vampires? She shook her head, dismissing the thought. Surely not—it was midday, and besides, the sun was out. She took another long look at David— strange man, remote warehouse, perfect setting for an assault— should she follow? Should she go? Her mind did the math at amazing speed, analyzing possibilities against probabilities faster than she could think them, but in the end, it came down to one simple variable: *I simply can't leave Brooke with that monster.*

Forcing herself to smile, she followed David inside the dark warehouse.

Once her eyes adjusted to the light, she saw a vast, empty space—a large, barren rectangle with small institutional windows too dirty to let in light. There was a single muted bulb dangling precariously inside a loose electrical socket right above a solitary metal desk. The desk was parked dead-center in the middle of the warehouse, and there were two folding chairs of the card-table variety facing it and one worn-out swivel seat with torn upholstery perched behind it.

Office much? she thought.

David led her to the desk, where he plopped into the swivel seat and gestured toward the folding chairs. "Have a seat, Matthews."

Tiffany took a deep breath and sat, ignoring the dust that was now getting intimately acquainted with her favorite jeans.

"I would offer you a cup of coffee or something, but we don't have anything," he said, his voice as serious as a heart attack.

Tiffany opened her mouth to speak, thought better of it, and closed it. Was there an appropriate response to a non-offer of a non-beverage? Once again, she forced a smile.

He leaned forward then and his dark, intense eyes met hers. "What we do here is serious business, Matthews. The information you've come across...very few people have, and it's important to keep it that way." He leaned back in his chair and placed both legs up on the desk, crossing his feet at the ankles. "Now tell me exactly what happened—what you saw."

Tiffany folded her hands in her lap, and, like a robot, she began to recite the events of the night Brooke was taken, careful to remain detached from her emotions. All she needed was to break down in front of this guy and have to dodge some perverted, military-style attempt at comfort. This was about Brooke and nothing else.

When she finished telling the story, she watched him for a minute. He had gone incredibly quiet, listening intently—and for the first time, she had seen something keen in his eyes. He might have been a quack, but he knew about vampires, and his militia was real: It registered in his very countenance.

He put his hand to his jaw and absently rubbed his chin with his thumb. "The males need incubators."

Tiffany waited for him to elaborate...until she realized that he wasn't going to. "What the hell is that supposed to mean?"

"Incubators. *Wombs.* The males. Sometimes they take human women and use them to reproduce. Sounds like what might've happened to your friend."

Tiffany blanched. She felt positively ill. "Do you mean that he took Brooke to use her as a breeding—"

"Depends," he answered.

Tiffany was on the verge of panic. She sat forward in her seat and placed her hands on his desk. "Depends on what!" she demanded.

"On what kind of vampire got her." He frowned, and his eyes showed a faint compassion. "There's more than one kind."

Tiffany was about to come unglued. "Kind? Just tell me what the hell you're talking about!"

He nodded solemnly. "Some vamps take a woman and keep her. Sure, they use her to breed, but at least she's still alive—until she becomes an undead blood-sucker like him that has to be put down—" He stopped abruptly.

Tiffany's mouth fell open, and her heart pounded in her chest. Not Brooke. That wouldn't happen to Brooke.

That had not happened to Brooke!

"Sorry," he said, and it sounded at least halfway sincere.

"What other kinds of vampires are there?" She cleared her throat and steadied her voice. "And what do they...do...to women?"

He looked away this time as he spoke. "The other ones are...let's just say, not something you ever want to meet. They rape their women to force breeding, and the hosts—the women—die forty-eight hours later when the babies are born."

Tiffany felt light-headed, and that was before the true

meaning of his words sank in. "Forty-eight hours? To have a baby? Impossible!" Because that would mean that—just maybe—Brooke was already…dead.

She quickly pushed the thought out of her mind.

That thing—the one who had taken Brooke—he was scary as hell, but evil?

Her head was spinning.

David sighed then. He reached across the desk and took her hand—and she was just upset enough to let him.

"Tell me everything you know about vampires," she urged. She might as well have the full story. She had to know what she was dealing with—what Brooke was dealing with—and she certainly didn't want any major surprises down the road.

David wrung his hands together and seemed to be thinking about whether or not to oblige her. After a few uncertain moments, he finally capitulated. "We think they had their origins in Europe," he stated…and then he began explaining the ins and outs of vampire evolution and their current societies.

He talked about how long the creatures had roamed the earth, how they behaved, and why their eradication was necessary…as was keeping the existence of their species a secret from the world at large. He explained how humans would panic if they knew about their undead co-inhabitants and how that knowledge would lead to widespread panic, vigilante murders of innocent people—not unlike the Puritan witch hunts—and ultimately, an all-out vampire war, which, at the present time, humans couldn't hope to win.

And that was where his militia—and others like it—came into play.

Their mission was to eradicate the demons one at a time, infiltrate their societies, and learn all there was to know about them before the two races collided.

It all sounded very Orson Wells.

Doomsday.

When he had finally finished, Tiffany couldn't tell myth from fact: So many crazy, hard-to-digest words had been used…like

104

demon, undead, feeding, and mind control. It was so sci-fi/futuristic that it made her head spin. And beyond that, something wasn't right.

Something was definitely off.

About David's militia, their understanding of the vampire species, and even their mission as far as she was concerned—but then, who really cared? Time was of the essence, and Brooke was all that mattered. She needed cold, hard facts, and she needed them now. How capable was David's militia of helping her? How was the organization structured? And who did she need to convince to get things in motion? As far as Brooke was concerned, what were the next steps?

Tiffany simplified and organized her questions in her mind: There would be time for emotion later. "Tell me about the militia and who you work for. Who is in control of your operation?"

David removed his legs from the desktop and planted his feet firmly on the floor, leaning forward to rest his elbows on his knees as he spoke in a hushed whisper. "What I'm about to tell you stays with us. You take it to the grave, capisce?"

"Yes," Tiffany answered. "I understand."

David shook his head. "No, I'm not sure you do. You speak a word of this to anyone outside this militia, and you *will* take it to the grave...*capisce?*"

Tiffany gulped, clearly getting his meaning. "Yes. I understand."

David nodded. "Good." He rested his elbows on the desk and folded his hands together. "There are regional, vampire-hunting militias all over the United States—the world, really—secret cells like ours led by individuals like myself...but financed and directed by covert operatives that we simply call Head Hunters." He smiled then. "Cute, eh?" The smile was just as quickly gone. "The operatives...the Head Hunters...seem to be national officials who answer to a council of governing nations, but no one really knows. Honestly? No one at the militia level really cares—as long as what needs to get done gets done." He

BLOOD POSSESSION

winked conspiratorially. "Each Head Hunter is in charge of recruiting and maintaining a handful of regional militias—usually groups of seven men, sometimes women—made up of ex-soldiers, bounty hunters, and retired special forces. We don't contact our Head Hunters; they contact us when and if needed." He sat back in his chair and drew in a deep breath. "They provide us with all the necessary background and training in the beginning until we're self-sufficient enough to plan and execute independent missions...until each militia can function independently as a cohesive vampire-hunting unit. I'm not a Head Hunter, but this is my unit, and I'm the man in charge."

Tiffany reached up to rub her temples. This was beyond comprehension, but at least she knew who she was dealing with now. What she was dealing with now. And she also knew that David was speaking the truth: The night she had been so desperate to find answers...a way to help Brooke...she had seen it in her dreams. It hadn't been clear who these people were or exactly what they did—but she had seen David Reed as clear as the day was long. And somewhere, fluctuating in the background of the dreamscape—almost, but not quite off-screen —had been another male: David's Head Hunter as he liked to call him.

The mysterious man had appeared as somewhat of a shadow, an enormous, imposing male with long, wavy blond hair like the wild mane of a lion. In the dream, his mouth had been set in a cruel scowl, and his eyes had appeared menacing. He never spoke, but David had called the Head Hunter by name in the dream: Tristan...something or other?

Oh yeah...Tristan Hart.

"Where is your Head Hunter now?" Tiffany asked, mostly out of curiosity.

David laughed, and then he shrugged. "Wouldn't tell you even if I knew, but I don't. Haven't heard from him in months."

Tiffany smiled then. "But that doesn't matter, right?"

He winked again, seemingly pleased that she got it.

And she did.

David Reed was the only person she knew even remotely

106

capable of trying to save Brooke, and she needed him. Fixing her best smile on her face, she leaned forward and met his gaze with pleading eyes. "David, I don't know any other way to say this: I really, really need your help."

ten

Napolean covered Brooke with a heavy wool blanket and walked quietly out of the living room. She had fallen asleep on the couch not long after they had returned from the ravine, no doubt as a result of so much emotional exhaustion.

Napolean was exhausted, too. As many times as he had watched a male from the house of Jadon meet his *destiny,* go through the full thirty days of the Blood Moon—with all that it entailed—and exit the other side far happier, more content…and even complete, it was still hard to see the finish line from where he and Brooke stood. Trust was a valuable commodity, and it was going to be very hard to earn.

Napolean opened the doors to the main floor veranda and stepped outside, needing a quick breath of fresh air. Brooke was practically inside of him now: Although he hadn't taken her blood yet, he had touched her, smelled her, and absorbed her essence. He would know if she woke up or moved. He was already that in tune with her.

A dead rose petal fell from an otherwise empty vine attached to a narrow piece of lattice above the veranda and landed at Napolean's feet, drawing his eyes upward to the sky. Absently, he offered a prayer of thanks to the goddess Andromeda for protecting his *destiny* so many years ago—it wasn't enough, of course. She should never have had to go through such a horrific experience in the first place, but it could have been much worse.

Much worse.

"Milord?" A soft, female voice interrupted his thoughts, and he spun around to find Vanya Demir stepping up onto the veranda.

His breath caught. She was a vision, wearing a soft, tapered, red velvet chemise over a sleek black velvet skirt, her long flaxen hair hanging loosely to her waist, interspersed with thick, plaited braids, each one secured with a minor black and red ornament. She looked like the royalty she was. "Vanya," he muttered, surprised to see her.

She smiled then, a sad but sincere expression. "You are surprised to see me, Napolean?"

He looked beyond her down the lane. "I'm surprised to see you alone. Tell me you were escorted here by—"

Vanya waved her hand and laughed. "Of course, milord." She threw up her hands. "Is there a warrior anywhere in the house of Jadon who will let me or Ciopori venture out at night by ourselves? I think not."

Napolean's eyes narrowed. "And in the day?"

She huffed. "No, dear king. We are sadly strapped with an entourage at all times if that pleases you."

The word *dear* caught him off guard, and he swallowed. They had shared a very brief but intense relationship—well, more like a heated moment of passion during a very vulnerable time— right after Ciopori had been kidnapped by Salvatore Nistor. In offering the princess comfort, much more had transpired. And it had taken incredible control for the two of them to make the rational, mature, and inevitable decision to part ways in order to spare each other considerable pain down the road.

At the time, Vanya had seemed so absolutely perfect for him. She still was—perfect, that is. But not for him. By all the gods, there wasn't a doubt in Napolean's mind that the woman who lay sleeping on his couch had been created from the very essence of his own soul. It was hard to explain, not something easily put into words, but when Brooke stood near him, his heartbeat slowed to match her rhythm...to beat in perfect time with her own. Napolean glanced at the doorway, knowing Brooke was still sleeping, but needing to verify her absence on the veranda with his eyes just the same.

He cleared his throat and regarded Vanya. Gods, she was an otherworldly beauty. "Princess," he began, his voice soft with regret, "I'm sure you've heard by now—"

"I saw the Blood Moon and Andromeda," she supplied.

"Forgive my interruption, milord, but I have no desire to hear you speak the words out loud."

Napolean nodded and the two stood in silence for a time. "Then why did you come?" he finally asked.

Vanya swept her hair behind her shoulder, raised her chin, and looked him in the eyes. "I needed to see for myself."

"See what?" he asked.

"*That...*" she answered, touching her left temple with her forefinger. "That look in your eyes."

Napolean remained silent.

She sighed. "That look that says you adore her...you want her...you already love her."

Napolean knew what was being asked of him, and he had no other choice than to say it out loud—to honor both Vanya and Brooke with the truth.

"Indeed," he exhaled. "She is my true *destiny*—and my first choice."

Despite her previous admission, Vanya blinked several times in quick succession, her eyes opened wide, and she placed an unsteady hand over her heart. Taking an inadvertent step back, she looked away. "Oh, well then..."

"I'm sorry," he said. "Gods, I am so bad with words."

Vanya laughed then. "You—the eloquent, ancient king of the house of Jadon—bad with words? I think not. But I understand; this is difficult territory."

"Very difficult," he offered, his voice thick with apology.

Vanya nodded elegantly. "Indeed." She wrung her hands together and turned to face him once more. "And that is why I have come to ask your permission for something."

Napolean raised his eyebrows.

Her shoulders sagged. "Well, that is not entirely true. I would, of course, like your permission—your blessing—but I shall follow my decided course of action with or without it."

Napolean waited to hear what she had to say. Although he was the sovereign king over the house of Jadon—and his word was law—Vanya, for all intents and purposes, outranked him.

BLOOD POSSESSION

She had been born before him in Romania; she was the daughter of King Sakarias and Queen Jade—not to mention the blood sister of Jadon and Jaegar Demir—and she was still of the original race: a half-mortal, half-celestial being with pure blood. Ciopori Demir, her sister, also maintained her celestial blood and powers; however, having mated with Marquis Silivasi, she had gone through the conversion under the protection of Lord Draco and was now a vampire as well. Ciopori was the embodiment of all they were—before and after the Blood Curse. Vanya, on the other hand, was a pure, living member of an otherwise forgotten race.

And while she would not live immortal as the Vampyr did, as far as the house of Jadon's healer could discern, her celestial origins gave her a slightly different physiology than her human female counterparts. Her immune system was stronger, and Kagen Silivasi was working feverishly to create a formula based on injecting small amounts of Vampyr venom into Vanya's bloodstream at systematic, safe intervals that would maintain her health and prolong her life without risking conversion…or jeopardizing her soul.

"As you know," she said softly, interrupting his solemn thoughts, "the Master Wizard Nachari has called upon his colleagues from the Romanian University to come to Dark Moon Vale and aid during this…tumultuous time." She linked her fingers together delicately in front of her.

Napolean nodded. "Yes. Niko and Jankiel. I'm aware."

She took in a deep breath and held it, clearly trying to gather her courage. When she finally let it go, she was steady and resolved. "What you do not know is that when Niko and Jankiel return to Romania, I intend to go with them."

Napolean gasped audibly and shook his head. "Vanya, there must be a better solution—"

Vanya held up her hand. "Milord, please…hear me out."

Napolean frowned. "Your sister and your nephew are here. Your people are here. By all the gods, I know this is a difficult situation, but—"

112

"If it were only that simple, my king." She rubbed her temples then. "If it was only about you...but it's not." She held both hands over her heart. "I miss my homeland—dreadfully so. You have to understand: I have no history or ties to this new land. All that I know is rooted in Romania."

"But your sister—"

"And it is far more than that, Napolean. The truth of the matter is: I am exactly who I am. I was raised from the time I was born to lead, to teach...to rule. I was educated in the history of our people and cultivated in the ways of celestial deities. I was taught to be a keeper of our magic, a charge that I took very seriously. You have done well, milord: Much has been passed down through the centuries within the house of Jadon, but males cannot pass down what they do not know. And our magic—our people's knowledge of the earth and physics, far beyond what is understood even by the Vampyr—cannot be allowed to die with me. Yes, Kagen may discover a way to prolong my life—perhaps indefinitely, should I choose such a thing—and Ciopori also holds the same knowledge—and she is now immortal—but her first responsibility is to her husband and her son...raising Nikolai. Not to mention, any other children they may have." Vanya threw up her hands and sighed. "I am more than a nanny or a sister, Napolean. Like you, I must do what I was born to do. And I can best do it at the University."

Napolean took a step back, considering her words. "Are you referring to taking a post...teaching formally?"

"Yes," she said, nodding her head adamantly. "Writing down the spoken history of our people in texts so that it will never be lost; reciting the magic incantations and charms so that all of our people will know who we are and where we come from. Reviving the ancient spiritual practices to further elevate our males." She took a step forward and reached for his hand. "The truth is, Napolean, I have searched my soul endlessly, wondering why Fabien saved me along with Ciopori: Why did the gods bring me to this foreign place and time, absent everything—and everyone—I have ever loved, except for my sister? And the answer is so clear—and it is so much bigger than me...or even you." She smiled then. "Understand, milord, that even if you and I had been *destined*, I would have returned to Romania to do this thing. It is what I was born to do, and it will be a legacy far more essential than being a citizen, or sister, or aunt." She quickly caught herself. "Do not misunderstand—I am all of those things, and that won't change—but you cannot stand there as the sovereign lord of our people and tell me not to go...that the knowledge I possess must not be taught and passed on formally from one generation to the next."

Napolean rested his fist on his chin and looked at her in earnest. Her rare, pale-rose eyes shone with the light of the truth, and the power of her spirit preceded her. Her soft, engaging smile beckoned his compliance every bit as much as her heart did. "No," he finally uttered, "I cannot argue with your conclusion." He paused. "But that doesn't mean I have to like it."

Vanya smiled and nodded knowingly. "Then I have your blessing?"

Napolean shut his eyes and cursed beneath his breath. After so many centuries, they had just found her, and now she was going back to the ancient homeland. He had hoped to learn from her himself, to find a place in the Hall of Justice to make full use of her wisdom. But that was selfish, and he knew it. Vanya deserved to be where she would shine the most...where she would be happy. "You do. Have my blessing, that is."

Vanya exhaled excitedly and wrapped her arms around him to hug him. "Forgive my impropriety, milord, but I am so relieved."

Napolean allowed his arms to enfold her and did his best to impart his warmth and good wishes.

She stepped back then. "And Napolean?"

"Yes?"

She glanced at the doors to the house and nodded her head in the direction of the front room. "Know that you also have my blessing." Her smile was radiant. "With your *destiny*."

114

Tessa Dawn

Napolean was at a loss for words.

There was no way to show her his deep appreciation and affection…to convey just how much her words meant to him. They were like a healing balm to his ancient soul.

Vanya Demir was truly dignity incarnated.

Beauty personified.

As the total awareness of all she had said—the true depth of just who was standing before him—became flawlessly clear to him, Napolean offered her the deepest sign of respect he could. He bowed his head, averted his eyes, and placed his right hand—bearing the ring with the crest of the house of Jadon on it—over his heart. It was a gesture of sublimation. A gesture he had not performed since he was a child in Romania standing before the royal family…much as he was now.

It was a gesture reserved solely *for him*…by others.

"God speed and keep you, my princess," he whispered reverently.

With tears streaming down her cheeks, Vanya gently removed Napolean's hand from his chest and kissed his ring. "God speed, my king."

eleven

Napolean watched as Princess Vanya headed briskly away from the veranda toward the winding, cobblestone pathway, where Julien Lacusta awaited to escort her home, and then seamlessly vanished from sight.

He sighed, contentedly.

For the first time in a long while, his soul was at peace.

"Peace is only afforded to the living." A deep, disembodied voice penetrated the serenity, sending instant chills up Napolean's spine. He spun around to face whoever was speaking to him, but there was nothing there but mist.

"Who are you?" he asked, speaking to the air.

A tragically sorrowful voice answered. "You do not know me, son?"

Napolean's voice hitched. "Father?" He turned in all directions, searching first with his eyes and then calling upon all of his heightened remaining senses—one at a time—in an effort to locate the entity.

"My soul cannot rest, Napolean."

Napolean's heart skipped a beat. "Show yourself."

A dark wind swept over the terrace. It tossed clay flower pots effortlessly into the air and leveled iron patio furniture like toy soldiers.

"Save me!"

"Fight!"

"Are you not a king?"

"Are you not a man?"

"Napolean?"

"Napolean!"

Voices came at him from all directions as if streaming from an endless vortex: male voices, female voices, old and young...

Some were clear, some nearly inaudible as they spoke in

unison, then individually, in turn.

"Napolean! Stop him."

"Save him."

"Change this!"

And then, the most familiar voice—and refrain—of all pierced the air: "*Napolean, run!*"

Staggering backward, Napolean drew a sharp dagger from a concealed hip holster. He absently massaged the expert carving in the hilt with his thumb—two crimson-eyed warriors with fangs, both perched and alert, prepared for battle—and then he spun the weapon in his hands. Ready.

Just then, a large crack resounded like thunder all around him, and the patio floor dropped out from beneath his feet. His powerful silver-and-black wings shot instinctively from his back, fluttering wildly in an effort to keep him upright, even as the house disappeared from view, and the surrounding trees began to sway like animated demonic spirits.

Limbs extended outward into wily arms. Knots gaped open as fanged mouths whispered hideous taunts. And brittle bark transformed into scaly armor—rough and reptilian like that of mythical dragons.

In the face of an anonymous evil, Napolean relied upon his battle-hardened core to remain steady and alert. He swiftly built his own power into a dangerous conflagration—carefully gathering harnessed energy, mounting his wrath, silently preparing to deliver a lethal strike at a moment's notice. He was itching to annihilate the enemy.

Even if he couldn't name it.

He was Napolean Mondragon, after all…

There was nothing on this planet that could best him. At least, not before now.

"What do you want with me?" he demanded. "Who sent you?" Despite his own unsettling guilt—the frequent occurrence of nightmares—it was still hard to believe that his once-loyal, loving father would approach him after all this time as a demon.

The invisible force struck first.

As if out of nowhere, Napolean's body launched backward. It hurled violently through the air and spun wildly out of control, as if propelled by an enormous malevolent force. Although it felt as if he were traveling a great distance, Napolean remained oddly fixed upon the veranda, and the conflicting perception destroyed his equilibrium. He shook his head in an effort to clear the vertigo, and then he blinked several times in quick succession as his vision blurred and a pair of imperial castle gates appeared before him. On some level, he knew what he was seeing could not possibly be there, but it felt and appeared so real.

A deep protest welled up in his throat, and he watched in horror as a terrified young boy caught his eye before scurrying into a small hole beneath the castle wall. The boy drew himself into a tight little ball.

"No!" Napolean warned. "Don't go in there!"

The boy was trying to make himself invisible, to hide his very essence from...*something*...horrific...while all around him a symphony of carnage rose in a deafening crescendo.

Haunting cries battered the air like thunder against a turbulent sky, and Napolean pressed his own hands to his ears, trying to shut out the noise—desperate to separate the past from the present.

The child shook uncontrollably.

Gods, he was so terrified...

So tortured.

So alone!

Absently, Napolean grasped the ring on his right hand and held it in a fierce grip. He remembered a long-ago pledge of fealty to Prince Jadon—how he had hoped and prayed and foolishly believed that he would somehow be spared from what was coming, *from the Blood Curse*—by swearing his loyalty to the favored twin.

But he had not been spared.

No one had.

"*Gods*, get out of there!" he ordered the child. His voice was hoarse with insistence, and his heart beat frantically in his chest now.

Fearful tears stung the boy's eyes as his gaze met Napolean's and he drew back in growing alarm, desperate to break free from the imminent violation. As the cruel, disembodied laughter came closer, battering the boy's ears—Napolean's ears—the past and present collided.

"No. No. No."

The child whimpered.

Napolean cried out.

They were spinning together now, falling as one—not into a hole, nor any physical time-space reality—but into some vast, invisible, nightmarish void, a world made of pure energy, powered by overwhelming, unbearable...emotion.

The child was moaning incessantly now, and although it appalled him to watch, Napolean strained to see. He was transfixed. He knew this scene so well.

Too well...

His heart broke in empathy as he *felt* the boy shake, knowing that his very bones rattled in his skin.

And then the fog approached.

Napolean swallowed the bitter fruit of fear, choking on it—it tasted like bile—as he began to wrestle in earnest to escape the void. He had to get to the child. He had to get out of this nightmare!

"No!" he protested, fully enraged. He would not live this again!

He could not live this again.

The fog swirled, became a miniature cyclone, rose up from the ground and dipped low—as if it had eyes that could see the little boy hiding.

"You think to escape, child?" The ghostly aberration hissed the words, even as Napolean spoke them aloud—in unison. There was no denying what was coming next, and there was no stopping it.

Laughter ricocheted through the small cavity.

It surrounded the child and engulfed the vortex...until at

last, Napolean and the child began to merge, to see through a single pair of eyes. Flames exploded from the center of the darkness, and in one last desperate act of resistance, Napolean manufactured cold icicles all around his body—the boy's body—in an effort to lessen the scorch of the flames.

"Die, little one! And be reborn the monster that you are!"

The child—Napolean—screamed until it felt as if his ears were bursting, yet the fog kept coming. Napolean felt his bones snapping, his organs reforming, his skin peeling back from his flesh like a pared apple. A gnarled, ghostly hand tore at his heart.

Napolean opened his mouth to command the spirits—surely, the gods would help him this time—but the fog entered his mouth and descended into his chest. He gagged and grappled for air.

"No! No! No!" There was acid flowing through his veins!

His very soul was on fire!

Napolean stared at the scorching flames consuming his childhood body—raging in spite of the perfectly formed icicles he had struggled to create—and for the first time, he let go…completely.

Welcoming death, he became the child, and they were lost together.

Suffering…praying…enduring…transforming.

Dying.

And then they were hungry—so very, very hungry.

They lapped at the blood on their hands like animals, gnawing on their own flesh in a crazed frenzy to devour more…

Blood…

They needed so much more blood.

And then just like that, they were transported forward in time until they stood as one, stunned and confused, in the village square, beside a familiar aged stone well.

"Napolean!" His father's voice beat in his head like a bass drum, ricocheting here and there in an endless, painful echo.

Napolean staggered to a halt beside the well and prepared to watch his father's murder all over again. He stared in resigned

BLOOD POSSESSION

horror as Prince Jaegar hunkered over his father's body and bent to his father's throat. The evil prince's eyes were wild with insanity—a familiar madness—as he drank his fill of Sebastian's blood.

Napolean couldn't help but wonder: What kind of son would just stand still for such a thing? Where in the name of the gods was his sword? *Blessed Andromeda*, why did he not have the courage to draw it and save the man? Sebastian was his father, for heaven's sake!

His beloved sire.

"Father." Napolean mouthed the words just like he had as a child. Only this time his father heard him.

Sebastian raised his head and met the child's eyes, and a desperate plea for mercy contorted his tortured face. "Save me!"

Napolean trembled. "I can't…"

"You can!" His father gurgled and choked on his blood. He spit out chunks of his own flesh—pieces of a battered throat that had caught in his mouth as he regurgitated in pain. "Please…son."

Napolean could stand it no longer.

He had lived the anguish of this very moment for twenty-eight hundred years—regretted it…buried it…tried valiantly to justify it—always knowing in his heart that his own death would have been preferred to his cowardice.

No more.

"Yes, Father," he promised, his words a solemn vow. "By all the gods, I will save you or die trying. Just tell me how."

His father's eyes opened wide, and a faint glimmer of hope flickered in them for the first time. "Your life for mine," he whispered. "It is the only way, son. You must make a trade."

Napolean paused, momentarily confused, but before he could question his father's words, Prince Jaegar withdrew his sword and yanked his father's head back by the hair, extending his neck as he brandished the glittering iron.

Napolean's life for his father's?

It was a trade he would gladly make, but how?

122

He was immortal—a vampire! Dispatching both the head and the heart was the only way, yet such a suicide would be nearly impossible.

Napolean steadied his resolve.

His head was spinning with confusion, but there simply was no time for reasoning why. It would take incredible strength, speed, and unwavering concentration to remove one's own heart while remaining focused enough to dispatch the head in the space of a single second—less than that, really—before the body toppled over and the heart ceased its beating.

But if anyone could do it, it would be him.

Prince Jaegar's sword rose high in the air, the male's strong arm flexing at the bicep with graceful, fluid power as he hefted the heavy iron with ease.

"Help me, son!" Sebastian's words were as desperate as they were imperious in their command: "Napolean…please; do it now."

There was no time for contemplation.

The moment was now…or never.

Napolean Mondragon lodged the tip of his dagger just below his heart and gathered every ounce of his being into focused concentration: He would have to thrust the blade—hard and fast—deep into his sternum in an exacting, powerful thrust—a violent, sweeping, upward motion—meant to penetrate, dislodge, and break free all in one fluid movement—the final swipe being a horizontal slash along the throat. Powerful enough to remove the head.

Prince Jaegar's arms tensed, threatening to come down in one final, wicked slash, even as a child's plaintive wail echoed in Napolean's memory: "Noooooooo!"

Bracing himself, Napolean counted backward: "Three. Two. One."

123

BLOOD POSSESSION

"Noooooooo!" Brooke Adams shouted at the top of her lungs.

She lunged for the sharp, archaic blade nestled against Napolean's breastbone, grasped the hilt with both hands, and tugged in the opposite direction just as he was beginning to thrust inward. If it had not been for the element of surprise, she would have never stood a chance against his brutal strength; but as it was, she surprised him and he relaxed his grip for just a fraction of a second. Long enough for the blade to slip. Just enough for it to slice sideways across his chest as opposed to impaling his heart.

He glanced down at his chest and tightened his hold on the blade.

With both hands glued to his shoulders, Brooke shook him as hard as she could while repeatedly calling his name. "Napolean! *Napolean!* What's wrong with you? Look at me!"

He was like a block of iron.

Relentless and unmoving.

He was no longer opposing her, but he wasn't releasing the dagger either. In fact, he had it locked in a death grip—it was as if he was stuck in some sort of trance.

"Napolean, snap out of it!"

He looked up at her then and snarled with unrestrained menace, his eyes turning a beastly red. Feral fangs shot out of his upper gums, and his lips twitched back as a savage hiss escaped his throat. "Go!"

She froze.

"Now!" he ordered, punctuating the word with a harsh, velvety growl.

The warning in his eyes was unmistakable.

He wasn't playing, and he didn't give a damn if she was his *destiny.*

In fact, he didn't appear to even recognize her, which made him—unquestionably—the most dangerous being on the planet...

And that was when—and how—she knew that she and this

vampire were truly, inexorably, linked.

Brooke could have gotten up and run.

She *should* have gotten up and run.

Every intelligent instinct in her body insisted that she do just that—take this perfect opportunity to escape, let this violent vampire die and finally gain her freedom—yet something far more basic inside of her simply could not let him go. Something so elementary it might have been primordial absolutely refused.

Brooke was terrified, but she would not let Napolean kill himself.

She released her death grip on his shoulders, drew back her right hand, and with all of the strength she could muster, struck him firmly across the face.

He didn't even budge. But it did get his attention.

Napolean blinked, let go of the blade, and slowly reached up to touch his inflamed cheek, stunned. And then he glanced left and right. "Father?"

Brooke knelt down in front of him, for the first time noticing the state of the patio, the disheveled furniture and décor; it looked like a tornado had swept through the yard. "No," she answered, keeping her voice steady and firm. "It's me, Brooke."

Napolean dropped his head in his hands and massaged his temples. "My father is here," he whispered, lowering his hands and scanning the deck. "Somewhere…"

"No," Brooke insisted. "It's just me...and you. Napolean?"

He stared blankly ahead.

"Look at me," she said.

He turned his head in her direction, but his eyes remained decidedly vacant—as if fixed on something that wasn't there.

Brooke swallowed hard and mustered her courage. She might regret this decision for the rest of her life, but she was still going to make it. God help her; she just couldn't let him suffer. She stood up, rose to her full height, and crossed her arms over her chest in a firm, unyielding stance. And then, in an authoritative, no-nonsense voice, she shouted his name:

BLOOD POSSESSION

"Napolean!"

He jolted.

"That is enough!"

He lifted his head and looked at her, his eyes finally making lucid contact.

"Get up! Now!" she insisted. Her heart was beating a mile a minute as she whispered, "Please...come back to me, milord. *I need you.*"

twelve

Salvatore Nistor picked up the heavy—expensive— crystalline vase from the center of the council chamber table and threw it across the room, hissing as the heavy object exploded into a thousand little pieces. And then he slammed his fist through the table.

"Are you done yet?" Oskar Vadovsky inquired, staring at his nails as if he were bored.

"Done?" Salvatore spat. "*Done?* No, I'm not done! I'm hardly getting started." He picked up his chair and smashed it to smithereens on the concrete floor, and then he grabbed a metal leg and snapped it in half just to punctuate his sentence.

"Very well—then you will stand for the remainder of our meeting."

Salvatore clenched his fists at his sides, threw back his head, and roared like a lion, shaking the light fixtures not only in the room but all the way down the hall. "How many women have we sacrificed?" He began pacing. "How many bodies have we drained? How much blood have we offered to the dark lord, Ademordna, in exchange for his malevolent blessings?" He spun around quickly, causing Demitri Zeclos to jump back in his seat, startled.

"I understand, Salvatore," Oskar murmured.

"No," Salvatore argued, feeling like steam was about to rise from his ears. "I honestly don't think you do. Magick spells are not like...McDonald's hamburgers," he ranted. "You can't just get another one around the corner!"

"*McDonald's hamburgers?*" Milano Marandici echoed. "Dude: You really need to chill!"

Salvatore met Milano's eyes with an icy glare. He appreciated his dark brother's presence on the council—after all, he, Demitri, and Milano had orchestrated a masterful coup to overturn the previous council chief not all that long ago—but now was not the time to screw with him.

He wasn't in the mood.

"Napolean Mondragon was *this* close"—he held his thumb and forefinger an inch apart—"to killing himself!"

No one spoke.

"And that...*bitch*! What in Hades was she thinking? She had her freedom! All she had to do was walk away."

Oskar slammed his gavel down on the uneven part of the table that was still standing. He had clearly had enough. "Are we going to replay the events all night, or are we going to hatch another plan?"

"Sure," Salvatore snarled. "Would you like that plain or with cheese? Perhaps I should hold the pickles!"

Milano shook his head and rubbed his temples. "Do you eat food or something now?" he asked, perplexed.

Salvatore folded his hands in front of him. "Sure I do—right after I consume a pound of flesh!" He dove across the table, snatched Milano up by the collar, and lunged at his neck. His fangs gnashed together as Milano flew back, barely causing him to miss.

"What the hell, man?" Milano shouted. "Damn, Salvatore!" He levitated backward and rose upward, his back brushing the wide expanse of the wall until he was at last hovering safely near the ceiling. "Pick another whipping post!"

Oskar sighed. "The next male who acts up in this room will have *me* to answer to." His eyes met Salvatore's squarely, and Salvatore quickly looked away. Everyone knew that Oskar Vadovsky was not one to toy with. He had been so incensed the day they had orchestrated their coup—at the audacity of a male in the house of Jaegar to actually attack another male for political purposes, to commit high treason—that he had punished each of them severely. Milano still had the scars where his missing eye had once been—Oskar had refused to let him regenerate—and Demitri, well, what he was missing kept him from comfortably riding horseback...or women.

And Salvatore…

He swallowed hard.

Salvatore had been the most insolent and defiant of the band, so proud of their treachery, in fact, that he had refused to show any remorse, not even a hint of repentance. He had taunted Oskar—flaunted his arrogance—until Oskar had eventually snapped…

And then the crazed, ancient Dark One had broken him.

Right there on the table.

In front of all the men.

Committing the ultimate act of violation and degradation … upon Salvatore.

Salvatore shook his head. It had been horrendous … unthinkable. An act so shocking and vile that no one ever mentioned it. He prayed no one ever thought of it. Such a thing had never happened in the house of Jaegar before, and it would never happen again.

They were all straight: heterosexual.

In fact, they had made a regular Olympic sport out of brutalizing human women—complete with organizing teams and keeping score—and he could only hope that everyone still held him in the highest regard…as a male. After all, he was still the most advanced sorcerer in the house of Jaegar—or at least that was his opinion—and his violence against human females was legendary.

Oskar narrowed his eyes and Salvatore looked away.

"Now then," Oskar said, "what do you have in mind to correct the situation, Salvatore?"

Salvatore snorted and ran his tongue over his teeth: Dark lords, what he wouldn't give for payback. "He's never going to kill himself now—not since he's found the woman…his *destiny*…bitch!" He closed his eyes and allowed himself to imagine. "Do you know what I would give for five minutes with Napolean Mondragon's woman…in a dark alley?"

The other males laughed.

Salvatore shivered. "I would probably be too worked up to

perform. I don't even know if a method of murder has been invented that is graphic enough for what I would do to that whore."

Milano nodded. "There's got to be a way to break Napolean."

Oskar raised his eyebrows. "Yeah…you and whose army? We tried that, and how many did he leave dead?"

He was referring to the day the warriors had come to rescue Ciopori from Salvatore's lair. Napolean had faced off with them in the hall, leaving eighty-seven soldiers—all strong Dark Ones, all once-powerful warriors—dead in his wake. Salvatore had to give credit where credit was due: The male was fearsome.

"It would take a dark lord himself to do it," Milano said.

Demitri nodded. "And even then, Napolean would have to cooperate."

Salvatore held up his hand. "Wait a minute."

Oskar sat forward. "Yes?"

"What would it take…" He started pacing as he considered the new dilemma, mentally consulting the Blood Canon in his head—now that Nachari Silivasi had stolen it, he could no longer open its dark pages. Thank the dark lords he had memorized it word for word.

A new idea began to unfold.

Smiling, he spun around and quit pacing. "Possession," he stated matter-of-factly.

"Excuse me?" Milano asked.

"Possession," Salvatore repeated, practically purring the word. "We call upon the Dark Lord Ademordna to enter, say, a human host in the form of a snake or a worm—and then we somehow get the human close enough to Napolean's body to transfer the worm. Ademordna takes over Napolean and kills his *destiny*—a far easier task than killing the whore ourselves."

"Then Ademordna relinquishes Napolean's body, and the king dies a very slow, painful death as a result of the Blood Curse." Oskar smiled. "I love the idea—the ancient king of the house of Jadon is taken out by the Curse for failing to make the required sacrifice: Of all the males to screw that up, it's poetic."

"It worked on Shelby Silivasi," Salvatore offered, remembering his late brother Valentine's successful plan to destroy the youngest Silivasi male by destroying his mate Dahlia—but not before he had used her well to produce a son of his own. "There you have it—since no one has a chance in hell of actually getting anywhere near Napolean's *destiny* to kill her, we simply let the love-struck king do it himself."

Everyone nodded except for Demitri. "Yeah, okay. It all sounds great in theory, but how the hell do we get this human—who is now possessed by a worm—anywhere near Napolean Mondragon? And even if we do, how the hell do we get Napolean to kill the human and swallow the worm? Doesn't the transfer have to take place at the exact moment of the host's death? Assuming we can beseech Lord Ademordna to grant such a thing—when was the last time any sorcerer in the house of Jaegar conjured a spell powerful enough to invoke Blood Possession?"

Oskar nodded and leaned forward, indicating that he was taking over the floor. "That is true, Salvatore. Assuming we could get close enough to Napolean to plant the worm—and assuming Napolean would actually cooperate by killing the human—how would you gain Lord Ademordna's assistance?"

Salvatore rubbed his chin, where a distinct three-o'clock shadow was beginning to grow. He had been too busy concentrating on destroying Napolean to shave lately. "I'll admit," he said cautiously, "the price for such a thing would be extremely high. Blood. Sacrifice. More blood than we've ever offered before. But with Oskar's recent directive to kill humans in Dark Moon Vale"—he nodded his regard to their council chief—"and to leave them in plain sight for the humans to find, we have collected more vials of sacrificial blood than ever before. Our storehouses are full."

"Which, if we're lucky, will be just enough to garner an audience with the Dark Lord—to get his attention: What will he require for the possession?" Oskar asked.

BLOOD POSSESSION

Salvatore took a deep breath and faced all the males at the table from the opposite end of Oskar. "How badly do you really want Napolean?"

Oskar cleared his throat. "What will it take, Salvatore?"

Salvatore frowned. "A firstborn son from a prominent family within the house of Jaegar...one for every day of possession we require."

Oskar scooted back in his chair, stood, and walked to the far wall, briefly turning his back to the table. When he turned around, his face was ghostly pale. "Sacrifice a firstborn son from our own colony? One every day just for the mere...possibility...of getting to Napolean Mondragon?"

Salvatore nodded. There was no way to sugar-coat it. "Yes."

Oskar blew out a long breath and shook his head. "Do we even have the power to make such a decree?"

"No," Demitri and Milano answered in unison.

"But," Salvatore added, "we do have the ability to put it to a colony-wide vote, to have the house of Jaegar pass the decree as a democracy. Do not underestimate the anger of our males toward the house of Jadon or their thirst to avenge the death of our warriors—not to mention our infants. I believe the males would vote for such an extreme measure and be willing to draw straws to see which families would...offer...a son, and in what order."

"Do the deaths have to be painful?" Oskar asked, outwardly cringing.

"No," Salvatore reassured him. "Dispatch the hearts while still beating, remove the head, and incinerate the body. We would immortalize them all as martyrs, build statuaries in their likenesses. Their families would be...compensated."

"How?" Oskar asked.

Salvatore shrugged. "I don't know...we'll think of something."

Oskar walked back to the table, placed both palms on the surface, and stared at Salvatore. His mouth turned up in a foul, wicked grin. "Are you sure you want to go forward with this,

Salvatore?" Before he could answer, Oskar added, "Think long and hard, Sorcerer: You are a firstborn son, remember?"

This time Milano whistled low beneath his breath.

"Would you die, Salvatore, to take out Napolean?" Oskar asked pointedly.

Salvatore closed his eyes.

It was true—he preferred to stick around for a long, long time. And if they all left well enough alone, and were careful to avoid the new hunting parties being organized by the warriors in the house of Jadon, they all had a good chance of achieving that goal. But then he thought of Valentine dying alone in the Dark Moon Vale lodge at the hands of Marquis and Nachari Silivasi, and his blood boiled. There could be no greater blow to any male in the house of Jadon—save perhaps the loss of his own mate—than the loss of their leader, Napolean. Napolean had no son. There was no one in the line of succession. The ripples would be astronomical...generational. Perhaps the sons of Jaegar and the sons of Jadon could at last go to war.

"Yes," Salvatore answered, "if it came to that." He shrugged then, already thinking of another angle. "But then the house of Jaegar would be without its most gifted sorcerer. Maybe an exemption is in order...for council members."

Oskar shook his head with disgust. "You never cease to amaze me, Salvatore."

The sorcerer smiled. "Then do we take it to a colony-wide vote?"

Oskar grunted. "Gather up all of the sacrificial vials and go consult Lord Ademordna. See if this thing is even possible before we approach our colony."

Salvatore nodded, but he already knew the answer.

Selling the need to sacrifice their own to the colony at large would not be an easy task; however, selling the image of Napolean Mondragon possessed by the evil spirit of the Dark Lord Ademordna would be another matter altogether. The possibility that he would then take the life of his own bitch...and leave the house of Jadon leaderless and vulnerable? It was simply too delicious to pass up.

The males would rant and rave—perhaps even commit violence—before they ultimately capitulated and voted in favor of the plan.

Tiffany Matthews sat at her desk at PRIMAR, doodling on a notepad and staring at her drawings. She had sketched images of everything but what she was supposed to be working on while her mind wandered—shadowed mountain peaks, snow-covered cabins tucked away in an eerie forest, dangerous men who hid in the shadows behind large boulders and haunted trees...*vampires* who pulled the doors off of cabs. She shuddered at the thought of it.

It was twelve o'clock on Monday, and she was too nervous—too fidgety—to eat her lunch. She had just outlined the sleek body of a mountain lion perched upon one of the distant boulders when her cell phone rang.

She checked the number of the incoming call: *private number, unknown.* She lifted the small device to her ear and depressed the answer-button with her thumb. "This is Tiffany." Her voice sounded professional if not slightly clipped.

"Ms. Matthews?"

"Yes."

"This is David. David Reed." He paused. "Is this a secure line?"

Tiffany rolled her eyes and shrugged. *As if? Who did this guy think he was—the CIA?* "Yes, Mr. Reed; it's secure." She humored him.

"I have good news for you."

She sat up in her chair, and her heart began to pound out an anxious rhythm. Her palms began to sweat. "You found Brooke?"

He sighed. "No...no, I'm sorry, we don't have those kinds

of resources."

She sighed, her disappointment evident. "Oh, I see. So, what's the good news then?"

He lowered his voice as if someone might be listening in. "We were able to get a bead on the male who took your friend: Napolean Mondragon, the leader of the...*vampire*." He whispered the last word.

Tiffany didn't respond immediately. She didn't want to get her hopes up too soon. Finally, leaning forward over her desk, she reached for a pad of paper and said, "Yes?"

"Like many of the others, he lives in the Dark Moon valley, but there's no way we're going to be able to get close to him. Just the same, we might be able to get him to come to us. To the warehouse."

Tiffany frowned. "How?"

"We're planning a short mission this coming Sunday. We're going to Dark Moon Vale to infiltrate the clinic."

Tiffany's senses were on hyper-alert. They were going back to that...place? She tried to overlook the use of the word *infiltrate*—to remind herself that it didn't matter if she had hooked up with a group of James-Bond-slash-Van-Helsing wannabes, just so long as they led her to Brooke. "I'm listening."

"We have wanted to gain access to the clinic for some time now. We believe there might be important information contained in those walls."

Good lord, James. "Like what?" she asked.

"Like tissue or blood samples that will help us determine the demon's weaknesses. Like records that will give us clues to their anatomy, perhaps stored venom...other chemicals...that might be made into effective weapons we can use against them."

Tiffany could hardly believe what she was hearing. "Okay, so how does that help with Brooke?"

"We are going to break into the clinic, take pictures...salvage whatever useful materials we can. If we get lucky and there are any patients being treated at the time, we might be able to get away with a hostage."

BLOOD POSSESSION

Tiffany sat back in her chair, alarmed. *A vampire hostage? Not if he—or she—was anything like the beings she and Brooke had met in the cab!* "How do you plan to—"

"Don't you worry about that, pretty lady. We know what we're doing."

Tiffany exhaled slowly.

"On our way out, we will leave a ransom note: a message offering to trade whatever monster we capture for your friend."

Tiffany did not like the sound of this foolhardy plan. She remembered vividly the strength and power of the male who took Brooke; the ease with which the male who had erased her memory controlled the humans around them. "What if there are...some of them...too many of them...at the clinic when you get there?"

He cleared his throat. "Then we plan to neutralize them." He sounded deadly serious—oddly confident—which only made Tiffany even more certain that the man was a fruitcake. Out of his mind. But what other option did she have? Brooke was gone, and unless they did something, she was never coming back.

"I want to go with you," she insisted, realizing she was as crazy as he was. But what if by some miracle Brooke was there? Or she happened to run across something or someone who had some information about where that vampire—Napolean—had taken her? She shivered at the thought. She knew it was a long shot, but there was no way she could stay behind and wait on Bond-Van Helsing to report back. "Will that be a problem?"

He sighed, sounding frustrated. "It's not safe, Ms. Matthews."

Well, duh! "I realize that, David, but I want to do this." The phone went quiet for so long that she thought he'd hung up. "Hello? Hello...David? Mr. Reed?"

"Yeah, okay: It's your call. But I can't be responsible for your safety."

She swallowed hard then. Was she really that desperate? Was she prepared to go straight into the lion's den on a suicide mission? "I understand."

136

Tessa Dawn

He cleared his throat and spoke in a deep, almost manufactured voice when he answered. "All right then. Be at the warehouse at o-eight-hundred hours on Sunday, not a minute later or we leave without you."

She started to respond, but he had already hung up. Depressing the call button, she slowly set the phone down on her desk and eyed her drawings. *God help us,* she whispered beneath her breath. *Please, God…seriously.*

Help us.

thirteen

It was midday on Wednesday when Nachari Silivasi swung open the heavy front door to his four-story brownstone perched at the end of a private, dead-end lane near the northern forest cliffs. There was an extra pep in his step, and his body felt rejuvenated. Ever since his twin brother Shelby had been indirectly murdered by Valentine Nistor—Valentine had kidnapped Shelby's *destiny*, rendering it impossible for the good-natured vampire to fulfill the demands of the Blood Curse—Nachari had more or less drifted here and there, unsure of what direction to take his life in next.

He had recently graduated from the Romanian University, becoming a Master in Wizardry, and was completing his post-graduate projects, but he hadn't decided what contribution he intended to make to Dark Moon Vale—to the local commerce—outside of his obvious role as a practitioner of Magick. While he stayed sufficiently busy assisting Napolean with containment—cleaning up the evidence left behind by the Dark Ones as a result of their local reign of terror—it wasn't exactly food for the body and soul. And Nachari Silivasi needed meaning as well as mental stimulation in order to feel alive after five hundred years...especially now that he walked the earth without his twin.

He absently clutched his amulet, a growing habit since the day Shelby had given it to him, and headed up the narrow row of stairs into the large, informal living room. A smile brightened his countenance as he thought about his recent decision to work part time at the Dark Moon Lodge & Ski Resort. Unlike Shelby, he had no intentions of providing private snowboarding lessons to children with disabilities—not only had Nachari grown a little bored with both skiing and snowboarding over the past few decades, but Shelby had possessed a special knack for connecting with children, fusing his instincts with theirs in such a way that their combined movements became a sort of graceful, intuitive dance, and Nachari would not dishonor his memory by trying to imitate something that was so clearly an innate gift.

No, Nachari had chosen a slightly different interest to get his juices flowing—the outdoor nature-challenge course—a program aimed at empowering individuals, families, and groups through rock climbing, rappelling, river rafting, and conquering challenging obstacles in nature. It was designed to build intimacy and cohesion between participants and to raise self-esteem.

And it really did work.

Nachari shoved a thick lock of raven-colored hair out of his face and plopped down on the soft leather sectional, his feet going instinctively onto the coffee table, heavy hiking boots notwithstanding. Having lost his parents at the young age of twenty-one, he understood what a difference a positive role model could make in someone's life. His brothers had really stepped in for him and Shelby, and the self-esteem that grew from their patient tutelage had served him all his life. He reached forward to pick up the latest issue of *Rock Climbing Magazine* and froze in place.

Sitting across the room in a deep, horrified stupor—frozen like a statue beneath an unlit lamp—was his adolescent roommate, Braden Bratianu: the once-human-child-turned-teenager he had been charged with caring for since his graduation from the University.

And the boy was not alone.

Sitting in front of him on the leather ottoman was a young girl—maybe eleven or twelve—with soft blond hair pulled loosely into two matching pigtails. She was sitting with her back to Braden, facing the wall…just staring straight ahead, blankly.

"What the—" Nachari caught himself before he cursed, not wanting to teach Braden any more bad habits. "Braden, what in the world are you doing? And who is that girl?"

Braden looked up at Nachari like he had been jolted out of a trance himself and blinked before smiling weakly. "Please don't be mad."

Nachari drew in a deep breath and steadied himself. *Gods, what had the boy done now?* Braden was rather well-known for his never-ending escapades that often led to trouble, which was why the council had given him to Nachari for a season to begin with—mentoring Braden was a test in patience, and it was also a test of insight...as beneath all of the fluff and chaos, the kid had a strong knack for Magick and many burgeoning spiritual gifts. "I'll try," Nachari bit out, holding out his hands palms facing up as if to say, *Well?*

Braden cleared his throat and bit his lower lip. He sighed, visibly raising and lowering his shoulders, and then plastered a misguided smile on his face. "This is Katie Bell." He pointed at the girl.

Nachari looked at the little girl in her skinny jeans and pink sweater and smiled. "Hi, Katie." He immediately became concerned when the girl didn't answer—or even look his way.

Transporting across the room in an instant, he knelt down in front of her. "Katie?" He waved his hand in front of her face several times, and she blinked.

"Hi," she said, extending her hand.

Nachari took it hesitantly. It seemed unbelievably small compared to his own. "It's nice to meet you, Katie."

She nodded, her eyes fixed on a point beyond his face.

Nachari whistled low and met Braden's stupefied gaze. "What's going on?"

Braden shrugged. "Okay, so...so check this out, bro: This is what went down—"

Nachari held up his hand to indicate *Stop!* Braden's urban hip-hop phase had been a last-week thing. Ever since he had helped save Marquis from being mated to the wrong *destiny*— helping to uncover a wicked spell of Black Magick crafted by Salvatore Nistor—he had been in full I'm-going-to-be-the-world's-greatest-psychic (after I'm done being a warrior) mode. Braden must be really nervous if he was reverting back to...last week. "Nix the slang and speak to me in plain English," Nachari warned.

Braden swallowed and nodded his consent. "Okay…yeah…no problem, Nachari."

Nachari gestured at the little girl, who was still more or less ignoring them both. "Katie Bell? What happened?"

Braden rubbed his hands together. "Okay, so you know all about the Dark Ones, right?"

"What about them, Braden?"

"About like this whole plot…to destroy the valley and kill the humans. You know, the reason you have to go around and clean up after them, replace people's memories and stuff."

Nachari nodded. "Okay."

"Well"—Braden lowered his head and looked down at the ground—"you also know how you and me—we're like…*this*"—he crossed his fingers and held them up—"really tight, and we have the same kind of skills and stuff."

Nachari rubbed his eyes. *Same kind of skills? Oh gods…* "Go on."

"Well, I kind of…sort of…wanted to see if I could learn how to do the whole memory swap-replace thing, too. You know"—he rushed the last words—"so I could maybe help you out with all the work you're having to do around Dark Moon Vale." He frowned and met Nachari's eyes. "I know how you called your boys from the University to come hang out and help you, and that's cool, but it's just…Marquis has been too busy with his new baby to teach me archery like he promised…and I thought maybe if I made myself useful, you would still want to hang out with me."

Nachari ran his hands through his hair and hung his head. Self-esteem, again. Why was this child such a yo-yo when it came to feeling good about himself, understanding his place in the world? He was deeply loved by the Silivasi brothers—ever since he had fought like a champion to save Nathaniel's destiny from a Lycan who had almost killed him in the process—and everyone was doing their best to shower as much time and attention on him as possible, indulging his latest fads, because they all

142

understood how hard it was for him to come into their society having been born a human. He was the first male vampire to be converted, a child by a previous marriage of a female destiny who was claimed by one of their males, and he was an all-around great kid, until he started to feel insecure—and came up with a lamebrained scheme.

Like this one.

Nachari looked at little Katie and tried to control his reaction: *What in the name of the gods had Braden done to her?* "Tell me absolutely everything," he instructed.

Braden looked at Katie then, and his face sank with remorse. "Well, she's human." Nachari raised his eyebrows and Braden laughed, insincerely. "Oh yeah, I guess you already know that."

Nachari nodded.

"And she goes to Tall Pines Junior High."

Well, it was at least a start, Nachari thought. Tall Pines was not that far from Dark Moon Vale.

"Me and some of the guys kind of…went to town for a while…you know, just to hang out?"

"Who drove?" Nachari asked.

Braden smiled. "Blade Rynich."

Nachari knew the kid's father; he was a warrior in the house of Jadon and an honorable man. "And?"

"And Katie was sort of walking home with her friends when we drove by."

"How old is she?" Nachari asked.

Braden shrugged.

Nachari placed his hand gently under her chin and lifted her head to catch her gaze. "Katie, how old are you, sweetie?"

She smiled but didn't answer.

He tried a different approach. Making the softest push he could against her mind, he whispered, "Tell me your age."

"Twelve," she said.

Nachari glared at Braden and frowned. "You boys stopped to talk to a group of twelve-year-old girls?" His disappointment was evident in his voice.

BLOOD POSSESSION

"No!" Braden insisted. "She was the youngest one in the group, I swear. I think it was her sister's friends or something because they were fifteen like me…like all of us…well, except for Blade, because he's sixteen and has a human's driver's license. But, honestly, the only reason I chose her was because she was the youngest—and I thought she'd be the easiest person to…practice on." He looked down, ashamed. "I swear, Nachari. I never meant to hurt her. You know me! I wouldn't hurt anyone—except a Dark One!"

Nachari nodded. "Tell me exactly what you did…and how she came to be here with you."

All at once, there was a subtle disturbance in the energy field around them, and Nathaniel Silivasi opened a telepathic link to Nachari: *Greetings, little brother: Is everything all right?*

Nachari held up his hand to make Braden pause and smiled. *Wow: Is my energy that bad?*

Not that bad, Nathaniel answered. *I was just closing the office at the lodge and putting some finishing touches on your paperwork—submitting the liability forms for the outward bound, nature-challenge program—so I was already linked into your energy when I felt your…uneasiness. What's up?*

Braden. Nachari answered. There was nothing more that needed to be said.

Ah. Nathaniel chuckled. *Anything serious? Do you need assistance?*

Nachari shook his head and sighed in frustration. *Not completely sure yet. Still assessing the damage. I'll get back to you.*

Nathaniel sent a stream of reassurance into Nachari's mind. *Very well—call me if you need me.*

Will do.

Be well, brother.

Be well, Nathaniel.

Nachari turned back to Braden. "Now where were we?"

"Who was that?"

"Nathaniel."

Braden frowned. "Did you tell him?"

Nachari was quickly losing his patience. *Slow-it-down,* he told himself. *It will all work out.* "Tell him what, Braden? You haven't finished telling me yet."

Braden looked at the little girl as if checking to see if she was okay before continuing. She wasn't okay—or not okay—she was simply there, like a bump on a log, an inanimate object, and Nachari could not act quickly enough to restore the girl to her normal state of mind: *if she could be restored.* At this point, there was no telling. Mind control was a common skill among the Vampyr, but in the hands of a novice, it could be extremely dangerous. "So what *exactly* did you do?" he asked Braden again.

Braden narrowed his eyes in concentration. "Well, we all just hung out and fooled around for a while, and then the other girls decided to go to the corner store to get a Coke. Blade and Tyce walked with them, but me and Katie weren't thirsty, so we just waited."

Nachari sent a deeper probe into the little girl, wanting to make sure she wasn't frightened or uncomfortable as they sorted things out. There was a clear presence of fear, but it was at a deep, unconscious level—she would be okay for now. "So, what happened when you and Katie were alone?"

Braden sat forward in his chair and rested his elbows on his knees. "At first, I wanted to see if I could erase her memory— you know like go back ten minutes, and see if it worked—so I did like you've described: pictured her thoughts as energy, connected to the individual strands, and followed them into her mind." He sat up, excited. "And once I finally got in there, I couldn't believe it. It was so cool. So I wanted to see if she would respond to suggestion, and she did! So, I made her do a couple of stupid things—"

"What kind of stupid things?" Nachari's voice was edged with anger, and his canines began to tingle in his mouth.

Braden's eyes opened wide. "Nothing bad. Honest! Meow like a cat. Tell me I was cute. That sort of thing."

Nachari had heard enough. "I'm really surprised by you, Braden. I can't believe you would do something like this. Do you think this is some kind of a game?"

BLOOD POSSESSION

The child visibly wilted, but Nachari didn't care. This was serious...and beneath Braden's character. Braden's eyes misted over, and even though he was a teenager, his bottom lip started to quiver, almost imperceptibly.

"I know," he murmured, his voice betraying his deep remorse. His eyes swept over the little girl, and his shoulders began to tremble. "And even while I was doing it, I knew it was wrong and I should stop." He struggled to hold his shoulders up and blink back his tears. "But I just kept thinking about what would happen to me if you and your brothers don't want me around anymore—if I don't keep proving that I'm useful—and so I couldn't stop. Because I needed to get good at it. Fast." He looked at the little girl then, and the sobs came out. "I'm sorry, Katie. I really am!"

She smiled like a paper doll, stiff and one-dimensional. And then her face returned to a blank slate.

"So, how did she get here?" Nachari asked.

Braden sniffled. "When everyone came back from the store, I tried to fix what I did...and I couldn't...so I started to really freak out, and Tyce said I should bring her back to you. We spoke telepathically so her friends never heard us."

Nachari was taken aback. "You held the telepathic connection for the whole group?"

"Yeah," Braden said, "and then I just imagined a kind of kinetic chalkboard and erased everything with the other girls. I told them that Katie had stayed after school and would come home later, and they just walked away....like she wasn't even standing there. They believed me over their own eyes, but I was really freaked out by then."

Nachari shook his head in disbelief. "When you made the mental suggestion to the girls, did you do it with your mind or with your spoken word?"

Braden considered the question before answering. "I said it out loud: *You will go home and wait for Katie*...type of thing. And they did."

Despite his anger and disappointment, Nachari was floored.

146

Braden's skill was nothing short of remarkable. Braden Bratianu was fifteen years old, and he had only been a vampire for ten of those. Where did these gifts keep coming from?

He walked over to the chair and placed a firm hand on Braden's shoulder. "Listen to me, son."

Braden looked up at him with the most trusting eyes Nachari had ever seen. The kid was such a paradox. "First of all, you don't ever have to prove yourself to me or anyone else in my family. We love you."

Braden's breath hitched, and he looked away, clearly embarrassed. Trying to play it off, he cleared his throat and muttered, "Cool."

Nachari knelt down in front of him. "Did you hear what I said?"

Braden nodded.

"And when your parents get back from vacationing around the world, we are still going to want you around...in our lives."

Braden raised his eyebrows, a hopeful look in his eyes. "Really?"

"Yes, really. We have already talked about working something out with your parents so that you can stay in Dark Moon Vale—continue your human studies at the academy here—instead of attending a human school in Hawaii, which Napolean has frowned upon all along."

Braden's Vampyr sire, Dario Bratianu, had been working at one of the house of Jadon's resorts in Hawaii when he had met his *destiny*, Lily, who happened to be Braden's mother. Following their current vacation, Dario and Lily hoped to remain in Hawaii for at least another five years; thus, creating the need to send Braden and his little brother Conrad—the child born of their Blood Moon—to a human school for their primary studies before transferring back to the Dark Moon Vale Academy for Braden's final year. The plan would require extensive home-schooling to make up for all the training the human education lacked—not to mention the additional instruction required between ages eighteen and twenty—and the Silivasi brothers were working earnestly to find a way to keep Braden with them until Dario and Lily were ready to move back to the valley.

Braden seemed to come alive at the news. Like a brand-new light bulb screwed into a lamp, his face lit up with joy. "Could I stay with you the whole time?"

Nachari shrugged. "I'm not sure about the whole time because I don't know what the future might bring, but between all of us, you will always have a home. And trust me when I tell you, Marquis is very excited about teaching you archery—I know he is because he mentioned it again just the other day." He paused and smiled. "Just keep in mind: Marquis's excited is another person's mad, so…it's all relative."

Braden laughed, and his chest puffed out a bit. And then just as quickly, he became serious. "So what are we going to do about Katie?"

Nachari surveyed the child on the ottoman, taking a quick read of her vital signs—pulse, body temperature, and blood pressure. He closed his eyes and thought about it for a second, and then he sat down next to her. His broad, muscular frame enveloped the entire space, and since that wasn't going to work, he gently pried her from the ottoman and repositioned her until she was standing directly in front of him.

"First things first," he told Braden, "I am going to enter your mind to retrieve all of your earlier memories, firsthand, which is something that is not done among males in the house of Jadon unless it is a true emergency: The mind is considered sacred territory, off-limits, but I will need to view your memories as if they are my own in order to know what to do for Katie." He placed his hand on her forehead, and she didn't blink. "I believe that you did such a thorough job of erasing her memory that you went too far: You went beyond the prefrontal lobe, which affects short-term information into the realm of the middle brain—the limbic system—which plays a role in dreaming. In essence, you disrupted the electrochemical pulses from her brain stem."

Braden's forehead creased in confusion and his top lip

turned up. "Huh?"

Nachari sighed. "In other words, Katie is more or less dreaming, even though she appears awake. Perhaps that's why she does not respond to outside stimuli unless pushed. Even though her eyes are open, it's as if she's asleep."

Braden grimaced. "*Damn*—I did all that?"

Nachari cut his eyes at him.

"Sorry."

Nachari nodded and reached for Katie's hand. He ran his fingers over her temples, massaging in slow, rhythmic motions.

"What are you doing?" Braden asked.

"Checking for any physical damage to the brain...making sure there is nothing irreversible."

Braden paled. "Gods..."

"Yeah—not a game," Nachari reiterated.

Satisfied that her mind was whole, Nachari released his touch and turned to regard Braden. "Once we have...put things back together...the way they belong, I'll retrieve her address from her mind, and we'll take her home."

"Really? How? Are you going to fly her home? Dematerialize with her in your arms?"

"Not so much," Nachari said in a calm tone of voice. "I think we'll take the Mustang."

"Oh," Braden replied, sounding dejected.

Nachari restrained his laughter.

"What will her family do when we walk up to the door?"

"Her family will not do anything when *I* walk up to the door," Nachari said sternly, his tone brooking no arguments. "I'll use a cloak of invisibility: They will never see me."

Braden's eyes grew wide, and his mouth turned up in an eager smile.

"No," Nachari said. "Don't even think about it!"

Braden crossed his arms and sat back in his chair.

"Braden, give me your word you will not attempt to use your...untested...powers again—at least not the more advanced ones—without consulting someone first?"

BLOOD POSSESSION

Braden frowned. "Yeah…okay."

"Braden?"

"Yeah…yes, I promise."

"Good." He gave Katie's hand a little squeeze—it wouldn't be long now—and then he turned to face his young cohort, adopted a slightly more formal posture, and linked their eyes in an unyielding gaze: The traditions in the house of Jadon were steeped in a rich history of unity, justice, and mutual respect—protocol was protocol—even when dealing with a silly young boy who might not understand it. "Braden Bratianu, son of Dario and Lily Bratianu, protected by Moniceros, the unicorn, and a fledgling in the house of Jadon?"

Braden swallowed and wrung his hands together, looking hesitant. "Yes?"

"I would ask permission to enter your mind for the purpose of healing this girl." Braden croaked out an unintelligible response, and Nachari's heart warmed. "What say you?"

Braden licked his lips, and then his eyes deepened with a shadowed hint of wisdom, a sliver of knowledge from somewhere deep within his genetic—vampiric—memory. He rose from his seat, approached Nachari, kneeled at his side, and reverently lowered his head. "It is with great humility that I grant your request, Master Wizard, even as I thank you for providing this service."

Nachari held the child in his gaze, noting the deferential posture, replaying the appropriate, acquiescent tone of his voice, and he knew that something monumental had just happened. A channel had opened, creating a bridge between Braden and the house of Jadon's ancient traditions—an extrasensory pathway that would offer the child full access to the Vampyrs' collective memories.

Nachari felt a sudden surge of enormous power and knew that Napolean Mondragon had somehow registered the occurrence at the same moment—taken note of the sacred gift that had been passed onto the boy.

The king would not invade their space or speak

telepathically.

He would not seek information that wasn't offered to him, but there could be no mistake: The surge of energy that had just passed through young Braden Bratianu was too powerful to go unnoticed by the heart and soul of the people—Napolean would remain linked to Braden on a highly acute spiritual pathway where he could carefully monitor the young acolyte's progress from now on.

Whew...

Would the surprises never end?

Nachari let out a deep breath. "Very well, then. Shall we begin?"

fourteen

Gabe Lorenz was strapped to a cold metal table, his arms and legs bound with tight, unyielding rope. His throat was sore and his mouth was dry as he continued to tug against his restraints and struggled to open his eyes.

"Where am I?" he croaked as his eyes began to focus.

The last thing Gabe remembered was walking out of the twenty-four-hour, fit-for-life gym after an extremely vigorous workout. He had been on his way to the shooting range to reassess his marksmanship skills before hiring himself out as a private bodyguard to a foreign dignitary. Being one of the best hand-to-hand combat experts in his early twenties—capable of killing a man in under five seconds with his bare hands—he had decided it was time to make some serious money. He was rapidly approaching thirty, and he needed to take advantage of his declining youth while he still had some stamina.

He blinked his eyes in quick succession, forcing them to open—and stay that way—and then his heart began to flutter wildly in his chest, momentarily seizing as if it were gripped in the clutches of an iron fist. He was in a dark, underground chamber illuminated solely by tiny flames—hundreds of black candles set inside deep, hand-carved crevices in an ancient stone wall—and a dense gray fog rose from the floor, swirling all around him.

His eyes narrowed their focus, straining to see through the fog, and his breath caught in his throat.

Standing directly to his left—and bending over the table with a curious and darkly evil expression on his face—was a giant of a man with coal-black eyes and muscles so defined that they rippled when he moved. He was wearing a tight black muscle-shirt over a pair of faded blue jeans, and he had the look of a warrior about him. Power practically oozed from his pores. And confidence? As far as this bad-ass was concerned, he owned the entire freakin' world.

Gabe grimaced. What the hell was up with the guy's hair? It was blacker than the night, and it shimmered with evenly dispersed bloodred locks, almost like it was a...living thing...and the color came from the roots—not some kind of hair-dye.

The dude leaned forward and smiled...or grimaced. Basically, he turned his lips up and then he bowed his head in an infinitesimal gesture of acknowledgment before purring his words: "Welcome, human. I am Salvatore Nistor, and you are a temporary...necessity...in the house of Jaegar. I do hope you enjoy your stay."

Human?

Gabe's terror was palpable in the room—and Gabe Lorenz *never* rattled—as his adrenaline and desperation kicked into overdrive. "Shit...*shit*...oh...what the hell...oh, shit!" The dude had *fangs* extending from his mouth, and his eyes glowed reddish-orange. And it wasn't from any contacts. "What the—"

"A vampire," the fanged giant answered wickedly, emphasizing the "V" and rolling the "R's" with a foreign accent for effect.

Vampire? Whatever the hell he was, Gabe knew instinctively that the dude was a sadist. He tugged harder at his ropes, even though he knew they weren't going to budge. He raised his head as far as he could and glanced around the rest of the room to see if there was any kind of—

"Sweet mother of God!"

He arched his back and bucked like a wild animal, fighting so hard to come off the table that his muscles tore and his wrists and ankles began to bleed as the rope cut into them. He rocked the table so hard it almost tipped over. Standing—no, *hanging*—to his right was another male just like the one bending over him: a tower of a man with black-and-red hair, only this guy's was cut short, and he was hanging by a short length of chain, both of his wrists shackled and stretched high above his head. The chain, in turn, was anchored to the ceiling by a large iron peg, and the guy was bare-chested and drenched in blood.

His throat, wrists, and inner thighs had been slit open, and the blood was running in pools from his major arteries into a large steel bucket positioned directly beneath his bare feet. The sadist was collecting his freakin' blood, and all around the base of the bucket, that strange, eerie fog continued to swirl, dip, and *hiss* as it spun around in a cyclone enveloping the offering.

Gabe shook his head to clear his vision. Holy…shit. There were strange objects surrounding the bucket, barely masked behind the smoke: engraved images of what appeared to be dark angels, various cut plants and herbs soaked in blood, and more black candles of every variety with mystic symbols carved into the hardened wax. In the center of the bucket of blood, there was an otherworldly fire blazing red, purple, and blue—burning not on the fuel of wood or coal—but from the very essence of the blood itself.

"Oh, hell no!" Gabe bellowed.

The vampire reached down and pinned both of Gabe's arms, holding him still against the table. "Do not waste your energy, human," he snarled. "You are going to need every ounce of your strength to complete the task you are about to be given." The vampire's strength was indefinable. In fact, he felt more like an iron tank than a man, holding Gabe to the table with effortless ease.

Gabe sucked in his breath and willed his heart rate to slow down—to maintain a steady, manageable rhythm—before he had a heart attack. What had the vampire said? He was going to be given a task?

This was good.

Very good.

If they needed him—if they planned to use him even temporarily—then that meant they weren't going to kill him…just yet. And if the task had anything to do with using his special combat or marksman skills, then he needed to make sure his arms, legs, and mental faculties remained functioning and intact. He needed to buy some time.

BLOOD POSSESSION

Gabe swallowed hard, pushing through the fear. "What kind of task?"

His question was met with a stunning blow to the jaw.

The impact rattled his bones and broke several of his back teeth.

"You do not speak to me unless I ask you to, human!" The guy literally growled like an animal. "Ever!"

Gabe turned his head to the side, choked on the coppery taste of blood, and spit out the loose fragments of his back teeth. Still coughing, he refocused his eyes on the *thing* in front of him...remaining deathly quiet all the while.

Lesson learned.

He was no idiot.

The vampire gestured toward the hanging male, and then walked over to stand next to him. "This," he practically sang in a lyrical voice that played over Gabe's body as much as it vibrated in his eardrums, "is Victor Dirga, the firstborn son of Octavio. He is honored among our kind, yet he will soon be sacrificed to our Dark Lord Ademordna. Do not overestimate your value, human."

When he spoke the name of the dark lord, the room went momentarily black.

A harsh, icy wind swept over Gabe's body, and his windpipe sealed shut, making it impossible to breathe, even as he felt the overwhelming urge to retch. He was filled with a sense of foreboding like nothing he had ever felt before; it was like being mired in a dark, emotional sludge, sinking in a malevolent quicksand made of mankind's most base emotions. Death, Murder, Addiction, and Insanity all took residence in his body at once. Guilt, Fear, Shame, and Hatred pooled in his gut like a living, breathing entity. And he felt the full force of each emotion as if he were living the experience right then and there—on the table—a sensation beyond illness, a pain beyond torture...his mind, body, and soul in an advanced stage of spiritual cancer.

The vampire fell to one knee, bowed his head, and the

156

suffocating energy lifted…although it didn't leave. Rather, it just seemed to hover, both along the ceiling and at the base of the bucket of blood.

Gabe sucked in the air that had returned to him as the vampire stood back up and ran a sharp fingernail—no, a claw—along the hanging male's chest. "Our lord will require one such sacrifice every day in order to answer our summons, so time is of the essence, is it not, Gabe?"

Gabe didn't dare answer. His stomach turned over in waves of nausea, and he felt like he might just black out, but he struggled to focus…and listen.

And then, the earth spun upside down on its axis, and all that was ever right in the world ceased to exist: The vampire drew back a powerful arm and plunged it through the hanging man's chest; he gripped the guy's heart in an iron fist and retracted it while it was still beating. The dying man's eyes fluttered open, and his mouth hung agape in a silent shout of terror.

Gabe screamed so loud his eardrums hurt as the vampire dropped the heart into the bucket, tenderly cupped the male by the face—almost as if he were going to kiss him—and then twisted his head off his body like it was nothing more than a dandelion on the end of a stem. "Forgive me, Victor," the vampire muttered, dropping the head into the basin. "Your sacrifice will not be in vain." He held both arms up to the sky, his head rolled back on his shoulders, and he began to chant over and over in a strange, primordial language.

And then, the vampire's hair began to flap behind him as if he were standing in a great gust of wind, and his words played like an orchestra, echoing from every direction at once in a macabre chorus of entreaty. The vampire cried out—he moaned like he was in horrific pain—and then just as quickly, he turned and headed toward Gabe and the table.

Gabe prayed for death.

The thing that approached him now was beyond *not-human*—beyond just a vampire—he was evil incarnate. His skin glowed from a deep, crimson halo, and a terrible fire danced about his hands and fingers. His face was contorted in an ecstasy so divinely evil that it almost appeared...beautiful...hypnotic. His eyes met Gabe's, and he seemed to pull Gabe's very soul from his chest, effortlessly dominating his will. "You will go to the address you are given. You will seek out the dark-haired lady who stands with Napolean Mondragon, and you will try to kill her." He swept his hand slowly over Gabe's belly—first, the back of his fingers, and then the front. Gabe's body convulsed, and the vampire moaned. "When Napolean Mondragon kills you for threatening his woman—and kill you, he will—you will release your soul...into his."

Gabe frowned, as confused as he was terrified...

Release his soul?

How could he release his soul?

When a look of abject terror swept over the vampire's face—even as he hovered above Gabe in a threatening manner—Gabe knew his goose was truly and permanently cooked: If this evil being feared something—anything—then whatever it was had to be unspeakable.

Gabe held his breath as the vampire slowly backed away from the table, retreated to the back of the room, and stood, terrified, his body flushed as flat as possible against the cold, stone wall.

Gabe clenched his eyes shut.

He couldn't take any more.

He wished the vampire would just kill him and get it over with.

"Come forth, my lord," the vampire shouted, his voice as thick with fear as reverence. "Accept this offering of blood...and come forth to do my bidding."

There was a great explosion, like a bomb going off, and Gabe's eyes flew back open. Not seeing was even worse than seeing...

Or so he thought.

"Blessed Mother, help me..." he whispered.

158

Tessa Dawn

The bucket was suddenly engulfed in intensely hot flames that flickered wildly before merging with the dark fog, consuming each of the elements that had been offered to it—and then the conglomeration began to take form.

"Hail Mary full of grace…" Gabe began to pray.

The form of a snake?

"The Lord is with thee…"

A reptile—no, a worm—began to emerge.

"Blessed art thou amongst women; and blessed is the fruit of thy womb—"

A hideous creature with horns and claws and hooves for feet shimmered slowly into view.

Gabe struggled to remember the prayer but forgot his place. "Pray for us sinners now, and at the hour of our death."

The face morphed in and out, taking on the visage of several other people—women, then children; boys, then young men—it was like the worm was consuming the blood of a dozen souls and becoming each as it absorbed their essence…growing more and more powerful with each offering.

And then the thing threw back its morphing head and roared like an angry lion, shaking the room in its wake.

Gabe heard a wretched, pitiable scream—a repetitious wail like that of a rotating police siren—sounding again and again in the room like nothing he had ever heard before.

And then he realized that it was his own voice.

Terror had fully consumed him.

As the worm made its way through the air—half slithering, half flying—only to halt and hover above his body, he felt as if his heart would simply explode in his chest from the shock, and relief would come at last. The horrible siren wailed on as the dark entity narrowed, dove down, and entered his mouth, burrowing all the way into the core of his body.

Gabe hacked and convulsed, and then he simply lay there motionless, deathly still, staring up at the ceiling.

BLOOD POSSESSION

Ademordna ripped the ropes from his hands and feet as if they were mere threads. He stood and sauntered over to his servant, who was still hovering in fear by the wall. When the male looked up at him, it was with such reverence…such uninhibited worship…that it felt like a wave of pure, unadulterated power washing over him, drenching him in self-adornment. Pleased, he snatched Salvatore by the hair, wrenched back his head, and bent to place a violent kiss on his mouth—exchanging a precious gift of his essence with his loyal servant. Such a talented sorcerer.

Black blood poured from Ademordna's mouth, filling the open orifice as Salvatore swallowed what was forced upon him. And then Salvatore began to choke. He fell to the ground and thrashed around on the floor in front of Ademordna, his body racked with mindless pain. Ademordna cocked his head to the side and licked his lips, watching as Salvatore clawed at his own skin in madness, tearing off large strips one at a time. He smiled in delight as the essence he had given the sorcerer regenerated the wounds as quickly as he could inflict them.

Such exquisite torture.

Such beautiful supplication.

Laughing wildly, Ademordna stepped away, and then he bent down to hover over the vampire. "You will be able to collect yourself well enough to provide the daily sacrifice, will you not?"

An oozing green trail of drool dripped from Ademordna's mouth and landed on Salvatore's face, burning a hole through his skin like acid. It regenerated, and Ademordna purred. He released a long, hideous claw, and slowly carved out Salvatore's left eye, watching with enormous pride as a new one grew back.

Salvatore trembled from the pain.

"Be still," Ademordna hissed. "I asked you a question." He bent to lick the inside of Salvatore's wrist, and the skin melted off to the bone, leaving fourth-degree burns. He gave the cells a command to heal much more slowly, gifting his faithful servant with hours more of excruciating pain before he would be released. "It is good, no?" he crooned. "You enjoy?"

Clutching his wrist and turning away in order to vomit more black blood, Salvatore forced himself to mumble the words, "Yes, my lord. Thank you."

The syllables came out distorted, garbled amongst all the black goo that oozed from Salvatore's mouth, but Ademordna found them acceptable, nonetheless.

"Does the purity of my essence taste as you thought it would?" Ademordna asked, intrigued.

Salvatore choked and gagged, still moaning in pain. "Forgive me, Lord"—he bit out the words—"but I think I'm going to have an orgasm."

Ademordna stood up, threw back his head, and laughed, the wicked sound ricocheting through the room like thunder clapping in a bottle. He watched as Salvatore writhed in pain…and pleasure…and the suffering was a balm to his dark soul. Even as the faithful sorcerer grew increasingly insane from his desperate need to escape his anguish, Salvatore embraced the darkness with every cell in his being. "Yes, my servant," Ademordna hissed. "You have truly pleased me this day." He groaned with approval. "Your sorcery grows stronger every hour; and if you survive this, it will only make you stronger still."

A fresh wave of pain struck the writhing vampire, and he vomited near Gabe's feet. Gabe spun around then, pleased, and closed his eyes. He ran his hands from the top of his head to the tips of his toes, reveling in what it felt like to dwell for the first time in a human body. Oh, that he only had the time to indulge himself in the simple pleasures of the flesh before completing his summons, but he knew he did not.

The spell was powerful, but it would not hold him.

The blood of so many women, children, and men had drawn him from his throne in the Valley of Death and Shadows, and the hideous sacrifice of the firstborn Dark One had purchased but one day on the earth. His twin energy, Andromeda, Napolean Mondragon's goddess and keeper, would not lie still for long.

Time was of the essence.

He would go to the ancient leader of the house of Jadon, possess his body, and kill his woman—as his servants had requested. And paid for in blood.

Yes, he would do all of these things.

He—the dark lord Ademordna, shadow god to Andromeda—would grant the supplication of his people. He would answer Salvatore's prayer, and the Curse would destroy the ancient king shortly thereafter.

As he familiarized himself with his body and dematerialized out of the sacrificial chamber, a faint voice echoed from deep within the walking corpse he now inhabited—

Ah yes, it was the remaining essence of the human male whose body he had taken. The eternal soul of the man named Gabe was gathering itself back to its original essence in order to enter the spiritual realm, to find freedom in death from this unholy union with Ademordna.

Ademordna laughed and casually relinquished the soul.

It wasn't like he needed it.

Gabe Lorenz was no more.

fifteen

Napolean shut and latched the door to the barn, leaving the stately horses safely behind them. He took several confident steps forward, then turned slowly and stretched out his hand, waiting for Brooke to catch up, hoping she would continue to walk at his side.

"The Dark Moon Stables account for about ten percent of our annual revenue," he said, enjoying the fact that he could talk business and Dark Moon Vale economy with Brooke as easily as any of his Vampyr proprietors. She had an amazing mind for figures and commercial concepts, and he found himself listening very carefully to her observations and off-handed advice. She wasn't completely comfortable with him yet—far from it, actually—but ever since that horrifying confrontation three days ago on the back veranda, there had been a sort of truce between them: Napolean knew that something deep in Brooke's soul had connected with him in that fateful moment. Although he was mortified to think of what she had seen, and beyond angry at whatever misuse of Magick had taken control of his mind, he was grateful that she had stepped in to save him. And more than that, he knew now that they were truly destined to be together. That the gods had created her for him, even if she didn't completely understand the depth of the connection...yet.

The whole incident had given him the confidence to pursue her more assertively, to push forward in an effort to get to know her better, to open his heart—allowing vulnerability—in order to move their relationship forward. While she still wasn't thrilled with her predicament, her heart was much more pliant, she no longer tried to escape, and with every hour that passed, she opened up to him just a little bit more.

"Surely not the trail rides alone," she said, staring off in the direction of the time-worn trails that led up into the steeper mountain ranges.

"What do you mean?" he asked.

"Ten percent," she answered. "With the jewelry factory and the casino, there's just no way horseback...*recreation*...accounts for ten percent of the annual revenue."

"No," Napolean agreed, shaking his head. "The stables are used for boarding, breeding, and private riding lessons as well as trail rides." He motioned toward a group of small log cabins that were evenly spread out along the bank of a winding creek about five hundred yards from the stables. "There's also a guest ranch associated with the horses. Families stay for up to two weeks at the ranch, taking advantage of custom vacation packages."

Brooke nodded her understanding. "And you incorporate white-water rafting, rappelling, rock climbing...that sort of recreation in the packages?"

"Yes, *cel intelept*," he answered.

She raised an eyebrow, looking as endearing as she was beautiful.

"Wise one," he answered, smiling.

She stared ahead at the cabins.

"Would you like to see one?" he asked, instantly turning in that direction. He had learned that her curiosity usually got the best of her.

Brooke took in absolutely everything.

She would want to know how the cabins were decorated; who was in charge of maintenance and grounds upkeep; whether or not the guest ranch was being publicized to the best advantage; and all the while, the inner wheels of her mind would be calculating revenues against expenses, doing an inner capacity-building audit—not because she had already invested her heart in Dark Moon Vale, but because her talent was just that raw and instinctive. She couldn't help herself.

"Sure," she answered as expected, falling into easy step beside him. They remained silent for a while as they walked toward the creek, and then she finally cleared her throat and glanced at him from her peripheral vision. "The stables are run by a human family, right? Kevin Parker."

Napolean smiled. "You have a memory like a steel trap, Brooke."

She shrugged. "Not so much. I just remember reading about the recent death of that young girl—the stable manager's daughter. What was her name?"

"Joelle," Napolean whispered.

"And she was killed by Marquis?"

"By Valentine Nistor," he corrected. "Marquis saved her from a horrific fate."

She shook her head. Clearly, she still had trouble processing the complexity of all she had been exposed to: the Vampyr, the descendants of Jadon versus the descendants of Jaegar, and the endless battles and treachery that were perpetrated between the two groups of descendants. "And Nathaniel's wife—Jocelyn—she actually saw one of those…birth rituals…up close and personal?"

Napolean stifled a growl. The murder of Dalia Montano and the consequent loss of Shelby Silivasi was still a sore subject. "Yes, she did." His answer was factual and without emotion.

Brooke blinked and looked off into the distance, dismissing the subject as if she understood.

Napolean stared at her then, studying her as she walked. He couldn't help it. She had such an easy grace…such a curious spirit. Brooke Adams was tall for a woman, at least five foot, nine inches, and she was slender, no more than one hundred thirty pounds: Every muscle was toned; every curve was accentuated; every movement was easy and relaxed. Despite such a troubled childhood, she had a quiet confidence that hovered about her like a halo. Her ebony, shoulder-length hair framed her face like a pair of hands embracing the chin of a lover, drawing attention to her soft, precisely sculpted bottom lip—the one she bit whenever she was nervous. Her impossibly blue, heavily lashed eyes stood out like a pair of brilliant sapphires, stunning in a face already graced with unusual beauty. Everything about her screamed *rare, exquisite... independent.*

BLOOD POSSESSION

She bit her bottom lip. "You're staring." There was no judgment in the statement.

Napolean drew in a deep breath. "I am." He stopped and reached for her hand.

Reflexively, she took a step back, her eyes scanning his face in rapid, nervous sweeps—as if to discern what he wanted before she responded.

"To kiss you," he answered the question in her eyes.

She blinked and swallowed. She opened her mouth to answer—perhaps to protest—but then she closed it without speaking a word. Instinctively, her eyes swept down to his lips before she quickly forced them back up to his eyes and blushed.

She shivered, but not entirely from fear.

Napolean reached out and brushed a soft but firm hand along her arm, tracing a gentle line down from her shoulder to her wrist, finally rubbing a small circle in the palm of her hand with his thumb. As the breath slowly left her lungs, he gently wove his fingers into hers and gave her a soft tug, pulling her into his body. Her breasts molded perfectly to his chest, and his breath hitched.

Careful, he told himself. She was still very much like a captured bird, wanting to trust yet terrified of being wounded. "By all the gods, *esti frumoasa,*" he whispered, his voice husky against her ear, "you are so…beautiful."

She was holding her breath now, listening, her senses fully alert. Napolean felt her pulse increase. He heard her heart thundering in her chest, and he felt the prickling of her skin— the undeniable evidence of her mutual attraction toward him. Indeed, the gods had chosen well.

He bent to her mouth slowly, his lips lingering just above hers, and their breath mixed as their eyes locked in a gaze of absolute vulnerability and need.

"I can't let you do this," she whispered, although she didn't pull away.

Napolean understood. His hands tightened around hers. "Because consenting to my kiss would be consenting to

166

our…destiny."

She started to speak, but her voice was hoarse. She cleared her throat and tried again. "Yes."

His right hand moved to the small of her back, and he cradled her more tightly against him, inhaling the scent of her skin as his eyes drifted closed. "But if I take it—without your consent—then once again, you will have no choice in the matter. Would that be easier for you, my queen? After all, you are still my—"

"Captive," she whispered, her lips nearly brushing his.

"Indeed," he breathed into her mouth as he closed the remaining distance between them, and his lips formed a soft seal over hers.

The kiss was warm yet tentative…at first.

He lifted both hands to cup her face, gently brushing the sides of her cheeks with his thumbs as he deepened the kiss, sought to taste her with his tongue, and let out a deep, feral growl in response to her pliant, almost inaudible moan.

His hands moved down to her hips, and he felt his body harden in response to the supple, luscious curves. He didn't try to hide his reaction. Pressed so tightly against him, she would feel everything, and he no longer cared.

Gods, he had waited *forever* for this woman.

A sudden snap-click-pop echoed in his head, and time slowed down into distinct, micro-increments: Snap—a thumb brushing over a safety. Click—a trigger cocking back. Pop—a bullet firing out of a chamber…speeding, whirring, sailing toward the back of Brooke's head.

Napolean spun their bodies around in a dizzying whir of speed, gasping as the bullet struck home right between his shoulder blades and penetrated his back. "Get down!" he ordered, shoving Brooke to the ground before spinning around to face the intruder.

Hiding less than fifty yards behind the wide foliage of a juniper tree was a human male, and he aimed the barrel of his gun, once again, at Brooke.

BLOOD POSSESSION

He fired: once, twice, three times in quick succession.

Each time, Napolean reached out with his left hand and caught the bullet. Each time, a searing heat burned his hand, eviscerating skin, bone, and tissue. Rage swept up from his toes to his head, then swirled around in his body, building a fire of its own. Napolean could hardly see through the red haze of fury as he held out his right hand and pointed his fingers at the male behind the tree.

The gun flew out of the male's steady hands, drawn from his grasp as if a powerful magnet had simply stolen it away. And then the human came next. As if tied to a marionette's strings, he rose off the ground and flew forward through the air toward Napolean. The king would not humble himself to go to his enemy. The enemy would come to him…

To embrace his death.

Napolean glanced over his shoulder, and his eyes took quick inventory of Brooke. "Are you hurt?"

"No," she croaked, her voice thick with fear, her body positioned wisely behind his. "What's going on? Is that another vampire…one of those Dark Ones?"

Napolean snorted. "No."

"Why is he trying to kill you?" Her voice raised an octave.

"He was trying to kill *you*."

Brooke gasped. "*Me!* But why? Who is he, Napolean?"

Napolean laughed then, a wicked, emotionless sound. "He is a dead man, my love. A walking corpse."

Ademordna, the twin demon to Napolean's goddess Andromeda, allowed the haughty king to lift him from the ground and draw him through the air like so much rubbage: talk about looking a gift horse in the mouth! Gabe Lorenz's body had served him well. It would have been nice to actually strike the woman with one of the bullets before his current form—

Gabe Lorenz's form—died, but in the end, this would be just as satisfying. The body Ademordna would soon inhabit would be more powerful than any other flesh currently animated on the face of the earth.

He would soon walk, breathe, and exist as the ancient one, Napolean Mondragon.

And until the end of Andromeda's Blood Moon—until Napolean failed to make the required sacrifice of the Blood Curse—Ademordna intended to take full advantage of Napolean's powerful physique, get his full mileage out of it, so to speak. He smiled in sweet anticipation. Let his servants in the house of Jaegar continue to sacrifice their firstborn, adult sons, shedding their own precious, evil blood to keep Ademordna alive for the remaining twenty-four days of Napolean's Blood Moon. Hell, it was good for them. It would teach them humility. And after all, Ademordna was a dark lord—every bit as divine as his ridiculous twin energy, Andromeda. He was owed the reverence. The homage was his due. Besides, the unbearable grief of those left alive would add an exquisite taste to this feast of supplication, a rare delicacy for his discerning palate.

Ademordna eyed the ancient king, and his heart hummed with expectation: The male was beyond impressive. In fact, Napolean's power was magnificent—unmatched—and it radiated outward from the vampire like the sun's aura in a noonday sky, so much greater than he had anticipated.

Much had been gained over so many centuries.

He could feel Napolean's magic pulsating all around him, his absolute command of the elements. He could practically taste his ancient knowledge of humanity and Vampyr alike. This male was more than a flesh-and-bone vessel. This king was very close to being a god.

Ademordna shuddered and shook his head as he drew closer to the sovereign lord of the house of Jadon. He hadn't expected to be so…*aroused*…at the thought of inhabiting Napolean's body, and he knew that he would have to amend his plans: Yes, he would fulfill the terms of the blood possession, remain in the

BLOOD POSSESSION

king's body for the remaining twenty-four days of the pact. He would see to it that Napolean Mondragon was no more at the end of the Blood Moon, but he would also take something extraordinarily invaluable away from the experience. And in doing so, he would deeply reward his faithful servants in the house of Jaegar for all their blood and sacrifice.

He would be a worthy lord, indeed, revered above all others.

Ademordna licked his lips as the plan solidified in his mind: He would use Napolean's body to mate with the human woman after all—just as the clueless king had intended to do, himself. He would allow the curse to proceed forward, using Napolean's seed to sire the promised twin sons: one child of darkness and one child of light. Then he would hand over *both* newborn babes—but not to the essence of the Blood Curse, the wicked, vengeful aberration that still demanded its pound of flesh millennia after the original sin—he would hand both babies over to the faithful Dark Ones of the house of Jaegar. A hallowed gift from the dark lords of the Valley of Death and Shadows. And what did or didn't happen to Brooke at that point would be of no consequence.

He laughed inwardly. The sons of Jaegar could raise, torture, or kill the lighter progeny however they saw fit; either way, Napolean would fail to make the required sacrifice, and the Curse would come to claim him through a vengeful, painful...and *final*...death, destroying the powerful patriarch once and for all.

And the evil child?

He would live!

Spawned from the essence of the Blood Curse, the child would be half abomination and half unadulterated power, the living essence of the greatest king—the greatest being—to have ever walked the earth. The child's power would be undeniable.

Unstoppable.

Purely and insatiably evil.

The Dark Ones would have a king of their own to worship one day—a male unrivaled by any other—a chosen, shadowed

170

soul to lead them to infamy. And with Napolean gone, the child would one day launch the ultimate battle of evil versus good. The final destruction of the sons of Jadon.

And all of this, courtesy of the Dark Lord Ademordna.

The demon licked his lips, practically tasting the victory yet to come.

Yes, this was beyond what even he had first imagined.

sixteen

Brooke huddled on the ground behind Napolean, still stunned by the sudden onset of gunfire—not to mention the fact that Napolean had caught each of the rapidly fired bullets in his hand, or that he had removed the gun from the assailant's grasp using only his mind to do it. She could still smell the burns where the missiles had seared his flesh, yet he showed no sign of physical distress. It was as if he was impervious to pain.

Looking up into his ruggedly handsome face, she was taken aback by the harsh, glowing red light that rimmed his dark eyes; the look of rage was so severe she almost felt sorry for their attacker.

Almost.

Survival was a powerful instinct—how well she knew. Only this time, she wasn't alone. This time, she wasn't helpless. This time, the towering male before her would make quick—and definitive—work of their enemy.

Her enemy.

The thought boggled her mind. Why would anyone in Dark Moon Vale want to harm her? It was the kind of thing that only happened in movies!

As the body of the male drew closer—drawn through the air like a mere feather in the wind, helpless against Napolean's barely restrained power—Brooke scrambled along the ground to hover directly beneath his powerful legs. The muscles in his back were bulging with pent-up aggression, and she had no doubt she was safe behind his towering frame.

The assailant's eyes were open wide in horror—and something else, something Brooke couldn't quite name: Excitement? Anticipation? Surely not.

As he lingered in the air, just above Napolean, he bent his head, straining to get a closer look at the woman kneeling behind

173

the king—straining to get a closer look at her. The man's dirty blond hair was slick with sweat, and it fell forward as his eyes sought hers. All at once, a pair of crimson-red beams—two harsh, buzzing lights—shot forth from Napolean's eyes into the assailant's, burning the man's retinas until his eye sockets burst into flames.

"You will not look at her!" Napolean commanded, and his voice echoed through the surrounding valley like so much thunder and lightning.

Brooke drew back, astonished…terrified…mesmerized by Napolean's enormous power.

The man cried out in agony as Napolean reached up and grasped his throat in one unyielding hand. Talons shot forth from the ends of Napolean's fingers as he squeezed even harder, yet the assailant remained eerily calm in the throes of Napolean's rage.

"Who are you?" Napolean demanded. "And who sent you?"

The compulsion in Napolean's voice was so powerful that Brooke felt an overwhelming need to respond to the question, even though she didn't know the answer. Her tongue danced in her mouth with the desire to obey the king's command.

The man smiled.

Smiled.

In all that pain.

"I am…Gabe Lorenz. I was sent by the Dark Ones' Council to murder your *destiny.*"

Napolean drew in a deep, discerning breath—as if he was *scenting* for truth. "There is no light left in your soul. It is no longer human. How is that possible?"

The man laughed then, loud and unabashed, even as he pressed his hands against his smoldering eyes and shuddered in pain. "Would you believe that I sold my soul—so to speak—for the chance to get my hands on her delicate human flesh?"

Napolean threw back his head and roared. Brooke covered her ears, and the ground shook beneath them. He placed a second hand on the man's throat and squeezed, watching with unbridled fury as blood and tissue oozed out between his fingers and bone snapped like twigs. And then he tugged in two opposite directions, his left hand pulling downward, his right hand twisting upward, and the man's head simply separated from his shoulders—blood spewing out like a geyser from the convulsing corpse.

Brooke opened her mouth to scream, but no sound came out. She covered her head with her arms in an effort to shield her face from the vile substance that rained down all around her.

As Napolean released his hold—his hands no longer had anything to grasp—the body fell toward the ground, and then, in a movement so fast it was only a blur, a mere impression of an action, Napolean plunged his right fist through the man's chest and withdrew his heart, tossing it aside before the torso hit the ground.

The body slumped, almost as if it were kneeling before the vengeful king, and then Brooke witnessed the most awful thing she had ever seen: The corpse began to shake violently. It jerked like it was being throttled by some great, unseen power, and a thick, inky darkness rose from the open wound at the neck, emerging as if from a tomb, copiously encased in blood and...malevolence.

Evil—pure and intemperate—rose from the body in the form of a gigantic worm with two narrow, glowing eyes, and the apparition danced in the wind like a cobra performing for a snake charmer. Even though the entity clearly had no mouth, a high-pitched squeal rang out from its throat—and the sound was deafening.

Soul wrenching.

Alarming all the way to the bone.

The worm rose up, poised to strike Napolean, and then it dove down with enormous strength and speed, piercing the king's mouth in an act so vile it could only be described as rape. It wriggled its demonic body—pushing, shoving, thrusting its way in—until, at last, it could no longer be seen, the ghastly form vanishing inside Napolean's throat.

BLOOD POSSESSION

Brooke's first instinct was to jump up and run.

She was desperate to put some distance between her and Napolean...and the burrowed worm, but then she stopped several yards away to consider...and watch. What if the apparition killed him—what would happen to her then? She couldn't possibly outrun so much evil. Her own heart was practically beating out of her chest, a feeling of desperation rising in her soul to the point of panic.

Dear God, she had to help him.

She didn't understand what was happening, but on some elemental level—somewhere her conscious mind no longer resided where her soul took refuge—it was like watching a lunar eclipse: The absolute life-giving warmth of the sun had been usurped by utter and complete darkness.

Something monumental had changed.

And the darkness threatened them all.

Napolean staggered back like a man being mowed down by a machine gun. His eyes grew so wide that the whites showed all around the edges. He gurgled and spit. His hands reached up to his throat, and he tried to claw the thing out, tearing at his own flesh in the process.

Brooke started to cry. She didn't know what to do. "Napolean," she whispered helplessly. "*Napolean...*"

His head fell forward against his chest, and he sank to his knees in front of her, silent and unmoving in the grass. Two or three more spasms rocked him, and then his face went slack...like he was dead.

Brooke swallowed the scream welling up in her throat, but her fear became a living, breathing entity.

"Napolean?" she whispered again, taking a tentative step forward.

His head snapped up in a serpentine movement, and a languorous smile curved the corners of his lips. He inhaled like a newborn infant drawing its first breath, full-throated and greedy, as if he couldn't get enough.

He stretched out his hand, and his eyes met hers.

Only they weren't Napolean's eyes.

They were two obsidian vortexes of pure, unadulterated evil.

"Come to me, *draga mea*." His voice was somehow different—thick, deep, and sultry as always—but so tinged with darkness that it assaulted her ears and prickled her spine as the tone rolled over her skin in crushing waves of…cruelty.

Brooke swallowed hard and took a step back.

He laughed then. Loud and wicked. And then he stood.

Brooke's feet were frozen to the ground. "Napolean, please…" She held up her hand to keep him at bay.

"Oh," he drawled, "make no mistake; I intend to please you…often." He licked his full lips, tasting the darkness that saturated them like black goo. "But first, I must make you as I am: Vampyr." The last word rolled off his tongue in a thick Romanian brogue, and it instantly conjured images of dark, musty castles and counts named Dracula.

Brooke shook her head and scanned the ground, searching for a weapon—a stone, a stick…anything. She couldn't possibly outrun him.

Before she could register his movement, he rose and stood in front of her, his arms reaching down to grasp her waist in a harsh, painful grip. When he opened his mouth and bent his head, with an obvious intention to kiss her, she could see the two yellow eyes of the worm staring out at her from inside Napolean's throat, and that high-pitched voice was laughing…

Mocking her.

The next voice she heard was not Napolean's but her stepfather's: "Shall I give you the kiss of human death?"

Brooke screamed until her throat felt raw as long, terrifying incisors shot from Napolean's mouth—the worm's mouth—and he struck her before she could break free and run.

Pain brought her back to attention.

It ripped the scream from her throat. Demanded her full awareness. Required her total concentration…if she hoped to survive. Like a woman caught in the throes of labor, she tried to focus—breathe—steady herself against what was coming in an effort to endure it.

There was an indescribable stinging sensation in her neck, and it felt like the venom of a thousand poisonous scorpions...a life-sized injection of a substance that was never meant to enter the human body. Despite her effort, she collapsed against him as the fluid began to flow into her veins, coursing in harsh, unrelenting waves of agony. She struck at him again and again—but to no avail. He tightened his hold around her waist, clamped her arms beneath his in an intractable grip, and moaned.

And just like that, her mind snapped.

Splintered into a thousand pieces.

Each one venturing outward in a different direction in a desperate attempt to do what her body could not...to flee the clutches of a possessed vampire.

seventeen

Nachari Silivasi turned the vintage Calypso Coral 1970 Mustang off the main drag onto a back road and headed toward home. He glanced at Braden sitting in the passenger's seat next to him and relaxed his tired muscles. They had returned Katie to her parents, and everything had gone as planned: Old memories had been erased, new ones supplanted, and all was right with the world again—at least until Braden found another mess to get into. He smiled at his young protégé as the boy bopped along to a rap song on the radio. Rhythm wasn't Braden's strong suit, but Nachari wasn't about to point that out.

"So I have your word then?" Nachari asked.

Braden looked at him through the corner of his eyes, his head bobbing up and down and side to side to the music—well, somewhere in the vicinity of the music—and smiled. "About what?"

"No more trying out dangerous, unused powers without consulting a Master first?"

Braden rolled his eyes, and surprisingly, the eye-roll actually coincided with the beat of the song. "Yeah…yeah…I already told you."

Nachari laughed. "Good. Then how about a movie tonight?"

Braden's face lit up. "You mean in an actual theatre?"

"Sure," Nachari answered. "Anything you want to see?"

"Oh yeah!" Braden exclaimed. "There's this crazy, siiiiick movie about these Roman gladiators who—"

His words cut off abruptly and Nachari smiled, pleased that the boy had, for once, tempered his own effusive language. Nachari had cautioned Braden repeatedly to go light on the urban accent. A little slang was par for the course with a human teenager, but Braden rarely did anything in moderation: When he really got going, he sounded like a cross between Snoop Dog

179

and Poindexter from Felix the Cat. Identity crisis 101.

"Go on," Nachari urged. "What movie would you like to see?"

Braden coughed and anchored his right hand against the dashboard, bracing himself against a sudden onset of spasms.

Nachari slowed the Mustang and turned to look at him. "Are you okay?" This didn't appear to be part of the dance, although Nachari had seen stranger things from the kid before.

Braden's left hand went to his throat, and his cough grew more insistent, rapidly developing into an uncontrollable hack.

Nachari pulled to the side of the road.

"Braden?" He searched the kid's face with growing alarm. Braden's skin was clammy, his eyelids were heavy, and a soft sheen of sweat had formed on his brow. Nachari closed his eyes and tuned in with his ears, relying on his hyper-acute hearing to assess the boy's condition: His airway was still open. His heartbeat remained steady. But something was rapidly making him ill. "What's happening, buddy?" he asked, placing a gentle hand on the kid's shoulder. "Talk to me."

Panting in distress, Braden doubled over in his seat. "Going to be sick," he mumbled. His right hand left the dash, and he pressed it to his stomach to quell the nausea. He bent over and moaned. "I mean it, Nachari. I think I'm gonna puke in your car."

With the supernatural speed of his kind, Nachari flew out of the Mustang, whizzed around to the other side, and yanked open the passenger door. "Have you been eating human food again?" he asked.

Braden shook his head. "No," he croaked. "I mean, yeah...sometimes...candy bars...but they don't bother me that much. It feels like—" His words cut off abruptly again as he shot forward in the seat, twisted to lean out of the car, and spewed a huge stream of vomit onto the ground, barely missing Nachari's boots.

It was just the beginning.

Wave after wave hit the boy with such violent intensity that his body shook with every surge, and the refuse began to spill out tinged with blood.

"Oh shit," Nachari muttered, instinctively holding Braden's hair back from his face. "What the hell?"

Vampires did not get the stomach flu.

They did not get sick—period.

Braden's body began to convulse, and his vomiting became a series of coarse gags. He fell even further forward, toppled out of the car onto the unpaved road, and began to writhe around in the dirt, screaming in pain between convulsions.

Nachari fell to his knees beside him and ran both hands through his hair in helpless frustration. *Kagen!* he called out telepathically to his older brother, the Master Healer, praying he would know what to do.

What's going on, Nachari? Kagen's reply was instant.

It's Braden. Something's really wrong with him.

Braden's affliction reached a fevered pitch.

Blood continued to seep out the corners of his mouth, and—as if it were even possible—his body convulsed more brutally. It appeared as if the kid was going to expel his organs through his mouth, and Nachari wished like hell he could trade places with him. The boy had suffered too much pain already in his short life.

Focus, Nachari. Kagen said in a steady voice. *Can you send me a visual image?*

Nachari forced himself to relax and open his mind. He took a moving picture of what he was seeing and hearing—not unlike a video camera recording the scene—and sent the full sensory stream to Kagen in a memory-transfer.

Kagen let out a short string of Romanian curses before quickly regaining his composure. *I'm not familiar with the scenery, Nachari,* he explained. *Where are you?*

Nachari glanced around. *Two or so miles east of Tall Pines— where the Snake Creek River forks just outside the county line... We turned off on River-Rock Road.*

Just like that, Kagen Silivasi shimmered into view next to his brother. He held his medical bag in his left hand, and his mouth was set in a severe frown, indicating that he meant business. He knelt beside Braden and quickly took his pulse, assessing all other vital signs in an instant with his heightened senses. "What brought this on?" he asked, incredulous.

Braden jerked away. "Help!" His lungs strained with the effort to speak.

"I'm here," Kagen assured him. "We're going to help you, but you have to tell me what's going on, son. Where does it—"

"Napolean!" Braden's words were forced. And panicked.

Nachari's eyes met Kagen's, and a twinge of dread passed between them. Nachari couldn't help but remember the odd energy that had…disturbed…their Sovereign during the meeting at the Hall of Justice. Unsure of what they were dealing with, he decided to bring Nathaniel and Marquis in on it.

He called out to both of them telepathically, careful to keep his voice at least moderately calm.

What is it? Marquis responded immediately.

I'm here, Nathaniel answered.

Something has happened to Braden, Nachari explained. *Kagen is already here, but I need you both to join us.*

Both warriors arrived in less than one minute, shimmering into view with stark looks of concern on their faces.

"What is it?" Nathaniel asked, immediately scanning his surroundings to check for danger.

Marquis strode directly to Nachari, already tense with anger, but before he could speak, he caught a glimpse of Braden and blanched. "What the hell happened?"

Nathaniel leapt the distance between them. "How serious is it?"

Sighing, Nachari brought them both up to speed: "We really don't know. We were just driving—talking about going to see a movie—when Braden got sick in the car. I pulled over to help him, and he started throwing up. Kagen came immediately, but we haven't figured anything out yet. And the only thing Braden has been able to tell us is that it might have something to do

Tessa Dawn

with Napolean."

"Napolean?" Marquis grumbled, confused.

Nathaniel turned to Kagen. "How does this possibly relate to our king, brother?"

"I don't know," Kagen answered, studying Braden intently. He felt the boy's brow for fever and then lightly pressed on his stomach, carefully feeling each internal organ for anomalies. He frowned. "I have to tell you, I don't think this is physical in nature."

"What do you mean?" Marquis asked. "The child is writhing around on the ground in a pile of his own vomit. It doesn't get much more physical than that."

Leave it to Marquis to provide a blunt, no-nonsense summary, Nachari thought.

"Is he going to be okay?" Nathaniel asked.

Kagen shrugged, and his dark brown eyes clouded with concern. "I don't know." He turned to Marquis. "And yes, warrior, the *symptoms* are physical, but the origin...I can't find it."

There was a moment of concerned silence before Nathaniel spoke up. "Nachari, you have mentioned Braden's emerging psychic gifts more than once recently. Could his...special abilities play a role in what's happening to him now? We all know that he divined the spell Salvatore used against Marquis and Ciopori with unusual insight."

A chilling, barely audible growl vibrated in the air—it was best not to remind Marquis of Salvatore's treachery. If the Ancient Master Warrior had his way, the sons of Jadon would stage a full-blown war against the entire house of Jaegar, lay waste to their underground colony at midday, and let the chips fall where they may—even if it left a dozen widows in the house of Jadon.

"Yes," Nachari replied, ignoring Marquis's reaction. "Anything is possible." A thought entered his mind. "In fact, just earlier today, something significant may have happened—"

"What?" Kagen asked, his fingers skimming lightly over Braden's psychic meridians, feeling for...gods knew what.

183

BLOOD POSSESSION

Nachari watched with fascination. "Earlier today, I needed to enter his mind because he had created quite a mess with this girl named Katie…" Nachari waved his hand in dismissal: The background information was irrelevant, and there wasn't time to waste. "Anyhow, I used formal decorum to request permission, and Braden fell right into it—like an ancient—word for word, gesture for gesture. It was uncanny."

A heightened silence fell among the brothers.

"But more than that," Nachari continued, "there was a surge of energy that moved through the room—through Braden. It's hard to explain, but more or less, a gateway opened, a bridge between Braden and the collective house of Jadon…our genetic memories…our living history. Our celestial…origins."

"What the hell are you saying, Nachari?" Marquis barked with growing impatience. "Quit talking like a wizard and get to the point!"

Nachari sighed. He was trying. Harder than they knew.

Trying to make sense of what was happening to the innocent kid in front of him.

Trying to come up with anything that might stop Braden's suffering.

After all, he had been the one charged with seeing to the boy's welfare, and if the origin of Braden's illness was not physical, then understanding any possible psychic connection was vitally important—it might just hold the key to Braden's recovery. And Napolean's well-being.

He tried again: "The point is, Braden became more than just psychic today; he became a portal—a link to the entire house of Jadon on a spiritual level." He shook his head in exasperation, sharing Marquis's frustration. "The only other male I've ever seen who was that…connected to all of us…is Napolean."

Nathaniel whistled low beneath his breath. "You're kidding, right?"

"No," Nachari replied. "I'm not."

"So then, you're saying he can read our minds and hear our thoughts without even trying? Shit like that?" Marquis asked.

"No," Nachari insisted, "not like that. I don't think even Napolean does that. It's more of a...knowing. Braden can pick up on the energy of a thing, its essence. He can *feel* what's happening to others, our common history and events, and he somehow channels information through those impulses." He sighed with frustration. "It's still too new...I honestly don't really understand it myself yet."

Nathaniel cleared his throat. "Very well. For the sake of argument, let's assume that his body is somehow experiencing these...impulses: No one in the house of Jadon is susceptible to physical illness, so it still makes no sense."

Marquis grunted, and then he squatted next to Kagen. "Braden," he said, his voice thick with authority, "I need you to pay attention, son. We need you to tell us what is happening."

Braden opened his mouth to speak, but before he could utter a word, he began to hack uncontrollably, writhing in horrible pain.

Nachari grimaced. "Can't you do something for him, Kagen?"

Kagen shook his head, and his dark brows furrowed with dismay. "I can't block his pain, brother. It's like it's locked up somewhere in a vault." He rubbed a soothing hand over Braden's forehead. "It's okay, Braden. Go easy...take your time."

Braden tried to nod. He focused hard on his next word. "Marquis?"

"I'm here, Braden." Marquis leaned closer. "I'm listening. We all are."

Braden pressed both hands to his roiling stomach and concentrated. He struggled onto his hands and knees and rocked back and forth in a heart-wrenching attempt to stop the vomiting. "My sickness," he bit out, "this...it isn't...mine." The spasms took him over with renewed force.

Slowly rubbing his back in soothing circles, Kagen coaxed, "Just breathe, son."

Braden slowly inhaled.

BLOOD POSSESSION

"That's it. Now let it back out...gently."

Braden gradually released the breath.

"Good," Kagen encouraged. "Can you try to talk again?"

Braden wiped his mouth with the back of his hand and sluggishly nodded his head. When, at last, he began to speak, there was a growing desperation in his voice, and it wasn't from the pain. "It isn't...me," he stuttered. "Not in my body. It's Napolean!" He moaned from the nausea and spat some lingering bitterness on the ground. "The cabins ... by the stables ... go ... to ... Napolean!"

Marquis's voice was as lethal as it was calm. "What is happening to Napolean, Braden?"

"Does it have something to do with his *destiny*," Nathaniel asked.

"Possession." Braden groaned the word aloud.

"*Possession?*" Kagen repeated.

Nachari could have heard a pin drop, and then Marquis exploded—

"From what? By whom!"

All at once, Braden fell to his back and cried out as his ribs began to snap one by one, the narrow bones bulging grotesquely through his skin.

"Damnit!" Kagen snarled. He ripped the boy's shirt off and scrambled for his medical bag. The others watched in stunned silence as he quickly lined up a syringe filled with medicine, an IV bag of saline, and some kind of kit containing a catheter. "I have to put him under," Kagen insisted. "Now!"

"Wait!" Marquis ordered. "We have to know what is possessing Napolean first."

"Son of a bitch!" Kagen scowled, turning to glare at Marquis. He took a cleansing breath, and his voice was suddenly calm. Too calm. "Get on with it then," he purred softly.

Nachari shuddered. He knew that placid tone all too well: the one that masked the barely leashed rage just beneath the surface. The all-too-reserved Dr. Jekyll who obscured the Mr. Hyde. He held his breath, eyeing Kagen warily: Whoever had

186

hurt Napolean—*whoever had hurt this kid*—would be better off facing Marquis, Nathaniel, and all the other warriors in the house of Jadon than this seemingly composed Healer.

Braden continued to scream.

Nachari said nothing.

He simply watched as Kagen pressed his hands over Braden's protruding ribs and gently held them in place. "I'm sorry," Kagen said earnestly, his eyes fixed on Braden's, "but before I can put you under—before I can stop this pain—we must know what has taken possession of our king."

Marquis scuffled a foot away from Kagen and took Braden's hand. He squeezed it to get his attention, and then he spoke to him in a voice heavily weighted with compulsion. "Focus on my eyes, son."

Braden's expression was stricken with anguish as he swallowed his pain, forced himself to stop screaming, and stared at Marquis.

"You have to be brave, son—just a little while longer—and tell us what you know: *What is possessing Napolean?*"

Braden trembled uncontrollably, and then he stopped to grind his teeth. "A worm," he ground out. His breathing grew shallow from shock. "The dark lord...Ademordna."

Kagen shut his eyes, then reopened them. "Thank you." With dizzying speed, he snatched the kit, ripped a sterile package open, and expertly inserted a long, thin needle into Braden's antecubital vein. He had just begun to attach the IV when Braden reached up and clutched his wrist.

"Wait!"

"What is it?" Kagen rushed the words.

Nachari placed a steadying hand on Kagen's shoulder. "Tell us, Braden."

"The dark lord has total control of Napolean," Braden said ominously. "He is going to...rape...his woman. He is going to kill our king!"

Nathaniel's eyes flashed red.

Kagen rocked back on his heels.

BLOOD POSSESSION

And Marquis was so angry he…smiled.

Holy shit, Nachari thought. All hell was literally about to break loose.

eighteen

Nachari Silivasi shut off his cell phone and sighed with relief. He dropped it into his front hip-pocket and considered the news: Katia Durgala, Kagen's head nurse, had assured him that Braden was going to be okay. The moment the anesthesia had taken effect, the brutal assault on Braden's body had ceased, and the boy had gone—blessedly—to sleep.

Kagen had then used powerful injections of vampire venom, as well as special poultices, to repair the teenager's broken ribs. Beyond that, Braden had been treated for dehydration, strained muscles, and a hoarse throat. Kagen had also given him a long-acting sedative in order to keep him comfortable, and according to Katia, he was now sleeping peacefully in a private room on the second floor of the clinic.

One less thing to worry about.

If only he could change what was surely coming next...

Nachari ran a weary hand through his thick, raven hair and turned his attention to the problem at hand: Napolean's possession by Ademordna and the imminent danger it posed to the house of Jadon. Not to mention to Napolean's future with Brooke.

He turned to watch his eldest brother Marquis, who was pacing restlessly—not unlike an angry tiger forced to remain in a narrow cage—about five hundred yards away. The male patrolled the banks of the Snake Creek River just beyond the cabin that Napolean—no, Napolean's possessed body—now inhabited with his new *destiny*, Brooke. Marquis's right hand was adorned with his favorite ancient cestus, and the sharp iron spikes gleamed in the waning sunlight as the Ancient Master Warrior clenched and unclenched his fists, again and again, to the rhythm of his impatient footsteps.

Although Nachari may have appeared calm on the outside,

189

in truth, he shared his big brother's sense of urgency, as well as his frustration.

They had been at it for hours.

Planning, strategizing, divining…

Trying feverishly to come up with a plan to subdue Napolean without harming his newly found mate.

The going was painfully slow.

After all, the stakes could not have been higher: Napolean was not just another member of the house of Jadon, and there was absolutely no room for error in their execution. The clock ticked painfully slow for Brooke—gods only knew what was happening to her inside that cabin—yet the males could not just rush in like a bunch of Wild West gunslingers and steal her from Napolean's arms. They had to face reality. Napolean Mondragon was the most powerful being on the planet, and he was absolutely unmatched in cunning, strength, and ability…not to mention supernatural powers. Putting it bluntly, to oppose Napolean—and make a mistake—was to surely die; and although Marquis, Nathaniel, and Ramsey were all formidable in their own right, none had forgotten how Napolean had singlehandedly annihilated eighty-eight warriors in the house of Jaegar during Ciopori's rescue, no doubt all accomplished fighters in their own right.

Blessed Perseus, and may the gods show mercy, Napolean could harness the power of the sun! He could kill with his rage alone.

Nachari winced.

While Ramsey and Marquis might be able to dance toe to toe with the ancient monarch for a short while, they would surely have to attack to kill in order to get Brooke away from him; and neither Napolean's death nor Brooke's were viable options. Not to mention, Napolean's powers were only half of the problem: There was also Ademordna and his wicked, supernatural powers to contend with. A fact Nachari Silivasi was becoming more and more aware of with every moment that passed.

A fact that might require more of Nachari than he was truly

Tessa Dawn

ready to give.

Ademordna was a shadowed deity: a demon.

A dark lord whose very soul embodied evil, and knowing that, Nachari shuddered at the thought of what he was about to be asked to do…

He had just decided to take a seat on the ground—a feeble attempt at calming his nerves—when two severe-looking vampires approached him, their faces grim with foreboding.

"Wizard," they greeted, speaking in unison.

"Niko," Nachari said softly, "Jankiel…" He stood back up. "I can't say I like the looks on your faces." He steadied himself. "Then what we discussed earlier…you consulted the fellowship, and they agree it is the only way?"

Niko Durciak momentarily averted his stone-gray eyes before forcing himself to meet Nachari's discerning gaze. "We have. And they do."

Jankiel frowned, the gesture revealing four horizontal age-lines in an otherwise youthful face, two creases on either side of his mouth. "You are by far the most powerful of the three of us, Nachari, or I would offer—"

Nachari politely waved his hand to quiet his friend. "There is no need to go there, Jankiel, although the sentiment is appreciated. It is what it is…yes?"

Jankiel nodded. "Yes…" What else could he say?

Nachari offered his fellow wizards a reassuring smile. "Very well then: I need to be the one to tell Marquis."

Niko looked beyond Nachari's shoulders and glanced at the warrior in question. He let out a slow, apprehensive sigh. "Agreed."

"Why don't you call all three of your brothers and tell them together," Jankiel suggested. "It will be more…expedient to explain it to all of them at once." His voice held a slight note of apology in it—but Nachari understood: Time was of the essence.

The decision would be difficult for his brothers to accept, and time was ticking. Just the same, he wasn't looking forward to the conversation.

191

BLOOD POSSESSION

Brothers, he said telepathically, *we need to speak...face-to-face.*

Marquis looked up immediately, no doubt recognizing the heaviness in Nachari's psychic voice. He turned to face the circle of wizards, took perhaps two dozen efficient strides, and then stopped abruptly in front of Nachari, squaring his shoulders as he did so. "What is it?" he asked.

Nachari waited for Nathaniel and Kagen to materialize beside Marquis before he started speaking. Once all three brothers were standing before him, he took a deep breath and steadied his resolve. "Thanks for coming so quickly," he said. "I think we're ready...we finally have a plan."

Nathaniel nodded, almost imperceptibly. "Okay."

"We're listening," Kagen said, his voice reflecting his concern.

"I assume you know how to go after the demon then?" Marquis asked.

Nachari nodded.

"We do," Jankiel answered.

"Then speak!" Marquis barked. He was clearly running low on patience, a virtue he wasn't blessed with a large portion of to begin with.

Nachari looked directly at Marquis, said a quick prayer to the gods, and measured his words carefully: "The warriors will follow the plan you, Nathaniel, and Ramsey already crafted." He squatted, picked up a stick, and drew a rough diagram in the dirt. "You will rush the cabin and create a decoy with only one goal—to distract Napolean long enough for Nathaniel to use Kagen's tranquilizer on him." He drew several circles on the diagram representing each male's position. "As we discussed earlier, you will only have a matter of seconds to get in and engage Napolean, so there should be no attempt made to either capture him or free Brooke: The whole strategy hinges on Kagen's ability to produce the perfect formula." He stood up, crossed his arms, and turned to regard his only brown-eyed brother. "Kagen, the dosage has to be exact. The anesthetic must put Napolean under—quickly and decidedly—on the first try. There are no second chances."

Kagen nodded, understanding. "I've been working on it all afternoon." He glanced at Nathaniel then Marquis in turn. "As long as one of you can get it in him, he'll go down."

"Good," Nachari responded. He took a deep breath. "Once Napolean is under, Kagen will need to…drain his life force—ensure that he actually flat lines—so that Ademordna will be compelled to leave his body."

"Excuse me?" Nathaniel asked hesitantly. "As in—"

Nachari held up his hand to stop Nathaniel's question before he lost his momentum. He needed to get this all out—finish explaining the plan—before he lost his nerve. "Brother, a possession spell requires a physical death in order to transfer a soul: Ademordna took possession of Napolean at the exact moment his previous host died, and it will require Napolean's brief death to cast him out. The dark lord cannot remain in an expired body."

Kagen cleared his throat, the expression on his face one of grave concern: "You realize we are more or less talking about *killing our king* in order to force his possessor out of his body. Some might consider that sedition. If something were to go wrong…" He couldn't finish the sentence.

"In a sense, yes," Nachari responded, "but you will bring him right back to life so quickly that there will never be any real danger of losing him." He narrowed his gaze and held it steady. "Napolean is immortal—an ancient vampire. It will take far more than a temporary…loss of blood…to end his existence." He eyed each of his brothers in turn, staring deep into their eyes to convey his conviction. "Our king's…lack of sentience…will be temporary and short, I assure you."

Niko Durciak stepped forward, cleared his throat, and added, "Ademordna will leave the instant Napolean flat-lines." His voice was firm and unwavering. "We would never propose such a thing if there was any doubt."

"Okay," Marquis said, sounding somewhat dubious, "so how do we keep Ademordna from jumping right back into

BLOOD POSSESSION

Napolean's body once we revive him?" He glanced around the circle. "And what is to stop him from possessing someone else?"

Nachari placed a hand on Marquis's shoulder. "You guys don't. I do."

"How?" Nathaniel asked, rolling his shoulders to relieve some tension. His brow was creased in a frown, and his midnight-black eyes reflected a host of unanswered questioned.

Nachari glanced from Niko to Jankiel, and the latter nodded his head in encouragement. "I will be there to meet the dark lord the moment he is forced from Napolean's body." Nachari's next words were clipped with an uncharacteristic staccato—probably because he was straining so hard to just spit them out. "I will do whatever I must to keep Ademordna from re-entering our Sovereign's body. And as for possessing someone else? He can't. The spell was specific to Napolean. It takes a tremendous amount of blood—not to mention sacrifice—to procure the sanction of a deity in an act of Possession: The Dark Ones have not paid for another soul, nor have they had time to conjure another spell." He tried to force a half-hearted smile in an effort to reassure his family. "Once Ademordna realizes that Napolean is protected—that our king is no longer vulnerable—he will do what is natural for him, return to the Valley of Death and Shadows."

A hushed silence fell upon the group.

After several minutes had passed, Nathaniel shifted his weight from one foot to another, kicked up a divot of grass with the steel toe of his boot, and slowly raised his head to stare at Nachari. "What aren't you telling us, little brother?" There was no trace of malice in his words, only concern. "As far as I know, you are an impressive wizard, but even you cannot consort openly with deities, nor can you see or talk to ghosts—at least, not last I checked. So how then do you plan to protect Napolean from a dark lord?"

When Marquis eyed him sideways, and Kagen raised his eyebrows, Nachari knew they were finally catching on. He swallowed a lump in his throat and briefly closed his eyes—the moment of truth had arrived. "You're right. I exist in the realm of the living, while Ademordna exists in the realm of the dead—it takes a spirit to confront a spirit—and that is why Kagen will need to drain my life force...before he drains Napolean's."

Nathaniel frowned, and—as if such a thing were even possible—his dark, ebony eyes grew even darker. A hint of red rimmed his pupils. "Come again?" His voice was clipped.

Jankiel stepped in then. "Nachari has to...cross over before Napolean does. He has to already be there—waiting on the other side—when Ademordna exits Napolean's body."

"He has to buy Napolean some time," Niko explained.

Marquis laughed—a humorless, wicked sound. When he spoke, a low growl edged his throat, and his jaw tightened. "You mean Nachari has to *die* long before Napolean does, and if you intend to bring him back to life—and I presume you are at least planning to humor us with such an attempt—Nachari's resurrection is to occur significantly *after* Napolean's. Unless, of course, my youngest brother is lost somewhere in the netherworld, tangled up with a demon lord." Leave it to Marquis to go straight to the heart of the matter.

Nachari ignored the sarcasm, recognizing it for what it was: a defense meant to deflect Marquis's concern...for him. "I fully intend to come back, brother," Nachari assured him. "Trust me, I have no desire to leave the earth right now, but our king's survival is far too critical: You know this to be true. When Ademordna steps out of Napolean's body, someone has to be there to prevent Napolean from being—"

"And why does that someone have to be you?" Nathaniel interjected tersely. His eyes were a full crimson red now, and the tips of his fangs had extended toward his bottom lip—which was also pulled back in a snarl. "I can't believe you are going to actually stand here and ask Kagen—your brother and my twin—to *kill* you, Nachari? To live with the consequences should you not make it back? Forgive me for asking, but are you insane?"

Nachari sighed. "Nathaniel...please...do not do this. Not now. Do not make this any harder than it already is."

BLOOD POSSESSION

"Why you?" Marquis demanded. He fisted his left hand tightly over his right—which was still gloved in an ancient cestus—causing blood to seep from his palm where the spikes bit into his skin.

Nachari concentrated on keeping his voice both respectful and calm: "Because I am a Master Wizard, Marquis. I am trained in second sight, and I have knowledge of both worlds. Not to mention, I also have possession of the Blood Canon—the ancient book of Black Magic—and I've read it from front to back. I know more about the dark lords than any of you." He rubbed his temples. "Even if I don't understand them, at least I recognize how sorcerers like Salvatore think—I see the intention behind their spells, the machinations beyond the darkness, the laws that govern the misuse of their power." Before Marquis could respond, he turned to face Nathaniel. "And to answer your question, brother, perhaps it is insane, but it is also the only way. We all know that the dark lord will not relinquish Napolean's body, just walk away and leave it behind, unless he is forced to do so. And he will not be forced to do so unless Napolean is truly—*and permanently*—dead. Would you let that happen, Nathaniel? Would you, Marquis?"

Marquis grinded his teeth together and then absently licked a trail of blood from the palm of his wounded hand. "But your death," he snarled, "this is acceptable?" He muttered something unintelligible beneath his breath.

Nachari shook his head. He understood that emotions were running high for all of them. "I won't die, Marquis." He quickly turned to look at Kagen, whose normally handsome face had turned gaunt. "I am hoping that this excellent healer will be able to sustain my body while I am...gone."

Kagen looked distressed. Clearly disliking Nachari's pitiful attempt at levity, he said, "Don't make light of this, Nachari."

Nachari placed a gentle hand on Kagen's shoulder. "I'm not, brother. *Trust me.* All I'm asking is that you keep me on life support while my soul travels. Maintain my heartbeat and provide oxygen to my brain...no matter how long it takes." He

196

tightened his grasp. "You can't resurrect me immediately—like you will Napolean—but that is only because my soul will not be available to reanimate my body; however, there is no reason why you cannot revive my body as soon as possible and keep it alive until my soul returns."

All three of his brothers became deathly quiet, and he knew that they were considering the facts—measuring the numerous possibilities, weighing each eventuality carefully in their minds, and he could only hope that none would be willing—let alone able—to risk Napolean's life. Simply put, they could not let Napolean die. No one could justify such a cowardly choice. Napolean Mondragon was the pulse —the very heartbeat—of the house of Jadon. And he had no successor. His *destiny* had finally come *after twenty-eight hundred years*, which meant that a true heir to Napolean's throne was less than one moon away from being born—an heir who would share Napolean's memories and powers, an heir who would intervene with the gods on behalf of the Vampyr.

They simply had to save Napolean.

The implications of his loss were too epic to even put into words.

And he knew all of his brothers understood this.

Nathaniel eventually spoke first, and when he did, his voice was a velvet whisper on the wind: "You cannot guarantee that you will merely go to the brink of death and return, can you, Nachari? The truth is, we may actually lose you…forever."

Nachari exhaled slowly, unaware until that moment that he had even been holding his breath. "Yes, Nathaniel. There is always a chance I might not make it back."

As if it were too much effort to remain standing, Kagen squatted down. He looked up at Niko and Jankiel then, regarding each wizard in turn. "Is this really necessary, wizards?"

Both vampires nodded, but it was Niko who spoke: "It is, Kagen."

Nathaniel squatted down next to Kagen, his movement both graceful and predatory. He stopped when they were eye to eye.

"I share your fears, my brother, but we must consider this carefully."

Marquis's eyes flashed red. "Fine. Then I will go in Nachari's place."

"With all due respect, Marquis," Niko spoke hesitantly, "the battle we must wage is one of light versus dark...wizardry versus sorcery." He kept his gaze respectfully averted downward and swallowed hard, his Adam's apple bobbing up and down as he avoided the Ancient Master Warrior's penetrating stare. "We are not talking about a battle of strength and agility—one warrior's skill pitted against another's. We are talking about doing battle with a dark lord."

Marquis Silivasi grunted and gestured angrily with his bloody hand. "And there is absolutely no way for one of us to confront this demon without dying first?"

"It will take a spirit to confront a spirit," Niko answered softy. He turned to offer a hand to Kagen, and when the healer accepted it, he helped him up. "Help us do this, Master Healer," Niko implored. "Please."

Kagen brought the back of his hand up to his eyes and let his head fall forward, struggling to restrain his emotion. He took a slow, deep breath and said, "I'm sorry: I cannot."

When he started to walk away, Niko and Jankiel gawked in disbelief and then stared pointedly at Nachari with a look of desperation in their eyes.

"Kagen," Nachari called, "healer...please, come back." When Kagen refused to turn around, he spoke to his back. "I don't want to die, brother"—his voice was heavy with conviction—"but I will do this thing with or without you." He lowered his voice then and whispered, "My chances are far better with you."

Kagen turned around slowly, and the look of defeat on his face made Nachari's stomach turn over in waves.

The truth had been spoken...aloud.

Nachari would risk his life to save Napolean, and no one could stop him.

He would fight like hell to survive, but there was no guarantee that he would.

Marquis rubbed the bridge of his nose, appearing suddenly weary as opposed to enraged. He took several steps back and stared at Nachari blankly, his eyes deflecting light like primordial stone. When he finally spoke, his voice was as vacant and hollow as an empty vessel. It was as if he had buried all emotion inside of a tomb. "I have not yet given you my blessing, Nachari." There was an implied threat of pulling rank in his words. "Nathaniel? Kagen? What say you each?"

Kagen shrugged and threw up his hands as if to say, *I surrender.* "Above all else, I am a healer for our people. I will help to subdue Napolean. I will even assist in draining his blood until he flat-lines, with the intention of bringing him back to life. And yes, I will do the same for Nachari: I will pump air into my brother's lungs and circulate it to his brain while he fights in spirit for our king." He stared at all three wizards, each one in turn, regretfully shaking his head. "But do not ask me to take part in the decision. This, I will not do."

Nathaniel's broad chest rose and fell with deliberate slowness. "We are brothers—always—but first, we are subjects, loyal to our king. I will ask this only once, Nachari, and I insist that you speak the gods' honest truth: *Is there any other way?*"

Nachari thought long and hard before answering. When he finally spoke, he did it with strength and conviction. "No, there is not."

Nathaniel stepped forward and pulled Nachari into a hard, unyielding embrace. He brushed the top of his head with a kiss so light it was almost indiscernible. *You are loved,* he whispered in his mind. "Go forth with my blessing."

"Thank you," Nachari said, nearly choking on the raw emotion. He turned to face Marquis then, and the look in the proud warrior's eyes almost shattered his resolve. If he could have knelt before his eldest sibling, pledged his loyalty, and promised to live a long, healthy life, he would have done it—just to erase the grief in Marquis's eyes.

BLOOD POSSESSION

But he could not make such a promise.

And so he waited...

Marquis gripped both of Nachari's shoulders and paused to consider his next words carefully. "I will also allow you to do this thing, but know this, little brother: If you die, I will never forgive you. Remember that."

Nachari recoiled, gasping. "Dear gods, Marquis...don't say that. Don't—"

"Remember that!" Marquis thundered.

Obediently, Nachari declined his head, averted his eyes, and nodded. Marquis was forbidding him to die in the strongest terms he knew. And it wasn't an empty threat.

Truly, Marquis could not even entertain the possibility of losing another sibling after Shelby, so what was there to argue?

Nachari placed one hand on each side of Marquis's face. His thumbs gripped the sharp planes of the warrior's jaw, and he tightened his grasp when Marquis squirmed in an attempt to break free from such an intimate gesture.

"*Marquis.*"

It was only one word—tenderly uttered—yet Nachari said more in those two syllables than any eloquent speech could have ever conveyed.

Trembling ever so slightly, Marquis slowly leaned forward until his forehead touched Nachari's. And then he placed his hands over Nachari's wrists and held them in a grip of iron.

"Come back to me...*brother*," he whispered.

nineteen

Brooke felt a sudden release as a powerful current of energy surged through her body, and the pain finally abated.

Dear God, the pain of conversion had been unbearable—unlike anything she had ever felt before. It had started the moment Napolean had bitten into her neck in the meadow, and it had continued long after they had entered the small log cabin by the river. She knew without question that she had died in those horrific hours.

Died.

One organ, one cell, one system at a time had expired, only to be remade by the substance—the venom—that had traveled through her veins like acid, burning away her cherished humanity to replace it with immortality.

She was a vampire now.

Yet the being that had done this to her—the creature that had treated her with such callous indifference—had not been Napolean. It had been a living, breathing demon: a disgusting, writhing worm that had entered Napolean's body.

How did Brooke know this for certain?

Because the truth had glowed in the thing's eyes just moments before it had taken possession: Evil had clung to its serpentine form like scales on the tail of a primordial dragon, and the coldness that had enveloped Napolean—his skin, his eyes, his gentle heart—the moment the worm took over, had been in such stark contrast to the warmth she had felt in his kiss.

Brooke blinked several times and pushed hard against the heavy, stone-like chest above her, hoping to finally wriggle free.

The demon gurgled, sighed, and laughed deep in the back of his throat. His razor-like fangs began to retreat from her neck, and she practically held her breath, waiting for the moment she would be rid of their constant invasion.

BLOOD POSSESSION

She gasped for air, drawing desperate, greedy gulps of it into her lungs, over and over, like a drowning woman who had just broken the surface. Napolean—no, the demon—stared down at her through amber and red eyes. He licked his lips, Napolean's firm, sculpted lips, and moaned.

"Did you enjoy that half as much as I did, my bride?" His voice was almost Napolean's—still rich and velvet—only heavily laced with strychnine.

"Where is Napolean?" she demanded. She sat up and tested her new body. Would the muscles work? Would the bones support her? Would her respiratory system sustain her? Despite her fears and the imminent danger of her situation, she couldn't help but register such a monumental change in her physical being. She felt…invincible. Strong. Healthy to her very last cell.

Powerful in a way she had never even imagined.

She could hear nuanced sounds from very far away—subtle shifts in the wind, the rustling of leaves on the branches of quaking aspen trees—and she could smell the scents of all the humans who had stayed in the cabin before her. While they were faint, they were still discernible.

Brooke jolted: *Humans?*

Had she just said humans?

Dear God, what was she?

What had Nap—*the worm-thing*—done to her?

The soft pad of a finger traced her bottom lip, jolting her back into the moment. The demon was bending over her now, appraising her with his gaze, staring straight into her soul with his evil eyes. "Please, my love: Call me Ademordna."

Brooke gagged. She scampered backward on the bed, twisting violently in an effort to break free. All at once, her body slid forward: Ademordna had grabbed her by the ankle and tugged her back beneath him. She kicked at him in vain, her newfound power proving worthless against his otherworldly strength.

"Going somewhere, my lovely?"

Brooke swallowed hard. It was maddening. When she looked

at him, she saw Napolean, and something deep in her soul—
something that had slowly been awakening from the moment
they had connected that day in the canyon by the waterfall—
reached out to him.

Needed him.

Knew him on a level more elemental...and real...than any
human connection she had ever experienced.

Until the demon had possessed him, she had not truly
understood why she had saved him that day on the terrace: why
she had chosen his life over her possible escape. Because
somewhere deep inside where eternity resides and the soul
remembers, she had recognized that her heart belonged to his.
That her life had been designed to merge with his. That the very
beat of her heart had adjusted to calibrate with his.

Brooke had fought it on both a conscious and unconscious
level. But now that his venom had passed through her body,
marking and claiming each of her cells as his own, she knew it
on an elemental level: A full awakening had occurred.

Brooke jerked her ankle free from the demon's grip and
looked up into his eyes. She was hoping to find Napolean's dark,
mystical orbs somewhere beyond the demon's gaze. "Napolean,"
she whispered tentatively, hoping against hope, "are you in
there?"

The male's eyes softened. He knelt beside her, reached out a
gentle hand, and lightly traced the line of her cheek from her ear
to her chin. He smiled Napolean's captivating smile: "Brooke."
His voice purred her name.

And then he brought down his open hand so hard against
her jaw that she felt her bones rattle, and blood squirted out of
her mouth.

Stunned, Brooke tried to focus. She had to get away. Crawl
off the bed. Get to the door. Yes, the door—it was...where?
Over there? She turned her head, and the room spun in dizzying
circles as black dots danced through the air.

She could hear Ademordna's laughter in the distance,
bouncing off the walls, echoing in waves of madness, rising to

BLOOD POSSESSION

the ceiling only to drop to the floor. His heckling was everywhere: deep and cruel and wicked.

He tore his shirt from his body, revealing Napolean's perfectly sculpted chest. Smooth skin gave way to lean muscle; rib after rib encased hard, molded sinew; and buttons flew all around her, making a sort of popping sound as they fell to the floor.

Another blow to her face. Another open palm. This one stung her opposite cheek before rattling her chin. *Damn, it hurt... Badly.*

Her lip felt swollen, and her mouth was numb.

When Ademordna drew back to look at her—to study his handiwork, Brooke supposed—she pulled herself into a sitting position, immediately rotated onto her hands and knees, and tried to crawl away. Once again, he grabbed both ankles and tugged, only this time, she clutched at the pine headboard for support, her fingers clinging to one of the four posts in a death grip. He yanked harder, wrenching her effortlessly from the post, flipping her back over, and pinning her sideways to the bed—her head and feet perpendicular to the headboard. With her arms stretched out above her, she felt like a pagan sacrifice, just waiting for slaughter.

"Napolean...please..." She slurred the words. They didn't sound right. Her jaw wasn't working correctly. She reached up to feel it, and saw Ademordna's open palm swipe down...again.

She tried to retreat...too late.

Darkness. More laughter. Cool air on her skin.

Was he removing her clothes?

"Soon, you will be the mother of the house of Jaegar, my dear queen," he crooned.

She heard more than saw his jeans come off, and somewhere in the back of her mind, she registered the horror of what was about to happen, but she couldn't quite connect with it. Perhaps he had truly slapped her silly. Perhaps her soul would not allow it. Maybe her mind was protecting her.

Please don't, she prayed silently. *Not with Napolean's body.* Not

204

with the hands she was just now learning to trust. *Oh God*, would no one save her?

Her eyes managed to focus on Ademordna's twin, glowing orbs for just a second, and the look of malice—the pure, unbridled hatred—that stared back at her wrenched a scream from her damaged throat.

He cocked his head to the side. "Hush, sweetling: Do not force me to beat you bloody before I take you."

Despite the warning, she screamed over and over…and over, the sound escaping as fast as she could take in air.

"Alas, my queen: You do not listen very well." He bent over her, licked the side of her face with his tongue, and then sat back up…and showed her his clenched fist. A terrifying look of perverse amusement swept over his face as he drew back his heavily muscled arm and snarled.

And then, in one powerful, hateful motion, his arm came down—

Brooke!

An imperious male voice pierced the icy silence. It penetrated her mind with such force that it jolted her out of the cabin, commanding her full attention…coaxing her from consciousness with enormous, magnetic power.

Brooke, follow my voice. Hear only my voice. Stay with me!

It was Napolean.

And he was there…all around her. Surrounding her, encasing her in his warmth, yet not with his body. It was more like—with his soul.

Napolean? She spoke with her mind, and she somehow knew that he heard her.

Yes, it is me, my love.

Where are you?

I do not know, he said. *I do not understand. I am not in my body, but my soul is not in a place I recognize, either. Ademordna has scattered it into a thousand pieces—it floats through the cosmos—waiting to be called back. But I have my mind—my consciousness—and you must stay with me until my warriors can get to you, do you understand?*

BLOOD POSSESSION

Brooke felt like she nodded her head, but she wasn't sure. There was only pain in her skull and fuzziness in her body. In the physical realm where the dark lord was now...beating her and—

She started to scream again.

Brooke!

This time, Napolean did more than call her—he somehow took her over. He merged whatever piece of his spirit he had access to with hers, and then he held her in an iron grip...far, far away...from the horror of that room.

Come, he beckoned. *Stay with me here—in this place between worlds—while we wait. Tell me of your childhood dreams. Let us plan for the future, reminisce about the past, share our stories and our secrets. Merge with me, Brooke.*

She did.

And they shared their lives—their pasts, their hopes, their individual dreams for the future. They exchanged precious memories: the first time Brooke rode a bicycle and how badly she had skinned her knees. The first time Napolean had successfully wielded a sword. She told him about her second-grade teacher, Ms. Krenny, and how the woman's perpetual kindness—and cherry-flavored Lifesavers—had given her young life purpose; and he told her about the time he had met Joan of Arc. He asked about her education—which classes she took, what she loved, what she hated—and then he told her about the rigors of dorm life at the Romanian University.

He learned about Brooke's career, her plans and aspirations; and she learned about the many nuances involved in governing the house of Jadon. She told him all there was to know about her best friend, Tiffany, and he described several of his most influential subjects.

Time must have truly stood still because it seemed like an eternity had passed when they finally stopped swapping stories...sharing secrets...yet that wasn't possible: Was it?

Finally, having gathered enough courage to broach the subject, Brooke asked: *Napolean, will my body survive what is being done to it?*

Napolean was deathly quiet...but only for a heartbeat. *As long as you are left alive—and that is a certainty—you will heal. My venom is the most potent in the house of Jadon.* He paused as if considering his words. *That is why your conversion was so rapid and...efficient. Painful.* There were dark shadows in his tone, deep pangs of regret. *Brooke, you will never know—there are no words—the way that you suffered...I am so very sorry. Know that I would have never treated you so harshly.*

Brooke held back her tears. On some level, she did know, but the memory was too recent, the confusion surrounding what was happening to her—even now—too acute. The male brutalizing her body was not Napolean—she got that; she really did—yet it was Napolean, his arms, his hands...his masculine flesh. Because she didn't know what to say, she didn't say anything.

Brooke? he said.

How do you know he will leave me alive? she finally asked.

Napolean sighed. *He must. He has plans—plans that require your basic physical health to be carried out successfully.*

Like what? Brooke asked, her unease growing.

Do not think about it, Brooke. I would tell you if I thought it would aid you in any way, but I do not wish for you to imagine such things...you will live...no matter what; and right now, that is all that matters.

Brooke was about to argue—she knew that Napolean was only acting according to his deep-seated nature; his first instinct would always be to protect her—but like it or not, they were in this together now. Without her consent, his world had become her world, and his enemies had become her enemies. She would have insisted on knowing every detail except she suddenly realized something far more profound: Napolean Mondragon was in terrifying, uncharted territory, and despite a lifetime of the king's practiced, rational leadership, the man was reeling from his own sense of helplessness...even as he tried to comfort Brooke. It was absolutely true. He did not want her to imagine what Ademordna was planning...because it was probably too hard to bear the thought of it himself. What man could?

They're coming, Napolean said abruptly, interrupting her train of thought.

Who's coming? Brooke asked.

My warriors.

She didn't dare hope. *How many? What will they do?*

Napolean's demeanor was instantly no-nonsense. *Only a handful, but it will be enough. They will enter the cabin with force and attempt to seize and subdue me before Ademordna can destroy them. Once they have me incapacitated, they will remove me from the premises and send in the women to care for you. To begin healing your body. This nightmare is almost over for you, Brooke—please hold on just a little longer.*

Brooke fought to swallow her fear: What if it was already too late? What if his warriors failed, and Ademordna killed them? Or what if their plan succeeded on all fronts—but Napolean never returned to his body? What would happen to her then? Would his people let her go? Would they blame her? Punish her? And even if they didn't, how could she ever return to her life...*as a vampire?* Oh God, what was going to happen? There was no good outcome to any of this.

Brooke, Napolean whispered. *Quiet your thoughts, draga mea. All will be well. All will be made well.*

She tried. She really did. She wanted to believe Napolean—hell, she needed to believe him...in order to keep her sanity—but there was a strange sense of foreboding washing over her, a distant, intuitive knowing somewhere deep in the pit of her stomach that simply would not let her go. Beyond all the things that were blatantly obvious, something else was terribly...*terribly* wrong. Something even more disturbing than the brutality her body had endured—something even more disturbing than no longer being human, if that was possible.

Something isn't right, Napolean, she insisted. *I mean, beyond the obvious. Please, Napolean: What aren't you telling me?*

Napolean sighed. His ethereal voice was deadly serious. *There will be time to deal with all that has occurred later, Brooke—I assure you. But first, you will need all of your strength to heal. Your body has been badly injured. I do not want your attention focused on anything other than getting well.* He paused, and her heart skipped a series of beats, sick with the anticipation of his next words.

Brooke swallowed hard. Was it really that bad? So horrible that he couldn't even tell her? She did a quick gut-check and knew that whatever she feared—her sense of terrible foreboding—went beyond physical injuries to her body. Needing to know, she let her mind begin to drift...back...back...away...farther and farther from Napolean's voice and his reassuring presence...concentrating, instead, on her body.

She began to feel some sensations: the heaviness of her physical form, a rawness in her throat, the coppery taste of blood. And then, all at once, pain washed over her like a tsunami crashing upon an unsuspecting shore.

Brooke! Napolean's will dominated hers. He seized her back from the room with overwhelming force, prying her awareness from the clutches of the dark lord, snatching her back before she could fully register what she had seen. *Stay with me just a little longer, my angel.*

Napolean, she cried. *What has he done to me?*

Brooke...

Napolean! Tell me!

Brooke...I...you—

Tell me! Now!

You already know.

She sobbed. She couldn't help it. Of course she knew—she had known all along—but the reality wasn't any less harsh now that it was an irrefutable fact: Ademordna had used her body...brutally and repeatedly. *Will I remember?* She croaked out the words.

No, Napolean assured her. *Never. Your mind—your spirit—wasn't there.* His voice was raw with emotion, thick with pain, and there was something else in his tone—something so vulnerable and regretful that it sounded as if his soul had been shattered. *Brooke, my heart is laid out on the ground by this atrocity, and I will never come to terms with the fact that I could not protect you—never—but that is my cross to bear. As far as your life is concerned, you must listen carefully to what I have to say, and you must hear with more than your ears.* He let the words linger before he continued. *I have lived a very long life; and in that time, there is little I have not seen—very little. And because of that, I have learned a very important truth: The body is only a temporary garment—one we wear to play out the various days of our lives—but the soul, the consciousness, it is the seat of all that is. Any time an injury lasts—or an insult continues to fester—it is because of the imprint it has left on the soul.*

He paused, as if for effect. *When a woman, a child—even a man—is abused, the body will heal completely in most cases, without any trace of the original sin. Any trauma that remains emanates from the soul—a broken heart, a shattered trust...the presence of fear where it once was absent. Self-recrimination, shame, and self-doubt—these are the true injuries sustained by victims of violence, no?*

Brooke swallowed hard, still listening. *Yes.*

By remaining with me, your soul remained untouched. It was simply not there at the time. You were simply not there at the time. And I swear to you on my honor that your heart and mind are unchanged—without memory, awareness, or sentience, there is no place for a lasting injury to take hold. Your body will heal, and you, too, will *be whole.*

Brooke understood what he was saying. She had known others over the years who had suffered physical violence, and he could not have described the mental aftermath better. But there was still something else. Something beyond the physical violation. Something permanent that he wasn't telling her.

Napolean?

Yes, he answered.

I have heard you, and I more-or-less agree with you, but there is still something...something you are not telling me...and I can feel it all the way down to my soul.

You are pregnant, Brooke. He spoke in a whisper. *Ademordna used my seed and my words to command your pregnancy.*

There was a brief moment of...nothing.

A small mercy.

That critical, surreal instant that occurs after a horrible accident when the mind simply shuts down and insulates the victim from the truth. They hear the words, experience the occurrence, or witness the act with their eyes, but it simply fails to register.

Rather, all becomes silent.

Time ceases to be.

And numbness rules.

With twins? she asked in a faraway voice. Her analytical mind was taking over robotically.

Yes, he answered.

Are they—she paused then, almost slipping into a dangerous rabbit-hole where panic loomed, gargantuan and real—*are they even yours? The babies? Or are they evil...like him?*

Napolean sounded sick to his stomach. *It is the same as if you and I had...the Blood Curse has not changed...there will be one child of light and one child of darkness...and the required sacrifice remains.* His next words were spoken with a gut-level disgust he clearly couldn't hide. *Although neither one of us gave our consent—and neither your soul nor mine was there—it was still our bodies that joined. The child will be ours—yours and mine—Ademordna cannot change that.*

Brooke bit her lower lip...or at least she thought she did. *I don't understand,* she said, sounding as confused as she felt. *If this demon...this dark lord...wants to use me to destroy you, why would he command a pregnancy? I mean, wouldn't it be easier for him to just kill me, leave you without the required sacrifice, and let the Curse come for you at the end of the thirty days? Why go through so much trouble...I mean, yeah, I get that he's a demon—so why not have some fun while he's in your body—but the babies? That part, I don't understand.*

Napolean waited a long time to respond, and with their intimate psychic connection, Brooke knew that he was fighting to regain his composure first. Her words had obviously cut him like a knife. *For so many centuries, our rules have been black and white: The males in the house of Jadon have two sons—one child of darkness and one child of light—and we are allowed to keep the child of light so our race does not vanish from the earth. The males in the house of Jaegar have made*

BLOOD POSSESSION

an abomination of the practice—violating innocent women who die horribly giving birth to two dark sons. Like us, they are required to sacrifice one of the two—in their case it is the firstborn—so they, too, keep a child to carry on their perverted lines. I believe that, in this instance, Ademordna intends to kill two birds with one stone: to remain in my body long enough to prevent me from making the required sacrifice, and to turn over both sons to the Dark Ones.

Brooke gasped. *That's why you're so sure he won't kill me, isn't it? He needs me to have the babies!*

Yes, Napolean answered.

Brooke began to tremble as the horror swept over her: all of it...

The conference.

Her trip to Dark Moon Vale.

Being taken by a *vampire*.

The day Ademordna had tried to kill Napolean on the terrace—the possession, her conversion...the violation. *The pregnancy.*

The Curse!

And what it now meant for her.

Ademordna intends...to turn over both sons to the Dark Ones.

Oh God, Oh God, Oh God...

She could lose her humanity, Napolean, and her child before it was over.

The enormity of it all was just too much to bear. Caught up in a whirlwind of panic, she slipped out of Napolean's psychic grasp and reappeared with a whoosh in the room. Her body was a broken, bloodied pulp, still stretched out on the bed, a pile of damaged bone, muscle, and skin...torn, slashed, bruised....and broken.

Stunned by the intensity of the pain, Brooke clutched her stomach with her arms and shouted her agony all the way to the heavens.

"Now!" Marquis Silivasi shouted.

Ramsey, Santos, and Saxson ripped the front wall off the cabin: The door exploded from its hinges, the window burst from its frame, and the crisscrossed logs shot out in one lightning-quick motion.

Marquis leapt into the center of the room, gloved fist raised, eyes and ears alert. He paused only for a fraction of a second—stunned by the scene in front of him: Napolean's *destiny* was laid out on the bed like a broken rag doll, bloodied and bruised and screaming like a woman mad with fear. The sovereign king of the house of Jadon knelt over her body, still naked with blood dripping from his fangs. He had recently fed at her…*thigh*.

"*Mother of Draco*," Marquis murmured.

This was not Napolean.

The thing on the bed was a dark lord from the Valley of Death and Shadows…a demon. Marquis stared into Napolean's absent eyes and shuddered; he could only pray that the demon was not as good with Napolean's body as Napolean himself would have been.

The dark lord whipped around and snarled, a spine-tingling sound that shook the remaining walls and the earth beneath them. Marquis didn't wait for an invitation. He lunged at the demon and swung his bare left fist with all the strength and speed he possessed. He was probably the only male in the house of Jadon that even had a shot at landing a blow.

As expected, Napolean caught Marquis's fist with his hand and squeezed. The king's bruised and bloodied knuckles tightened around Marquis's fist, bearing down hard in an effort to crush the warrior's bones.

Because every single action had been planned out ahead of time, the warriors had a slight advantage: Marquis gritted his teeth against the overwhelming pain and countered the move by driving the spiked cestus skyward in a powerful uppercut that connected squarely with Napolean's chin. The whole scene seemed to unfold in a fraction of a second: Napolean clutched Marquis's throat, and his eyes began to glow as he prepared to incinerate the warrior where he stood.

Nathaniel Silivasi struck fast.

Having entered the cabin under a cloak of invisibility, he materialized behind the dark lord, plunged the syringe into his bicep, and injected the full dose of anesthetic all in one swift motion.

Ademordna roared his rage. He spun around and backhanded Nathaniel with such incredible force—such overwhelming fury—that the temperature in the room dropped at least ten degrees, and Nathaniel's body shot through the opposite wall, blasting splintered chips of wood in all four directions.

And then the dark lord staggered, momentarily dazed and disorganized. Ramsey, Marquis, and Santos seized the moment, taking Napolean to the floor. They held him there with dogged determination, furiously fighting to restrain his arms and legs, as Saxson Olaru slipped a heavy, black velvet hood—one that happened to be embroidered with dozens of carefully placed, studded diamonds—over Napolean's head to block his powerful eyes. No one wanted to be incinerated.

Napolean bucked beneath them. With one swift kick, he booted Ramsey all the way to the ceiling, and then he began to twist and turn his hands, rotating his long claws like a set of nunchucks—effortlessly slicing the wrists that held him. Hissing, Napolean sat up and reached for the hood.

Marquis threw another punch then. This time, he connected front and center with Napolean's jaw.

The possessed king only laughed.

"Son of a jackal!" Marquis growled, as exasperated as he was astounded. "Go to sleep, already!"

Maybe it was time for plan B.

Marquis reached into the front pocket of his long, leather coat and drew out a vial of chloroform encased in a silk handkerchief. He broke it in his hand, and before Napolean's hood could come completely off, shoved it up the length of the cloth and forced the anesthetic over Napolean's eyes and nose.

A pair of painfully sharp fangs sank into his hand, and an even sharper set of claws pierced his breastbone, puncturing his chest cavity on the way to extract his heart.

Marquis Silivasi did not let go.

He could feel the painful daggers digging…clawing…finally grasping his beating organ in an iron fist, and he braced himself, prepared for the pain—prepared to die—as he knew Napolean would immediately incinerate the organ before any of the warriors could attempt regeneration. In that frozen moment, Marquis understood—far too clearly—the sacrifice Nachari had been willing to make…

It had never been a choice.

Fortunately, the combination of Kagen's sedative and the chloroform spared Marquis from such a fate.

The iron fist relaxed around his heart, and he was able to extract Napolean's hand, holding the arm up and away from his broken, bleeding chest as the king's eyelids grew heavy and his body began to slump to the ground.

"See you in hell," Napolean whispered as he finally went unconscious.

Marquis exhaled deeply and sank to his knees.

A pair of strong arms caught him from behind. "Be still, brother," Nathaniel whispered in his ear. "Allow me to heal you so we can get the women in here to attend to Brooke—and move on to the real battle."

Marquis nodded slowly. "Warrior," he whispered. "You may have been right to give Nachari your blessing."

Surprised, Nathaniel paused for a second, then chuckled softly. "I'm sorry, but did you just say I was *right?*"

Marquis grumbled. "Do not misunderstand—"

"Brother," Nathaniel teased, "as far as I am concerned, it is the chloroform speaking."

As much as Marquis ever did, he smiled.

And then he passed out.

BLOOD POSSESSION

Napolean's disembodied spirit had hovered helplessly over Brooke's battered body—unable to wrench her from the room, unable to help his warriors—as they had battled to subdue Ademordna.

Brooke's screams of terror and pain—the shock and revulsion she had felt the moment her spirit had re-entered her damaged flesh—had pierced the ancient king's heart. And he had poured every ounce of his considerable power into blanketing her frail form…absorbing her pain…willing her into a deep state of unconsciousness.

Now, as he replayed the battle-scene in his mind, Napolean felt more than just a little pride for his warriors.

Son of a gun, his males had been clever…and skillful…and quick.

Marquis had managed to engage him while Nathaniel had injected him with some sort of tranquilizer, and the sentinels had neutralized his powers with a diamond-studded hood. Wisely, they had kept Ademordna from using Napolean's eyes to incinerate them on the spot. And when the anesthetic had not worked quickly enough, Marquis had followed it up with a powerful dose of chloroform.

Excellent strategy.

Expert execution.

Despite Ademordna's furious resistance, Napolean's able warriors had won the hasty, life-and-death battle.

Napolean would have expected no less from this group of vampires.

He mentally sighed. Step one was over. Now all that was left was to pray…

Pray for the women to provide Brooke with swift and competent care. Pray for his *destiny's* peace. Pray for his unborn child.

And pray that Nachari Silivasi—an incredibly talented, but relatively untested Master Wizard—would win the favor of the gods. For the male was about to engage in the spiritual battle of his life, and everyone else's future depended upon the outcome.

twenty

Nachari Silivasi reclined against the stiff cot and tried to relax while Kagen hooked machine after machine up to his naked body. He adjusted the tubes that would drain Nachari's blood from his major arteries onto the ground several times before he appeared satisfied. He ran an IV to the vein in his left arm and lined up several syringe packets next to a set of carefully marked glass vials. He took out *another* container filled with Marquis's powerful venom—*just in case*—and then, oddly, moved Nachari's thick, wavy hair away from his neck, as if he didn't want it to come in contact with his blood.

This was not going to be a neat procedure, no matter what lengths Kagen went to, and all of the preparing, double-checking, and rearranging was beginning to make Nachari even more nervous than he already was.

He glanced up at the sky and searched the heavens for courage, praying for the fortitude to do what had to be done. It was around six in the evening, the sun had recently set, and the sky was a beautiful, mystic blue—deep, dark, and enchanting—stars sparkling like jewels in a divine auditorium. It was as if the earth itself knew.

And waited.

Nachari closed his eyes and concentrated on his breathing, reveling in the rise and fall of his chest, the simple movement of air flowing in and out of his lungs, such an effortless gift, so often taken for granted. His eyes blinked open, and he regarded Kagen thoughtfully. If he hadn't known better, he would have sworn the healer was sweating: His brother's nerves were completely frayed, and he hadn't even begun.

He lifted his right hand and clutched Kagen's forearm, wanting his full attention. "It's going to be okay, brother."

Kagen nodded and wiped the back of his forearm across his

forehead, drawing it slowly downward. Maybe he really was sweating. "I think everything is ready," he mumbled.

Nachari forced a smile. "I know it is." He glanced across the field at the second cot—the makeshift bed holding Napolean Mondragon's sedated, unconscious body—and reminded himself of why he was about to do this. "Let's not procrastinate," he said, hoping Kagen understood his urgency. This had to be done before he lost his nerve.

Kagen reached for a bottle of iodine, poured it on a square, cotton cloth, and cleaned Nachari's neck just above his jugular. And then he repeated the process on the flat of his wrists and just above the femoral artery at both inner thighs.

Nachari sighed. "Iodine, brother? Vampyr do not get infections."

Kagen shrugged. "I know, but I just want to cover every contingency…just in case."

"Kagen."

The tall, muscular, but lean vampire blinked his dark-chocolate eyes, brushed his soft brown hair away from his face, and nodded. "Yeah, okay." He lifted a sharp titanium scalpel from a steel tray lying next to the cot and tested the weight in his hand. His eyes met Nachari's and a thousand unspoken words passed between them.

Nachari nodded and held his breath.

Kagen bent over, gently tipped Nachari's chin back, and pressed the steel blade against his flesh just above the artery. He gulped and steadied his hand.

"Ramsey." It was Marquis's voice that pierced the silence. His firm hand intercepted Kagen's before the healer could make the incision, and the massive blond warrior with spiked hair, crazy eyes, and the demeanor of a pit bull stalked to the side of the cot.

"What's up, Marquis?"

"You do it," Marquis said.

Ramsey didn't hesitate. He rarely did. He brushed the dirt from his hands, squatted down beside the cot, and gave Nachari a crooked smile. "Sorry about this, friend." And then in businesslike fashion, he took the blade from Kagen, leaned over, and sliced his throat in one deep, harsh gash.

Nachari jolted, shocked by the sudden invasion and the severity of the pain. And then he instinctively tried to sit up, his free hand going to his throat as he choked on his own blood.

Kagen caught Nachari's arm even as Marquis held his head in place. "Try to relax," Kagen said, "don't fight it."

Nachari's eyes grew wild with discomfort and fear. He thought he had been prepared, but he was wrong. Ramsey made quick work of both his wrists, and Nachari felt certain he was about to lose it.

Just then, Nathaniel appeared at his side. "Look at me, wizard."

Nachari's eyes latched onto Nathaniel's like the hands of a circus acrobat latching onto a trapeze two hundred yards above the ground: He was clinging for dear life.

Nathaniel restrained Nachari's bloody hands—both to comfort and control him—as Ramsey made two swift cuts along the length of his left femoral artery. Despite the sharp pain, the sensation in his thigh was nothing compared to his throat—he still wanted to breathe...

He desperately *needed* to breathe.

"*Can't breathe,*" he gasped, part audibly, part telepathically.

Nathaniel shifted uncomfortably, but held his gaze. "I'm here." He indicated Kagen, then Marquis with a nod of his chin. "We are all here."

Nachari nodded rapidly, then steadied himself as Ramsey sliced his remaining femoral artery, and the added pain made him dizzy. Or was it the loss of blood? His eyes shot back and forth from one brother to another; he was searching for reassurance, pleading for...something...he couldn't name.

Son of a jackal...it hurts! he thought.

Nathaniel's hand tightened around his own, and Nachari thought he heard strange, distant sounds in the background—like gurgling, choking...stuttering—and then he realized that the sounds were coming from him. His throat no longer worked. It didn't...belong. It was making everything impossible...so impossible. He couldn't swallow or breathe—or make the pain stop.

He needed to concentrate.

Shit, he was really about to lose it—something he had never done in battle before—but then, he had never prepared to battle a dark lord before...

Holy deities, he was going to completely—freak—the—hell—out!

Great Perseus, he couldn't do this! "Stop!" he tried to shout.

"Shhh!" The smooth sound of Marquis's voice echoed in his mind. "You have lost a tremendous amount of blood...very quickly." Marquis's voice was unbelievably steady despite his inevitable emotional turmoil. "It won't be long now. You can do this."

Nachari felt his body shaking and wished he could make it stop.

He couldn't.

It won't be long now...

That was what Marquis had said.

He could hold on just a little bit longer. Yes, hold on...just a little bit...

Longer...

His skin was sticky and wet. It was so uncomfortable. He thought—absently—that he would really like a shower.

When Kagen's demeanor suddenly changed, Nachari knew something major had happened. But he wasn't sure what. He had expected some grand finale—a chorus of trumpets or a bright white light—something to herald the transition from one state of existence to another, but there had been nothing other than the telltale signs of his brother, the healer, going into serious-as-a-heart-attack doctor mode. Kagen was furiously checking the monitors now, rapidly connecting fresh blood to transfuse through an IV...steadily preparing a BMV resuscitator—or Ambu bag—to begin breathing for Nachari.

In other words, he was in the process of placing Nachari on full life support. Which had to mean it was over.

Nachari had already died.

And his spirit had already left his body.

After all, Kagen would never risk stabilizing him too soon, not after all they had gone through to insure his…demise.

Nachari was momentarily confused.

"Time is short, wizard. Quit dallying." A crisp laughter echoed through the meadow, and Nachari looked up to see the most brilliant, serene green eyes he had ever seen, shining peacefully in a chiseled face framed by soft blond curls.

"Shelby," he said, smiling from ear to ear, as all of his pain and fear instantly abated.

Shelby held out what appeared to be a very firm, corporeal hand, and Nachari took it. His twin pulled him straight up—out of his body and onto his feet—where he was suddenly clothed again, and the two brothers embraced like it had only been minutes since they were last together. Side by side, they became reanimated—as males, as brothers—two powerful beings no longer walking the earth, but both vibrantly alive and infused with joy and energy.

"You look well," Nachari said. He didn't have any other word for it.

"Well?" Shelby mocked. "I look better than you!" He held out his arms to showcase his magnificently sculpted frame. He positively glowed.

Nachari threw back his head and laughed, his thick mane of hair swaying from the vibration. "I thought you knew, Shelby…"

"Knew what?"

"Nobody looks better than me—haven't you heard the women talk?"

Shelby's answering laughter was hearty and unrestrained. "You mean no one looks more girly, wizard!"

The two males collided playfully, arms reaching up to lock each other's heads in a simultaneous wrestling hold, bodies circling in an attempt to gain physical advantage. They had wrestled like this a thousand times over the years, and there was nothing strange or otherworldly about their coming together now. It all seemed so easy.

So pleasant.

As if Nachari had simply walked from one side of the creek to the other to meet his twin.

There was just no great transition.

And now that the pain and fear were gone, there was no hesitation or regret, either.

They wrestled until they were winded and their ethereal bodies were covered in dirt. Until a pair of distant but distinct—and gravely serious—voices interrupted their play: "Nachari!" The urgent tone grabbed both of the twins' full attention.

"Oh gods," Nachari said, chastising himself for getting distracted, even for a moment. He spun around, searching the meadow. "Niko? Jankiel?"

Niko's voice rose with alarm. "Nachari, Napolean has already bled out! He has already died, and Ademordna has stepped out of his body!" He was speaking as a medium.

Nachari spun around warily. "Where is the demon?"

The grief in Jankiel's voice was inconsolable. "The dark lord has already reclaimed possession. I'm afraid it may be too late to save our king."

"No," Nachari lamented. "No!"

Dear Celestial gods, what had he done?

Nachari scanned the meadow, trying desperately to see what he needed to see: the cot containing the body of his Sovereign. Everything was blurred in subtle, shadowy form. Not dark—just not clear.

Shelby held out his hand. "It is an acquired skill, brother."

Nachari took Shelby's hand, and the land around them fell into immediate focus. Together, they jogged to the side of the king's body. Napolean looked so…still…lifeless.

Harmless.

And then his eyes popped open and a dark, evil presence regarded the twins as two orange balls shone from behind the king's pupils. "I win. You lose," the malevolent voice purred.

Napolean's body sat up on the cot—or at least it did on this side of the world—and he licked his lips as if tasting a delicacy.

"How do you figure?" Nachari asked.

The body laughed, and it was alarming—hearing Napolean's pure voice being used by such a wicked being. "You're dead, wizard, and I still have the king."

Nachari stared at the evil lord gloating before him. He scanned Napolean's body, taking careful measure of every chakra—the colors of his aura—assessing any breaks or holes in the energy. The dark lord's essence was firmly planted in Napolean's body. In fact, it had taken such firm hold that the fit appeared almost seamless.

Almost.

But not quite.

Just below the heart chakra, there was a weakness—a break. A place where the goodness of the male who had animated the body for so many centuries had not completely given way to the absolute and irretrievable hold of the darkness. Napolean's integrity and his growing love for the human woman, his *destiny,* were still imprints in his heart, and that was Ademordna's vulnerability.

Nachari exchanged a quick glance with Shelby, who nodded almost imperceptibly. In the blink of an eye, both brothers extended their fangs, released their claws, and leapt at the dark lord—Nachari from the front, Shelby from the back. They struck his chest with unbridled force. They impaled his breastbone, dug up and under his ribs, and clutched at the black demon heart for all it was worth.

"Now!" Niko and Jankiel's voices rang out in their ears, and both brothers wrenched back with all they had—twisting the false heart from opposite directions—yanking, turning, and jerking it free from the possessed cavity.

The blood turned thick and gooey, and worms began to crawl along Nachari's arms, each maggot sinking sharp, jagged teeth into the wizard's skin like a frenzied parasite. The demon lord shouted his rage as his form broke free from Napolean's body, and a pure, pink heart began to grow—and beat—in the place of the diseased one.

As Napolean's pure heart took firm root once again in the body of his birth, the possession came to an end.

And then suddenly, they had a much greater problem.

Napolean Mondragon, the sovereign lord of the house of Jadon, was free once again to return to his people, his *destiny*, but Nachari Silivasi was still in the spirit world, standing face to face—toe to toe—with the unrestrained, immortal demon, Ademordna. The maggots, which were microscopic fragments of the dark lord's blackened heart, leapt from the hands of the twins—back into their familiar, immortal, shadowed form; and then the shadow grew in height until it stood at least ten feet tall, the evil growing darker...and darker...until, at last, it shimmered an inky, iridescent black.

Ademordna's features were so repugnant that it burned Nachari's eyes to look upon them; and then the dark lord's tongue began to slither about his mouth, like a snake on a vine, wagging its tail in some gruesome, erotic parody. He was hideous yet handsome at the same time—clearly not human or Vampyr.

Nachari instinctively reached for Shelby, using their familiar telepathic line of communication, but there was no answer to his call. He spun around, his senses flaring out. "Brother!"

Still no answer.

"Shelby!"

The demon cackled loud and abrasive, and the meadow shook. The surrounding trees grew arms in place of their branches and began to reach out for the wizard, clawing at his flesh with jagged fingers.

Nachari fell into a low, fighting stance, rotating to the balls of his feet—he was ready to strike or defend at will—and then he closed his eyes, calling on his second-sight to see what was truly there.

"Your brother is no longer beside you," the dark lord hissed on the cold tail of a foul wind. "What did you think would happen once you made things right—as it were—dear wizard?" The words dripped with venom. "You returned the king to the land of the living, and myself—the dark lord Ademordna—to the throne of the abyss." He groaned, and fire shot out of his mouth in a steady stream like the red-hot flames of a blowtorch.

Nachari felt for the truth of the dark lord's words—demons were notorious for lying—but this one was telling the truth.

"Shelby is *dead*...despite your pitiful desire to believe otherwise," Ademordna purred with satisfaction. "His eternal soul has been retrieved by the Valley of Shadow and Light"—he rubbed his chest as if the words suddenly brought enormous pleasure to his wicked heart—"and good for him, really. He was such a generous soul...when he lived." He whistled a discordant tune, and the notes fell upon Nachari's ears like fingernails against a chalkboard, the reverberation crawling up and down his spine like blades cutting into the vertebrae.

Slowly, incipiently, Ademordna reached out with a sharp claw to scrape the underside of Nachari's chin. Nachari tried to avoid the demon's obscene touch, but it was as if he were powerless to move. It was like being caught in an awful nightmare, where every step is mired in quicksand, and any effort to move or resist becomes herculean...and pointless.

"Ahh." The demon lord rolled his head back and forth on his shoulders, allowing long locks of oily hair to sway back and forth, each strand undulating like a writhing serpent along his shoulders. "How I wanted the king..." He sucked wind between rotting teeth. "How I wanted his sons..." he moaned. "But to feed for all eternity on the light of a Master Wizard—a soul so pure it would trade its life out of duty for another..." He gyrated his hips against the oppressive, humid air. "Mmm, yes. It will do."

Nachari swallowed a lump in his throat and looked around,

warily.

Shit.

And more shit!

Ademordna wasn't lying.

Nachari had died on that cot, despite the fact that his body still breathed. And the world between worlds—where Shelby had met him, laughed with him, and helped him to exorcize Napolean's demon—was no longer where he stood.

He felt the ground beneath him ooze.

Demonic power gushed about his feet, and, as the sludge passed over, his skin, his toes, and ankles—even his bones—collapsed beneath its weight…disintegrating, painfully decomposing…only to regenerate and break again.

Perpetual suffering.

Perpetual injury.

Endless death, eternal agony, and punishment…

Nachari Silivasi was in the domain of the dark lords of the underworld. He was standing in the heart of the Valley of Death and Shadows. He had traded his soul for Napolean's, and Ademordna had accepted the trade. The moment the demon had relinquished the king's body, he had been cast back into his own private hell…and Nachari had gone with him.

Shelby, on the other hand, had returned to the Valley of Spirit and Light, where his soul would remain forever. It was a matter of degrees. Shelby was truly dead—his soul was already at rest—and as such, he could not enter the shadow of the abyss: He had already been claimed by the light.

"But you…my beautiful, exceptional wizard…" Ademordna circled Nachari and crooned to him like a baby. He reached out, snatched a handful of his hair, and sniffed it, causing blackened blood from his nostrils to seep out and soak the strands. It burned Nachari's scalp like acid. He licked a dollop of the blood from behind Nachari's ear, and Nachari jerked his head away in disgust. The saliva ate at his skin, but he refused to cry out. "You are neither alive nor dead, Nachari Silivasi. Your soul was traded before it was appointed." Heckling, Ademordna gripped

Nachari's shoulders with both hands and clamped down hard, breaking the fine clavicle bones in two.

Nachari gritted his teeth against the pain and fought not to faint.

He would not give the demon the satisfaction.

His eyes rolled back in his head as he struggled to maintain consciousness. *Dear celestial gods,* was he really going to spend all of eternity in the Valley of Death and Shadows? Away from his brothers? Never again to see Shelby? Sentenced as Ademordna's prisoner…forever? Had his eternal soul really been the price of Napolean and Brooke's freedom? Had he truly made the *ultimate sacrifice* for the house of Jadon?

Even as he asked, he knew the answer.

Yes.

And his heart wept for Nathaniel and Kagen—for Marquis.

Dear Gods, for Braden.

The dark lord rearranged his molecules then, shrinking his giant form down to a human size, to stand as a man—albeit a giant, enormously powerful man—before Nachari. He held up both hands in a casual gesture. "Should you desire to try and escape, I will wait…and watch…with great enthusiasm."

Nachari looked around him. The sky was black—not dark with iridescent beauty like on the earth—but black as in absent of form and light. There was no horizon, only vapor and mist so that nothing could be seen beyond a couple hundred yards. All was smoke and mirrors. Dark illusion and fog. This place did not contain the body—it imprisoned the soul.

The land and the vegetation were solid, but not with the intelligent energy of creation like on the earth; rather, with the cold, inky presence of evil—of creepy, crawly, scream-in-the-night-from-terror electricity—the kind that made one's stomach churn and the hair on the back of one's neck stand up. There was nowhere to go. All space was but a portal, looping in an endless circle of evil…of perpetual night.

Nachari drew in a deep breath. "Is any other form of death possible here?"

BLOOD POSSESSION

Ademordna laughed raucously. He seemed genuinely entertained by the question. "Ah, yes, wizard: Suicide would be so much easier, would it not?"

Nachari didn't show any emotion, although he wanted to rip the demon's heart out—again—to take them both out of their misery...together...permanently. But it couldn't be done. Ademordna was already dead.

And so was he.

"No, Silivasi; I have something far richer planned for you." Ademordna smiled—a look at complete odds with his twisted features.

Nachari closed his eyes and prayed, hoping somewhere, somehow, a celestial god or goddess would hear his petition. He reached out for his brothers—for Niko, then Jankiel, for Napolean—just to know that the king still lived, that his sacrifice had not been in vain.

No one answered.

Ademordna extended his arm—two decrepit hands flexed and contracted with demented grace—and then he covered Nachari's eyes. "See your future, wizard."

The world spun in dizzying circles, and Nachari felt as if his body lifted off the ground—but he couldn't be sure. Then just as suddenly, he was transported to a castle where all kinds of demonic creatures and animals roamed the halls. He ended up in a great stone chamber, a throne room, staring down at his own naked body, manacled to a cold slab of stone. The stone sat beside Ademordna's throne, and he knew that he was to be displayed for all time as the dark lord's trophy—the prized soul he had stolen from the house of Jadon, the pure one, the magic one—as an eternal show of power...darkness defeating light.

There were spikes and swords, daggers and javelins piercing his body at the joints and through the bones...like an eternal crucifixion. And the myriad of puncture wounds—from his neck to his thighs...to the thin membranes surrounding his scalp—left no doubt that he would be continuously fed upon by countless demonic creatures, perhaps the various dark lords themselves, evil beings hungry to consume his light.

Next to the stone stood a cache of crude implements of torture, some rusted, some jagged, all designed to inflict the greatest amount of suffering possible. Inhabitants of the valley would pay for the privilege—for the pleasure of cutting him open, peeling back his skin, breaking his bones, and making him scream.

Despite his courage—his uncommon resolve—Nachari Silivasi sank to his knees and wept.

The horror of it was too much.

The loss of his brothers even worse.

He felt utterly destitute of hope, broken before his enemy.

Yes, he was a fighter. A male in the house of Jadon. A Master Wizard and a *Silivasi*! And he would struggle like the powerful being he was—he would use his magic, and he would wield it well. He would weave spells to lessen the pain. He would create illusions to deceive his mind. And he would strike back whenever he could, causing as grave of injuries to his enemies as possible.

But it would all be a perpetual dance without end.

Nachari Silivasi was a prisoner of hell…

And there was no Magick that could change that fact.

twenty-one

Napolean Mondragon flung open the door of his master bedchamber and stood silently on the threshold. It had been two days since the sentinels had moved Brooke from the cabin to the manse after treating the worst of her injuries. Almost forty-eight hours since his *destiny* had been impregnated by Ademordna.

It had taken Napolean just as long to completely recover from the possession, to regain full awareness in his body, and there was simply no measuring the eternity that had come and gone since Nachari Silivasi had left his lifeless, inanimate body—breathing but unoccupied—on a stiff cot...in a cold meadow. An unthinkable sacrifice for the house of Jadon.

Napolean saddened at the thought, even as he brought his attention back to his bedroom and stared for the first time at the trio of women before him: Brooke lay unconscious in the center of his bed, Jocelyn Levi sat next to her on the edge, gently leaning over and stroking her hair, while Ciopori Demir knelt on the floor beside her and dipped a cool washcloth into a shallow basin.

When Jocelyn turned around, her stunning hazel eyes were cloudy with concern. "Hi, Napolean." She forced a smile.

Napolean knew that Jocelyn was not entirely comfortable around him to begin with. Under circumstances such as these, he could hardly blame her. He inclined his head in the faintest intimation of a nod. "Thank you for being here, Jocelyn. How is she?"

Jocelyn opened her mouth to speak but apparently thought better of it. She averted her eyes instead.

Ciopori glanced up from where she knelt on the floor. "Greetings, milord." Her words were measured but kind. "I'm glad you were able to make it before the birth—it does my heart good to see you." She glanced at Brooke. "She's healing nicely."

BLOOD POSSESSION

Napolean took a modest step forward, relieved. "Thank you, Ciopori." He noticed for the first time that there were no other medical personnel present—none of Kagen's apprentices accompanied the women. "Is it only the two of you?" he asked, concerned.

"Yes." Ciopori nodded.

"Where is Vanya?" He frowned. "I thought she would...want to be here."

"She's with Storm and Nikolai," Jocelyn said.

"I see." Napolean narrowed his eyes with apprehension, and then he took a longer look at Brooke. "And the two of you were able to provide her with all the care she needed...on your own?"

Ciopori shook her head and gestured toward the door. "Kagen's nurse is outside on the veranda with Ramsey. She has kept her well sedated, and Ramsey has seen to her...comfort."

Napolean knew that Ciopori was referring to the responsibility of a male vampire—usually the woman's mate—to assist with the progression of her pregnancy. In order to assure the female's absolute comfort from beginning to end, the males held all of the sensations in their own bodies throughout the extremely short—but intense—forty-eight hour gestation period. Normally, Napolean would have been the one to do it, but he had been trapped between this world and the next, fighting to get back to his body.

Ciopori tucked her thick, flowing hair behind her shoulder in a somewhat nervous gesture. "Marquis shared his venom as well. We wanted to keep the room quiet and dark...peaceful for the baby."

Napolean swallowed a curse. He should have been the one there, taking care of Brooke...in every way. "Has she been unconscious this entire time?" he asked.

Jocelyn shook her head. "No. She's been in and out. She knows what's happening." She locked eyes with Napolean, and he knew that she held her tongue out of great respect...and maybe a little fear. Either way, her thoughts were not hard to read: Although Ademordna had been the one

Tessa Dawn

to…violate…Brooke, the thought of such suffering occurring at the hands of the fearsome leader was…well, unfathomable. As women, they couldn't help but be badly shaken up by the possession, and Brooke's violation.

Napolean summoned his fortitude and walked to the other side of the bed. He looked discerningly at Brooke, and his very soul trembled. The women had done an incredible job of healing her injuries—over the last forty-eight hours, her bones had mended, her cuts had sealed shut, and her puncture wounds had closed—but the evidence of her struggle was still there. If only as faded remnants of the trauma, pale bruises still reminded all who looked of the viciousness of her captivity.

Napolean swallowed his anger and kept his voice neutral. "Leave us."

The women looked slightly taken aback, and he immediately regretted the brusqueness of his tones. In truth, he wanted to inquire about Brooke's mental health—ask more about her state of mind. He wanted to thank both women from the bottom of his heart for taking such loving care of his *destiny*, but he could not give voice to those sentiments just yet. He wasn't at all sure that he could hold it together, and as the sovereign lord of the house of Jadon, he could not afford to lose control in front of his people. They needed him to be their rock—a constant certainty in an uncertain world—and Brooke would need his strength to get through what was soon to come.

"Yes, milord," Ciopori finally whispered.

"No problem." Jocelyn stood up.

Napolean shook his head then. "Do not go far. The time is close. In less than—" He hesitated.

Oh hell, what was the exact hour?

He should know.

He would know…if he had been there at the conception.

Ciopori seemed to sense his consternation. "It can't be more than a half an hour, milord."

All eyes went to the prominent rise at Brooke's middle, the obvious pregnant belly that protruded beneath a soft, silk gown,

235

and if someone had dropped a pin in the room, it would have sounded like a grenade.

Ciopori appeared to measure her words carefully before continuing. "I would never question your wisdom, Napolean, but I do feel that it would be best for a woman...for myself or Jocelyn...to be here when the babies are born."

Napolean exhaled and tilted his head back and forth on his neck, releasing tension. His jaw was set at a firm angle. "Brooke has seen and been through far too much trauma. I will not put her through the pain of the sacrifice. When the moment arrives, I will call my sons to me while she sleeps; I will have Marquis take the Dark One to the Chamber of Sacrifice and wait for me; then we will meet our true son together."

Ciopori raised her chin and cleared her throat. "Please reconsider, Napolean."

He looked at her then, really looked at her. There was nothing harsh or judgmental in her eyes, only compassion.

Jocelyn shared the same look. "I don't mean to speak out of turn, but it's really a hard thing...the sacrifice...a terrifying moment for a human being, Napolean. You have to keep in mind: You have had thousands of years to understand the Curse, to know how truly evil it is and how dangerous that Dark Child will be. You have had centuries to accept the fact that there is absolutely no choice in the matter, but we don't have near enough time to absorb it that deeply. That kind of magic doesn't exist in the human world. And I don't know if Brooke will be able to forgive you unless she sees it for herself. Maybe...at least...just consult her."

Napolean interlocked his hands, stretched his fingers backward, and cracked his knuckles. "I don't want to take anything away from Brooke." He wondered if he looked as weary as he sounded. "I just want to spare her further pain."

Ciopori nodded her understanding, grasped Jocelyn by the forearm, and nudged her toward the door. "You will make the right decision, milord." She smiled empathetically. "We will be close by if you need us."

Napolean inclined his head politely. "Call Marquis," he said. "One way or the other, I will need someone to take the Dark One from the room immediately until I can…attend to what must be done."

Ciopori nodded. "Very well."

Jocelyn tapped a nervous foot against the floor, and then she walked away with a compassionate wave.

Napolean ran the pads of his fingers lightly along the surface of Brooke's skin as she slept. He was memorizing every bruise, reliving every injury, using his highly tuned senses to recreate each moment of trauma from its faint cellular imprint.

He had to know what her body had endured.

Even though he had spared her soul—kept her mind from any conscious awareness of the brutality—it had been his body, his fists, his manhood that had violated her…and he had to know what had been done.

Every nuance.

He had to feel the pain because his body had inflicted it.

He had to experience the horror because someone needed to.

He had to relive each moment in order to reinstate balance, to adhere to his own deeply entrenched sense of justice.

Carefully—reverently—Napolean used his own venom to treat the remaining bruises and wounds, taking the energetic vibration of each act of violence into his own muscles, skin, and tissue as he went along, forever removing it from Brooke's awareness, even at a molecular level. His eyes clouded up several times, but he refused to cry. He was too powerful of a being, and such depth of emotion would be too great: The earth would respond with storms unlike any the valley had ever seen.

So he measured his breaths—slowly drawing in air, then gently letting it out—as he set about healing whatever injuries remained in his *destiny*. When he was confident that her body had returned to a perfect state of health, he kissed her lightly on the forehead and whispered a command to awaken in her ear.

Brooke's eyelids fluttered, opening and shutting several times like the wings of a butterfly, before their stunning blue depths finally registered awareness.

"Napolean?" She tried to speak, but her voice was scratchy.

He smiled. He couldn't help it. The situation was as grave as any could be, but the sound of her voice, the sudden emergence of her spirit in the room, was like the rays of the sun shining through a cloud after a heavy, violent storm. She radiated beauty.

She promised hope.

"Yes," he whispered, adjusting his frame on the bed so that he was turned to face her. He ran his fingers along her cheek and held her gaze, unwavering. "How are you feeling?"

She swallowed and reached for her throat. "Okay, physically." She looked down at her belly, and her eyes betrayed her fear. "But this...I'm scared to death."

Napolean leaned forward. He extended his hand and was about to place it on her protruding abdomen, when he hesitated. "May I?"

She paused as if thinking it over. "Yes." She didn't sound altogether confident.

Napolean sent a strong wave of serenity into Brooke's body with his touch, eliciting a grateful, unconscious sigh from her soft lips. "I don't remember anything that happened in that cabin," she whispered, "or even how I got to this room." She looked left then right, appearing to notice for the first time that the two women were gone. "Where did Ciopori and Jocelyn go?"

"They're just outside the door," Napolean reassured her. "I wanted some time alone with you...if that's okay."

Brooke nodded, and then a slow, mischievous smile creased the corners of her mouth. "Did you really get your head stuck between two stones in a castle wall when you were a boy?"

Napolean drew back, surprised, and then he chuckled.

"Woman, I return from the brink of hell after being possessed by a demon—just in time to share the birth of our first child—and this is what you ask me?"

She smiled broadly, and it made her face positively radiant. "No, it's not that, it's just"—she reached out to touch him, her fingers tracing the line of his chin—"your head is not that big."

He opened his mouth and started to speak, and then he closed it, at a complete loss for words.

"No," Brooke said quickly, "I mean, it's big enough…" She bit her bottom lip and looked away.

"Thank you…I think," he said. He took her hand in his, lifted it to his mouth, and bent to gently kiss the top of her knuckles. When his lips brushed her skin, she drew her hand away in a nervous, reflexive gesture, like a schoolgirl who had suddenly become shy, and Napolean's chest swelled with emotion. He could hear the pitter-patter of her heartbeat, the quickening of her breath, the slight rise in her blood pressure that made it obvious she was attracted to him. Very attracted to him. Despite everything that had happened, their growing, innate connection had not been damaged. Brooke still reacted to the closeness of his body…to the feel of his touch.

When she looked back at him, there was an unmistakable tenderness in her eyes. "How did you do it?" she asked.

"Excuse me?" he said. "How did I get my head wedged between two stones?"

She shook her head and laughed. "No. *This*." She gestured toward him…toward the room…toward the land outside the window. "How did you keep me from…experiencing…what happened in that cabin?"

Napolean shifted his weight and sighed. "I willed it with everything I had."

Brooke held his gaze with growing intensity. "I don't understand that kind of power—the kind that vampires have. The kind *you* have."

Napolean kept her hand sheathed in his, and when she tugged—as if to pull away—he tightened his grip—not enough to hurt, just enough to heal. "You have them, too, Brooke. You are as I am...now."

Her eyes grew wide, but she didn't panic—not like she might have a week ago. "Unfortunately, I remember that part."

Napolean felt his shoulders tense. Although he wanted to look away with shame, he owed her more accountability than that. "The conversion." He brought her hand to his mouth and breathed warm air into the center of her palm before holding it to his own cheek. "I will not ask you this day to forgive me for so much suffering, but I will promise to spend the rest of my life making it up to you, earning your trust."

Brooke blinked. "No, Napolean. I don't blame you."

He hesitated, considered her words, and then frowned. "How is that possible?"

She shook her head and shrugged. And then she ran her thumb against his cheek in a slow, natural caress. It was the first time she had ever initiated such innocent affection with him. "I don't know," she answered honestly. "I should resent you. I should be scared to death of you. I should want to run away from you...as fast and as far as I can." She sighed. "For all intents and purposes, I should hate you for dragging me into this insane world of demons and magic...and blood...and *so much* violence. But when I look at you, I just...don't."

He leaned back and cocked his head to the side. "Tell me why, Brooke—if you can."

She took a very slow, deep breath and bit her lip. "When that man started shooting at us in the meadow...when I crawled behind you to take cover..." She paused as if carefully considering her words, and then she cleared her throat and continued: "For just a split second—for the first time in my life, really—I felt protected. Safe. Like the world might explode around me, but I had something...*someone*...invincible to protect me. And it felt...right. In the middle of all that danger, it felt *right*."

Napolean closed his eyes and rested his head against the warmth of her hand. He tried to disguise his regret. "But you weren't safe...Brooke." He opened his eyes because he needed to face her. "Apparently, I wasn't as invincible as either one of us thought. By all the gods, I am so sorry...if I had known the man was possessed—"

Brooke withdrew her hand from his, placed her forefinger over his lips, and shushed him. "No, you weren't invincible. For the second time since I met you, you were vulnerable—*real*—like me. And in that split second, when that *thing* shot out of the man's body and possessed you, I felt like I was watching a nuclear bomb go off. Like life as I knew it would never be the same." She struggled to sit up, and Napolean quickly propped several stiff pillows behind her back, helping her get comfortable in a new position. She shook her head, frowned nonsensically, and fingered a lock of her hair. "I don't get it. It doesn't make any sense, but that's when I knew this Curse was real—that I am who you say I am—because when I thought you had died, I almost... I felt...like a part of me wanted to die with you."

He tried to take her hand in his once again to reassure her, but this time, she withdrew from his touch. It didn't appear to be out of anger or revulsion; it was more like the contact was just too much at that moment...as if her words had simply made her too vulnerable.

Looking away, she continued, "I survived the conversion because I knew you were out there somewhere, maybe needing me." She forced her gaze to his. "This whole thing has terrified me, and the last seventy-two hours have been a living hell, but I realize that I do know you, Napolean. I feel you"—she placed her hand over her heart—"in here."

Napolean released the unconscious breath he had been holding. Leaning forward, he braced one arm on the left side of Brooke's body, one on the right, and tensed his muscles to keep his weight off her stomach. "Ingerul meu. Destinul meu. Regina mea," he whispered breathlessly. "My angel. My *destiny*. My queen," he repeated. "Let me love you, Brooke. I have waited millennia to love you."

With that, he dipped his head and allowed his lips to meet

hers. They were soft and receptive, and he felt a hunger like nothing he had ever known well up inside of him. A deep, throaty growl vibrated in his throat—he couldn't stop it—as he gently swept his tongue inside her mouth and tasted her total willingness for the first time. She tasted like a spring breeze after a long, barren winter, and he moaned into her. "Gods, I want you," he murmured, cupping her cheek in his hand and gently massaging her skin with his thumb.

He drew back and kissed her chin, her nose, the sides of her jaw up to her ear, where he gently nipped the lobes with a fang and swirled his tongue over the blood. "Forgive me, Draga mea; I had to taste you." Exercising incredible restraint, he pulled away. He smiled when he saw that she looked lost...like someone in a dream. He bent to her belly and gently kissed the protruding mound. "It is almost time, Brooke, and there is much we need to talk about."

She brought her hand up to her mouth and lightly touched her lips as if testing to make sure he had really been there, and then she slowly nodded her head. "Tell me what's going to happen." Her voice betrayed her fear.

Napolean sat upright and took both of Brooke's hands firmly in his. "Do not be afraid, my love. I will not allow you even the slightest discomfort. As you know, vampires can dematerialize—expand their molecular structures to the point where they dissipate into a million detached particles, then transfer them, together, as a whole, and redistribute them someplace else. I will call our sons from your womb when the time is right, and they will dematerialize from inside of you and rematerialize here in my arms."

Brooke nodded like a soldier receiving battle orders, scared to death of what was to come, yet determined to face it with courage and obedience. "Okay." The word was shaky.

Tessa Dawn

Napolean became deathly serious then.

He sent his power flowing into her with his eyes, and then he held her in a gentle stream of warmth…and compulsion. It was necessary. "You read about the Curse when you went through the annals of our people. You know what comes next—and why."

Brooke swallowed and tucked her hair behind her ear with a nervous hand. "I—I—I'm not sure I'm going to be able to handle that part, Napolean."

Napolean nodded, understanding.

How could she?

How could she understand the breadth of the original crime committed so many years ago: the slow, systematic slaughter of female after female until an entire civilization had been at the brink of extinction? How could she possibly imagine the suffering the women had endured at the sacrificial stone, kneeling like broken slaves with their hands tied taut around the rock, their heads forced down against the cold slab, bleeding out from their throats as the males stood silently and watched. Then drank.

The Curse had been severe, to be sure.

But the punishment had been deserved.

If Prince Jadon had not pleaded for mercy, there would have been no souls left to save. But he had—and this was the price—returning the Dark One to the Curse as atonement. Right or wrong, just or evil, it didn't matter. The blood sought and took its vengeance. If it couldn't have the child, it would take—and torture—the father.

There was simply no other way.

Still, over the centuries, several males had perished trying to get around it: They had traded their lives to save both firstborn sons, only to leave grieving widows who later died of broken hearts, mourning their eternal mates. Or worse—they left widows who survived only to raise dark sons who, ultimately, had to be hunted down and destroyed as they grew older. Napolean had since passed a law forbidding the practice.

243

BLOOD POSSESSION

The dark twins were evil to their core.

Predatory abominations without conscience or soul that preyed upon the weak—the strong, the young, and the old...both vampire and human alike.

"You cannot feel remorse for the dark twin," Napolean explained. "He is not what he seems."

Her eyes held doubt, but she remained silent...listening.

Napolean searched for a way to explain: "In the human protestant religion, there is the concept of god's enemy—an evil being who seeks to destroy, who wears many faces. Sometimes he appears as an angel of light, other times as the malevolence he is; but always, he is a deceiver. So it is with the dark twin attaching himself to his brother of light. It is part of the Curse— the punishment—a cruel twist of illusion meant to shock, hurt, and horrify each one of us as further retribution for the original sin. The dark lord who possessed my body, who took you so cruelly, who waged such violence...*that* is the kind of spirit I will take from this room this night. Do you understand?"

Brooke took her hands from his and folded them in her lap, at least what was left of it. When she finally spoke, her tone of voice said everything...

She got it.

"I do understand; and because I understand, I want you to do something for me."

Napolean brushed his fingertips gently along the line of her jaw and smiled. "Anything, Brooke. Anything."

She steadied herself. "I want you to use the power of your mind—however you have to—to protect me: stop time, erase my memory, put me in a trance, whatever it takes. I don't want to see the Dark One, and I don't want to watch you take him away, either. Is it possible for me to...be asleep? Can you...call our sons...alone...and then wake me up when...the bad stuff is over?"

Napolean smiled. Truly, this woman had been chosen for him by the gods, for clearly their minds and hearts were as one. "Consider it done," he said.

244

With that, he placed his hands over her belly and began to chant a series of incantations in Romanian—the sacred words that would call his infant sons from his *destiny's* womb. As the energy around him began to swirl and congeal into a brilliant vortex of color, light, and wind, without hesitation, he spoke a firm command in Brooke's ear: "Dute la culcare."

Sleep.

twenty~two

Brooke turned off the water and stepped out of the dreamy marble shower in Napolean's master bathroom. She wiped some steam off a large oval mirror that hung over an elegant, English chestnut vanity, slipped into the pink cotton pajamas she had packed for her trip to the valley, and began to gingerly towel-dry her hair. As she rubbed the soft towel through her thick, dark tresses, she tiptoed to the open door and peered into the room. She gawked—in total awe—at the small, ornate bassinette by the window...and the tiny bundle sleeping soundly inside.

A sense of wonderment swept through her as she glided across the floor to the edge of the cradle and peeked at the child...for the umpteenth time. The perfect baby slept soundly on his back. His arms were bent at the elbows, resting to his sides, and his little knees were curled around his diaper so that the heels of both feet touched one another. She sighed and shook her head. It was simply—and utterly—unbelievable. The fact that this beautiful, living being was hers.

Her son.

When just weeks ago, she had been single—and definitely not pregnant.

The reality was almost too much to grasp.

When the babe drew in a soft, carefree breath and cooed on the exhale—still fast asleep—Brooke almost giggled like a child herself. For the past several hours, her emotions could only be described as giddy. She had never given much thought to marriage and a family. In fact, building her career had been the only goal in her foreseeable future, yet now, every time she stared at her son's soft, pliant skin, allowed herself to gape at those perfect, heart-shaped lips, or found herself awestruck by that silky head of raven hair, she felt like someone who had just fallen in love: Her heart fluttered; her palms began to sweat; and a feeling of such powerful yearning swept over her.

Perhaps God—the celestial gods?—had programmed the response into her DNA. Who knows? She only knew that she couldn't stop staring at the child she and Napolean had created together just over forty-eight hours ago. She shook her head as if to dismiss the thought: The awareness of the horrors that took place in that small cabin, the way her son had actually been conceived, was not something she cared to think about. But even as she fought to insulate herself from the memory, she already felt completely divorced from it. Napolean had plucked her soul from Ademordna's grip and held her far away—safe and untouched, as it were—using nothing more than his sheer will to do it. And he had somehow absorbed every bruise, every injury—every memory of the event—at a cellular level.

There was simply nothing there to recall.

It was like telling someone with amnesia that they had been in a terrible car accident. While they could still see the evidence of the mangled vehicle, in the absence of any memory or remaining physical injuries, the depth of trauma just wasn't there. On a gut level, she knew that she should be broken inside—shattered—and probably in need of many years of therapy, but the feeling-place of the event had been completely removed from her consciousness at the most rudimentary level: Her mind would never replay the terror or torment her incessantly. She would never be haunted by visceral nightmares…or fear. She would never remember the incredible suffering.

For all intents and purposes, it was as if the horror had never happened.

And her baby—the evidence of that horrific circumstance— could not possibly be compared to a mangled car. Looking at him now, she felt oddly thankful—not for the past several days, the disgusting Blood Curse, or the way she had been taken from her previous life—but for the gift of something so incredibly precious and innocent.

She smiled.

Tessa Dawn

She wanted to just sit for hours and listen to him breathe. In fact, she craved the touch of his little hands and fingers so much that she was almost tempted to wake him. Good Lord, what would Tiffany think? What would she say? She could hardly wait to tell her, but she knew that they needed to wait just a little bit longer—she actually agreed with Napolean on that fact: Until Brooke understood her new powers...her body...the world she was now immersed in, she wouldn't be able to merge it with her former life. And she did want to reconcile the two as best she could. She needed to know how to answer Tiffany's questions before she exposed her innocent human companion to too much at once. Whether or not her best friend could ever know the full extent of the truth—whether Tiffany would be trusted by the Vampyr to keep such a critical secret—still remained to be seen.

In deference to her better judgment, Brooke stepped away from the bassinette. The child had only been in the world for four hours—since 6:30 p.m. on Friday, October sixteenth: *her son's* birthday—surely his miraculous body knew what it needed. If he was sleeping, he probably needed to sleep. Besides, Brooke really didn't have a clue what to do with a newborn baby, let alone a vampire. Of course, Napolean had promised to provide her with help, and Jocelyn and Ciopori had been downright generous with a myriad of their own offers, promising everything from baby clothes and furniture for the nursery to hands-on tutorials on what they had learned in their short time as new Vampyr mothers. And Brooke fully intended to take them up on it...once she had settled in.

She wandered back into the bathroom and stared at herself in the mirror. She held her breath, leaned forward, and bared her teeth, half expecting to see a set of fangs gleaming back at her. When nothing but her traditional pearly-whites sparkled in the reflection, she tried growling low in her throat.

Okay, now that just sounded ridiculous.

Not to mention embarrassing.

She ran her tongue along her upper front teeth and tried her hand at the best Transylvanian accent she could muster: "I vant to drink yer blood." She quickly glanced around the room, nervous. Although she knew no one was there—no one could possibly have seen or heard her idiocy—she still needed to be sure. She peeked into the bedroom and sighed, vowing inwardly to never, ever do that again—what if Napolean had caught her? God, she would have to curl up and die.

She took a step back from the mirror then and brought her hand in front of her face—no claws at the ends of her fingers. Thank God. She steadied herself, remembering what Jocelyn had told her: The males of the species were the more aggressive ones. They were far more likely to display primal characteristics such as glowing eyes, fangs extended in anger or lust, and the emergence of claws and wings. In fact, the female *destinies* did not get wings—although no one knew why. While they had gained the same perfect health, the same tremendous power, and the same need for blood—as well as immortality—the females' instincts were softer, and their hunger could be sated by their mates. Unless truly angered or provoked, they weren't nearly as combative or primitive. Perhaps something of their human nature survived the transition after all.

Brooke closed her eyes and thought about the way vampires traveled when they weren't using their wings—and where did those glorious feathers come from, anyway?—their backs looked as smooth as anyone else's through their clothes. In fact, when Napolean had held her that day in the meadow, she hadn't felt anything rough or unusual. She sighed: just another question to add to her list.

She glanced at the hand in front of her face and tried to concentrate on the bedroom, visualize the bassinette the way Jocelyn had explained transportation—well...sort of. As she thought of the room and pictured her son, she began to imagine herself beside him. And as the image became clearer and clearer, she tried to relax, releasing her connection to the physical world. Somehow, she tried to intend her *being-ness* somewhere else. In an instant, her hand began to fade in front of her eyes—going all pliable, soft, and misty—until distinct sections shimmered completely out of view.

Brooke shrieked and jumped back. She waved her arm in the air and shook her hand wildly, as if she could somehow knock the spell loose. "Holy cow!" she muttered. She grasped her hand and squeezed it, begging the limb to stay on her arm.

And then she swore beneath her breath.

In the throes of her panic—the midst of her antics—she had cleared off the entire bathroom counter, scattering spray bottles, a curling iron, and an open case of makeup all around the room. The disturbance had made quite a racket—not to mention quite the mess. She stared at the chaotic pile of toiletries and grimaced.

Shit, Brooke, are you crazy?

What if she had managed to transport only one part of her body into the other room—or worse yet, several random parts? What would have happened to the rest of her? Or what if she had disappeared somewhere in never-never land, beamed up into outer space, or dematerialized beneath the ocean—and no one had ever found her? The thought gave her chills.

What if she had taken her body apart and then couldn't put it back together?

She swallowed a lump in her throat.

There was a loud knock at the bedroom door, and her heart sank into her stomach.

Oh, damn.

Ramsey.

The imposing sentinel had been stationed right outside the bedroom door since the moment Napolean left to go to the clinic—to see Nachari and the Silivasis.

"Yes?" Brooke called, trying to sound calm and in control. *As if…*

"Is everything all right, milady?"

Brooke frowned—my lady? *Really?*

She tried to put some reassurance in her voice. "Yeah, sure—I mean, yes." *You betcha, Mr. scary-as-hell-warrior! I just almost*

251

BLOOD POSSESSION

beamed my butt up to Mars, but everything is hunky-dory. She shuddered then, thinking of the fearsome male on the other side of the door...

Ramsey Olaru was truly one of the most menacing-looking men she had ever laid eyes on. She had feared the spooky guy from the first night she had seen him driving Napolean's Land Cruiser. There was just something...harsh...in his eyes, something that said the vampire would gladly eat you for breakfast, spit you out if he didn't like the taste, and devour your quivering children—all before he finished his morning coffee— while never missing a bite of crumb cake in the process.

"Should I come in?" Ramsey asked in that rough, nearly baritone voice.

Now she really did wish she could beam up to Mars.

"No!" she insisted. "Really, I'm fine." She paused and forced herself to smile—she had given enough presentations to know that smiling was a sure way to put a reassuring note in one's voice. "Thank you, though...Ramsey."

The vampire was quiet for a moment, and Brooke half expected him to rip the door from the hinges and fly in on angry wings, but then, of course, he could just materialize into the bathroom if he wanted to, couldn't he?

The thought scared her to death.

She needed ample warning in order to deal with something like that—a big, husky vampire suddenly appearing in the bathroom, hovering like a velociraptor, flexing giant muscles in her face...and towering over her with big, bad *fangs*. The Stephen King movie about a slobbering, rabid Saint Bernard suddenly came to mind. *Cujo*—yeah, that's what it was called— the one where the crazy dog tried to eat all the actors, and—

She quickly dismissed the thought and checked herself in the mirror, measuring the number of buttons fastened on her pajama-top to make sure she hadn't left one undone—because that really mattered...why?—and then she shook her head.

Calm down, Brooke: It isn't going to happen! He won't just...materialize...in here.

252

Tessa Dawn

Ramsey was the devil-in-blue-jeans type, a two-hundred-forty-pound raging bull with lethal horns charging through a china shop, not because he was clumsy—in fact, quite the opposite—but just because he could. If this male decided to come into the room, he wouldn't politely…quietly…appear. He would do it with a sufficient amount of force.

Brooke bit her bottom lip and waited.

Nothing happened.

"Very well then," Ramsey finally grunted.

She let out a deep, relieved sigh. "Yep, very well then," she responded, wondering why she couldn't just shut up. As if her tongue had a mind of its own, it kept going: "Yes, indeedy…very well…everything is super…very…well." She clasped her hand over her mouth. *Everything is super very well? What does that even mean? Stop talking, Brooke!*

Ramsey didn't appear to notice. Or maybe he noticed, but he was just too ornery to care. "Napolean asked me to tell you he is on his way home," he added.

Brooke's heart literally skipped a beat.

Her eyes grew wide and she spun around, staring at the mess she had made of the bathroom. She looked down at the front of her clothes, and then fingered her wet hair. Oh, hell… "How do you know?" she asked. "I didn't hear the phone ring. Did he say how soon he'd be here?"

"He didn't call," Ramsey grunted. "He"—the spooky vampire paused, as if searching for the right words—"spoke to me directly."

Brooke gasped. "Then he's already here?"

Ramsey chuckled then—actually *chuckled*—as if he found the whole situation amusing. Clearly, he had no idea just how sinister his laughter actually sounded. "No, milady—in my mind," he said.

"Huh?"

"Napolean spoke to me directly," he repeated, "in my *mind*." When she didn't respond, he added, "Telepathically."

"Oh," Brooke answered, sighing. She wondered absently

253

why Napolean hadn't chosen to speak to her, instead. After all, she was a vampire too, now, wasn't she? "Okay, thanks."

"Is there anything else you need, milady?" This time, his voice was both polite and respectful.

Brooke chewed on her bottom lip. "*Brooke*," she said, in an equally pleasant tone.

"Excuse me?" he asked.

Brooke smiled. "You asked if there was anything else I needed—just for you to call me Brooke."

Ramsey cleared his throat. "Oh..." He snorted. "As you wish...milady."

Wow.

Brooke held up her hands, shrugged, and rolled her eyes. "You're going to make someone a very attentive husband someday, Mr. Olaru," she whispered beneath her breath, sarcastically.

"Pardon me?" he growled.

Brooke blanched.

Was he in her head? Could he read her thoughts? Shit! She held her breath, too afraid to answer, unwilling to think...anything. *Blah, blah, blah, blah—blah, blah, blah...*

After a time, Ramsey walked away from the door, and his heavy footsteps could be heard slowly receding down the hall.

Brooke exhaled. This was all going to take some getting used to.

She felt positively faint and more than a little dizzy—the way she sometimes became when she was under an enormous amount of pressure. She peeked into the bedroom one more time, glanced at the bassinette, and heaved a sigh: By some stroke of luck, their son was still asleep. And then she looked in the bathroom mirror—at the mess that was her appearance. For reasons she couldn't comprehend, she almost felt like crying.

What the heck is wrong with you? she wondered. *You are acting absolutely...idiotic...childish.*

Positively insane.

She gazed at the face in the mirror, feeling mildly queasy at this point. And then she realized what was wrong…

Napolean was coming home.

To her.

To their son.

To their bedroom…and their new life…together. For all intents and purposes, the man was her husband now.

Brooke had already been converted. She was no longer human, and there was no going back. The demands of the Blood Curse had already been fulfilled, and as far as his kind was concerned, they were well and truly mated. And she got what that meant—she knew what came next…

In that eager, frightened, excited-yet-overwhelmed way that women had, Brooke knew that their relationship was about to go to another level.

The level.

And she knew that it was inevitable.

Imminent, even.

There was nothing at this point that could stop it—because she no longer possessed the willpower, or the desire, to say no.

Napolean Mondragon, the Ancient Master Justice and dominant leader of the most powerful race of beings she had ever known—the most commanding, and let's just face it, sexy male she had ever seen—was on his way home to her…to be with his wife for the rest of the night. And one way or another, they would end up making love.

Brooke Adams tried to ignore the swarm of butterflies that fluttered around wildly in her stomach as she set about cleaning the bathroom, drying her hair, and lightly applying a soft application of makeup, all in record time. Relying upon her newly enhanced, preternatural speed, she stepped out of her cotton pajamas and into a tasteful yet form-fitting silk-and-lace nightgown: She wondered if it wasn't a bit too obvious but decided to keep it anyway. She brushed her teeth, moistened her full lips with a hint of gloss, and dabbed on a few drops of her favorite perfume before finding a comfortable—albeit nervous—position in the lazy armchair beside their son's bassinette.

She felt ridiculous.

Excited.

Nervous enough to pass out.

Drawing in a deep breath, she folded her hands in her lap and switched her attention from Napolean, the man—and what he was coming home to—to Napolean, the king, and what he was coming home *from*. Not only had he been in charge of the birth, having to call their sons from her womb while keeping her unconscious at the same time—as she had asked him to—but he had then been faced, alone, with the unthinkable: remitting the Dark One to the Curse for the sacrifice.

Brooke's hand rose absently to her stomach in both wonderment and trepidation: wonderment because it seemed so impossible—a miracle, in fact—how her body could be so firm, fit, and perfect just hours after creating life; trepidation because it seemed so implausible—evil, without question—how that same magic could have used both her and Napolean to spawn something so abhorrent, so wrong, as the evil twin. For no other reason than to carry out a primordial, vengeful punishment that was ultimately much darker than the original crime.

She shut her eyes and shivered. Napolean had taken that dark being, disguised in a body of light, and seen to its end. And it was right. It was necessary. After all, death, one way or another, was inevitable.

The Curse had seen to that so many centuries ago.

Either the dark infant would be sacrificed, alone, or Napolean would be tortured, mercilessly, to death in the Dark One's place.

And the latter would only buy a miniscule amount of time for the dark child anyway—releasing something so horrible into the world as a result, that the father's sacrifice was hardly worth it.

She had read the annals of the house of Jadon, the detailed accounts, and she knew with certainty that the dark twin would grow up to murder, rape, and destroy…to prey on humans unchecked, unrestrained…that ultimately, the sons of Jadon would be forced to destroy it anyhow.

Brooke shuddered at the thought. Even though she understood the reality, she also realized that knowing and doing were two very different things. The bottom line was—Napolean had been forced to carry out the sacrifice alone, and that had to have been horrific for such a transcendent being.

Brooke shifted in the soft, leather armchair and hung her head as a new—yet just as disturbing—topic entered her mind….

Nachari Silivasi.

The other burden weighing heavily on the king's mind.

The young Master Wizard had saved Napolean's life. He had died in order to free Napolean's spirit—in order to wrench the blackened heart of that hideous thing, the dark lord they called Ademordna, from Napolean's body. Nachari's sacrifice had enabled the true soul of the king to return; and the other wizards, warriors, and his brothers had counted on bringing the brave vampire back to life, returning him to his own waiting body once the king was safe…

But something had gone horribly, horribly wrong.

Brooke hadn't understood all of what Jocelyn and Ciopori had told her, but she had sensed enough in Jocelyn's tone, seen the depth of pain reflected in Ciopori's eyes, to know that the loss to the house of Jadon was beyond monumental. It was epic. According to Jocelyn, the Silivasi family had suffered the loss of Nachari's twin only two months before, and the grief had almost destroyed them.

Before he had left the mansion, Napolean had tried to hide his turbulent emotions from Brooke, for her own sanity's sake, but even a blind man could have seen the truth: The king was racked with guilt and remorse over what had happened to

257

BLOOD POSSESSION

Nachari. He was overwhelmed with a sense of helplessness and determined to do all that he could to help the family...and his people. As it stood, all he could do was sit with the brothers and their *destinies* at the Dark Moon Clinic, wait and watch in solidarity—pray to the celestial beings for Nachari's return—yet even Brooke knew that with every moment that passed, the chances of the wizard's return grew slimmer.

Despite her total lack of experience with a newborn baby, as well as her recent emergence into the Vampyr world as one of their species, Brooke had urged Napolean to take all the time he needed with the Silivasis, to return only when he grew tired or needed a break.

"How is our son?" Napolean's deep, husky voice echoed through the room, and Brooke almost came out of the chair in fright.

"Holy cow! You scared me!" she exclaimed.

She hadn't seen him enter the room...or even materialize into the space. He was just suddenly there, standing on the other side of the bassinette, looking like silk and fire, stealth and grace—and utter male perfection—all wrapped up in a black muscle-shirt and dark jeans, leaning over their son as he slept.

"I'm sorry," he whispered, his words wrapping around her like a velvet caress. "I didn't mean to—"

All at once, his eyes grew wide. They swept over her body in an instant, and his mind seemed to...freeze...as if trying to make sense of what he was seeing. He stared at the small silk straps of her nightgown, and then his eyes roamed over her otherwise bared shoulders before following the sleek lines of her collarbone down to her breasts, pausing at her waist, and then settling on the exposed flesh of her thighs. His appreciation showed in his quick intake of breath as his gaze moved slowly back up the nightgown, lingered at her neck, and finally met her flustered stare. He opened his mouth to speak, and then closed it, seeming to have forgotten his words.

He cleared his throat, and his tongue swept over his full bottom lip, moistening his mouth in an inadvertently sexy

258

Tessa Dawn

gesture. And then a brilliant smile curved along the corners of his mouth.

"Dear gods, Brooke: You are devastating."

twenty~three

Napolean could hardly breathe.

He had returned home expecting to find his destiny somewhat anxious, and maybe even a little bit upset, by his unavoidable, prolonged absence. Instead, he had walked in on a beautiful, heartfelt scene: the miraculous sight of his son, lying peacefully in an antique bassinette, his soft eyelids closed in contentment, his tiny arms and legs spread out to the sides. And his woman—his *destiny*—sitting lovingly in the large armchair beside the child, enchanting, like an angel, luminous and surreal, with her hands folded peacefully in her lap.

And then he had noticed what Brooke was wearing...

His body had hardened instantly, and he had scarcely been able to draw air through his lungs.

The soft, silk nightgown had rendered him speechless, but it was the look of flushed anticipation on her exquisite face—a look that he hadn't expected to see for many weeks to come—that had caught him completely off guard.

He had told her she was devastating...because she was.

Now he wondered if he hadn't been too forward with his eyes...his appreciation.

After all, their relationship was still very fragile. A lot had happened in a very short span of time. And they were still getting to know each other as friends.

Brooke shifted nervously in her seat and brought her hand up to her chest, partially covering the exposed skin that robbed him of breath. Clearly, she was uncomfortable, perhaps even a little afraid, yet she had dressed in the most beautiful scrap of silk—*for him?*—and her thick, dark hair smelled of lavender and vanilla, the soft tresses swaying gracefully just above her delicate shoulders as she turned her head to look at him.

"Thank you," she whispered.

BLOOD POSSESSION

He smiled tenderly, not wanting to disquiet her further with his words.

Unable to hold the very eye contact she had initiated, she smoothed a lock of hair anxiously with her fingers, swept a graceful hand into the bassinette, and straightened the corner of their son's blanket. "He's been sleeping most of the evening." Her voice was a mother's gentle caress.

Napolean followed her gaze then, reveling in the sight of the child they had created together—whether or not they had chosen the manner of his creation. "He also takes my breath away," he said.

Brooke smiled, relaxing. "Mine, too." Her eyes positively sparkled, and she sounded like a child, then—so full of uninhibited joy and wonder. "I have no idea what to do with a baby, Napolean." She laughed. "But, I already…" She paused and met his eyes once again. "I already love him."

The words settled deep into his soul.

With her hand still resting just above her heart, she added, "He's already in here."

Napolean nodded. "I know what you mean." His eyes feasted on her beauty, and he knew he could not contain his passion much longer. He would try to be tender…and gentle…but she was fully converted now—completely and irrevocably his—and he wanted her in every way. Sending a strong psychic suggestion to the baby—imploring him to remain asleep—he held out his hand. "Come here."

Brooke visibly paled, and she cleared her throat. "Excuse me?"

Napolean chuckled then, low and deep, not meaning to add to her consternation but unable to restrain his amusement. "Come to me, Brooke."

She smoothed the skirt of her nightgown, and then her eyes nervously scanned the room, stopping to stare in desperation at the matching robe lying alongside the edge of the bed. "Um, let me go get my robe," she muttered. She stood up and quickly stepped aside, walking slightly backward all the way to the bed,

262

as if he might do something hasty if she turned her back on him.

What? he wondered. *Pounce on her like a hungry lion?*

Or a thirsty vampire…

He restrained a smile. "Are you still afraid of me, Brooke?"

She laughed insincerely. "No, of course not. I"—she quickly slipped the robe over her bare shoulders and tied the sash loosely around her waist—"I'm just cold." She rubbed her hands over her arms. "I think I caught a chill."

Napolean swallowed a chuckle. Indeed, he had noticed several goose bumps on Brooke's arms—just before the robe had concealed them. It was true, she did have chills—but she wasn't cold. His body heated with the knowledge. "You waited up for me?"

She shivered, but she didn't respond.

"Thank you."

He took a measured step forward, and she retreated, the back of her legs meeting the bed at just the right height so that her knees bent and she fell backward onto the mattress in a seated position. She looked up at him with enormous blue eyes. "I…I knew you would want to see our son."

"Mmm…I see," he murmured, holding her gaze.

As if the nonsensical explanation suddenly occurred to her, she abruptly changed tactics. "I mean…I knew that we would probably have…there were things we should talk about…about our son."

Napolean's heart skipped a beat.

She was lovely in her indecision.

Beautiful beyond compare as her desire warred with her sense of modesty…and her curiosity battled her unspoken fear.

Her perfect breasts rose and fell beneath the light, silk robe, and despite her reluctance to allow passion a foothold, her nipples hardened beneath the cloth. She was aroused and pulling herself in opposite directions: One wanted him to touch her—no, needed him to reassure her that all of this was real, that he would take infinite care of her heart as well as her body from this moment forward—and the other was lost and confused...and so overwhelmed by the power of their bond that she probably wanted to run.

"So," she breathed, clearly searching for a distraction, "what happened? At the clinic, I mean."

Napolean shook his head.

He wanted to tell her.

Gods knew he needed her comfort.

The weight of the grief he had encountered in that cold, sterile waiting room, the palpable terror that had radiated from the Silivasis and their *destinies*—from young Braden and even Kristina—had shaken him to the core. He shook his head again, forcing his thoughts from the clinic back to the bedroom. "Later," he whispered. "I will tell you later. It is...too much...right now."

Brooke looked up at him with so much compassion that he couldn't help but close the short remaining distance between them, gliding as much as walking to the side of the bed. He reached down and took her hand in his. "I need you, Brooke."

She stiffened, however slightly, and dropped her head, and her thick wealth of hair created an easy, natural barrier, hiding her gaze from his. "Napolean, I—"

"You what?" He cupped the back of her hand in his, brought her palm to his mouth, and slowly kissed the center, over her lifeline—a line that would now reflect immortality. Releasing her hand, he lightly stroked the length of her wrist, softly brushed the curve of her elbow, and then ran the pads of his fingertips along her upper arm to her shoulder, where he slid the back of his fingers along her neck to her ear, then fingered her hair. With his other hand, he tipped her chin to force her gaze. "Don't turn away from me, Brooke."

She tried to smile, but couldn't quite manage it. "I'm not trying to turn away, it's just..."

He waited for her to finish speaking, his heart warm with longing. When she didn't continue, he whispered, "It's just...what?"

She licked her lips. "It's just that I'm not sure if I'm ready

Tessa Dawn

for…all of this." She shrugged her shoulder out from under his hand—albeit gently—and gestured around the room. "Our life together. Our son." She gripped the sides of her robe and drew the silk together, holding it tightly against her chest. "I'm not sure if I'm ready for…us."

Napolean knelt in front of her, never losing eye contact, and she almost squirmed in an effort to back away. He could feel her determination—the effort it took to remain seated, to hold her ground and face him—and he was blown away, as always, by her bravery.

"I know what it looks like." She smiled sheepishly. "What I'm wearing…the room." She glanced at the blazing fire across from the bed, and then she turned to glimpse the low-lit lanterns above the nightstands, hanging as decorative sconces. The walls were adorned with evenly spaced electric candles, crafted to imitate the real thing, and their pale yellow reflections created a soft, golden halo about the bed.

Baby sleeping or no, Brooke could have left the overhead lights on, but she hadn't.

She sighed then. "I thought I was ready for all of this. I mean, for heaven's sake, we have a child together…and it doesn't get much more intimate than that, but…" She rubbed her forehead with her fingers. "But I think I'm just overwhelmed."

Napolean waited, still and unmoving.

He said nothing.

He simply remained in front of her and waited for her to raise her head, meet his eyes, and…slowly begin to relax.

"Brooke," he finally whispered.

She raised her eyebrows.

"Don't you know that I would never hurt you?"

She swallowed hard and nodded. "Yes."

He shook his head. "No, don't just answer—do you really know that I would never…ever…hurt you?"

She nodded. "I think you would die for me, Napolean." She gestured toward the crib. "And for our son."

BLOOD POSSESSION

He brushed her hair back behind her ears and stroked the side of her cheek with the back of his hand, causing her to shiver. "Then what are you afraid of?"

She shrugged. "I really don't know." She swallowed hard, deliberately released the iron grip on her robe, and clasped her hands together in her lap. "It's just too soon."

Napolean shook his head and leaned closer. The heat of his body mingled with hers. He brushed the tips of his fingers gently along her collarbone. "Your heart says you're ready." It was beating like a bass drum. He traced the swell of her lower lip. "Your mouth says you're ready." Her lips were quivering. He glanced at her breasts, quietly admiring the two delicate peaks that revealed her true arousal, and then he gently averted his eyes to avoid making her nervous—although gods knew, he wanted to take one into his mouth right then and there through the silk. "Your body is ready," he added. He rose up on his knees, took her narrow waist in his hands, and pulled her against him so he could whisper in her ear. "What is it that you need from me, Brooke?" The feel of her lush curves against his chest sent electricity coursing through his veins. "Tell me," he rasped.

She groaned, melding her body to his.

Her resistance was melting like butter.

"Your soul," she whispered breathlessly. And then she spoke so softly, her words were barely audible. "You are so strong, Napolean." Her hands swept over his rugged chest and lingered there for a moment. "Powerful...in so many terrifying ways." She drew back to look into his eyes. "I don't question your desire"—a quick glance downward left no question as to what...desire...she was referring to—"but Napolean, there has been so much...violence...and pain. I need to know your heart. Your tenderness." She sighed as if exasperated—and maybe a little embarrassed. "I need to have a clear sense of your conviction all around me...to trust it as surely as I breathe."

Napolean rocked back on his heels, inching away—not far enough to remove his warmth—but just enough to meet her scrutinizing gaze. As he stared into her eyes—such beautiful, haunting sapphires—the truth of her words reflected back at him, and the need they revealed was as stark as their beauty.

Brooke needed to *feel* Napolean's devotion beyond her five senses.

And there was nothing he could say to her, give to her, or demonstrate with his touch alone that would take the place of that deep, intrinsic knowing.

She had to feel it in her bones.

He paused, considering…wondering what under heaven could convey such deep, soul-stirring conviction.

He sighed: If only he could give her the moon, perhaps the graceful ebbing of a purple sunset, receding over snowcapped mountains. In his ancient memory, he recalled the hauntingly lovely drone of bagpipes playing on a rainy day so many centuries ago in Ireland; he still heard the heart-stopping rhythms of the Native American drums shortly after his species had arrived in the New World; he still felt the harmonious concerto of an orchestra he had once seen in New York while traveling on business—the graceful crescendo of the wind instruments, the beguiling entreaty of the strings, the cello's bass…the viola's allure…the violin's wings soaring beyond the theatre…

If only he could transport Brooke to the past.

Because music was the only thing he knew of that could break down such powerful barriers, transcend fear and trepidation…reveal the heart and bare…the soul.

The corners of Napolean's mouth turned up in a smile, and Brooke gave him a curious glance.

He began to compose a gentle melody in his heart—an allegory of such powerful longing and love that it was certain to stir her soul—and then he took her face gently in his hands and began to transfer the haunting stream of music into her mind.

She gasped, clearly startled. "You can play music in my mind?"

He nodded.

Her eyes grew large, and a look of such deep passion

267

alighted in their depths that he was almost afraid to breathe.

"That song," she whispered. "It's yours…you're composing it, aren't you?"

"Yes," he answered, wondering if she understood just how exposed he truly was. He leaned forward until his forehead rested against hers, and then he sighed. "I want you to feel my need." He lifted his head and gently brushed her mouth with a kiss. As their warm breath mingled together, her eyes fell shut, and her body became pliant in his arms.

Napolean nuzzled the hollow between Brooke's chin and shoulder. He softly grazed her delicate skin with his fangs. And then he slowly kissed his way up the back of her neck to her ear, where he used his voice as both sound and touch—pitched in a sultry lilt—to caress and lure. "I want you to *share* my need."

He continued to play the melody in her mind, sending the sweet, poignant chords right through the center of her body, allowing them to settle at the very core of her being. When she arched her back and moved slowly against him, a low growl escaped his lips, and he felt his arousal kick for the first time, straining for release.

He nipped her lightly on the neck then—just above her shoulder—and she moaned.

Moaned.

He shifted, trying to make room in his jeans to accommodate his growing erection. And then, his hands swept up to cup the weight of her breasts, his thumbs found her nipples, and he began to massage them…in soft, arousing circles.

Napolean Mondragon had waited an unfathomable lifetime for this moment.

For this woman.

For the refrain that continued to rise from his soul.

And as their passion grew deeper, the timeless song became richer…and purer…until a distinct set of lyrics began to emerge—

"I'll be your moonlight in the night;

I'll make everything all right.
I'll give you love; protect your heart; fulfill your dreams…
Can't you see I've always been
that imaginary friend,
the knight who still defends his treasured queen…"

Napolean sang the words directly into Brooke's ear, and then
he sought her mouth again, this time deepening his kiss with the
full breadth of his need.

His lips teased hers in tender, passionate play, even as his
tongue led her through a slow, erotic waltz. At times she
followed, at other times she led. But more and more, she began
to yield to his touch, moving instinctively against him with
burgeoning need.

His song grew with her desire…

"And when time has come and gone,
countless settings of the sun,
my love will be the wind beneath your wings…
As we soar beneath the skies,
I'll live a lifetime in your eyes;
the destiny *who charmed an ancient king."*

He trembled from the restraint it took to complete the
song…

"Won't you listen to your heart,
for the truth lies in your soul…
in the passion that we share—
feel the hunger as it grows,
and come into my arms…
Oh, come into my arms."

Brooke gasped, breathless, her hands moving longingly over
Napolean's body. She traced his arms, his shoulders, his
thighs…until he involuntarily growled into her mouth and
pushed her back against the bed, blanketing her body with his.
In an effort to draw him closer, she encircled his shoulders with
her arms, pressed her breasts against his chest, and coiled her
legs around his hips.

Barely clinging to his sanity, Napolean Mondragon sent up a

BLOOD POSSESSION

silent prayer of thanks to the gods.

BLOOD POSSESSION

silent prayer of thanks to the gods.

twenty-four

The male sang like an angel, kissed like a demon, and stirred Brooke's passion with an intensity she had never known in all her life.

Desperate to feel his skin against hers, she grasped at his shirt and tugged the hem free from his jeans. When he swiftly pulled the garment over his head—revealing that immaculate, chiseled chest—Brooke's breath left her lungs with a whoosh. Her lips parted in admiration, and her mouth fell, temporarily, open.

This wasn't a man.

This wasn't a vampire.

This was a finely honed work of art...

Every muscle, every angle, every strong plane was perfectly formed as if sculpted from clay—molded beneath the very hands of God. Napolean Mondragon was absolutely magnificent. His skin. His coloring. His utter...maleness.

Brooke's womb constricted like a tightened fist, and a fiery heat pulsed between her legs. Heaven help her, she was aching for him. Her body was on fire. As strong hands gently slid the silk straps from her shoulders, exposing her breasts to the cool air, she twisted on the bed and fought not to squirm beneath him: She didn't want to writhe in supplication like one of his subjects, begging to feel his unleashed power, desperate to have him inside of her.

But she was.

And the intensity of her longing was unsettling.

His warm mouth closed over her nipple, and she almost cried out. What in the name of his species—their species—was he doing with his tongue? His teeth? She felt the slow drag of his fangs lightly scoring her skin, and she wanted to arch into him, force him to take her, beg him to just do...*something*...

271

BLOOD POSSESSION

More.

Bite her?

The primal thought startled her at first, but as her nipple stretched—as Napolean took it deeper and deeper into the warm cavity of his mouth—Brooke lost all ability to think rationally. His erection had grown huge—solid, long, and thick beneath his jeans—and it was now pressing hard against her stomach. A brief pang of fear disturbed her passion as she wondered if making love to Napolean might be...painful. After all, the man wasn't large—he was enormous: And just where had he been keeping all of that, anyway?

Determined to appease her curiosity, she reached down to tug on the zipper of his 559's. With a sharp inhale, he gently pushed her hand aside and then hastily wrenched the denim from his hips, kicking his snug boxer-briefs and his heavy black boots off along with the jeans. The sundry pile hit the floor with a thud, and Brooke smiled.

Despite his intimidating size—or perhaps because of it—she groaned at the feel of his bare erection directly against her stomach. It felt like tempered steel, iron sheathed in fine satin— a jeweled sword encased in silk, crowned with a glorious, thick head—and she wanted the silk nightgown gone.

Now.

In spite of her blatant, growing desire, Napolean kept up the torture: He continued to torment her breasts with ever-imaginative machinations. His hands molded, caressed, and fondled. His mouth tasted, suckled, and lavished. His teeth grazed, nipped, and teased—until the ecstasy became unbearable. Crying out, Brooke grasped at his thick mane of hair and tugged, pulling him fiercely to her mouth. She needed him like she had never needed...anything.

"Oh gods, Napolean!" She was almost crying.

Crying.

What was he doing to her?

"Please," she whimpered.

His deep, throaty growl betrayed his satisfaction at hearing her utter the word. "Please what, *Iubita mea*?" he purred.

She panted in response, and they scooted further onto the bed. He sat up and knelt over her body, his massive erection standing so tall and proud, teasing her with its promise of pleasure, and then slowly, maddeningly, he released a sharp talon from his right index finger and cut through her nightgown and panties. He parted the silk from her body like a man unwrapping an expensive present at Christmas, and then he just stared.

Closed his eyes.

Moaned…a guttural cross between a purr and a snarl, crazy-making in its glory, magnificent in its raw, uninhibited hunger.

He was pure, primal perfection.

Everything she had ever imagined a dream lover could be and more. And in this state, it actually hurt to look at him. She reached up to touch his striking face, to trace his harshly perfect mouth.

Slowly licking his lips, he drew her finger into its warmth, and then he nicked the tip with his fangs—on purpose.

She gasped and drew back her hand, but her heart raced with arousal…and anticipation.

There was nothing playful left in his eyes now—just a stark, animal hunger: a need so primitive that it practically radiated from his pores.

Brooke swallowed hard and watched as Napolean's fangs extended from the crown of his mouth, his arousal grew to an impossible length, and his eyes began to glow a deep, coral red.

She held herself still, mesmerized by his power, absorbed in rapt fascination by his…splendor.

And then he buried his face between her breasts once again and took torturous turns pleasuring one, then the other, until he finally began to work his way down her ribs to her waist…then lower still…

His tongue took its first taste of her core, and she screamed and bucked beneath him, her body rising off the bed. He held her down with primitive male satisfaction, anchoring her hips to the mattress with arms as strong as a vise as he gratified her with his mouth.

After the third orgasm, Brooke began to weep.

Real…inexhaustible…tears.

He had managed to bring her to climax again and again, producing a greater need for release each successive time, until at last, he had stirred a hunger so fierce that nothing would slake it but the joining of their bodies.

It was beyond teasing.

It was pure, unadulterated torture.

When, at last, she couldn't stand it any longer, she clutched his arms and dug her nails into his skin. "Why are you doing this?" she whimpered, beginning to feel foolish.

"Doing what?" he asked in a spirited, husky tone, his eyes boring into hers with deep, feral hunger.

"You know what," she whispered. "Teasing me…denying me." She groaned against his chest.

Napolean growled deep in his throat, and then he slowly rose up over her body until he was suspended directly above her. "I'm not trying to torture you, *Iubita mea*. I only want—"

His voice cut off.

Brooke held his face in her hands and stared into his luminous eyes. "You want what, Napolean? Tell me now because I'll never survive this torture."

He shook his head, and then he rose up to kneel above her. He lifted her legs, placed them gently over his shoulders, and then, while massaging the backs of her thighs, he gradually pulled her forward until the head of his shaft pressed hard against her core.

Brooke's heart stopped beating as she measured his warmth and his size. He was hard as a spear and slick with the first drops of pleasure. She held her breath then…waiting. When nothing happened, she whispered, "What! What is it?"

The look in his eyes told her he was teetering on the edge of control. "You are mine," he ground out between gritted teeth. "Say it."

She felt the large, blunt head of his shaft prodding against her core, vying for entry, and she could hardly gather her thoughts, let alone speak. Napolean looked positively possessed with lust and passion.

And love…

Was that really possible?

Her heart opened completely then, and she knew her body would follow. "I'm yours," she whispered.

His hips ground against her in a harsh circle, and he slid inside, stretching her a glorious several inches before stopping once again. His powerful thighs trembled from the exertion it took to restrain his invasion. "Say it louder, Brooke." He bit down on his bottom lip. *"Mean it."* There was a harsh, almost guttural desperation in his voice, and all at once, she understood…

This man had a lived a solitary existence for longer than she could conceive of.

Forever.

He had carried the weight of his people on his shoulders in stoic silence, and he had seen to everyone's needs but his own, always putting the concerns of others first. He had protected the Vampyr from both outward and inward threats, leading his subjects through radical changes in time, place, and ideology…without anyone there to stand at his side.

Or return the favor.

His power was so immense that all who knew him feared him, making it virtually impossible for him to freely express his wants and needs.

To openly share his life.

This was the first time Napolean had ever had a place of refuge or a haven of pleasure, and he needed to know that it belonged to him…

And him, alone.

"I'm yours, Napolean." Her voice was thick with conviction.

He blinked several times in quick succession, and she knew he was fighting to hold back tears.

"Forever and always until the end of time," she added in a

BLOOD POSSESSION

whisper. And then she reached haphazardly into his mind, blindly trying to draw information from his memory in a desperate attempt to find a way to tell him what she felt in his native tongue: "*Regele meu frumos si neinfricat.*"

She hoped she had said it right: *My fearless, beautiful king.*

Napolean dropped his head and surged forward, driving deep into her welcoming heat. A low moan escaped his throat as his shoulders tightened, his head fell back, and he began to thrust in a soulful rhythm.

Brooke cried out as the heavenly sensation enveloped her. At the overwhelming satisfaction of being filled so deeply by so much raw power. And then, Napolean nuzzled her neck; his lips found her pulse; and his mouth formed a tight seal directly above her carotid artery.

Brooke braced herself.

She knew what was coming next.

The one thing she had feared the most—and anticipated the most—ever since she had learned what Napolean was.

Ever since she had learned what it meant to be his *destiny.*

The bite didn't come.

At least not how she expected.

To Brooke's surprise, he released the seal—almost as if he had changed his mind— and began to kiss her sweetly … reverently … along her vein, descending ever so slowly toward her collarbone.

Then lower still.

Until he paused, perched just above her left breast, raised his head, and met her impassioned gaze with a fierce, feral hunger of his own.

Their eyes locked in something so primal—so ancient and fundamental—that it robbed her of breath.

And then he bit her.

Not in the throat.

Not in the carotid artery.

But right through the soft flesh of her breast—penetrating her heart in one swift, almost serpentine motion.

276

Tessa Dawn

The orgasm that tore through Brooke's body was positively mind-numbing. She was certain every male and female in Dark Moon Vale heard her scream, and she prayed that Napolean had used his nearly celestial power—as she suspected—to keep the baby sleeping.

She tried hard to be quiet, but she just couldn't suppress her pleasure.

The climax wouldn't stop.

As long as Napolean's mouth tugged at her heart, her body continued to shatter into a million pieces. It contracted and released in powerful waves of ecstasy. It vibrated—almost violently—as if there were a million bolts of electricity pulsating through her core...all at once.

She writhed and bucked and cried out. She ripped at the sheets, pulled his hair, and scored his back with her fingernails, but he still continued to drink...taking long, drugging pulls like a man possessed until, at last, he had taken his fill.

Until it was crystal clear to Brooke that he was not, in fact, human but a powerful, dominant male—an *amazing* preternatural being—claiming every aspect of the female he called his own. Demanding nothing less than her absolute surrender.

"Yes, yes...yes," she whimpered as tears of release poured down her cheeks. "Oh gods, yes..."

Napolean reacted voraciously to her cries of pleasure: He retracted his fangs, drew her hips into a fierce, iron hold, and began to pump furiously—almost feverishly—into her body. The crimson essence of her heart stained his beautiful mouth as he panted and groaned, and then he threw back his glorious head and shouted his release as his powerful seed pumped over and over inside of her.

They both collapsed in exhaustion. And utter contentment.

Taking Brooke with him, Napolean rolled onto his back and held her tightly against his chest. Whispering soft words of endearment in her ear, he raised his free arm to his mouth and scored his wrist with his fangs, causing blood to trickle out in a steady rivulet.

BLOOD POSSESSION

"The heart is the sweetest of all delicacies," he purred, "but I'm afraid you may have lost too much blood." He placed his wrist to her mouth and gently stroked her hair with his other hand. "Drink, my love. Replenish your body with the strongest blood of our race."

Brooke knew that she should have been revolted.

That whatever part of her had once been human should have rebelled at the thought of drinking blood, but the feel of him, the smell of him, the power of him was just too addictive.

She wanted it all, and she wanted it forever.

As if she had done it a thousand times before, Brooke latched onto Napolean's wrist, formed a seal with her lips, and drank. As renewed vigor coursed through her body, she gently closed her eyes...and drifted off to sleep.

twenty~five

Kagen Silivasi swept his hands through his dark brown hair and stared at the date and time on the stainless-steel clock: *Sunday, 12:05 p.m.* His youngest brother, Nachari, rested peacefully beneath the starched white linens of the adjustable hospital bed—in fact, Nachari looked almost too tranquil, too lifeless—and Kagen had the overwhelming urge to check his vital signs...again.

But he already knew what they would say.

Heart rate, steady. Blood pressure, good. Respirations—even.

They would be the exact same as they had been five minutes ago.

And five minutes before that...

He rose from his bedside chair and began pacing.

"Why don't you sit down, Kagen," Marquis grumbled from the back of the room. He copped a lean against the far wall—for all intents and purposes, he looked calm and relaxed—but Kagen knew his eldest brother was a powder keg ready to go off at the slightest provocation.

"I've got too much energy," Kagen argued. "I can't just sit here."

Nathaniel Silivasi, who was seated on the opposite side of Nachari's bed, shifted impatiently in his chair. He crossed and uncrossed his legs at least three times as if he couldn't get comfortable. "Both of you need to go and get some air," he suggested.

"And leave Nachari here alone?" Kagen asked. His voice was sharp with irritation, his own temper far too fragile. "And what if he wakes up?" he snarled. "I don't think so, brother." Needing something to do with his hands, he headed toward the porcelain sink in the corner of the room.

BLOOD POSSESSION

Nathaniel refused to be baited. "It was just a suggestion."

"Yeah, well," Marquis said, "when we want some advice, we'll ask for it."

Kagen washed and dried his hands, tossing the crumpled paper towel into the wastebasket. He leaned casually against the counter and stared at Nathaniel, who rested his elbows on his knees and intertwined his fingers in order to form a chin rest. Kagen thought his twin looked tired: His dark, shadowy eyes— as deep as the night and just as troubled—were heavy with concern. And fatigue.

"So, this is how we're going to play this?" Nathaniel asked, speaking to no one in particular.

"Play what?" Marquis snapped.

Nathaniel met Marquis's steely gaze. "Deal with this … tragedy."

The room fell silent.

"By tearing into each other…because there's no one else to go after," Nathaniel added.

Marquis pushed off the wall and walked to the foot of the bed; he covered the ground in two even strides. "I'm not the Master Healer—the one who said he could bring him back. Give me someone to kill, and I'll handle it. Unfortunately, Nachari needs a doctor."

Kagen's fangs shot from his mouth with deadly intent. He felt his normally dark brown eyes flash with heat, and he knew they were glowing a deep, crimson red. "What the hell is your problem, Marquis?" He came within mere inches of the Ancient Master Warrior's face, his muscles twitching in anticipation as they stood nose to nose. "That's a hell of thing for you to say to me!"

Nathaniel jumped up from his chair. "Whoa…whoa…my brothers…"

Marquis held up his hand and took a step back, a rare sign of retreat—and respect—offered in the heat of the moment. "Forgive me, Kagen." He grabbed two fistfuls of his own hair and tugged in frustration. "I don't know what I'm saying." The words had barely left his mouth when he pounded an iron fist into the back wall of the room, sending drywall and metal splintering in all directions.

The clinic was a fortified stone structure—a virtual fortress excavated from solid rock—covered in drywall and plaster only to give the appearance of being a normal, aesthetically pleasing building. Knowing that the sons of Jadon were directly connected to the earth through their powerful emotions—that an intense bout of anger, rage…or grief…could set off anything from an earthquake to a flood—the clinic had been carefully constructed out of the side of the red cliffs in an effort to contain the intense fluctuations of energy.

Marquis's fist was broken and bleeding as he drew it back—only to slam it home again.

Nathaniel moved swiftly…but carefully. He placed one firm hand on Marquis's shoulder and another on his straining bicep to stop him from slamming it home a third time. He opened his mouth to speak, and then he closed it. Apparently, he knew better than to say anything that might further set Marquis off. No doubt, he had no desire to trade places with the wall.

Kagen couldn't let the subject go that easily. "Do you really blame me for this, Marquis?"

Marquis growled. He shrugged free of Nathaniel's grip and went back to leaning casually against the wall, ignoring the steady droplets of blood that fell from his broken hand onto the sanitary tile floor. Despite the casual pose, he looked like a tightly packed stick of dynamite, all lit up with sizzling fire, burning on a finite fuse, and destined to explode.

"Do you?" Kagen asked again.

Marquis waved his good hand in a dismissive gesture. "No."

Kagen wasn't convinced. "Brother, I have to know if—"

"*No.*" Marquis's eyes met Kagen's in an apologetic stare. They were pained with frustration and ripe with regret. "I should have never said that." He shifted his weight from one foot to another. "If anything, I blame myself." He let out a deep breath. "Hell, Kagen. I just want to kill someone. But not you—never you."

Nathaniel seemed to relax a bit. He took his seat and stared at the quiet body lying so peacefully on the bed. "What the fuck went wrong?" The question was rhetorical.

Kagen returned to Nachari's side. He sat down on the bed, reached for his wrist, and began to take his pulse...again. *He had to do something.* "I don't know, but whatever it is...it's really, really wrong. He looks so serene, but he's not at peace."

"Do you think the dark lord somehow...got him?" Marquis asked, his voice betraying his dread.

Nathaniel whistled low beneath his breath and shuddered. "I don't know. I'm trying not to think about it, but did you guys see Napolean's face Friday night?"

They both nodded.

"He felt something. He sensed something—I'm sure of it. And whatever it was, it was too awful to speak of."

Kagen recorded Nachari's pulse on his chart, wondering why the hell he was bothering with such useless and redundant behaviors: Had he totally lost his grip on reality?

Marquis pumped his fist, testing his broken fingers. "Someone has to go after him."

"Go after him?" Nathaniel asked.

"Yeah," Marquis answered, "follow him into the spirit world. Maybe if you or I took Niko or Jankiel with us—"

"Nachari might be a wizard," Nathaniel interrupted, "but he's one of the strongest fighters I know—a true warrior in his own right. Whatever happened, if he could have fought his way out of it, he would have."

Marquis grumbled. "He is not my equal, Nathaniel. Nor yours."

Nathaniel shook his head. "You're going to die, too, brother?"

Marquis shrugged. "If that's what it takes."

Nathaniel smiled then, although the light never reached his eyes. He gestured toward the door. "Your wife is right outside that door, Marquis, and your son is home with his nursemaid.

Would you leave Ciopori without a mate? Would you allow Nikolai to grow up like Nachari and Shelby did—without a father to teach him?"

Marquis threw his hands up and sighed. "Then what are we going to do?"

Nathaniel frowned and looked away. He grasped Nachari's hand and clutched it in a grip that was probably too tight, but Kagen wasn't about to say anything. "Where are you, brother?" Nathaniel whispered. "It's time to come back."

Kagen scrubbed a hand over his face. He had to get the hell out of there—he was coming apart.

Time to come back?

It was way past time to come back!

It had been four days now, and while Kagen was working overtime to keep oxygen flowing to Nachari's brain, to force his lungs to expand and contract with air, he still knew the truth of the matter: Technology—and technology, alone—was all that was keeping Nachari...viable. He wasn't alive. His spirit no longer inhabited his body. And the moment his family stopped forcing the issue, they would have to face the inevitable.

"Damnit!" Kagen shouted, jumping up and heading for the door. "I've got to get some air." He tried to ignore the stunned faces of his brothers as he reached for the doorknob. It would be the first time since Nachari...had left his body...that Kagen had left Nachari's side. And his outburst was certain to betray a deeper truth: As Nachari's brother—and his doctor—Kagen was losing hope. "I'll send Katia in behind me," he murmured, trying to salvage their confidence. "I'll only be gone a few minutes." One glance at his brothers' faces told him he had failed: Nathaniel's skin was pale, and Marquis's eyes were stricken with horror.

Neither brother responded.

Pretending not to notice, Kagen sauntered out the door.

To hell with it!

He was grateful to be out of the stifling room.

Unfortunately, the moment he stepped across the threshold,

a new set of challenges awaited him in the receiving area: His brothers' mates, Jocelyn and Ciopori, immediately rose to their feet; and Nachari's young protégé, Braden Bratianu, who was curled up in a chair in the corner all by himself, looked up at him through bloodshot eyes.

No one spoke a word, but their fear was palpable.

"Nothing's changed," Kagen said in a rush. "Nachari is still...stable. I just need some air."

Jocelyn shot a sideways glance at Ciopori, and he knew that the females were interpreting his behavior the same way as his brothers had...

Hell and damnation, he did not want the women to lose hope.

He did not want Braden to lose hope.

He was running a hundred miles an hour to stay ahead of his own fears so that *he* didn't lose hope.

But *gods*, he was tired. The situation was untenable, yet he couldn't give up.

Nachari couldn't leave them.

Not now. Not so soon after Shelby. Not ever! He would keep his body breathing for a hundred years if he had to—

For the sake of Auriga, what was wrong with him? He was seriously messed up.

"Healer?" Ciopori's lyrical voice swept over him in a soothing caress as she took several steps forward and gently laid her hand on his shoulder.

"I'm fine," he grumbled, eyeing the clinic's front door. He had to get out of there. Now.

"Brother," she said more firmly, "look at me." Her soft golden eyes sparkled with an unearthly amber light. "Let me see you, Kagen." She sent a healing wave of energy so powerful into his body that it almost shook him where he stood, and he was unable to disengage from her spell. All at once, her subtle gaze became penetrating, and a deep, unspoken truth passed between them: Ciopori saw the extent of Kagen's fear—the depth of his hopelessness—and she closed her eyes, breaking the connection.

Does Marquis realize? she asked on a private telepathic line, no doubt wanting to shield Braden from their conversation.

Kagen felt a strange, stinging sensation in his eyes and wondered what it was—surely, not tears? He stilled his body and forced himself to breathe evenly—draw a slow breath in, let a deep breath out—careful to contain his volatile emotions. *Realize what, sister?* he asked, biting his bottom lip so hard he tasted blood. *There is nothing to realize. Nachari is coming back, and that is all.*

Kagen, Ciopori whispered compassionately in his mind, *it's okay if—*

I said, That is all.

He leveled a harsh, unyielding glare at her, and then he turned toward the tall, slender nurse standing quietly in the corner. "I'll be back shortly, Katia." He spoke in an eerily quiet voice and motioned her inside the room with his head. "Stay with Nachari until I return." Gently removing Ciopori's hand from his shoulder, he regarded her one last time with a cordial nod. "I'll see you later, sister," he said.

And then he walked briskly out the front door.

Jocelyn Silivasi watched the brief interplay between Ciopori and Kagen with a heavy heart. "Oh, God," she murmured as Ciopori sat back down.

Ciopori nodded. "Indeed."

"They're all coming completely apart?" She phrased it as a question, but she already knew the answer. Nathaniel had been a bastion of strength, but even he was certain to unravel soon if Nachari didn't—

"What?" Braden asked in a timid voice. "What is it? What isn't Kagen telling us?"

Ciopori drew her shoulders back like the regal princess she was. She raised her chin in a gesture of utter confidence. "Nothing at all, Braden." Damn, she was good. "Kagen just needed some air. Nachari is fine."

BLOOD POSSESSION

The boy nestled deeper into the huge leather chair. He sniffled and quickly turned his head away, not wanting the females to see that he had been crying—as if anyone had missed that fact. In an effort to play along, Jocelyn glanced around the waiting room, pretending she hadn't noticed the tearstained tracks on his cheeks.

As she eyed their surroundings with clinical interest, she observed that the normally warm, welcoming space seemed somehow cold all of a sudden. Sure, the pliant leather armchairs still sat in perfect, peaceful arrangements—cozy with their matching ottomans on a slate-stone floor, rich in rustic textures, and soft with muted earth tones—but their welcome was as muted as their color. And yes, sparse but tasteful art still hung within expensive frames in perfect increments on the clinic walls—displaying scenic pictures of snowcapped mountains, forest trails, and rushing waterfalls—but their once-tranquil appeal was noticeably absent. A non-obtrusive, flat-screen TV, an inviting beverage table, and a guest computer station were still arranged in perfect order; but there was no order to their lives anymore. Her new family was in a freefall of uncertainty, and if Nachari didn't recover, they might not ever know peace again.

Feeling restless and fidgety, Jocelyn glanced once again at Braden: He had finally managed to restrain his tears. She sighed, knowing that Braden's effort was also Ciopori's burden. Her sister-in-law, as it were, had been gathering and shielding Braden's energy for days. Although the boy was still young—and his powers were by and large untapped—Braden possessed some incredible spiritual gifts, and his attachment to Nachari was…elemental, for lack of a better word. Even inside the fortified clinic, Braden's chaotic, unchecked emotions had the ability to cause great havoc on the land around them, and that was why Ciopori was keeping such a close eye on him.

It was also why both she and Ciopori had chosen to leave their infants at home with their nursemaids: Emotion was simply too high—too raw—there were too many unknown variables playing out in real time. If young Braden, with all of his power—

286

or hell, even one of the Ancients—actually lost it, the women didn't want the added concern of protecting their children from the fallout. Not that their mates would ever hurt them, but the Vampyr were intrinsically connected to the earth, and Jocelyn had seen firsthand what too much raw emotion could do.

Dismissing the thought, she stood and headed toward the refreshment center. Despite being converted nearly two months ago, she still enjoyed an occasional indulgence—she might as well make herself another cup of coffee. She glanced at Ciopori. "Are you worried about Marquis?"

Ciopori nodded almost indiscernibly. "The noise we heard. I felt a surge in Marquis's energy; I am certain he hurt someone or something...most likely himself."

Jocelyn sighed. "It's hard...not to go in there right now."

"It is," Ciopori agreed, "but I fear that if they do not come together in this difficult time—find a way to draw strength from one another—those bonds will be severely injured."

Jocelyn shook her head. "I don't know. I've never known any family that loved each other more."

Ciopori brushed a piece of lint off her blouse. "It isn't a matter of love; it is a matter of pain tolerance...grief tolerance. This is more than any one of them can bear alone. Perhaps more than they can bear together."

Jocelyn couldn't stand it another second.

She had to reach out to Nathaniel.

Baby, she whispered soothingly on their private telepathic bandwidth, *how are you holding up?*

Nathaniel sighed—a deep, slow, exasperated exhale. *Ah, tiger-eyes; this is...so hard.*

Jocelyn swallowed a lump in her throat. *I know. Kagen is a mess. How is Marquis?*

He broke his hand against the wall, and he hasn't even thought to heal it yet.

Jocelyn clenched her eyes shut. *Oh God, do you need me to come in there?*

Nathaniel chuckled, a laugh absent of joy. *Always,* Iubita

BLOOD POSSESSION

mea. *I need you...always. But give us a little more time. When Kagen returns, we are going to talk...perhaps pray.*

Even though Nathaniel couldn't see her, Jocelyn nodded instinctively.

Angel? he said.

I'm here, she assured him. *Just outside the door. I love you, Nathaniel.*

Mmm, he purred, and the sound was like soft velvet caressing her ears. *And I, you, angel.*

Just then, the clinic doors flew open and a red-headed whirlwind in three-inch heels stormed through the entrance. "Hey, Joss. Hey, C. What the hell is up with Kagen?" Kristina Riley-Silivasi stood in the doorway in a short pink miniskirt and matching pumps, her Corvette keys still dangling in her hands. "Is Nachari okay?"

Kristina was the de facto sister of the Silivasi brothers after having been mated to Marquis for less than a week in what could only be described as an utter disaster: The Dark Ones had used black magic to gain the assistance of the dark lord Ocard in reversing the Blood Curse in order to fool Marquis—basically, they had switched Kristina and Ciopori, leading Marquis to believe that the wild redhead was his *destiny.* Luckily, Nachari had figured it out before Marquis and Kristina had consummated the union—before she had become pregnant with his twins—and they were able to reverse it in time. Unfortunately, Marquis had already converted her, unknowingly, under the protection of the dark lord, and she had become a full-fledged vampire: It had been too late for Kristina to go back to her human life, although, truth be told, it hadn't been the greatest life to begin with.

Knowing that Kristina shared their blood—and their vampiric existence—the Silivasi brothers had adopted her as their sister, and Marquis had agreed to take care of her financially for the rest of her life. And the rest, as they say, is ongoing history.

"Kagen is trippin' for real," Kristina explained, gesturing wildly with her arms. "I walked up to him and was like, *Yo Kagen,* and he just looked right through me. So I was like, *dude, do you not hear me talking to you?* And he practically yelled, *Nachari is fine!* I was like, *okay, Mr. Hyde…*shit!"

Jocelyn smiled. "He's just overwhelmed. Nachari is the same."

Kristina nodded. Then she walked right past the women, went straight to Braden, and knelt down in front of him. "Hey, Bray," she whispered in a voice so kind it could hardly be recognized as hers. "How's my favorite little brother?"

Braden smiled briefly, then shrugged. "Okay, I guess. Nachari still hasn't…" His voice faltered, and he didn't try to finish the sentence.

Kristina reached for his hand. "Yeah, I know. But that's okay. He's probably just busy somewhere…you know…out there in the spirit world kicking some serious demon ass. You know Nachari: If he's having a good time, then we're just gonna have to wait."

Her words brought a genuine smile to the boy's face, illuminating his soft burnt-sienna eyes. "You think so, Kristina?"

She nodded convincingly. "Yeah, I do. For real." She stroked Braden's hand lovingly. "He's not gone. Not Nachari. No way."

Jocelyn looked at Ciopori and smiled. "Some wonders never cease."

"How very true," Ciopori said. "It is odd—the relationship she has with the boy—although, I suppose not so much when you consider how much time she spends at Nachari's place." Her face constricted with sorrow when she spoke his name. "I imagine there is somewhat of a bond there as well."

Jocelyn nodded. "Yeah, I think so."

Kristina, for all her crude, elementary, and in-your-face ways, had made a strong impact on everyone in the family, including Marquis. Maybe the time they had spent together had meant something after all; although, whatever Marquis and Kristina had shared, it was nothing compared to the love he felt for the beautiful woman standing in front of her.

Jocelyn sighed. "I kind of like her myself."

BLOOD POSSESSION

Ciopori laughed, then. "Yes, me too."

Kristina turned around and rolled her eyes. "Newsflash, everyone: I'm not human anymore. I can hear you!"

Jocelyn and Ciopori laughed.

Just then the door to Nachari's room opened, and Katia stuck her head out. "Excuse me, but Marquis is about to inject some venom in his hand to heal it. However, before he seals it up, I would like to remove some metal fragments that are lodged in the bone. Would one of you mind fetching a pair of tweezers from the basement supply closet for me? There aren't any in here, and I can't leave Nachari unattended—"

"Just leave the damn things in there!" Jocelyn heard Marquis grumble from inside the room.

She cringed.

Ciopori shook her head. "Try to be agreeable, warrior," she called, loud enough for him to hear her. He responded with a deep, throaty growl, and she smiled. Placing her hand on Jocelyn's arm, she winked at the nurse. "Jocelyn and I will both go fetch the tweezers—we could use the exercise, anyhow."

"Speak for yourself, sister," Nathaniel mumbled, his witty voice echoing from inside the room.

Ciopori huffed. "That is not what I meant!" She gave Jocelyn an apologetic glance. "I didn't mean you needed exercise—"

"I know what you meant," Jocelyn teased. "Where do we find the tweezers, Katia?"

"At the end of the hall, through the last door on the right. They're in the glass cabinet on the third shelf down."

"Got it," Jocelyn replied. Turning to Ciopori, she took her by the hand and hauled her in the direction of the stairs. "Come on, C," she said, mimicking Kristina, "let's go for a short walk." Raising her voice, she added, "We could *both* use the exercise, anyway."

She heard Nathaniel's chuckle as the door to Nachari's room swung shut.

twenty~six

Tiffany stood directly behind David Reed as he shimmied open the back door to the clinic, making fairly easy work of it—either vampires were not very concerned with high-quality locks, or they were not very afraid of intruders. She had a sick feeling it was the latter.

Having arrived with David and five other soldiers from the vampire-hunting militia about fifteen minutes ago, the team had been forced to wait while a brown-haired male wandered further away from the property after speaking briefly to a red-haired woman. Tiffany didn't know for sure what a vampire looked like—she had only seen the ones that had taken Brooke—but watching the way the tall, handsome male moved, the barely leashed power that radiated from his body and the easy gait of his steps, which mimicked a lion on the prowl, she had no doubt that he was one of them. The militia had gone to great lengths to mask their scent with a special blend of herbs created just to fool vampires, and then David's team had moved with an uncanny stealth and grace all their own.

"Shh," David cautioned. He held a finger to his mouth and then ushered her ahead, gesturing for her to enter the building just behind his men. Apparently, he was going to take the rear. "If there's anyone here, we're prepared for them; but keep in mind, they have incredible hearing." He whispered the words in a barely audible voice. "I'd rather catch one of them by surprise than be caught by surprise myself. Understand?"

Tiffany swallowed hard and nodded, noting the sweat beading on David's forehead. They were prepared—beyond prepared—with their dangerous cache of weapons: His team had brought tranquilizer guns, each filled with enough tranquilizer to bring down an elephant in three seconds flat; semiautomatic nine-millimeters, each one loaded with a full magazine of diamond-tipped bullets; lethally sharpened stakes; and long, curved machetes used for...beheading. She shook her head in disbelief. She had to admit she had been impressed by the arms they carried—she couldn't even imagine what a diamond-tipped bullet must cost.

Just the same, it was hard to believe they were really here—that all of this was really happening.

A part of her still insisted it wasn't real.

Yet she knew that it was.

Brooke had been gone for ten days now, and there was no mistaking what Tiffany had seen in her dream; there was no mistaking the similarities between the predatory male who had been walking outside of the clinic and the terrifying ... creature ... who had taken Brooke away the last night of the conference. Vampires were real. And her best friend was in the clutches of one now. She shivered and murmured a quick prayer, fingering one of the three crosses she was wearing. Sure, David had told her that the whole crosses and holy-water thing was a myth—one that might just get her killed if she relied on them—but she figured a little extra protection couldn't hurt. Better safe than sorry.

"Hang in there, Brooke," she whispered beneath her breath, "we're going to find something useful here today, and these men won't rest until you're back home safely. Neither will I."

They had just entered the building and were walking down a long, narrow corridor, when they heard a door open at the far end of the hall. The voices of two women carried through the hollow space, and two distinct sets of footsteps could be heard descending a staircase. David held up two fingers. With eyes as sharp as an eagle's, he pointed to the right, signaling for two of his men to take cover in a nearby room. He directed the remaining three to the left, just across the hall, and then he backed into a doorway, pulling Tiffany tight to his side and eyeing her with a stern warning: "Stay right here. No matter what happens, do not confront one of the vampires." He withdrew his tranquilizer gun and held it up against his chest. "If things get ugly, get the hell out of here…as far away as you can."

Tiffany's eyes grew wide. "You said there wouldn't be any vampires around, and if there were, they would be sleeping at midday."

David shrugged. "Yeah, well, I guess I was wrong."

Tiffany tried to calm her racing heart. Panicking wouldn't do her any good. She tuned into the hushed murmurs of the women and listened: They sounded relaxed, like friends…normal. "What if they're human?" she asked, her heart suddenly sinking into her stomach. "You're not going to shoot first and ask questions later, are you?"

David stared right through her. "If you wanna ask one of those things to identify itself before you strike, that's your business; but I prefer to live to see tomorrow." He held his arm out across her body and pushed her further back in the doorway. "Now, shut the hell up, or we're both going to die."

Tiffany frowned. *What the hell had she gotten herself into?*

The voices grew louder as the women exited the stairwell and began to walk down the corridor. Shit, they seemed to be walking this way—coming all the way to the end.

David shifted the tranquilizer gun to his left hand and slowly withdrew a long, sharpened wooden stake. He nodded at one of the soldiers across the way, and some kind of unspoken communication passed between them: a plan of action.

Good God, was he going to try and stake one of the women?

This was insane!

These were *normal* people—not vampires—and in her desperation to find Brooke, she had all but joined a fanatical cult.

Tiffany was just about to turn and run—get the hell out of there and away from these overzealous nut-jobs—when the hair on the back of her neck stood up. She stopped and held her breath, listening to her intuition. She didn't know exactly what it was, but something was off—and it felt very much like the night Brooke had been taken.

BLOOD POSSESSION

There *was* something different about these women.

She backed up as far as she could, trying to mold herself to the door—make herself invisible—as she continued to hold her breath. The women drew closer, caught up in the rhythm of their conversation...completely unaware of what was waiting for them.

As the first of the two passed in front of the doorway, Tiffany's eyes met hers in a frozen moment—it was as if everything ground to a sudden halt and then began again in slow motion: The woman was positively stunning, and her eyes were almost unnatural. She had golden pupils with amber-hued lights dancing in the centers, appearing very much like sunlight reflecting through diamonds. Her long, raven hair swayed as she walked, and her face was almost...antique...in its beauty, as if not of this time.

The woman's eyes grew wide, and she started to turn and run, but not before David bounded out of the doorway. He raised his arm high above his head, grasped the wooden stake solidly in his hand, and threw his entire weight into the thrust, impaling the beautiful woman right over her left breast. And then he gripped the end of the wood with one palm and used the other to drive it home.

The woman gasped and stumbled backward. Stunned, she slowly looked down at her chest and stared in disbelief at the protruding wooden object. When she staggered back a few more steps, the second woman rushed forward and caught her.

Shocked and incredulous, the second woman slowly lowered her friend to the ground. *"Ciopori...Ciopori..."* The second woman kept repeating her name...and then it was like someone flipped a switch in the second woman's head, and full recognition of the situation suddenly kicked in. The woman went into some deep, instinctual mode—like auto-pilot on an airplane—and the calm, focused look on her face said it all: This woman was no stranger to combat, and their small group was in trouble.

Evan Turner, one of the three soldiers hiding on the left—

and the closest man to the second woman—shot out of the opposite doorway with a similar stake in hand, but before he could connect with the pretty, brown-haired female—drive the stake in from behind—she spun around and delivered a lightning-fast roundhouse kick to his head.

Tiffany screamed as Evan's feet left the ground, his body slammed into the wall, and his skull imploded upon impact. The woman looked straight at her, and she took two steps back. Dear God, what had just been beautiful hazel eyes had turned a deep, coral red, and there was a low, unnatural rumble in the woman's throat. The two remaining soldiers shot out of the doorway in an effort to pin the woman where she stood, but she quickly bent down, swept Evan's gun out of its holster, and turned, while spraying the room with bullets at the same time. And then she did some sort of back flip—walking it off the freaking ceiling— as she landed further down the hall in the midst of the men and snapped one of their necks before he even saw her coming.

David released a tranquilizer then, scoring the woman directly in the shoulder. She pushed the remaining soldier off her and turned to face David, bringing the gun up in an expert, two-handed grip. She knew exactly what she was doing, but before she could squeeze the trigger, the two soldiers who had been hiding in the doorway to the right opened fire, unloading their magazines into her jerking body.

The remaining soldier from Evan's group hit the deck even as David snatched Tiffany by the waist, threw her to the ground, and covered her body in an effort to protect her from ricocheting bullets. And then, after what seemed like thirty seconds or so, the room was quiet.

"Is she dead?" the disheveled soldier from Evan's group asked. He sat up on his knees and eyed the second woman's body warily.

David scurried to his feet. "Hell no," he barked. "Neither one of them is dead." He dropped his tranquilizer gun and motioned toward the soldier's hip, where he kept a sheathed machete. "Take her head—and then her heart—before she regenerates!" He drew his own machete from its scabbard and motioned one of the soldiers to his right, forward. "Get over here, Roger." He held out the machete.

The short, stocky man walked quickly to his side. "Yes, sir?" He took the weapon from David.

"We don't have much time to case the place now; you finish this one, while Miss Matthews and I try to retrieve what we came for." He turned toward the only other remaining militia member. "Don, you stay here in the hall and keep a lookout."

Don reloaded his gun and nodded.

Roger looked down at the raven-haired beauty—the one the second woman had called Ciopori—and a slow, vindictive smile curved the corner of his mouth. "No worries, sir. This one is as good as dead."

Nathaniel Silivasi heard a woman scream in the basement of the clinic, but it wasn't Jocelyn or Ciopori. "What the hell—"

Before he could finish his sentence, there was a loud explosion. The sound of bone splintered off a wall, footsteps reverberated on the basement *ceiling*, and an utter explosion of gunfire erupted down below. His heart skipped a beat. "Marquis!"

The Ancient Master Warrior was already gone, dematerializing out of the room.

Nathaniel, Kagen, and Marquis materialized at the same time, each appearing at the bottom of the basement staircase. Although it felt like an eternity, in truth, it only took the males a fraction of a second to analyze the situation with all five of their senses—and take in all the details...

And what they saw stole the air from their lungs.

Ciopori was slumped over at the far end of the hall. She was lying on her side like a broken rag doll in a shallow pool of blood, and there was a thick wooden stake protruding out of her chest. The stake had penetrated all the way through the cavity to her back, and it stuck out from the rear like a macabre pole on a carousel. She appeared dead, yet less than six inches away, a human male stood over her with a garish, curved machete held tightly in his hand, preparing to do her further damage.

A second gunman stood in the middle of the corridor—his feet spaced evenly apart, a nine-millimeter semiautomatic in his right hand—like some sort of Johnny-come-lately prison guard patrolling the hall. He had a tight black skull-trim, and his weapon had been recently fired. With sweat trickling down his anxious brow, he stood at an even distance between Ciopori and—

Jocelyn.

Oh dear, goddess, no!

Nathaniel felt a cold surge of rage sweep over his body, and he had to force his mind to focus: Jocelyn was also lying in an unnatural heap in the middle of the hall. Her body was riddled with bullets, there was a red tranquilizer dart sticking out of her left shoulder, and a tall human male with a Mohawk was looming over her, his face distorted with hatred. The machete in the man's hand was raised high, held taut, and ready to swing. He also possessed a nine-millimeter that was tucked into the back of his waistband, and Nathaniel could still smell the gunpowder from its recent use. Nathaniel's body practically hummed with the need to spill the human's blood.

Both women were about to be beheaded.

Unwilling to risk the heartbeat it might take to get to his mate's side, Nathaniel waved his hand through the air and froze Jocelyn's assailant in place. Glaring at the flesh-and-bone statue, he threw back his head and roared his rage. His fangs punched out of his mouth with such force that his gums began to bleed as he stalked down the hall toward the breathing corpse about to behead his *destiny* in front of him.

Marquis moved just as swiftly.

In a series of movements so sudden they could hardly be seen, he materialized beside Ciopori, plunged an iron fist straight

BLOOD POSSESSION

through her attacker's solar plexus, clutched his spine with his fist, and pulled. In one harsh, angry tug, he tore the man's spinal column free from his body and tossed it aside, away from Ciopori. In a final moment of irony, the body remained upright—still standing, machete in hand—as if it had not yet recognized it was no longer living, and then it slumped to the ground in a lifeless pile. And Marquis kicked it aside.

Kagen approached the guard in the middle of the hall calmly. Too calmly.

His fangs remained retracted, his eyes a solid, deep brown. He didn't growl or snarl or make any threats; he simply strolled down the hall in a leisurely manner, smiling and licking his lips, until he stood like a lifelong friend in front of the alarmed human. "Good afternoon," he drawled pleasantly, as if welcoming the intruder into his home.

The human freaked out.

He shoved his gun into Kagen's ribs and began to unload a fresh magazine.

Kagen jerked in surprise…and then he laughed. "Well, I'll be damned; you've got diamond dust in those bullets." He waited until the magazine was empty, and then he reached down, palmed the hot piece of iron in his fist, and crumpled it like a piece of paper, tossing it to the side. He ran his fingers along the fresh wounds in his side. "How rude," he growled, leaning forward to speak directly in the man's ear. And then he held out his hand as if to make a formal introduction. "And you are?"

Petrified—and completely off balance—the human took his hand. "Uh…Donald."

Kagen gripped Donald's hand, smiling as he crushed the bones into dust.

The man's face grew pale, and he cried out in agony.

Kagen clucked his tongue three times and shook his head. "Shh, Donald—no need for all that drama." He lifted him by the neck, crushed his vocal cords, and then held him high in the air in front of him, dangling by the strength of one hand. "You see, this is my clinic—my home." He glanced at Ciopori and Jocelyn.

"And these are my sisters." His fangs elongated, dripping with lethal venom. "And you, sir, are not welcome." He drew back his arm and slammed the man's face into the side of the wall, flattening his head like a pancake. As he dropped the twitching body, he booted it to the ceiling, where it actually stuck for a couple of seconds before falling down.

Nathaniel thought very little about what he had just seen: His mind was too consumed in its own red haze of rage. He had reached the man with the Mohawk, unconsciously releasing him from his paralysis, and the human had dropped his machete, screamed like a girl, and started to run. Nathaniel had side-stepped in front of him to block his path.

Now, as they continued to do a back-and-forth dance, Nathaniel remained acutely—and only—aware that the fool was blocking his path to Jocelyn. As he stared absently at the *destiny* he loved more than his own life, lying injured and still on the floor just beyond the ridiculous human, his vision went blurry— a deep, hazy black—and then it slowly dialed back into focus.

He shook his head to clear the cobwebs. "I have neither the time nor the inclination to play with you, human." His voice sounded distant, even to his own ears. "I have never met anyone so eager to be killed, to suffer a slow, endless torment, yet I haven't the time to accommodate you." He smiled a hate-filled grin. "I tell you what; ask me for your death, and I will give it to you swiftly." Each word was punctuated on a feral hiss.

The human trembled in his boots, unable to reply. A quick glance into his mind told Nathaniel that the man was beyond coherent thought. He was in shock. And utterly desperate to live.

As if…

Shoving his way so hard into the human's brain that it instantly caused a migraine, Nathaniel implanted a powerful compulsion: "Beg me for your death *now*, and let us get on with it."

Clasping his ears with both hands, the man fell to his knees. "P…p…please…kill me, sir. I beg you."

Nathaniel bent over, picked up the man's dropped machete,

BLOOD POSSESSION

placed it in his right hand, and shoved him face-down on the floor. Pitching his voice in a deep lilt of persuasion, he whispered: "Do it yourself." When the human looked confused, he gestured at the machete. "Remove one body part at a time. Start with your feet and work your way up...but save the vital organs for last, lest you die too soon." He spat on the back of his neck. "Oh, and stack the pieces neatly in a pile...since you won't be around to clean up the mess." He shrugged. "I guess I changed my mind about killing you...*swiftly*."

As he stepped over the horrified human on his way to Jocelyn, he caught a glimpse of Marquis and Ciopori: His brother had just lifted his *destiny* into his arms and was about to examine her piercing, when they all heard the soft scrape of a chair coming from the supply room at the end of the hall.

"There are more of them?" Kagen asked, incredulous.

Nathaniel turned and snarled. "By the gods, we don't have time for these fools."

Marquis was shaking with the need to kill, but he stayed exactly where he was: Clearly, he wasn't about to leave Ciopori's side. "Kagen, find them—and bring them out alive." The tone of Marquis's voice brooked no argument as he glanced down at his mate and swiftly pulled the stake free from her chest. "The man I killed was not the one who did this." He placed his hand firmly over the wound and applied pressure to staunch the bleeding. "Whoever did this is mine."

Kagen nodded, turned on his heel, and started down the hall toward the supply room.

"Wait," Nathaniel called, his voice thick with anguish. "Let me go after them." He removed the tranquilizer from Jocelyn's shoulder and gathered her tight against his body, wrapping his warmth around her in a gentle embrace. "I don't trust myself to heal her right now." He realized how absurd that sounded. After all, how many battles had they been through? How many life-threatening wounds had they healed? But he just didn't care. This was not a hardened warrior from the house of Jadon. This was not even one of his beloved siblings.

Tessa Dawn

This was his *destiny*.

"Jocelyn needs you now, healer...right now," Nathaniel implored.

Kagen stopped abruptly and rushed to Jocelyn's side.

"Gods...there are so many bullet wounds," Nathaniel murmured, slowly lowering her back to the floor so Kagen could take over. He looked up at his twin and frowned. "She's losing so much blood. Too much blood. You have to stop the bleeding, Kagen—I want you to remove the bullets—*now*."

Kagen placed a firm, reassuring hand on Nathaniel's shoulder and nodded. "Then let me take her to surgery, Nathaniel. I can work far more efficiently upstairs." He inclined his head toward the supply room. "Tie up the captives; secure the clinic; and meet us up there."

For the first time, Nathaniel noticed Kagen's injuries as well. His twin's torso was littered with bullet wounds, diamond-encrusted bullet wounds, which had to burn like hell, not to mention sap his strength. Kagen had also lost a great deal of blood—and was still losing it—yet he acted as if nothing had happened. How was he still standing? "Can you work like this?" Nathaniel asked, ashamed that he hadn't considered his twin's health sooner.

Kagen nodded. "I am in no danger of passing out...at least not for a while. And the pain is tolerable."

Nathaniel knew that his twin was lying. He knew that it was only a deep, abiding love for his family that kept Kagen upright, and he also knew that Kagen would never accept assistance until the women were out of danger...and any further threat was eliminated: Kagen may have been a healer, but like all the Vampyr, the warrior's code was bred into their DNA.

Nathaniel met Kagen's eyes and held his gaze. And then he bowed his head, however indistinctly, and averted his eyes in a show of profound respect. "You honor me, brother." He reached down and took Jocelyn's hand in his own, gripping it with a fierce protectiveness. "Do not let her—"

"Don't even speak it," Kagen cut him off, his voice clear and

301

insistent. "Nathaniel Jozef Silivasi, her head is intact. Her heart is intact. You are in my clinic, and I have plenty of stored blood and venom—Marquis's venom, *Napolean's* venom. She will live."

Nathaniel nodded, but he didn't let go. "I know. It's just..."

Kagen's voice brushed gently against the warrior's mind in a private, intimate communication: *Nathaniel, there is no contingency in which your destiny leaves us this day. On the honor of the house of Jadon, I pledge this to you: She will live. I will heal her.*

Nathaniel swallowed hard and rocked back on his heels, releasing Jocelyn into Kagen's care. "Okay," he mumbled, "do not let her suffer, Kagen...block her pain."

Kagen smiled faintly. "I will care for her as you would."

Nathaniel nodded and looked down the hall toward Marquis and Ciopori. Marquis was bent low over Ciopori's chest, holding her in his massive arms like a boneless doll—her back sharply arched, his fangs full extended—as he furiously injected venom directly into her heart.

"Marquis?" Nathaniel called quietly.

She hasn't lost as much blood as Jocelyn, Marquis answered telepathically so that both brothers could hear. *The stake acted as a cork, blocking the flow. But the injury was to her heart, and that is very serious.*

Kagen stood up, hefting Jocelyn as if she weighed no more than a feather. "Was it punctured or was it severed?" he asked Marquis.

What do you mean? Marquis answered.

"Her heart: Was it severed from the chest cavity by the stake, or was it merely punctured?"

Merely? Marquis growled in anger.

Nathaniel sighed. "Marquis, please, answer the question: Kagen needs to know."

The heart is still attached, Marquis said.

"Good," Kagen said. "Then as awful as it looks, she is not critical. Continue to infuse her with venom until the opening repairs itself and all the wounds close. Then bring her upstairs to exam room three. I will have Katia attend to her, but odds are she will heal completely on her own."

Marquis growled his consent and continued pumping life-giving venom into his mate.

"I'll be with you shortly, my love," Nathaniel whispered into Jocelyn's ear. He gently brushed his hand over her cheek as Kagen walked away with her, heading toward the stairs.

The bottom dropped out of Nathaniel's heart, and a silent fury enveloped his soul as he turned to measure the progress of the man with the Mohawk—the human who had dared to attack his *destiny*. The man was sawing at his right foot and shaking like an earthquake, his body clearly in shock as he continued to hack away at his limbs. The left leg sat in a bloody heap next to him, the foot was chopped off at the ankle, and the calf was dissected just below the knee...the thigh torn chaotically away from the pelvis. Sweat poured down the man's face in painful rivulets, and his mouth hung open in a silent scream of terror—and unspeakable pain—yet he continued to dismember himself against his will, caught in the vampire's compulsion. Since Nathaniel had also seized his vocal cords, there would be no sound to accompany his agony.

Satisfied, Nathaniel headed toward the supply room.

He stopped just outside the door, closed his eyes, and concentrated fully on his hearing. There were two separate sets of heartbeats in the room. The first came from a large, expansive chest. The second, from a narrow, smaller cavity. One male and one female.

Interesting.

Curiosity swept over him as he fed the information to Marquis. It was hard to believe that a female could have gotten the best of either Jocelyn or Ciopori.

No matter.

She was as dead as the male.

BLOOD POSSESSION

Nathaniel drew closer to the room and pressed his ear against the door: Their breaths were shallow and quick, rapid from fear...racing with desperation.

Good.

Alive, Marquis reminded him. *I want them alive.*

I cannot promise not to harm them, brother. But I will bring them out alive, Nathaniel answered telepathically, in order to remain quiet.

Rendering his body invisible, he passed through the supply room door and rose to the ceiling, where he hung like a spider, spinning a web for his prey. He could see as clearly in the dark as an owl, and it took less than a second to locate both of the intruders—a dark-haired man huddled in the corner next to a terrified blond female. Their backs were pressed hard against the wall, and the male gripped a loaded firearm in his hand as if his life depended upon his grasp.

Silly rabbit.

Based on his body language, Nathaniel determined that the guy was a soldier of some sort, a fighter—well, as much as any human could be against a vampire. The point was: He was clearly determined to fight to the death, whereas the female looked like she might just die any moment from fright.

She certainly didn't belong in this scenario.

Such stupid, stupid humans, Nathaniel thought. What in the world would make these fools believe they could prevail against such a powerful species? That they could come to Dark Moon Vale, harm the mates of ancient warriors, and still walk away with their lives?

And why in the world had this clearly terrified woman consented to go along with such an ill-begotten plan?

No matter.

Both of them had made a fatal error in judgment. And there wasn't an argument either one could present that would convince Nathaniel—or Marquis—to spare their lives.

Anticipation heated Nathaniel's blood as he slowly descended from the ceiling.

twenty~seven

Careful to remain invisible, Nathaniel Silivasi landed on the floor in front of the cowering intruders. He plucked the gun out of the unsuspecting male's hand and pitched it across the room, well out of the fool's reach. The female screamed in surprise. She shrank further into the corner and covered herself up in a tight little ball.

But the male came out swinging.

He threw wild, desperate punches in Nathaniel's direction, one careless jab after the other, each one easily deflected or blocked. Irritated by the idiotic confrontation, Nathaniel stepped out of the fool's reach and searched the room until he located a folding card table in the corner. With supernatural speed, he flew to the table, broke off a metal leg, and snapped it in half. Wielding both pieces like batons, he twirled them absently in and out of his fingers as he slowly approached the male from behind. In a matter of seconds, he had both of the human's arms crossed behind his back and tied in an inescapable knot made out of the first half of twisted metal. The human spun around wildly. He kicked at Nathaniel's legs and tried frantically to free his hands, all to no avail. Further annoyed, Nathaniel swept the human's legs out from under him, lifted him upside down by the ankles, and secured both feet with the remaining piece of metal. Hog-tied and no longer dangerous—as if he ever was—Nathaniel threw him across the room into the toppled-over card table and bared his fangs at the female, slowly shimmering into view. His low, feral growl spoke volumes: *Stay in line.*

The woman looked like she had just seen the devil.

She began to scream like a broken siren, one short blast after another rising to a fevered pitch until it became evident that she was about to hyperventilate. "Shut up!" Nathaniel hissed, glaring at her with eyes he knew were gleaming red. "Shut up—or I'll shut you up."

The blonde swallowed a gasp and pressed her hand tightly over her mouth in an attempt to quell her unrelenting cries. Tears streamed down her face in rivulets as she removed her hand and whimpered, "Please...oh please, don't—"

Nathaniel's glare stopped her short.

A second hand came up to cover the first, and both were pressed hard against her mouth in a feverish attempt to stay silent. She nodded furiously, demonstrating her compliance. Shaking his head with disgust—yet confident that the female would remain obedient—Nathaniel turned back to the male.

The dark-haired human was sprawled out on the floor in an extremely awkward position: His back was twisted sideways against the cold tiles, and his head was propped upright and forward, braced against the top of the table, which now stood parallel to the floor. Praying the man hadn't died that easily, Nathaniel hovered over his twisted body and squatted down to make eye contact.

The man squirmed.

Good.

He tried to scoot away, but there was nowhere to go. Not to mention, his legs were too tightly bound to assist him.

"Who are you?" Nathaniel growled, his voice so thick with vehemence he hardly sounded coherent. He tried again, slower this time: "Who—the—hell—are—you?" When the man didn't immediately respond, he added, "You have three seconds to answer before I rip your throat out."

He knew he couldn't actually do it.

Marquis had ordered him to keep both intruders alive, but the human didn't have to know that.

"Screw you, vampire," he spat.

Surprised, Nathaniel stood up. He took a step back and regarded the human thoughtfully. Studying his features with keen interest, he took in his full measure: Dark, hawkish eyes glared back at him with as much contempt as fear. There was a brazen defiance in his gaze that revealed both a stiff spine...and extremely poor judgment. Moreover, the man's slightly dilated pupils betrayed a lack of balance, the fact that he wasn't altogether...wrapped too tight...for lack of a better term. His thin, pursed lips were as cruel as they were stubborn, meaning he was capable of just about anything; however, his sallow complexion exposed an internal weakness: The man thought of himself as a leader—a rebel belonging to some sort of worthy cause—but in reality, he was nothing more than a follower, an easily brainwashed devotee, ultimately under the control of others.

Nathaniel crossed his arms in front of his chest. "Well, now, I must admit you have...courage. You're stupid as hell, but courageous." He knelt down in front of him, grabbed him by the throat, and squeezed, falling just short of crushing his trachea—after all, destroying the man's larynx would make it a little hard for him to talk. And then, he wrenched the man's head back by the hair, dipped his head, and sank his fangs so deep into his throat that they scraped against his vertebrae. He ripped out tissue before releasing his bite, repositioning his mouth, and sinking his fangs once again into the artery.

Nathaniel took long, drugging pulls of the man's blood, aiming to inflict as much pain as possible—which was a great deal: Without a vampire's assistance—the mind control that dulled the pain and reduced the initial sensation—there was nothing tolerable or romantic about being bitten by the Nosferatu. A bite felt like exactly what it was: two long, thick spikes being driven into the side of one's throat.

The pain was beyond excruciating, and the human started to convulse. He shrieked like a newborn baby, and his eyes darted around the room in panicked horror.

Unwilling to risk draining him dry, Nathaniel sustained the bite as long as he could, and then he finally withdrew his fangs...and waited.

"Oh God...oh God...oh God," the man panted hysterically. "Please...no more...*please*." He writhed in pain. From the look in his eyes—and the frenetic way his hands strained behind his back—the human desperately wanted to reach up and apply pressure to his burning throat, ease the unrelenting pain—but he was unable to give himself even the slightest relief.

Nathaniel licked his lips. "That's better." He crossed his arms and struggled to take his bloodlust down a notch. He felt a rivulet of the man's blood trickle out the corner of his own mouth but made no effort to wipe it away. "The brown-haired female"—Nathaniel spoke with absolute dominance and contempt—"the one with the hazel eyes...did you shoot her?" Despite his promise to Marquis, he was trembling in anticipation of the male's answer: If the guy said yes, then all bets were off. Even Marquis would have to understand how restraint, in such a circumstance, was too much to ask. Nathaniel's lips twitched as he waited.

The human shook his head adamantly back and forth. "No...no! *God, no...*I swear it."

"What about the other woman!" Marquis Silivasi threw open the supply room door and stormed into the room, followed by a reluctant Braden Bratianu. "Did you impale that beautiful, dark-haired woman...*through the heart*...with a wooden stake?"

Nathaniel looked up at the angry Ancient Master Warrior: Marquis's rage was simmering...on the edge of boiling. "Brother," Nathaniel said in greeting. And then he instantly switched to telepathy, not wanting to give the human the satisfaction of knowing the extent of the injuries he had caused their mates: *Marquis, what is happening? How is Jocelyn? Where is Ciopori?* He paused to look at the young vampire standing nervously at Marquis's side and frowned—Braden looked both dazed and apprehensive. *Why did you bring the boy with you?*

Marquis growled so low in his throat that Nathaniel took an instinctive step back, and Braden instantly scurried to stand on the other side of the room. *Jocelyn is still in surgery, but Kagen says it is going well. Ciopori is sedated and sleeping in an adjacent room. Julien and Ramsey are guarding her.*

Julien Lacusta was the valley's best tracker and a fierce Master Warrior in his own right, and Ramsey was a crazy-as-hell

308

bastard who could inflict the most hideous torture while whistling a happy tune at the same time. Ciopori was in good hands. *And Braden?* he asked.

"Braden is now a son in the house of Jadon, and the Vampyr are his people." Marquis spoke out loud, obviously wanting the human to hear his words. "An attack against our women is an attack against him." He looked across the room at the adolescent, who now stood with his chest puffed out, no doubt trying like hell to appear braver than he felt. "He is not too young to stand with us in solidarity…or to kill with us…in pleasure."

Nathaniel nodded. Braden Bratianu might only be fifteen years old, but he had a lot to learn in a very short time in order to catch up with his vampire peers of the same age. As the only human son of a female *destiny* ever converted to their species, as opposed to being born that way, nothing came easy for the awkward boy. He had to learn what others took for granted, and Marquis had taken a special interest in him ever since the kid had helped save Jocelyn from the Lycan hunters.

"Very well," Nathaniel growled, giving Braden an approving nod before turning back toward the table.

Marquis was instantly there, looming over the terrified human male. "I asked you a question: Did you stake the other female?"

The human looked precisely like what he was—a man being forced to stare his own death in the eyes. Wisely, he didn't answer the question.

And his silence told Marquis all he needed to know.

Marquis slowly lifted his hand, and a thin red beam of light shot out of his index finger.

"Wh…wh…what are you doing?" the man asked, his horrified eyes trained on the light.

Marquis shrugged. "Taking the image from your head." He focused the narrow beam of light on the sweat-dampened skin of the human's forehead and began to burn a deep cut into his skull as if with a scalpel. As Marquis's finger moved slowly to the right, the male's scalp opened in its wake, and the fetid stench of burning flesh began to fill the room.

"No! Stop!" the man screamed, tossing his head back and forth in a futile attempt to avoid the laser. He fell on his side and began to vomit, choking on the refuse as it passed through his throat.

"Cry me a river," Marquis snarled, and then he snatched the man by his shirt and tossed him onto his back, leaving him prone on the floor like a pagan sacrifice. Marquis straddled the human's body and forced him to meet his heated gaze. He held his finger directly above a blood-soaked eye and made a circular motion, as if to say, *This comes out next,* and then he spat in his face. "I won't ask again: Did you stake the other woman?"

The man choked out the word with unfathomable regret: "Yes."

Marquis hung his head and released a long, slow, deep breath. In what appeared to be a herculean effort, he rocked back on his heels and briefly retreated from the confrontation; and then he reached up and rubbed the bridge of his nose as if in deep concentration.

Nathaniel had no doubt Marquis was struggling to contain an absolute explosion of emotion, and he would have placed a steadying hand on his brother's shoulder, except he wasn't at all sure he would get the hand back in its present condition. After sixty seconds or so had passed, Marquis cleared his throat and looked back at the waiting human.

His expression was as cold as stone.

His eyes were both hollow and impassive.

And his voice held a dark-velvet promise in its depths: "I am going to sever your head from your body—*with my teeth*—but first, you are going to answer three questions: Who are you? Why are you here? And why did you try to murder my wife?"

The man wet his pants.

"Talk," Marquis snarled. His voice was laced with compulsion.

"Mm...muh...my...name is David...Reed. I'm the head of

the Midwest vampire-hunting militia." In a torrent of piteous words, David explained the organization, how they had come to learn about Dark Moon Vale through their regional Head Hunter—a government operative named Tristan Hart—and how they had hoped to find something in the clinic to help destroy the vampire species: perhaps a sedative made specifically for their race, tissue or blood samples that revealed information about their anatomy, a secret about vampire physiology that could be used against them in the future. He explained how they had been caught off guard by the women, and he assured Marquis that they had never intended to attack the females—or anyone else for that matter.

As if that mattered in the least…

After collecting all the information he needed—or wanted—Marquis bent ever-so-slowly over the man's body and…smiled.

"Please…please, I'm begging you…for God's sake…I—"

Marquis held his finger over the man's lips to silence him. "You tried to kill my woman," he whispered, and then he placed one hand on either side of the man's shoulders. "Oh, and by the way, your so-called Head Hunter—the one who recruited you to help rid the pure, human race of monsters—was a Lycan." He laughed, a deep, wicked sound that echoed through the room. "Tristan Hart isn't a government operative any more than you are: He's a *werewolf*, you fool—or at least he was before my brother killed him." He paused. "Perhaps you will meet up in hell."

Marquis locked eyes with the human, and then he released his fangs and bent his head oh-so-slowly to his neck. With a calm that was more frightening than any rage, he bit into his throat in one clean bite, his jaw enclosing both sides of the jugular at once. He breathed quietly and evenly, deeply inhaling the man's scent; and then a deep, guttural growl rose from his very soul and his eyes flashed crimson-red—glazed over like no one was home.

Marquis Silivasi ripped the man's larynx out in one horrible mouthful.

BLOOD POSSESSION

He spit out the torn flesh, licked his lips, and bit into him again—this time with a feral, unrestrained rage. With both palms braced flat against the floor, evenly spaced on either side of the man's head, Marquis Silivasi tore out the human's throat like a rabid animal—biting, tearing, spitting, and snarling—ravaging with such unbridled fury that even Nathaniel had to look away. When he turned back, Marquis was kneeling—silent and still— the base of the man's spinal column clasped between his teeth like a bone in the jaws of a dog. And the human's head was fully decapitated from his body.

As he'd promised, Marquis had done it all with his teeth.

He snapped the spine in half with his molars and spit out the remains on the man's torso, and then he spun around, noiselessly, and leapt across the room, landing in a low, feral crouch in front of the petrified woman, who still sat tightly huddled in the corner.

He cocked his head to the side and smiled. "And to think they call you the fairer sex." He reached out to stroke her cheek with a bloody finger. "You didn't think we forgot you, did you?" He held out his hand in front of him, lifted the gory finger to his mouth, and slowly licked off the blood. "Time to face the music, human." Eyeing her from head to toe with disdain, he grunted, snatched her by the front of her shirt, and roared, "Get up!" And then he plopped her into a chair, slid it across the floor with a kick, and laughed when Nathaniel halted the careening motion with his bent knee and pulled up a chair of his own to take a seat in front of her.

"Alas, we meet again," Nathaniel drawled wickedly, waiting for Marquis and Braden to join him in front of the woman.

Braden Bratianu stifled a gasp and quickly shuffled over to Nathaniel's side. "Hey…but…but…she's a—"

Marquis turned to glare at Braden, his eyes flashing a stern warning. "But what?"

Braden shook his head and averted his eyes.

Marquis nodded and sighed. "You are right, son; she's a woman. And unless we are directly threatened or in imminent

Tessa Dawn

defense of our females, we don't *ever* hurt a woman." He threw back his head and bellowed toward the ceiling: "Kristina!" The sound ricocheted off the walls like thunder—shaking the building for several seconds before it was replaced with an equally frightening silence.

The five-foot-six redhead materialized instantly in the outside hall.

Her sharp heels could be heard clicking against the tile floor as she promptly made her way to the supply room and opened the door. To her credit, her eyes swept the entire room in an instant, yet she didn't react.

At least not in response to the woman and the decapitated body. "What—the—hell—was—that—*thing*—out—in—the—hall?" she asked, incredulous.

Nathaniel frowned. "What thing?" Had they overlooked another attacker? He started to move toward the door but was stopped short by her wild gestures and bulging, bright blue eyes. "That pile of feet...and knees...and an arm!"

"Oh that," Nathaniel said. "Is he still alive, by the way?"

Kristina's eyebrows creased in consternation, and her mouth dropped open. "Uh...that would be a no. He's still got a machete in his hand, but...yeah, I'd say he's...passed on."

Marquis shrugged. "Nathaniel has always been the...creative one."

"Yeah, well, remind me never to make him mad," Kristina said, shaking her head with disbelief.

Marquis gestured toward the seated woman with a sweep of his hand. "This is why I called you."

Kristina looked down at the terrified blonde in the chair, and then she paused—almost as if her mind was trying to process the details. With a sudden start, she strode across the room in four, long measured steps, as graceful as they were powerful, drew back her arm, and slapped the woman so hard that she flew out of the chair. As the blonde slammed into the nearest wall, clearly breaking a bone in her arm, Kristina shouted, "You bitch!"

313

BLOOD POSSESSION

The woman cried out in pain, and then, clutching her arm to her chest, she scrambled to turn around and face Kristina. Her words were scarcely audible beneath her heart-wrenching sobs. "Please...please...I didn't do anything."

Kristina closed the distance between them. "Didn't do anything? Didn't do anything! One of my sisters is in surgery right now, and the other one had to have a stake pulled out of her heart! What do you mean, you didn't do anything?" Her fangs shot out of her mouth, and she lunged at the woman's throat, literally flying through the air toward the floor.

Nathaniel caught her by the waist, pulled her away, and sat her down slowly in his chair. "Hold on, Kristina," he whispered as he squatted in front of the woman. "Talk. *Now.*"

The woman opened her mouth, cleared her throat, and stuttered. She opened it again, this time swaying so hard that Nathaniel had to steady her shoulder to keep her from falling over. The moment he touched her, she began to throw up, heaving over and over while clutching her arm—trying desperately to talk the entire time. "I promise...I didn't...didn't do anything." She wiped her mouth with the back of her hand and stared at the floor, too afraid to look any of them in the eyes. "I didn't come here to hurt your sisters, and I swear, I didn't do anything to either one of them."

Nathaniel leaned back on his heels and stared at her. "She's telling the truth." He leaned forward again. "Then why are you here?"

She lifted her head, met his gaze, and started to hyperventilate.

Nathaniel scrubbed a hand over his face. "Breathe," he whispered.

She gulped air, furiously trying to take it in, but it only made matter worse.

Sighing, Nathaniel placed the palm of his hand over her lungs and slowed her breathing for her. "Just breathe," he repeated.

The woman sat there for almost sixty seconds doing just

that. When she finally caught her breath, she looked up at Kristina with pleading eyes. "I didn't come for your sisters." She turned to Marquis, then Nathaniel. "Or your wives. I just wanted...I just wanted to find Brooke! I swear that's all. A...a...vampire...took my best friend—he kidnapped her—and I wanted her back." She was sobbing uncontrollably now. "I found the vampire-hunting militia, and they said they could help me. I don't know...I don't know what I was thinking. I just want Brooke." She looked up at Kristina before collapsing on the floor. "She's like a sister to me, too. The only one I have. I just want Brooke."

"Oh, gods," Nathaniel said on an exhale, standing up.

Kristina took a step back, and Braden looked like a kid who had just been caught with his hand in the cookie jar.

Marquis blanched. "How do you know all this—about Brooke?" He stared pointedly at Nathaniel. *Why is her memory intact, brother?*

I don't know, Nathaniel answered. His psychic voice revealed his frustration. He called out telepathically to the warrior who had been with Napolean the night of his Blood Moon—the one who had also been charged with erasing the memories of any witnesses: *Ramsey!*

The dangerous sentinel answered the summons immediately: *Nathaniel?*

Nathaniel didn't waste any time getting to the point: *The night Napolean claimed his destiny, did you not see to her friend—her coworker in the backseat? Did you erase—and replace—her memories?*

Of course, Ramsey answered, sounding slightly irritated. *Why?*

Because she's sitting right here in front of us in the basement, and she remembers everything.

Silence hovered in the air.

Finally, Ramsey Olaru growled deep in his throat and swore in Romanian. *I'll be right down.*

No! Marquis interjected. *Stay with Ciopori. We will let you know when we have more information. What is the woman's name by the way?*

Ramsey paused for a moment, and then he said,

BLOOD POSSESSION

Tiffany...Tiffany Matthews.

Nathaniel closed the communication and watched as Marquis brusquely helped a stunned Tiffany up from the floor and led her back to the chair. After righting it, he helped her sit down. "Tiffany," he said in a low, soothing voice—well, about as soothing as Marquis could get—"how is it that you can remember what happened to Brooke? At any time, did you ever experience a...lapse in your memory?"

Tiffany looked up then, as surprised to hear her name as she was at the sudden gentle treatment. She choked back her tears and cleared her throat. "I...yes...I...that guy...the blond man with the chin-length hair, he erased my memory that night. I know because—"

"Because what?" Nathaniel asked, not waiting for her to finish.

"Because I saw it all in a dream."

Marquis raised his eyebrows. "You saw it in a dream? What does this mean?"

Tiffany swallowed then, her eyes cautiously lighting with a faint spark of hope. "I have like...what you would call a gift...dreaming...dream weaving. I can see the future and the past—anything really—in my dreams. They come to me to give me information whenever I need it. I didn't remember what happened to Brooke until I went to sleep on Friday night, and then I saw it all replay clearly in front of me: The vampire that took her, the one that tried to erase my memory...all of it."

"How did you know we were vampires?" Marquis asked.

"My dream—"

"Told you," Marquis supplied. He shook his head and walked away.

"Shiiiiit," Braden said, whistling.

Nathaniel raised his eyebrows and regarded the youngster appreciatively. "Well said."

Marquis crossed his arms in front of him. "Brother, have you ever heard of such a thing—humans dreaming with that much psychic accuracy?"

316

Nathaniel shook his head. "No, I have not. Wizards? Yes. But humans?" He sighed, and then he placed his hand gently on Tiffany's arm and began to absorb her pain, drawing it slowly into his own body until her suffering diminished. "Is that better?" he asked.

The blonde looked up at Nathaniel with both apprehension and wonder in her eyes. She was clearly confused by all the sudden changes in behavior yet far too afraid to question the meaning of it. "Yes," she whispered timidly. She appeared to be holding her breath.

Marquis cleared his throat. "Nathaniel, do you know if Kagen has another medic on call? Katia is still with Nachari; Kagen is with Jocelyn; and when he does finish, he will need medical attention himself."

Nathaniel thought about it.

There were plenty of males studying Healing at the Romanian University, but the revived interest was new—something that had just cropped up over the past several centuries. Less than a handful of males had actually completed their schooling and returned to Dark Moon Vale to apprentice. He thought harder. "Navarro Dabronski," he finally said. "He's back on break to celebrate his parents' anniversary. He's a competent medic, at least as long as Kagen is present to supervise."

Marquis nodded, his anger having somewhat abated. "Good. Call him." *Let's address the human's wounds first—then contact Napolean*, he added privately. *We do not dare manipulate her mind—or erase her memories—until we hear how our king would like to proceed.*

Very well, Nathaniel replied. He turned to Tiffany and crouched down slowly in front of her. "Tiffany," he said, lifting her chin to get her attention.

Her teeth chattered but at least she was breathing. "Your friend Brooke is alive and well."

Her eyes lit up and she appeared to momentarily forget her predicament. "Oh, thank God!"

Nathaniel smiled, surprised by her resilience. "Kristina is

317

going to take you upstairs to one of the medical rooms so we can treat your arm and check you for other injuries, and then we will call Brooke."

The look of surprise on her face was utterly priceless. She exhaled slowly and nodded. And then she turned to look at Kristina. "No," she said, shaking her head emphatically. "Please, not her..." She pointed at Marquis, thought better of it, and then changed her selection to Braden. "Him. I want him to take me upstairs." She paused as if all at once remembering her place. "Please..."

"Oh, so it's like that," Braden said in frustration, "like I can't do any damage? Like I can't even bite or slap—"

"Braden!" Nathaniel chastised. The poor woman was likely to be irreversibly traumatized as it was.

Braden shrugged. "Just sayin'."

"Shut up, Braden," Marquis growled.

Braden huffed and rolled his eyes. "Fine."

Marquis gave the kid a stern, unyielding glare.

"I mean, yes sir," he said, looking down at the floor.

Nathaniel turned back to Tiffany. "The boy will take you upstairs—without incident—you have my word." He turned to look at Marquis then, and an unspoken thought passed between them: *By all the gods,* what would be the fallout when Napolean's mate learned what had been done to her friend? As two mated males, they both understood implicitly just how precarious the beginning of a relationship with one's *destiny* could be.

Not to quote Braden, Nathaniel muttered on a private telepathic line, *but shiiiit!*

Indeed, Marquis responded.

twenty-eight

Although Brooke was eager to get to her best friend, Napolean needed her to stand by his side as he observed protocol with the Silivasis before she attended to Tiffany: There was still much she needed to learn about his duties as the sovereign leader of the house of Jadon—a life where the good of all of the people sometimes came first. They had looked in on Jocelyn first, and Brooke had handled the delicate situation with both poise and grace: Her light-hearted manner and gentle spirit had been deeply appreciated during those sensitive moments when Jocelyn had recounted the details of the attack...what had taken place...and in what order they had happened.

Jocelyn had been the most critically injured of the two, yet she had come through surgery nicely and was healing at a very rapid pace. There were no words adequate to thank the ex-detective for what she had done down in that basement—in effect, Jocelyn had saved Ciopori's life as well as her own—yet Brooke had managed to express Napolean's sentiment perfectly. In fact, she had expressed it better than Napolean could have expressed it himself.

They had met with Ciopori and Kristina next: Thanks to Marquis's powerful venom—as well as his bull-headed determination—Ciopori had already fully recovered from the heinous injury she had suffered at the hands of the vampire-killing militia. Though seriously shaken up, Napolean knew Ciopori had been through far worse in the past. Still, the idea that something so grave, so unthinkable, could have happened to one of the original females—right in the basement of Kagen's clinic, right under the noses of two of their strongest warriors—was more than a little unsettling. Napolean had decided right then and there that something substantial would have to be done to further protect all of the *destinies*—something far more

319

permanent than posting guards or sentinels, something that rose above the innate guardianship of their protective mates.

He had used his time with both women as a sort of debriefing—gathering enough information to begin smoking out the vigilante members of the so-called militia and ascertaining the nuances of their tactics well enough to combat future attacks. Satisfied with what he had learned, he and Brooke had stopped to offer a few words of encouragement to Braden Bratianu, and then they had headed to an empty examination room where Marquis and Nathaniel waited to speak with their leader—and his new mate—in private. Having been treated for his own nasty injuries by a medic, Kagen had excused himself from the intimate meeting in order to return to Nachari: a request Napolean could hardly refuse. After all, gods knew, Napolean would have healed the Master Wizard with his own hands if he could have.

Pushing aside that ever constant concern, he knocked lightly on the door to the examination room and then swiftly opened it without awaiting a response. Marquis stood leaning against the far wall at the back of the room, while Nathaniel leaned against a high countertop containing a sink, a soap dispenser next to a jar of small cotton balls, several unopened syringes, and suture materials. Both men immediately stood up straight and declined their heads, averting their eyes to the floor, as Napolean ushered Brooke in before him. She seemed unusually nervous to Napolean—maybe because she remembered the role the Silivasis had played in rescuing him from the dark lord Ademordna—maybe because she remembered the role they had also played in rescuing her. Regardless, he reached out and took her hand in support.

"Greetings, warriors," he said solemnly.

"Milord," both males answered in unison.

Napolean nodded his approval and placed a firm hand on the small of Brooke's back. She shifted nervously from foot to foot but stood her ground. "I would like you to formally meet my *destiny*." He took her left arm and gently turned over her wrist, displaying the complex set of markings that clearly revealed her as his. "A daughter of the goddess Andromeda, the mother of my son—who is heir to my throne—and your queen: Brooke Adams."

To Brooke's utter surprise—and seeming embarrassment based on the way she suddenly blushed and shot an inquisitive sideways glance at Napolean—both warriors bent to one knee and bowed their heads.

As the eldest of the two brothers, Marquis reached for her hand first, and then he reverently kissed the back of her ring-finger—the one displaying a braided platinum band with the royal crest from the house of Jadon on it. It was a solemn acknowledgment of her relationship to Napolean. "It is an honor, milady," Marquis said.

Brooke drew in a quick intake of breath.

Still averting his eyes, Marquis released her hand and continued to bow his head.

Nathaniel took it next. "I am also honored, milady." His kiss was equally reverent, and then, being the youngest male before them, the burden of an apology fell to him. "I speak now for myself as a servant of the house of Jadon; for my twin, an Ancient Master Healer; for my sister, who is newly converted to our race; and for my eldest brother Marquis, also an Ancient Master Warrior: We would beg your forgiveness for the offense we committed against your friend, Tiffany Matthews." His eyes met hers and they were brimming with conviction. "Milady, our wives had been attacked. We did not know the reason for the attack, the origin of our enemy, or what relationship the female was to you. Nonetheless, it does not erase the injury, and we deeply, deeply apologize."

Brooke's brilliant sapphire eyes grew wide, and her mouth fell open in astonishment. As silence hovered in the air like a mist, she turned to Napolean and raised her eyebrows. "What—"

Shh, Napolean whispered in her mind, no doubt surprising her with the easy, intimate communication. They were mated now, linked for eternity in mind, body, and spirit: Even their thoughts could be effortlessly shared. *What he does is a great act of humility. It is best honored with silence.*

She looked at him quizzically, not understanding.

Place your right hand on his left shoulder.

Hesitantly, Brooke did as he said.

Now simply nod your head.

She nodded and both men stood with a polished grace, their bodies rising in perfect synchronicity. Brooke gulped, clearly overwhelmed by the casual show of animal prowess before her.

Indeed, Napolean thought, the Silivasis were a sight to behold.

When Brooke actually took a step back, inadvertently drawing closer to Napolean as if for protection, he immediately slipped his arm around her and smiled…inside. *It is done,* he explained, nuzzling her hair—it was so soft, so beautiful—*the transgression has been forgiven and will never be spoken of again: While it may be acceptable to discuss the events, to hash out further details if the information proves important, the transgression itself—the actual fact that my subjects caused injury to you through their mistreatment of your friend— has been unconditionally forgiven…and thus, irretrievably forgotten.*

Brooke nodded, demonstrating her understanding, and Napolean kissed the top of her head. Although everything in him wanted to keep her in his arms, he gently stepped away. "Brooke, would you mind leaving us alone to talk for a while? I'm sure Tiffany is anxious to see you."

Brooke bit her bottom lip; her eyes lit up; and her stiff shoulders relaxed with relief. "Sure, no problem. Kristina said she'd be happy to take me to Tiffany's room whenever I was ready." She turned to Marquis and Nathaniel and smiled. "It was nice…meeting you both." Although her rapidly beating heart betrayed her underlying disquiet with the males, Napolean knew that it would come in time.

"Nice meeting you," Nathaniel said in his usual, relaxed, charming voice.

Marquis grunted what sounded like an affirmative, forced a

half smile—which, for him, was a social milestone—and nodded.

Napolean could not have asked for more.

"Okeydoke," Brooke exhaled, holding Napolean's gaze a little longer than she needed to.

Are you all right, my love? he asked her then. *Do you need me to go with you?*

"No," she answered out loud, immediately catching the error. She turned toward Marquis and Nathaniel and shrugged. "I don't quite have the whole talking-to-each-other-in-your-heads thing down yet." She cringed. "I mean, I do—I *can* do it—but I just don't remember *to* do it…" She turned to Napolean and blanched, her eyes ripe with apology, as if she had just embarrassed him horribly.

He laughed out loud then and pulled her into his arms right in front of his warriors.

Stunned by the outward show of emotion, they both looked away.

"You, my love, are perfect," Napolean said.

Brooke's answering smile lit up the room.

As Brooke made her way out the door, Nathaniel and Marquis turned back around to face Napolean. *"Wow,"* Nathaniel murmured beneath his breath, "I don't think I've ever seen you—"

Napolean gave him a cross look, cutting his words off mid-sentence. "Do not forget your place, warrior," he warned. "*She* is my mate—you are not."

Nathaniel nodded. And then he bit down on his bottom lip, trying to contain a smile. "Yes, my love… I mean, milord."

Napolean chuckled. "Okay…okay. If you've had your fun, let's move on." He turned to Marquis and gave him an expectant look—waiting to see if the Ancient Master Warrior had any teasing of his own to add. "Marquis?"

The large vampire frowned. "What?"

Napolean just shook his head—of course Marquis had missed the joke.

BLOOD POSSESSION

Napolean's manner became all at once serious as he changed the subject: "What happened here today—in the basement of this clinic—is a wake-up call we can no longer afford to ignore."

"Agreed," Marquis grunted.

"Since the moment I heard of what happened, I have been able to think of nothing else," Napolean continued. "And we all know that the only reason the women still live"—he eyed both males with deep concern and empathy—"is because of Jocelyn's former training with the police department." He nodded his appreciation to Nathaniel. "Her reaction to the attack was exceptional—and instinctual. She managed to neutralize two enemies before she was—" He was about to say *gunned down* but caught himself; fortunately, he pulled back the words before they were uttered. "Before she was hurt." He folded his hands in front of him. "Her actions bought the time the women needed for reinforcements to arrive—I can't even allow myself to think of what would have happened otherwise." He slowly shook his head and regarded each male in turn with a somber stare.

Marquis growled low in his throat, and Nathaniel's eyes flashed briefly red before settling back into their normal, dark hue, yet both males remained quiet. No doubt, they understood the grave implications on a level far deeper than Napolean.

"That said," he continued, "the best course of action—that which any one of our warriors would have taken instinctively— would have been to immediately cloak her appearance the moment Ciopori was injured. Having rendered herself invisible, she might have eliminated the humans one by one, or at the least, she might have been able to construct a protective holding cell around the two of them while calling for help. She might have been able to begin administering healing venom to Ciopori immediately." He sighed. "And she would have never been shot herself." Sharpening his tone, he added, "I believe it is time to provide our women with much more training in the use of their powers. It is no longer enough to accept the basics: Our enemies have become too bold."

Marquis sighed and Napolean felt his frustration: All male

vampires were hardwired to be the protectors of their women and their families. It wasn't sexist so much as it was a genetic trait of the species—just as a female lioness hunted while the male protected the pride, so did the male Vampyr protect what belonged to him.

The need to defend was as inherent as the need to possess.

Far beyond a value judgment or a narrow-minded gender assignment, it was a deep-seated instinct, one that had been programmed into the very DNA of the species. Like it or not, Vampyr were not human, and as much as their forms—and even some of their traditions—mimicked their human counterparts, their primary characteristics more closely mirrored the various predators of the animal kingdom.

"Perhaps, milord…" Marquis clearly weighed his words carefully, "but how many thousands of drills does a warrior go through before such instincts become automatic? Before life-or-death decisions are made on a dime—encompassing the full range of our powers?" He turned to Nathaniel. "How many centuries did it take before you were able to construct a perfect holding cell in less than five seconds, one with no energetic leaks or inherent weaknesses, that could be easily taken apart by your enemies?"

Nathaniel frowned. "I agree with Marquis. Take the ability to stop a bullet, for instance: It is one thing to discern the difference between a subtle energy shift and a slightly harsher disturbance—say, a finger flexing back on a trigger versus the vibration that occurs a fraction of a second later when the bullet is actually leaving the chamber—yet it is another thing altogether to get ahead of the bullet and intercept it before it strikes." He paused. "When I think of what I went through, all of the years and trials—not to mention the excruciating injuries I sustained in the process of learning such things…" His voice trailed off.

Napolean strode across the room, listening. He leaned back on the exam table, crossed his arms in front of him, bent his left knee, and rested his right foot on the floor at the ankle. "The way I see it, the problem is our women inherent all of our powers—there are few abilities we possess that they do not also possess—however, without the benefit of the same extensive training, they rarely learn to wield them as we do. We concentrate on telepathic speech, tracking, feeding—perhaps enhanced speed and strength—and travel: the ability to move, seen or unseen, through objects. We want them to thrive as vampires, to speak to us and our children with their minds, to enjoy their enhanced senses, and to materialize and dematerialize; but that's as far as we take it because we know we cannot put them through what we have been through." He waved his hand through the air as if to dismiss an obvious, yet unspoken, argument. "And not because they are too weak or because we wish to control them. On the contrary, I shudder to imagine our females—one such as Kristina—after four hundred years at the University. Good gods—"

"We would all have to move," Nathaniel offered, smiling.

Marquis nodded. "Ciopori would be...frightening."

Napolean smiled. "Suffice to say, they are our equals—if not our superiors—in every way, but the Curse is as it is; and within thirty days of being claimed, they become mothers...they bear our sons. And that is an added responsibility, even a liability if we are to look at it logistically in terms of warfare, that we do not have to deal with during our initial training. Consider how much higher the stakes are for our mated males, even the warriors, once they take on a mate and are gifted with a child. I have seen even the most instinctive warrior think twice about his next move because his death may leave a widow—or his mistake may cost him a son. It is not the same carefree, independent mindset our unmated males enjoy throughout their training. The stakes are simply higher with a family." He shrugged and held up his hands. "But what we can give them, we must." His voice dropped to a low, throaty purr and practically vibrated with focused intent. "Never again will I place any female in the house of Jadon in such danger—surrounded by an enemy, facing life or death without her mate at her side—armed with anything less than her full potential."

Both Nathaniel and Marquis nodded.

"Four hundred years is not an option," Napolean added. "But six months to a year is." Marquis raised his eyebrows. "At the University, *in Romania?*"

"No," Napolean answered. "Of course not, but we have the necessary facilities right here in Dark Moon Vale. We can utilize the gymnasium and the outdoor training fields at the local Academy." He turned to face Nathaniel then. "Nathaniel, Marquis, and Ramsey are already overseeing the hunting expeditions, our new initiative to find and eliminate Dark Ones, to ultimately seek their full extermination. You will oversee the creation of a new program—a self-defense program here in the valley—for every female inducted into the house of Jadon. They may not be able to get in front of a bullet after only six months of training, but they can learn to deflect one. If a complete holding cell is too tall an order, a temporary wall is not. They are stronger, faster, and far more keen in their senses than any human on this planet; they should be well trained in hand-to-hand combat, in the most efficient and lethal ways to kill, maim, or disable at will using their preternatural abilities. Telekinesis is no longer optional: A gun can be removed from an enemy's hand from a great distance away, and while the total invasion of a human's mind is an energetic feat of enormous ability—what is it now, the junior year before our males are even allowed to attempt such a thing?—the ability to influence, nudge, or even put a human to sleep is doable. It's hard to fire a gun when you're lying unconscious on the ground. Do you see my point?"

Nathaniel nodded. "Absolutely, milord."

Napolean relaxed his shoulders, unaware until now that they had been tense. "Very well. Work with Mateo Devera on this. Create a six-month training program to maximize every gift our women possess, and see that it is started immediately." He paused then. "Train your *destiny* first, Nathaniel. I know Jocelyn was interested in getting back into some sort of PI work soon, but I believe this is something she will willingly sink her teeth into. And the females will be more comfortable with a male-female training team. She can teach beside you or Mateo, depending on time constraints."

A low growl of disapproval escaped Nathaniel's throat, but he quickly reined it in.

"I cannot afford to tie up any of the remaining sentinels," Napolean said by way of an explanation, brushing off Nathaniel's territorial behavior. "You will learn to live with the arrangement, warrior—and I will hear no objections or alternative solutions."

"It's a good plan," Marquis added.

"I believe so," Napolean agreed. He then glanced at Nathaniel. "See it done."

"Yes, milord," Nathaniel said.

Satisfied, Napolean turned to leave the room. As he grasped the handle on the door, he stopped, glanced back at the Silivasi brothers, and spoke in a soft, almost reverent tone of voice: "We have already discussed what took place these last days—the indescribable sacrifice Nachari made on my behalf—so I will not beat the drum unnecessarily, but I want you both to know that there is not an hour that goes by that I do not intercede with the gods on his behalf."

Nathaniel turned away and rubbed his jaw, suddenly seeming weary.

Marquis met the king's stare, but his eyes were vacant, carefully concealing whatever pain was buried behind them.

"I would not have chosen this for him...for your family," Napolean said quietly. "Nathaniel, Master Warrior, look at me."

Nathaniel looked up.

"No matter how old or proficient Nachari becomes, both you and Marquis continue to see him as your little brother, and this I understand. But you must each recognize that he is far, far more powerful than you know. Nachari did not choose wizardry—it chose him—because of his gifts...because of his spirit. His story is not over."

Nathaniel held up his hand to stop the king from speaking, and Marquis finally looked away. "I know you want to help,"

Nathaniel mumbled, "but we are not children to be patronized. Please, just—"

"Hold your tongue, warrior!" Napolean commanded, his voice rising with a heat so intense that the room reverberated from the surge in energy and the lights blew out. "You are not in an ordinary state of mind, so I will forget what you almost said."

Nathaniel looked away, clearly apologetic.

Napolean sighed and released the door. He strode toward Nathaniel, quickly closing the distance between them, and placed a gentle hand on the warrior's shoulder. "Nathaniel…"

Nathaniel stood unerringly still…listening.

"Nachari's—story—is—not—over," Napolean repeated, carefully emphasizing each and every word. He waited for Nathaniel to fully process what he was trying to convey before going on. "I do not know what has happened, but on several occasions, I have sensed his life force…somewhere…surviving. Kagen is right to keep his body viable. If there is any soul in the house of Jadon that possesses the raw talent—the absurd command over the laws of nature and the unseen world— necessary to beat this thing, it is your little brother. You must not give up hope."

The silence in the room was tangible, raw…edgy. What had been laid out was too weighty for words.

"Your presence is not required at my son's naming ceremony," Napolean whispered as he steadily returned to the door. "I have already given Kagen leave to remain at the clinic— I understand that he must maintain the life-support effort, and I am in full agreement with that decision. However, there will be no insult taken if your entire family chooses not to attend, your children and your *destinies* included."

Marquis started to speak, but Napolean held up a hand. "That said, to see you both there would do my heart good."

Marquis frowned. "Why?"

"Because it would mean that you've finally reclaimed your faith."

"What faith?" Nathaniel asked.

BLOOD POSSESSION

"Faith in Kagen to remain vigilant in your absence...faith in *Nachari* to fight this battle as he now must—on his own." Opening the door once again, the sovereign king sighed. "There is great love and loyalty in your family, and I would always see it so—but sometimes love requires faith, and faith, in turn, requires *acting* like you believe in someone. Believing in them as deeply as you love them."

He didn't turn around to see their reactions.

He simply whispered a silent entreaty to the gods—praying for peace and understanding—and then he let the door shut softly behind him.

twenty-nine

"Hey, you," Brooke whispered, her voice warm with tenderness. Smiling from ear to ear, she slowly entered Tiffany's room and sat on the edge of the bed.

Tiffany sat up gingerly, adjusted the large, fluffy pillows behind her back, and carefully studied Brooke's face. Her entire body relaxed with relief, and then her beautiful sea-green eyes clouded with tears. "Brookie..." She forced a smile, and the dark circles that rimmed her eyes brightened. "Come here, you," she said, slowly lifting her left arm to attempt a hug. Her right arm remained closely tucked to her body, encased in a hard plaster cast. "I can't believe you're real."

Brooke embraced her best friend, careful not to jiggle her injured arm. "Yep, it's me." She almost giggled from the joy of being reunited. "And I'm real."

They held each other for a long time, neither one wanting to be the first to let the other go, and then Brooke finally pulled away. She smoothed the thin cotton blanket resting over Tiffany's lap and reached for her hand. "Are you comfortable, Tiff? Is there anything you need?"

Tiffany sniffled and raised her casted arm in a token show of exhibition. She glanced down at the fresh plaster and shrugged. "I won't lie—I've been better. But now that you're here, I'm not complaining."

Brooke laughed then. She couldn't help it. "Ah, Tiff..." She sighed. "What happened in that basement? Can you tell me?"

Tiffany shook her head and her eyes grew narrow. "Hell if I know." She blinked several times as if bringing a mental moving picture into focus. "In a nutshell? Some redheaded girl beat the stuffing out of me."

Brooke shut her eyes and frowned. "Kristina...but why?"

Tiffany shrugged. "Oh, God..." She paused to steady

herself. "Because she thought I played a part in attacking those two beautiful women." She shivered then. "OMG, Brooke—it was awful! David staked one of the women right through the heart, and the other guys—they shot this brown-haired lady like she was nothing...like a dog." She shut her eyes as if she could also shut out the memory. When she opened them, they were wide like saucers, and her voice rose in pitch: "It was so crazy after that! You wouldn't believe all the things I saw, Brooke."

"Shh," Brooke whispered, patting Tiffany's hand to calm her. "I know. I heard." She shook her head slowly. "I'm just so surprised—and grateful—that you're still alive."

Tiffany sagged against the pillows. "Yeah, me too."

Brooke smiled then and glanced at Tiffany's cast. "Your arm will heal very quickly, trust me. Kagen sealed it in plaster, but not before—"

"He spread some kind of nasty slobber all over my skin?"

Brooke smiled sheepishly. "Yeah, I guess that sums it up nicely."

Tiffany's expression all at once became serious, and she slowly shook her head. "Brooke, what in the hell? These things are vampires."

Brooke looked away. "Not *things*, Tiffany. Males and females. They're not so—"

"The man who took you, Brooke? He was a vampire! What did he want with you?"

Brooke considered the question, all the while wondering just how much of the truth her friend could handle. She measured Tiffany with a scrutinizing gaze while remembering a previous conversation she'd had with Napolean. They had spoken about the importance of bringing Tiffany fully into their lives, and Brooke had made her position crystal clear: Under no uncertain terms would she be willing to give up *all* the elements of her past.

Some things were just too important...

But they had hoped to have more time to ease Tiffany into it.

Brooke cleared her throat. "There's so much you don't know, Tiff. So much you have to learn."

Tiffany squeezed Brooke's hand. "Then tell me, Brooke. Because I swear, I'm going to go crazy if you don't."

Brooke nodded slowly and sighed—she owed her friend at least that much—perhaps she should just let the chips fall where they may. After all, fate had already guided them this far. She withdrew her hand from Tiffany's, wrapped both arms around her sides, and stared nervously ahead. "I hardly know where to begin."

Tiffany set her jaw in a stern slant. "How about at the beginning...the last night of the conference...that Friday night in the cab: What in the heck was that?"

Brooke took a slow, deep breath and pushed forward. "That was the man—the male—who was intended to be my ... husband ... my other half ... finding me and claiming me."

Tiffany's mouth hung open, her forehead wrinkled in consternation, and her eyes narrowed with disbelief, but to her credit, she did not interrupt.

Brooke swallowed hard. She squeezed her midriff tighter for comfort while wondering just how one set about telling an outrageously fantastical, undeniably terrifying story without making it sound...well, outrageously fantastical and undeniably terrifying. "His name is Napolean Mondragon, and he's been a vampire for a very, very long time." She paused, trying to think of the best way to explain it. "He wasn't always that way, and pretty much everything we have ever heard about vampires and the myths that surround them isn't true..."

Her speech drifted into an easy rhythm, and a hollow echo filled the room as she relayed the story, the words reverberating all around her as if told by someone else. Her own voice seemed foreign to her ears as she told of the celestial beings and the original people. The crimes committed and the resulting Curse. Jaegar's arrogance...and Jadon's mercy. She was surprised at the firm grasp she had on the history, and her cadence took on a slight singsong lilt as she continued to explain Napolean's past, the structure of the house of Jadon, and the varied roles of its many members.

The way the Vampyr lived.

The successful industries they ran…

And the families they raised and loved.

She knew that it all sounded like a bizarre fairy tale—or perhaps a never-ending nightmare, depending on one's point of view—as she shared the events that had taken place, starting the night Napolean had taken her from the cab. Several times, Tiffany had looked overwhelmed, and Brooke had stopped talking in order to let her friend process the incredible events…regain her perspective. It was a lot to absorb, but Tiffany maintained an attentive, calm demeanor throughout the entire story, especially when it came to the part about how the curse ultimately played out for a male and his *destiny*—and the necessary conversion.

Finally, Brooke said, "But all that stuff about garlic, holy water, and coffins…it's not even like that. *Really*. Well, the sunlight can be a problem—but only if you're a Dark One…which I'm not. We're not. So…" She eyed her friend nervously, twiddled her thumbs, and smiled sheepishly. "Uh … comments? …questions? …psychotic meltdowns or religious tirades?" She laughed insincerely. "Feel free to interject anytime." Despite her pitiful attempts at humor, she practically held her breath, praying she hadn't just lost her dearest friend. The mere thought of having to ask Napolean to erase Tiffany's memories—to somehow alter her brain to insulate her against her dreams—to send her on her way in peace was, well, unthinkable.

Tiffany stared at Brooke like she was an alien.

She cleared her throat and tried to speak, but nothing came out.

She tried again. "So, then, you're…you are…you're a…" Her voice trailed off.

"Vampyr," Brooke supplied, careful not to blink. "Like the ladies in the basement."

Tiffany nodded and stared at the ceiling...the walls...the door handle, anything but Brooke. "Alrighty then. So uh, yeah. Okay."

Brooke placed her hand on Tiffany's shoulder. "Tiff, I'm the same person I've always been." She smiled then, trying to lighten the mood. "Just way faster and stronger." She tossed her head in a mock hair-flip and smiled as if posing for a camera. "And way, way sexier, don't you think?"

Tiffany laughed insincerely, and then she raised her hand to cover her throat protectively. "Are you going to bite me, Brooke?'

Brooke sighed loudly. "No, Tiffany. *Never.* I swear—"

"But then, how—"

"Anything...I need...I'll get from Napolean."

Tiffany blanched and wrinkled her nose. "No offense, but *eww.*"

Brooke laughed and waved a dismissive hand. "Trust me, Tiff. You didn't get a good look that night. When you see him...well, let's just say, you're gonna want one for yourself."

Tiffany raised her eyebrows. "Uh...don't think so." Her face suddenly paled, and a look of deep concern shadowed her eyes. "Oh God, now that I know, do you have to...convert...me, too?"

Brooke laughed. She couldn't help it. "I already said I would never bite you. And no, it's not even possible. Only a male's *destiny* can be converted...or I guess in rare instances, like the boy you met in the basement, if the woman already has a child of her own blood, then the kid can be converted. But regular people? Can't be done. At least not unless the person being converted willingly relinquishes their soul."

Tiffany held up her hand. She had clearly had enough. "My brain can't absorb any more of this," she said. "Just stick to the facts—me, you, and Napolean." She ran her hand through her short blond hair nervously, leaving the sharp, precise layers mussed in its wake. "So, if he's a king, then that makes you a...queen." She laughed, and the laughter soon rose to hysterics, a much-needed release of nervous energy. When she had finally spent all of her anxiety, she looked at Brooke, tilted her head to the side, and frowned. "What about PRIMAR? You're going to leave me alone with those vultures now, aren't you?"

Brooke laughed softly. "Well, I haven't completely decided. I'm pretty sure I won't be going back to work in San Francisco." She shrugged. "Not only is my home here now...with Napolean...but it really wouldn't be safe."

"The Deep Ones?" Tiffany asked.

"Dark Ones," Brooke corrected.

"Yeah, yeah. The demon spawn." She shivered.

"Exactly," Brooke said. Crossing both arms in front of her stomach in a gesture of determination, she addressed the original question. "I'm not going to let go of all my hard work—or my recent project. Napolean believes I can work independently as a contractor, and that we can negotiate fair terms for my ideas and contributions: In other words, PRIMAR can finally pay me what I'm worth, and to hell with their titles and promotions. I'll have my own marketing business."

A sly smile curved the corners of Tiffany's mouth. "And if they don't want to give you what you're asking for, then you can just send hubby to do a little Vulcan mind-melt." She giggled conspiratorially, and Brooke couldn't help but join her.

"I'd rather not," Brooke said. "I want to earn everything I get fair and square."

Tiffany rolled her eyes. "Since when do Jim Davis and Lewis Martin play fair and square?"

Brooke shrugged her shoulders and held up her hands, knowing she looked mischievous. "I said that I want to *try* and earn everything fair and square. I didn't say that I might not...have a little fun...if the good ole boys still refuse to play ball."

They both snickered then, and the mirth cut through the remaining tension.

"And," Brooke added, "if I do go into business for myself, then there's a certain graphic artist that I would love to hire right

Tessa Dawn

off the bat."

Tiffany's eyes lit up. "Would you pay me a fair wage?"

Brooke frowned. "No." She shook her head vigorously. "Absolutely not."

Tiffany pouted, confused.

"I would pay you a ridiculously obscene wage—just because."

Tiffany laughed, and then she sighed. "So, you're not gonna just leave me then? Toss me aside for some dark, handsome blood-sucker?" She smiled ruefully.

Brooke rolled her eyes. "No, silly. Never." She held up her hand. "But there would be a lot to talk about before we could go forward with something like that." She stood up from the bed and stretched, grateful to be past the worst of it now. "It's not a small thing...coming here as a human...having full knowledge of the community and who lives here. I'm not even sure if Napolean would agree to it. It would depend on just how loyal and committed you were willing to be to the Vampyr—whether or not they felt they could trust you implicitly." She sighed. "Whether or not you would even want to assume the risk—or danger—that comes with knowing. Whether you could accept the level of protection—and let's face it, intrusion—that would be necessary. It's a lifelong decision and a lot to think about."

Tiffany looked overwhelmed, and Brooke reached out to smooth her friend's hair back into place—the fierce, dramatic style still looked good even mussed up in a hospital bed. "But enough of that for now. I can't do any more of the serious stuff." She bit her bottom lip, trying to stifle her enthusiasm as she stood up, backed toward the door. "There's someone I want you to meet."

"Napolean?" Tiffany asked warily.

"Just wait," Brooke answered.

She opened the door, held it steady with her hip, and gestured toward Katia, who stood just outside with her beautiful newborn baby. Taking him carefully into her arms, she formed a secure cradle around his delicate body and wondered, once

337

again, what in the world she was going to do with him. The love that swept through her rendered the questioning insignificant. She was going to ride the blessing all the way to heaven.

She slowly spun around, took a careful step into the room, and let the door close behind her. Smiling like a giddy clown, she gently approached the bed. "Look!" she exclaimed proudly.

Tiffany's eyes grew wide with wonder. "Oh my God, what a beautiful baby." She reached up with her healthy hand and offered her index finger to the infant, then giggled when the baby took hold of it with a firm, steady grasp and smiled at her. "I don't think I have ever seen such a beautiful baby. Whose is he?"

Brooke hesitated and took a deep breath. "He's mine. Remember?"

Tiffany's eyes swept from the baby's face to Brooke's, then back again. "Come again?"

Brooke swallowed hard and raised her chin, hoping to project more confidence than she felt. The whole situation was simply overwhelming—no matter how she presented it. "He's mine. My son. Mine and Napolean's."

"Oh, yeah…" Tiffany nodded…and she almost smiled.

And then she fell gently back on the bed, her good arm dangling to the side, and passed out.

thirty

Napolean looked out upon the remarkable sea of powerful males, the *destinies* of those who had mated, and all the children who had been born to the house of Jadon and stood silently. As his eyes swept the grand Ceremonial Hall, he couldn't help but think, *All is well.*

Despite so much turmoil, the incessant battles—the endless centuries since the original Curse—the lighter Vampyr had flourished.

When he turned to regard his *destiny,* who was standing beside him holding their baby—his thriving newborn son—he took a quick intake of breath, and his heart fluttered in his chest.

Brooke was a sight to behold.

Beautiful.

Majestic.

As stately as any female born to royalty. As genuine as the night sky. As beautiful as the sunset.

Her ebony hair shone like silk against her flawless skin, even as her dazzling blue eyes complemented her elegant gown—from the filmy, split-cap shoulders all the way down to the gracefully flared hem. Her smile was positively radiant, and the only clue that betrayed her nervousness was the soft bite of her upper teeth against her lower lip.

Napolean suppressed a smile.

In the short time he had known Brooke, he had come to love that quirky habit—and that full bottom lip. His lower body stirred at the thought, and he quickly redirected his thoughts: not the kind of show he had come to put on.

Standing to his left, Ramsey cleared his throat. *Damn hyper-intuitive vampires!* On his right, Julien and Saxson smiled knowingly. A low, almost inaudible warning growl checked all three males in an instant, three sets of eyes respectfully finding

339

the floor.

That was better.

Napolean drew back his broad shoulders and squared his body to the audience. When his eyes surveyed a special set of attendants, he couldn't suppress his smile: Marquis and Ciopori stood in the front row with Nikolai held lovingly in Ciopori's arms. Beside them, Nathaniel and Jocelyn held hands, and young Braden Bratianu stood proudly holding Storm.

And the wizards—Niko Durciak and Jankiel Luzanski—those who had come to Dark Moon Vale to aid Nachari in saving their king, stood next to Braden in a show of solidarity, representing both Nachari and his absent brother, Kagen.

Napolean placed his hand on the small of Brooke's back, and together, they took a step forward.

The room fell deathly silent.

Not even a breath could be heard.

Once the anticipation had grown to an agonizing peak, Ramsey Olaru raised his chin, swept a hand out over the audience, and began to speak in a proud, commanding voice: "My brothers; fellow descendants of Jadon; Ancients, Masters, and Fledglings; our beloved children and revered mates; the soul of our house—our *destinies*—I welcome you to one of the most important occasions we will ever witness." He chuckled softly then—well, as softly as a severe male such as Ramsey could. "After more time than Napolean would like me to mention, I have the distinct honor of *finally* presiding over our sovereign and very, *very* ancient lord's marriage ceremony as well as the naming ceremony of his newborn son."

The crowd chuckled, and Napolean smiled graciously—hoping to maintain some semblance of dignity in the sacred ceremony: He knew Ramsey Olaru would never be able to stick strictly to the script, and, honestly, he was so filled with pride and joy that he just didn't care. He nodded his approval, and Ramsey continued.

Turning to face the royal couple, Ramsey swallowed nervously. "It is with great joy, and on behalf of the entire house

Tessa Dawn

of Jadon, that I greet you this day, milord, my brother, a fellow descendant of Jadon and Ancient Master Justice, mate to the daughter of Andromeda, father to this newborn son of Aries the Ram, who makes his home along the celestial stars Alpha, Beta, and Gamma. What name have you chosen for this newborn male?"

Napolean swelled with pride. "Should it please the house of Jadon and find favor with the Celestial Beings, the son of our lord Aries is to be named Phoenix Lane Mondragon."

Brooke's exquisite blue eyes glazed over with tears at the mention of their son's middle name, and Napolean reached out to take her hand. They had chosen his middle name in honor of Brooke's grandmother, the woman who had raised her with so much love and care: Lanie Adams.

It is a worthy name, he whispered telepathically to his *destiny*.

Brooke smiled.

And Ramsey nodded. "The name pleases the house of Jadon, and since you are the one who intercedes directly with the gods, I will assume that there is no objection from the Celestial Beings."

Napolean chuckled and shook his head. "There is no objection."

Having formally accepted the name, Ramsey took Phoenix from Brooke's arms and handed him to Napolean, who held him firmly in front of his body. As Napolean's fangs elongated, he slowly bent his head and drank for the first time from his son's wrist.

There was a soft inhale from the crowd.

As far as anyone knew, it was the first time a child had remained silent—had not instinctively cried out—in response to the brief but intense pain of Napolean's bite. It was an unexpected confirmation of royalty—a regal show of restraint from one so young—and it pleased the house of Jadon immensely.

Napolean gently withdrew his fangs and met his son's happy gaze with overwhelming pride. He knew in that moment that a

BLOOD POSSESSION

lifelong bond had been formed, a connection far beyond that of sovereign and subject: the priceless bond of father and son.

Lifting his child high so that all could see the now squirming bundle, Napolean said, "Welcome to the house of Jadon, Phoenix Lane Mondragon. May your life be filled with peace, triumph, and purpose. May your path always be blessed." He handed the child to Ramsey, who repeated the greeting before gently passing him to Saxson...then Julien...then Santos...to do the same. As the valley's sentinels and sworn protectors of the king, the Olaru brothers had been honored with officiating the ceremony...and being the first to greet the young prince.

Once all three brothers had finished welcoming Phoenix, Santos kept the babe in his arms, and Ramsey turned once again to regard them as a couple. "By the laws which govern the house of Jadon, it is my privilege to accept your union as the divine will of the gods and hereby sanction your mating." His soft hazel eyes—so paradoxical to his harsh, stormy manner—fixed on Brooke. "Brooke Adams Mondragon, do you come now of your own free will to enter the house of Jadon?"

For the first time since the ceremony had begun, Napolean became a bundle of nerves. He held his breath...listening...for that strong yet soothing voice: *Oh gods, please let her say yes...*

Brooke nodded and flashed an endearing half smile. "I do."

Napolean slowly exhaled, and then he closed his eyes in wonderment: Was this actually real? Did this woman...and this child...really belong to him? He was startled by the depth of his emotion.

"Hold out your wrist," Ramsey instructed.

Tentatively, Brooke did as she was asked, and to her obvious relief, the male who took her arm was Napolean, not Ramsey. As the sovereign lord of the house of Jadon, the blood of every member ran through Napolean's veins. Having taken the essence of each soul, he could not only locate them in an emergency, but tap into the deepest recesses of their being—it was a unique, if not divine, privilege granted solely to him. And it reinforced his enormous power and responsibility over the Vampyr. Brooke

342

was not only his mate now but a member of his species—his people. And, of course, they didn't need to know that he had already drunk…indulgently…from her heart.

On more than one occasion.

Napolean was careful to keep his grip on Brooke's wrist exquisitely gently, and his long, shimmering, silver-and-black locks fell over her arm fortuitously, creating a tent of privacy as he bent to pierce her delicate skin. As always, he struck swiftly and cleanly, his fangs sinking deep, as he formed a tight seal over the wound and drew three steady, but powerful drags. While the initial bite was inevitably painful, the immediate contact with his lips flooded his *destiny* with peace. He felt her tense…then relax. And just like that, it was over.

He effortlessly withdrew his fangs and sealed the wound with his venom, the transition between canines and incisors so smooth it could hardly be seen. When his eyes met hers, he felt a love so deep that he almost swayed where he stood.

"Congratulations," Ramsey said, bowing deeply before stepping back.

Santos and Saxson did the same, the latter still cradling Phoenix in his arms.

Napolean kissed the underside of Brooke's wrist, turned to face the crowd, and held up her arm for all to see. "Let all souls present recognize the mated *destiny* of your king, and in the presence of the celestial gods, here and forevermore pledge your fealty to your queen: Brooke Adams Mondragon."

Brooke's face paled as all eyes in the house of Jadon suddenly focused on her like a collective, supernatural laser. *Oh. My. God*, she whispered. *Please tell me you're kidding.* Apparently, she was so freaked out by the moment that she didn't even realize she was speaking telepathically—without any effort.

Napolean smiled.

You forgot to mention this part of the ceremony, Napolean, she chastised.

Shh, he responded, his deep melodic laughter echoing in her mind. *Just breathe, Brooke.*

BLOOD POSSESSION

Before she could freak out any further, Santos stepped forward and handed the baby to Napolean. He took his son in the palm of both hands and slowly held him up before the assembly. "Let all souls present recognize my firstborn son—the chosen and rightful heir to my throne— and in the presence of the celestial gods, from this moment unto eternity, pledge your fealty to your prince: Phoenix Lane Mondragon."

As if the moment had been perfectly choreographed, one by one, the males in the house of Jadon descended onto their right knees, each vampire bowing his head in a continuous wave that swept from the front row to the back in perfect harmony. When the last knee had touched the ground and the last head had bowed, all right hands covered their hearts, all left hands covered the right, and a sea of identical rings, bearing the crest from the house of Jadon on them, were displayed to the king in a demonstration of devotion.

The moment was surreal.

The love. The respect. The good fortune.

And like the calming of a turbulent sea after an endless storm, a great peace settled upon Napolean...and he finally understood.

What he should have always known.

That on that fateful day so many centuries ago, his father had commanded him to run because he loved him. Because nothing mattered more to Sebastian than saving his son—and the legacy that would live on through his line. Perhaps Napolean could have confronted Prince Jaegar on that frightful day—and died along with his father—but then none of this would have happened. And his father's death would have been in vain.

Napolean swallowed hard.

Struggling to maintain his composure, he searched for his voice, but he couldn't find it...

Twenty-eight hundred years.

He had waited an eternity to make peace with his father's death.

He looked down at his son. He had waited an eternity for

344

this child—for Sebastian's grandson.

He offered his hand to Brooke and felt both amazed and honored when she took it: Where had this blessing come from? When had all of this happened?

It had been worth all of the ceaseless doubts…both dying and suffering possession…living so many endless centuries alone…to finally find her.

He had waited an eternity for this woman.

"I love you," he whispered hoarsely, not caring if the whole house of Jadon heard him say it.

Brooke squeezed his hand, and one look in her stunning eyes told him all he needed to know: His *destiny* saw…and felt…all the same things.

They were home.

Napolean cleared his throat. He raised his hand and slowly waved an arm over the crowd, releasing the kneeling spectators. "Be at ease," he said.

The males stood, visibly relaxed, and waited to hear more from their king.

Napolean cleared his throat again, this time adding a calming breath to the mix. He nodded his appreciation to his males and their *destinies* alike. "Know this, all who are present: This day, my heart is fuller than I ever thought possible. There is not a soul in this hall that I do not live for, nor a soul in this hall that I would not die for. Serving you is my greatest honor, and living amongst you has been a constant privilege. We have suffered much over the years, but we have learned much as well. We have grown much." He turned to Brooke. "And we have loved much." Telepathically, he added. *My queen, would you like to say anything to your people?*

Brooke looked hesitant.

She leaned in close to him, seeking the shelter of his body, and then instinctively, she reached out for their son and gathered him close in her arms. Brushing her lips softly over Phoenix's brow, she gazed up at Napolean and nodded.

This was the Brooke he knew.

BLOOD POSSESSION

The woman who would make a magnificent, gracious queen. The savvy intellectual who didn't hesitate to compete in an industry full of corporate sharks. Napolean beamed with pride.

Brooke took a graceful step forward, and then she smiled cautiously. "I'm standing in a room full of vampires," she began, deliberately projecting her voice, "married to a guy I didn't even know existed a couple of weeks ago, holding a baby I never thought I'd have—and truly have no idea how to care for...yet." She laughed, and the sound infused the air around them with joy as the audience joined her. "Hell, I even have fangs."

This time, Napolean laughed.

"But the truth is, despite all of my career goals—all I have worked to achieve in the past, and all I imagined for the future— all my life, I've only wanted one thing..."

When she paused to brush away a tear, Napolean had to resist the impulse to sweep her into his arms, fly them both back to the manse, and make love to her until her tears were but a memory.

He listened, instead.

"All my life, all I've ever wanted—yet never dared to hope for—is a family. Someplace to belong. Someplace where I was loved and truly wanted." She raised her chin and stiffened her back, clearly determined to get the words out. "I have all of that and so much more now."

When she glanced at Napolean and smiled, his heart warmed with gratitude and awe. And he knew that she actually got it: The house of Jadon was her family now. The males did not serve out of some shallow sense of obligation, ceremony, or pretense, and they did not make empty promises. Theirs were a species bound by honor, loyalty, and family, and they would freely give Brooke their allegiance out of a true generosity of heart.

This family would never intentionally hurt or betray her.

And gods save any other who did.

Brooke blinked rapidly, still struggling to hold her tears at bay. "You know, from the outside looking in, people might think I've experienced a nightmare: that a very, *very* scary man

346

Tessa Dawn

forced his way into my world and uprooted my life." She glanced at Napolean and chuckled. "But they would be so very wrong. The truth is: while it may have been rough getting here, I've awakened to a dream. The most incredible man in the world came into my life and gave it back to me." Turning to face him, her eyes softened, and she whispered, "You have awakened me to a happiness I never dreamed possible, Napolean. You have helped me make sense of the past and given me an incredible future to look forward to." Blushing, she smiled and bit her bottom lip.

And Napolean's heart soared.

"Napolean," she whispered, "I love you, too."

Epilogue

Nachari Silivasi gripped the iron stakes on either side of his hands and shouted his pain as the harsh lash bit into his skin again and again. And again.

He would not beg.

He would not give them the satisfaction.

His body shook against the hard granite beneath him, and his back arched in unnatural contortions as his spilled blood pooled beneath his naked belly. It felt warm against the otherwise cool stone.

It had been three long months.

Three long months since he had descended into the Valley of Death and Shadows—and entered hell—in order to save the Vampyr king of the house of Jadon from a dark possession.

It had been three agonizing months since he had seen his brothers.

The lash struck again, catching him off guard on a violent exhale, and he almost passed out. His amulet, the one Shelby had given him, was cutting into his skin—it always did when they laid him face-down against the stone for his lashings—but he didn't dare take it off. Once, a minion of the dark lord had tried to wrench it from his neck, and it had burned the demon's hand like a hot branding iron.

As the lash struck lower this time, falling somewhere between his upper thighs and his buttocks, he heard himself whimper, and he cursed his momentary weakness. If only he could die. If only his brothers would renege on their promise to continue providing life support to his body until he returned. If only he could be free.

If Nachari could have laughed at the irony—which he couldn't—he would have: In their desire to keep him alive, to hold him to the earth, his brothers were keeping him instead in a vampiric version of purgatory. As long as his earthly body remained safe and healthy, awaiting his spirit's return to Dark Moon Vale, he could not fully die. Once dead, his corporeal body, which was holding his soul at bay, and his ethereal soul, which was projecting a corporeal form in order to sustain the endless torture, would merge. He would be one entity in one place, and the Dark Lord Ademordna could no longer enslave him.

Granted, he would be dead, never to return to his precious valley in the Rocky Mountains, never to see his Romanian homeland one last time, never to meet his *destiny*, but he would at least be at peace—for the dark lord who had taken him into the Valley of Death and Shadows could not hold him as one integrated being. His eternal soul would find its solace in the Valley of Spirit and Light where it belonged. With Shelby.

As the next stroke of the lash fell into the same exact groove as the previous one, Nachari inadvertently bit his tongue: *Great celestial gods*, how much more could he endure? Day after endless day. Knowing his body would regenerate again and again only to prepare him for more torture.

Unable to withstand another moment of his torment, Nachari chose to take the only way out available to him...however temporary. Indeed, it was an escape he had taken one hundred times before. He threw back his head, his glorious mane of thick, raven hair spilling around his face and shoulders in wild waves of blood-crusted locks, and slammed his forehead against the stone.

The pain was indescribably profound.

Literally and figuratively stunning.

And then—mercifully—he collapsed against the stone, and the entire underworld went black.

Deanna Dubois knelt on her living room floor in deep

concentration, rocking back and forth on her heels as she stared at the new set of drawings in front of her. She sighed in frustration and more than a little trepidation. The only reason she could call these drawings *new* was because she had drawn them last night—as opposed to the night before...

Or the night before that.

There was nothing new about her disturbing, ever-growing obsession.

She twirled a thick lock of ash-brown hair around her finger, noticing a particularly stark amber highlight, before turning back to the paintings.

Dear God, what was wrong with her?

She needed help.

And it was getting harder and harder to deny it.

She reached for the thin, light-weight computer beside her, drew it on top of her lap, and used the mouse to enlarge the webpage she had opened—and left open—almost two weeks ago: Psychiatric Clinics in New Orleans.

Just pick one, Deanna, she told herself. *You need help!*

She glanced once again at the pictures before her and tried to see them in a new light, maybe, with an eye for self-analysis—it was time for some serious introspection. Setting the laptop aside, she laid the drawings out in order—sort of like a progressively animated comic strip—and then sat back and studied them.

On the far left was the most beautiful man she had ever seen, a tall, incredibly well-built Adonis with deep green eyes and a face so utterly perfect she wasn't sure God could actually create such a being—let alone endow her with the ability to draw it. His hair was unnaturally thick and silky, and there was a strange air of confidence swirling around him even in the drawing—not quite arrogance, but definitely pride—a regal-like quality. He was simply breathtaking. Actually, more than that: He was arresting...almost disturbing in his appeal.

The next sequence of drawings was more benign, and she drew them the same every time: pine trees, rock outcroppings, skies filled with dark, mottled clouds, and endless miles of forest.

BLOOD POSSESSION

Nothing especially interesting or disturbing there. They reminded her of pictures she had seen of Colorado.

She turned to the next drawing, the one immediately to the right of the last forest picture, and she shivered. In this frame, the ground had opened up beneath the handsome man, and he was falling into a dark, endless hole…being sucked into some evil netherworld. The hands that were reaching up to grab him were skeletal and demonic; and, of course, this is where the metaphorical comic strip began to deteriorate and her own mental health came into question: In the subsequent set of photos—the largest sequence that she drew night after night— the ungodly beautiful male was depicted in all kinds of horrific scenarios and positions being tortured.

And by *tortured*, she meant hideously tormented in ways that no stable human being could possibly come up with—let alone draw in such brutal detail—unless that artistically disturbed woman was seriously going insane.

She rubbed her face with her palms as if she could scrub away the anxiety and stared apprehensively at the farthest picture to the right. Something in her gut turned over as her eyes connected with the images…

It was as if it were real.

As if it were happening right now.

As if, right this second, the man was lying face-down against a cold stone, bound by four heavy lengths of chain, with diamonds—of all things—embedded in the links. And God almighty, was he writhing in pain as his flesh was literally torn from his body by a spiked lash. Yet never—not even once in all of her drawings—did the guy beg his tormentors for mercy. For lack of a better term, he took it like a man.

A man forged from iron.

Whoever her phantom captive was, he clearly had the heart of a lion.

Deanna reached out and swept the drawings into a haphazard pile, purposefully disturbing the order in a desperate attempt to erase the madness that had become her nighttime—

and more and more often, daytime—obsession.

"Who are you?" she whispered, pleading with heaven-knows-what for just a moment's peace. "And why are you haunting me?"

One of the earlier-sequenced drawings seemed to rise to the top as if it were trying to answer her question by floating above all the other images…speaking in some cryptic, metaphysical way. "It's just random, Deanna," she reassured herself. "From the way you messed them up… You are not *that* crazy!" She emphasized the last five words while momentarily squeezing her eyes shut. And then she began tapping the back of her foot nervously against the floor in a frenetic, repetitive rhythm as she cringed. "What's wrong with me…what's wrong with me…*what's wrong with me?*"

She continued to stare at the most prominent drawing.

"Fine," she finally spat, reaching for the picture and lifting it up to study it more closely. "I'll bite. Show me some great hidden meaning, then." Shaking her head, she whispered, "Show me just how psychotic I am so they can lock me away…forever."

As she turned the drawing over and over, observing it at different angles, she began to notice a strange pattern in the sky: There was something hidden within the shadows of the dark clouds…the ones that loomed ominously over the forested valley—the place from which the man always fell into the black hole. And the hidden pattern wasn't something Deanna had added to the picture; rather, it was a deliberate omission—white space that remained empty, uncovered by pencil marks.

An outline emerged in the absence of color.

Frowning, Deanna leapt up from the floor and went to get her magnifying glass in order to take a closer look. As she held the drawing beneath the lens, she bent way over to study the vacant space…and froze.

What in the world?

The spaces were letters.

And the letters spelled very distinct words.

BLOOD POSSESSION

Wondering if she wasn't about to open Pandora's box—and whether or not she might be better off leaving well enough alone—Deanna reached for her pencil and flipped over another drawing in order to transcribe the letters on the back, one at a time…

DARK-MOON-VALE-CLINIC.

She sat back and stared at the words, and then she picked up the magnifying glass and verified each one a second time, making sure she hadn't overlooked anything. Yep, that's what they said all right: Dark Moon Vale Clinic.

She set down the magnifying glass and shrugged. At least they hadn't spelled out Sybil or Three Faces of Eve. At least they hadn't spelled out *Redrum, Redrum, Redrum* over and over and over: "All work and no play makes Deanna a very dull girl," she whispered, shivering at the inappropriate reference to *The Shining*—a terrifying book written by Stephen King in the 1970s that was later made into a movie. That was later remade at a remote Colorado hotel…

Near the Rocky Mountain National Park…

Just outside the Roosevelt National *Forest*.

Deanna swallowed a lump in her throat, set the magnifying glass aside, and slowly reached for her laptop again. This time, she ignored the intimidating list of local psychoanalysts in favor of trying a different search: Colorado Clinics. When she didn't find the one from her drawings, she began to breathe easier. *Okay, this is good. The clinic isn't real.*

Even as she thought it, an uneasy feeling grew in her belly, and she continued to try various word combinations in the search engine, absently seeking to discern whether or not the *place* was real, even if the clinic wasn't.

And there it was.

Right beneath Mountain Hotels and Accommodations: *Dark Moon Vale Lodge.*

Damnit! she thought, her trepidation growing. It was time to research the place in depth.

Despite some frantic voice screaming deep within the

recesses of her mind, *Stop! Don't go any further. This is one of those forks in the road—one of those ominous moments in life from which there is no turning back—don't do it!* she was helpless to stop herself.

Because something far deeper within her, something far more fundamental and compelling than fear, was spurring her on—inexplicably drawing her to the suffering male in her sketches. To the haunted eyes of that masculine figure.

And nothing in this world—or the next—was going to keep her from solving the mystery...if, in fact, it could be solved.

Even as Deanna clicked on the link and prepared to read further, she already knew she was headed for Colorado: She was going to Dark Moon Vale.

Somewhere...the victim in her drawings did exist. And she was going to find him even if it killed her.

If she had harbored even the slightest doubt before, it was now completely gone: Deanna Dubois was absolutely—*certifiably*—insane.

About The Author

Tessa Dawn grew up in Colorado where she developed a deep affinity for the Rocky Mountains. After graduating with a degree in psychology, she worked for several years in criminal justice and mental health before returning to get her Masters Degree in Nonprofit Management.

Tessa began writing as a child and composed her first full-length novel at the age of eleven. By the time she graduated high-school, she had a banker's box full of short-stories and books. Since then, she has published works as diverse as poetry, greeting cards, workbooks for kids with autism, and academic curricula. The Blood Curse Series marks her long-desired return to her creative-writing roots and her first foray into the Dark Fantasy world of vampire fiction.

Tessa currently lives in the suburbs with her two children and "one very crazy cat" but hopes to someday move to the country where she can own horses and a German Shepherd.

BLOOD POSSESSION

Writing is her bliss.

Books in the Blood Curse Series

(In order of publication)

Blood Destiny

Blood Awakening

Blood Possession

Blood Shadows (Coming Soon…)

If you would like to receive notice of future releases,

please go to the Blood Curse Series Website

www.TessaDawn.Com